Praise for Lars Kepler's

STALKER

"Fast-paced . . . the type of writing that makes the hours disappear. . . . Kepler's unflinching prose gives lucid rendering to scenes of suspense, graphic violence, and hand-to-hand combat, elevating the sense of unease or excitement they produce."
—*Mystery Tribune*

"As in the other books in the superb Joona Linna series . . . there's not an ounce of flab on *Stalker* despite its heft, which accommodates both scrupulous character development and elaborate scenes of derring-do."
—*Shelf Awareness*

"Short chapters, nightmarish murders and a tantalizing, suspenseful mystery. . . . The best legal drug you could possibly ask for."
—*Bookreporter*

"Super creepy. . . . *Stalker* keeps up the pace with super short chapters that build a sense of urgency."
—*CrimeReads*

"The reveal of the stalker's identity is a genuine gut punch. . . . Kepler . . . does a masterly job of elevating the serial killer thriller beyond genre clichés and tropes."
—*Publishers Weekly* (starred review)

"Kepler delivers a page-turning hunt for an expertly camouflaged killer that draws shocking connections between the hallowed halls of the Karolinska Institute, Stockholm's prostitution and drug scene, and Sweden's rural churches. The author's dark, complex procedurals are must-reads for readers drawn to Stieg Larsson, Mons Kallentoft, and Michael Connelly."
—*Booklist* (starred review)

Lars Kepler

STALKER

Lars Kepler is the pseudonym of the critically acclaimed husband-and-wife team Alexandra Coelho Ahndoril and Alexander Ahndoril. Their number one internationally bestselling Joona Linna series has sold more than fourteen million copies in forty languages. The Ahndorils were both established writers before they adopted the pen name Lars Kepler and have each published several acclaimed novels. They live in Stockholm, Sweden.

ALSO BY LARS KEPLER

The Joona Linna Series

The Hypnotist

The Nightmare

The Fire Witness

The Sandman

STALKER

STALKER

A Joona Linna Novel

LARS KEPLER

Translated from the Swedish by
NEIL SMITH

Vintage Crime / Black Lizard
Vintage Books
A Division of Penguin Random House LLC
New York

FIRST VINTAGE CRIME/BLACK LIZARD EDITION, JANUARY 2020

The Library of Congress has cataloged the Knopf edition as follows:
Names: Kepler, Lars, author.
Title: Stalker : a Joona Linna novel / Lars Kepler ;
translated from the Swedish by Neil Smith.
Description: First United States edition. | New York : Alfred A. Knopf, 2019.
Identifiers: LCCN 2018027587 (print) | LCCN 2018028517 (ebook)
Subjects: BISAC: FICTION / Suspense.
Classification: LCC PT9877.21.E65 (ebook) | LCC PT9877.21.E65 S8313 2019 (print) |
DDC 833/.92—dc23
LC record available at https://lccn.loc.gov/2018027587

Vintage Crime/Black Lizard Trade Paperback ISBN: 978-0-525-43306-4
eBook ISBN: 978-1-5247-3227-1

www.vintagebooks.com

Printed in the United States of America
10 9 8 7 6 5 4 3 2 1

STALKER

It wasn't until the first body was found that anyone took the video seriously. A link to a YouTube video had been sent to the National Crime Unit's public email address. The sender was impossible to trace. The police secretary followed the link, watched the video, assumed it was a rather baffling joke, and entered it in the records.

Two days later three detectives gathered in a small room on the eighth floor of National Crime headquarters in Stockholm, as a result of that very video.

The clip they were watching was only fifty-two seconds long.

The shaky footage, filmed with a handheld camera through a bedroom window, showed a woman in her thirties putting on a pair of black tights.

The three men watched the woman's movements in embarrassed silence.

To get the tights to sit comfortably, she took long strides over imaginary obstacles and did several squats.

On Monday morning the woman had been found in the kitchen of a terraced house on the island of Lidingö, on the outskirts of Stockholm. She was sitting on the floor with her mouth grotesquely split open. Blood had splattered the window and a white orchid in its flowerpot. She was wearing nothing but a pair of tights and a bra.

The postmortem concluded that she had bled to death as a result of multiple lacerations and stab wounds that were concentrated, in a display of extraordinary brutality, around her throat and face.

THE WORD *STALKER* HAS EXISTED SINCE THE EARLY 1700S. In those days it meant a tracker or poacher.

In 1921 the French psychiatrist de Clérambault published what is widely regarded as the first modern analysis of a stalker, a study of a patient suffering from erotomania. Today a stalker is someone who suffers from obsessive fixations, or an unhealthy obsession with monitoring another individual's activities.

Almost ten percent of the population will be subjected to some form of stalking in the course of their lifetime.

Most stalkers have or used to have a relationship with the victim. But in a striking number of cases, the fixation is focused on strangers or people in the public eye, and coincidence plays a key role.

Even though the vast majority of cases never require intervention, the police treat the phenomenon seriously because a stalker's pathological obsessiveness brings with it inherent danger. Just as clouds rolling between areas of high and low pressure can turn into a tornado, a stalker's emotional swings between worship and hatred can suddenly become extremely violent.

1

IT'S A QUARTER TO NINE ON FRIDAY, AUGUST 22. AFTER THE magical sunsets and light nights of high summer, darkness is encroaching with surprising speed. It's already dusk outside the National Police Authority.

Margot Silverman gets out of the elevator and walks toward the security doors in the foyer. She's wearing a black cardigan, a white blouse that fits tightly around her chest, and long black pants whose high waist is stretched across her expanding stomach.

She ambles toward the revolving doors in the glass wall.

Margot's hair is the color of polished birch wood and is pulled into a thick braid down her back. She has moist eyes and rosy cheeks. She is thirty-six years old and pregnant with her third child.

She's heading home after a long week. She's worked overtime every day and has received two warnings for pushing herself too hard.

She is the new police expert on serial killers, spree killers, and stalkers. The murder of Maria Carlsson is the first case she's been in charge of since her appointment.

There are no witnesses and no suspects. The victim was single and had no children. She worked as a product adviser for Ikea and had inherited her parents' unmortgaged town house after her father died and her mother went into a nursing home.

On most days, Maria traveled to work with a colleague. They would meet down on Kyrk Road. When she wasn't there that morning, her colleague drove to her house and rang the doorbell, looked through the windows, and then walked around the back and saw her. She was sitting on the floor, her face covered in knife wounds, her neck almost sliced through, her head lolling to one side, and her mouth strangely wide open.

According to the postmortem, there was evidence to suggest that her mouth had been so arranged after death.

When Margot was appointed to head the investigation, she knew she couldn't seem too aggressive. She has a tendency to be overeager.

Her colleagues would have laughed if she'd told them she was absolutely convinced that they were dealing with a serial killer.

Over the course of the week, Margot has watched the video of Maria Carlsson putting her tights on more than two hundred times. All the evidence suggests she was murdered shortly after the recording was uploaded to YouTube.

Margot can't see anything that makes this video special. It's not unusual for people to have a tights fetish, but nothing about the murder indicates that sort of inclination.

The video is simply a brief excerpt from an ordinary woman's life. She's single, has a good job, and takes cartoon drawing classes at night.

There's no way of knowing why the perpetrator was in her garden, whether it was pure chance or the result of a carefully planned operation, but in the minutes before the murder, he captured her on video.

Given that he sent the link to the police, he must have wanted to show them something. He wanted to highlight something about this particular woman, or a certain type of woman. Maybe it's about all women.

But to Margot's eyes, there's nothing unusual about the woman's behavior or appearance. She's simply concentrating on getting her tights on properly.

Margot has visited the house on Bredablicks Road twice, but she's spent most of her time examining the video of the crime scene before it was contaminated.

The perpetrator's film almost looks like a lovingly created work of art compared to the police's crime scene video. The forensics team's minutely detailed recording of the evidence is relentless. The dead woman is filmed from various angles as she sits with her legs stretched out on the floor, surrounded by dark blood. Her bra is in shreds, dangling from one shoulder, and one white breast hangs down toward the bulge of her stomach. There's almost nothing left of her face, just a gaping mouth surrounded by red pulp.

Margot stops as if by chance beside the fruit bowl, glances over at the guard, who is talking on the phone, then turns her back to him. For a few seconds, she watches the guard's reflection in the glass wall, then takes six apples from the bowl and puts them in her bag.

Six is too many, she knows that, but she can't stop herself. It's occurred to her that Jenny might like to make an apple pie that evening, with lots of butter, cinnamon, and sugar.

Her thoughts are interrupted when her phone rings. She looks at the screen and sees a picture of Adam Youssef, a member of the investigating team.

"Are you still in the building?" Adam asks. "Please tell me you're still here, because we've—"

"I'm sitting in the car on Klarastrands Road," Margot lies. "What do you need?"

"He's uploaded a new video."

She feels her stomach clench and puts one hand under the heavy bulge. "A new video," she repeats.

"Are you coming back?"

"I'll stop and turn around," she says, and begins to retrace her steps. "Make sure we get a decent copy of the recording."

Margot could have just gone home, leaving the case in Adam's hands. It would take only a phone call to arrange a full year of paid maternity leave. Her fate is hanging in the balance. She doesn't know what this case will bring, but she can sense its gravity, its dark pull.

The light in the elevator makes her face seem older in the reflection of the shining doors. The thick, dark line of mascara around her eyes is almost gone. As she leans her head back, she realizes she's starting to look like her father, the former commissioner.

The elevator stops at the eighth floor, and she walks along the empty hallway as fast as her bulging stomach will allow. She and Adam moved into Joona Linna's old office the same week the police held a memorial service for him. Margot never knew Joona personally and had no problem taking over his office.

"You have a fast car," Adam says as she walks in, then smiles, showing his sharp teeth.

"Pretty fast," Margot replies.

Adam joined the police force after a brief stint as a professional soccer player. He is twenty-eight years old, with long hair and a round youthful face. His short-sleeved shirt is untucked.

"How long has the video been up?" she asks.

"Three minutes," Adam says. "He's there now. Standing outside the window and—"

"We don't know that, but—"

"I think he is," he interrupts.

Margot sets her heavy bag on the floor, sits down on her chair, and calls forensics.

"Margot here. Have you downloaded a copy?" she asks. "Listen, I need a location or a name. All the resources you've got. You have five minutes—do whatever the hell you want—just give me something, and I promise I'll let you go so you can enjoy your Friday evening."

She puts the phone down and opens the pizza box on Adam's desk. "Are you done with this?" she asks.

There's a ping as an email arrives, and Margot quickly stuffs a piece of pizza crust into her mouth. A worry line deepens on her forehead. She clicks on the video file and maximizes the onscreen image, pushes her braid over her shoulder, and rolls her chair back so Adam can see.

The first shot is an illuminated window shimmering in the darkness. The camera moves slowly closer through leaves that brush the lens.

Margot feels the hair on her arms stand up.

A woman is in front of a television, eating ice cream from a carton. She's pulled her sweatpants down and is balancing on one foot. One of her socks is off.

She glances at the television and smiles at something, then licks the spoon.

The only sound in police headquarters is the computer fan.

Just give me one detail to go on, Margot thinks as she looks at the woman's face. Her body seems to be steaming with residual heat. She's just been for a run. The elastic of her underwear is loose after too many washings, and her bra is clearly visible through her sweat-stained shirt.

Margot leans closer to the screen, her stomach pressing against her thighs, and her heavy braid falls forward over her shoulder.

"One minute to go," Adam says.

The woman sets the carton of ice cream on the coffee table and leaves the room, her sweatpants still dangling from one foot.

The camera follows her, moving sideways past a narrow door until it reaches the bedroom window, where the light goes on and the woman comes into view. She kicks her pants off. They fly through the air, hit the wall behind an armchair with a red cushion, and fall to the floor.

2

THE CAMERA ZOOMS IN SLOWLY AND THEN STOPS RIGHT outside the window, swaying slightly as if it were floating.

"She'd see him if she just looked up," Margot whispers, feeling her heart beat faster.

The light from the room casts a slight flare across the top of the lens.

Adam is sitting with his hand over his mouth.

The woman pulls her shirt off, tosses it onto the chair, then stands for a moment in her washed-out underwear and stained bra. She glances over at the cellphone charging on the bedside table. Her thighs are tense and pumped with blood after her run, and the elastic waistband of her pants has left a red line across her stomach.

There are no tattoos or visible scars on her body, just faint stretch marks from a pregnancy.

The bedroom looks like millions of others. There's nothing worth even trying to trace.

The camera trembles, then pulls back.

The woman takes the glass of water from the bedside table and brings it to her mouth. Then the video ends abruptly.

"Fuck, fuck," Margot repeats irritably. "Nothing, not a goddamn thing."

"Let's watch it again," Adam says.

"We can watch it a thousand times," Margot says, rolling her chair farther back. "Fine, what the hell, go ahead, but it's not going to give us a fucking thing."

"I can see a lot of things. I can see—"

"You can see a detached house, twentieth century, some fruit trees, roses, triple-glazed windows, a forty-two-inch television, Ben & Jerry's ice cream," she says, gesturing toward the computer.

It hasn't struck her before, the way we're all so similar to each other. Seen through a window, a broad spectrum of Swedes conform to the same pattern, making them interchangeable. From the outside, we appear to live exactly the same way. We look the same, do the same things, own the same objects.

"This is totally fucked up," Adam says angrily. "Why is he doing this? What the hell does he want?"

Margot glances out the small window, where the black treetops of Kronoberg Park are silhouetted against the hazy glow of the city.

"There's no doubt this is a serial killer," she says. "All we can do is put together an initial profile, so we can—"

"How does that help her?" Adam runs a hand through his hair. "He's standing outside her window, and you're talking about profiling!"

"It might help the next one."

"What the fuck?" Adam says. "We have to—"

"Just shut up for a minute," Margot interrupts, picking up her phone.

"Shut up yourself," Adam says, raising his voice. "I have every right to say what I think. Don't I? I think we should get the papers to publish this woman's picture on their websites."

"Adam, listen. Much as we'd like to be able to identify her, we have nothing to go on," Margot says. "I'll talk to forensics, but I doubt they're going to find anything more than they did last time."

"But if we circulate her picture to—"

"I don't have time for this now," she snaps. "Think for a minute. Everything suggests he uploaded the clip directly from her house, so there's a theoretical chance of saving her."

"That's exactly what I'm saying!"

"But five minutes have already passed."

Adam leans forward and stares at her. His eyes are bloodshot, and his hair is on end. "Are we just going to give up then?"

"We have to think before we act," she replies. "We can't make any wrong moves."

"I know," he says, annoyed.

"The perpetrator is confident. He knows he's way ahead of us," Margot explains as she picks up the last slice of pizza. "But the better we get to know him . . ."

"Get to know him? Fine, but that's not really what I'm thinking about right now." Adam wipes sweat from his top lip. "We couldn't trace the previous video, we didn't find anything at the scene, and we won't be able to trace this one either."

"We're unlikely to get any forensic evidence, but we can try to pin him down by analyzing the videos and the brutality of his MO," Margot replies, feeling the baby move inside her. "What have we seen so far? What has he shown us, and what's he seeing?"

"A woman who went for a run and is now eating ice cream and watching television," he says tentatively.

"What does that tell us about the murderer?"

"That he likes women who eat ice cream?!" He sighs and hides his face in his hands.

"Come on, now."

"Sorry, but—"

"I'm thinking about the fact that the murderer uploads a video showing the period leading up to the murder," she says. "He takes his time, enjoys himself, and wants to show us the woman alive, wants to preserve her on video. Maybe it's the living he's interested in."

"A voyeur." He feels his arms prick with discomfort.

"A stalker," she whispers.

Adam turns to the computer and logs into the police database. "Tell me how I'm supposed to filter this list of scumbag ex-cons," he says.

"A rapist, violent rape, someone with obsessive fixations."

He types quickly, clicks the mouse, and types some more. "Too many results," he says. "Time's running out."

"Try the first victim's name."

"No results." He runs a hand through his hair.

"A serial rapist who's been treated, possibly chemically castrated," Margot says, thinking out loud.

"We need to check the databases against each other, but that'll take too long," he says, getting up from his chair and pacing. "This isn't working. What the hell are we going to do?"

"She's dead," Margot says, leaning back. "She might have a few minutes left, but . . ."

"We can see her," Adam says. "We can see her face, her home. Christ, we can see right into her life, but we can't find out who she is until someone finds her body."

3

SUSANNA KERN FEELS HER THIGHS TINGLING FROM HER RUN as she pulls her sweaty pants down and kicks them toward the chair.

Since she turned thirty, she's run five kilometers three evenings each week. After her Friday run, she usually eats ice cream and watches television, since Björn doesn't get home until ten o'clock.

When Björn landed the job in London, she thought she'd be lonely, but she fairly quickly came to appreciate the hours she had to herself in the weeks Morgan was with his dad.

She needs this downtime more than ever since she started taking a demanding course in advanced neurology at Karolinska Institute.

She undoes her sweaty sports bra. She can't remember a summer this hot before.

A scratching sound makes her turn toward the window.

The backyard is so dark, all she can see is the reflection of the bedroom. It looks like a theater set or a television studio. She has just made her entrance and is standing under the floodlights.

Only I forgot to put any clothes on, she thinks wryly.

She stands for a moment, looking at her naked body. The lighting is dramatic and makes her reflection seem thinner than she actually is.

She hears the scraping noise again, as if someone is running their nails across the windowsill. It's too dark to see if anyone's out there.

Susanna stares at the window and walks cautiously toward it, trying to see through the reflection. She grabs the dark blue bedspread and holds it up to cover herself. She shivers.

Reluctantly, she leans her face closer to the glass. The backyard becomes visible, like a dark gray world.

She sees the grass, the tall shrubs, Morgan's swing moving in the wind, and the panes of glass behind the playhouse for the sunroom they never got around to building.

Her breath mists the window as she straightens and closes the dark pink curtains. She lets the thick bedspread fall to the floor and walks naked toward the door. A shiver runs down her spine, and she turns back toward the window. A strip of glass is shimmering in the gap between the curtains.

She picks up her phone from the bedside table and calls Björn, and as the call is put through, she can't help staring at the window.

"Hello, darling," he answers far too loudly.

"Are you at the airport?"

"What?"

"Are you at—"

"I'm at the airport, I'm just having a burger at O'Leary's, and—"

His voice vanishes as a group of men in the background shout and cheer.

"Liverpool just scored again," he explains.

"Hooray," she says without enthusiasm.

"Your mom called me to ask what you want for your birthday."

"That's sweet," she says.

"I said you'd like some see-through underwear," he jokes.

"Thanks."

She stares at the shimmering glass between the curtains as the phone line crackles.

"Is everything okay at home?" Björn's voice says into her ear.

"I was just feeling a little scared of the dark."

"Is Ben there?"

"In front of the television," she replies.

"And Jerry?"

"They're both waiting for me." She smiles.

"I miss you," he says.

"Make sure you don't miss the plane," she whispers.

They talk some more, then say goodbye and blow kisses to each other over the phone. The line goes dead, and she finds herself thinking about a patient who was brought in last night. A young man who had crashed his motorcycle when he wasn't wearing a helmet, resulting in severe head injuries. His father had come straight to the hospital from his night shift. He was still wearing his dirty overalls and a breathing mask dangled around his neck.

Holding her pink kimono in front of her, she walks back to the living room and closes the heavy curtains.

Silence settles over the room.

The curtains sway in front of the windows, and she shudders as she turns away from them.

She tries the ice cream. It's much softer now, just right. The rich taste of chocolate fills her mouth.

Susanna sets the carton down and walks to the bathroom. She locks the door and turns the shower on, then loosens her ponytail and sets the scrunchie on the edge of the sink.

She lets out a sigh as the hot water washes over and envelops her body. Her ears are roaring as her shoulders relax and her muscles soften. She washes herself and runs her hand between her legs, noticing that the hair has already started to grow back since the last time she waxed.

Susanna wipes the steam from the glass door so she can see the handle and lock of the bathroom door.

Her mind keeps coming back to what she thought she saw in the bedroom window just as she was pulling the bedspread around herself.

She dismissed it as a trick of her imagination. She couldn't even see through the glass.

The room was too bright, and outside it was too dark.

But in the reflection of the dark bedspread, she thought she saw a face staring back at her.

The next moment it was gone, and she realized she must have

been mistaken, but now she can't help thinking it might have been real.

It wasn't a child, but maybe it was a neighbor out searching for their cat, who then stopped to look at her.

Susanna turns the water off. Her heart is pounding as she realizes the kitchen door is open. How could she have forgotten that? She's had it open all summer to let in the cool evening air, but usually shuts and locks it before taking a shower.

She wipes steam from the glass again and checks the lock on the bathroom door. Nothing has changed. She reaches for the towel and thinks she'll call Björn and ask him to stay on the phone as she goes through the house.

4

SUSANNA CAN HEAR APPLAUSE ON THE TELEVISION AS SHE leaves the bathroom. The thin silk of the kimono sticks to her damp skin.

There's a cold draft along the floor.

Her feet leave wet footprints on the worn parquet tiles.

There's a dark shimmer from the dining room windows. Black glass sparkles behind the hanging ferns. Susanna feels like she's being watched but forces herself not to look out. She doesn't want to scare herself even more.

Nonetheless, she keeps her distance from the closed door to the basement as she approaches the kitchen.

Her wet hair is soaking through the back of the kimono. It's so wet that it's dripping inside the fabric, trickling down her butt.

The floor gets colder the closer she gets to the kitchen.

Her heart is pounding hard.

She finds herself thinking again of the young man with serious head injuries. He was sedated. His whole face was crushed, pushed up toward his temples. His father kept repeating that there was nothing wrong with him. He could have used someone to talk to, but Susanna didn't have time.

Now she is imagining that the stocky father has found her, that he blames her, and is standing outside the kitchen door in his dirty overalls.

A different song is on the television now. She recognizes it as the theme song to a popular singing competition.

There's a breeze blowing straight through the kitchen. The door is wide open, and the vertical blinds flutter into the room. She walks slowly forward. It's hard to see anything behind the blinds.

She holds her hand out, pushes the blinds aside, slips past them, and reaches for the door handle.

The floor is chilly from the night air flowing into the kitchen.

Her kimono slips open.

She sees that the backyard is deserted. The bushes are moving in the wind, the swing swaying rhythmically.

She quickly closes the door, not bothered by catching part of the curtain in it, and hurriedly locks it, then pulls the key out and backs away.

She puts the key in the bowl of loose change and adjusts her kimono.

At least it's locked now, she thinks, as she hears a creak behind her back.

She spins around and then smiles at her own reaction. It was just the window in the living room shifting when the flow of air stopped.

On television, the audience is booing and whistling at the judges' decision.

Susanna thinks about getting her phone from the bedroom and calling Björn. He should be waiting at the gate by now. She wants to hear his voice as she searches the house before settling down in front of the television. She won't be able to relax otherwise. The only problem is, there's no reception in the basement. Maybe she could put it on speaker and leave it halfway down the stairs.

She tells herself that she doesn't have to sneak around in her own home, but she can't help moving quietly.

She passes the closed door to the basement, sees the dark windows in the dining room from the corner of her eye, and continues toward the living room.

She knows she locked the front door after her run, but she still wants to go and check.

There's a whistling sound from the open window in the living room, and the curtain is being sucked back toward the narrow opening.

She walks toward the dining room and notices that the wild-flowers in the vase on the heavy oak table have run out of water. Then she comes to an abrupt halt.

Her whole body feels like ice.

The three windows of the dining room act as large mirrors. The overhead light illuminates the table and eight chairs, and behind them there's a figure.

Susanna stares at the reflection of the room, her heart pounding so hard, it almost deafens her.

Someone is in the doorway holding a kitchen knife.

He's inside. He's inside the house, Susanna thinks.

She locked the kitchen door when she should have escaped.

Susanna moves slowly backward.

The intruder is standing completely still with his back to the dining room, staring at the hallway to the kitchen.

The large knife is hanging from his right hand, twitching impatiently.

Susanna backs away, her eyes fixed on the figure. Her right foot slides across the floor, and the parquet squeaks slightly.

She has to get out, but if she tries to get to the kitchen, she'll be visible. Maybe she can get to the key, but she may not make it.

She continues backing away cautiously, keeping her eye on the reflection.

The floor creaks beneath her left foot, and she stops and watches as the figure turns around to face the dining room. He looks up and sees her in the dark windows.

Susanna takes another slow step back. The intruder starts to walk toward her. She lets out a whimper as she turns and runs into the living room.

She slips on the carpet and hits her knee on the floor, putting her hands out to break her fall and gasping with pain.

There's the sound of a chair hitting the dining table.

Susanna knocks over a lamp as she pulls herself up. It hits the wall before clattering to the ground.

She hears rapid footsteps behind her.

Without looking around, she rushes into the bathroom and locks the door. The air in there is still warm and damp.

This can't be happening, she thinks in panic.

She hurries past the sink and toilet and pulls the curtain back from the little window. Her hands are shaking as she struggles to undo one of the catches. It's stuck. She tries to force herself to calm down. She fiddles with it, tugs it sideways, and manages to get the first catch open as she hears a scraping sound from the lock on the bathroom door. She rushes back and grabs the lock just as it starts to turn. She clings to it with both hands.

5

THE INTRUDER HAS SLIPPED A SCREWDRIVER, OR POSSIBLY the back of the knife blade, into the little slot on the other side of the lock. Susanna is holding on to the handle, but she's shaking so badly that she's scared of losing her grip.

"God, this can't be happening," she whispers to herself. "This isn't happening, it can't be happening . . ."

She glances toward the window. It's too small for her to be able to just throw herself through it. Her only hope of escape is to run to the window, undo the second catch, push it open, and then climb up. But she can't let go of the lock.

She's never been so terrified. This is a bottomless, mortal dread, beyond all control.

The lock feels hot and slippery under her tensed fingers. There's a metallic scraping sound from the other side.

"Hello?" she says toward the door.

The intruder tries to open the door with a quick twist, but Susanna is prepared and manages to resist.

"What do you want?" she says, in as composed a voice as she can muster. "Do you need money? If you do, I can help you. It's not a problem."

She gets no answer but hears the scrape of metal against metal and feels the vibration through the lock.

"You're welcome to look, but there's nothing especially valuable in the house. The television's fairly new, but . . ."

She stops speaking, because her voice is shaking so much it's hard to understand what she's saying. She clutches the lock tightly. She must stay calm. Her fear is dangerous, and it might provoke the intruder.

"My purse is hanging in the entryway," she says, then swallows hard. "A black bag. Inside it there's a wallet with some cash and a Visa card. I just got paid. I can give you my pin number if you want."

The intruder stops trying to turn the lock.

"Okay, listen, the pin is three-nine-four-five," she says to the door. "I haven't seen your face. You can take the money, and I'll wait until tomorrow before I report the card."

Still holding the lock tightly, Susanna puts her ear to the door and thinks she can hear footsteps moving away across the floor before a commercial break on television drowns out all other sounds.

She doesn't know if it was stupid to give him her real pin number, but she just wants this to end. She's more worried about her jewelry, especially her mother's engagement ring, and the necklace with the big emeralds she was given after Morgan was born.

Susanna waits behind the door and keeps telling herself that this isn't over yet, that she can't lose her concentration.

Carefully she changes hands on the lock, without letting go of it. Her right thumb and forefinger have gone numb. She shakes her hand and listens carefully. It's been more than half an hour since she told him her pin number.

It was probably just a junkie who saw an open kitchen door and came inside to look for valuables.

The show is ending. More commercials, and after them the news. She changes hands again and waits.

After another ten minutes, she lies down on the floor and peers under the door. There's no one standing outside.

She can see a large stretch of the parquet floor, and she can see under the sofa. The glow of the television reflects off the varnish.

Everything's quiet.

Burglars aren't violent. They just want money.

Trembling, she gets up and grabs the lock again, then stands still with her ear to the door, listening to the news and weather forecast.

Grabbing the squeegee from the floor as a weapon, she steels herself and cautiously unlocks the door.

The door swings open without a sound.

She can see most of the living room through the hallway. There's no sign of the intruder. It's as if he's never been there.

She leaves the bathroom, her legs shaking with fear. Every sense is heightened as she approaches the living room.

She hears a dog bark in the distance.

Carefully she moves forward and sees the light from the television play on the closed curtains, the sofa and the glass coffee table with the carton of ice cream.

She's planning to go into the bedroom and get her phone, then lock herself in the bathroom again and call the police.

To her left, she sees the glass-fronted cabinet containing the collection of Dresden china that Björn inherited. Her heart beats faster. She's almost at the end of the passageway, where she'll be able to see into the hall.

She takes a step into the living room, looks around, and notes that the dining room is empty, before realizing that the intruder is right next to her, just one step away.

The stab of the knife is so fast, she doesn't have time to react. The sharp blade goes straight into her chest.

Her muscles spasm deep inside her body.

Her heart has never beat so hard. Time stands still. She still can't believe this is happening.

The knife is pulled out. She presses her hand to the wound and feels warm blood pumping out between her fingers. The squeegee falls to the floor as she reels to one side. Her head feels heavy, and she can see her blood splattered across the raincoats hanging in the entryway. The light seems to be flickering, and she tries to say that this must be some sort of misunderstanding, but she has no voice.

She turns around and walks toward the kitchen. She feels quick jabs to her back and knows she is being stabbed repeatedly.

She stumbles sideways and knocks the display cabinet against the wall, toppling all the porcelain figures with a clattering, tinkling sound.

Her heart is racing as blood streams down the kimono. Her chest hurts terribly.

Her field of vision shrinks to a tunnel.

Her ears are roaring, and she is aware that the intruder is shouting something, but the words are unintelligible.

Her chin flies up as the intruder grabs her hair. She tries to hold on to an armchair but loses her grip.

Her legs give out, and she hits the floor, collapsing onto her back.

She can feel a burning sensation in her chest and coughs weakly.

Her head lolls sideways, and she can see there's some old popcorn lying in the dust under the sofa.

Through the roaring sound inside her head, she can hear strange screams. She feels rapid stabs to her stomach and chest.

She tries to kick free, thinking she has to get back to the bathroom, but the floor beneath her is slippery, and she has no energy left.

She tries to roll over onto her side, but the intruder grabs her by the chin and jabs the knife into her face. It no longer hurts. Her head is spinning. She can't believe this is happening. Shock and dislocation blur with the precise and intimate feeling of being cut in the face.

The blade enters her neck and chest and face again. Her lips and cheeks fill with warmth and pain.

Susanna realizes that she's not going to make it. Ice-cold anguish opens up like a chasm as she stops fighting for her life.

6

PSYCHIATRIST ERIK MARIA BARK IS LEANING BACK IN HIS pale gray sheepskin armchair. He has a large study in his home, with a varnished oak floor and built-in bookcases. The dark brick villa is in the oldest part of Gamla Enskede, just south of Stockholm.

It's the middle of the day, but he was on call last night and could use a few hours' sleep.

He shuts his eyes and thinks about when Benjamin, his son, was little and liked to hear how Mommy and Daddy met. Erik would sit on the edge of his bed and explain that Cupid really did exist. He lived up among the clouds and looked like a chubby little boy with a bow and arrow in his hands.

"One summer's evening Cupid gazed down at Sweden and saw me," Erik explained to his son. "I was at a college party, pushing my way through the crowd on the roof deck, when Cupid crept to the edge of his cloud and fired an arrow down toward the Earth.

"I was wandering around at the party, talking to friends, eating peanuts, and talking to the head of the department.

"And a woman with strawberry-blond hair and a champagne glass in her hand looked in my direction. At that exact moment, Cupid's arrow hit me in the heart."

After almost twenty years of marriage, Erik and Simone had agreed to separate, but she was the one who really wanted it.

As Erik leans forward to switch the light off, he catches a glimpse of his tired face in the narrow mirror by the bookcase.

The lines on his forehead and the furrows in his cheeks are deeper than ever. His dark brown hair is flecked with gray. He ought to get a haircut. A few loose strands are hanging in front of his eyes, and he flicks them away with a jerk of his head.

When Simone told him she had met John, Erik realized it was over. Benjamin was pretty relaxed about the whole thing and used to tease him by saying it would be cool to have two dads.

Benjamin is eighteen now and lives in the big house in Stockholm with Simone, her new husband, Benjamin's stepbrothers and -sisters, and the dogs.

Erik turns from the mirror and looks at his old smoking table. On it is the latest edition of the *American Journal of Psychiatry* and a copy of Ovid's *Metamorphoses*, with a half-empty blister pack of sleeping pills as a bookmark. He pulls the pills from the book and pops one into his hand, trying to figure out how long it would take his body to absorb the active substance, then gives up. Just to be sure, he breaks the tablet in half along the little groove, blows the loose powder off to get rid of the bitter taste, then swallows half of it.

The rain streams down the windows as the muted tones of John Coltrane's "Dear Old Stockholm" flow from the speakers.

The tablet's chemical warmth spreads through his muscles. He shuts his eyes and enjoys the music.

Erik is a psychiatrist who specializes in psychological trauma and disaster counseling.

He worked for the Red Cross in Uganda for five years. He has spent four years at Karolinska Institute leading a groundbreaking research project into group therapy involving deep hypnosis. He is a member of the European Society of Hypnosis and is regarded as a leading international authority in clinical hypnotherapy.

At the moment, he is part of a small team studying acutely traumatized and post-traumatic patients. They are regularly called in to help the police and prosecutors with victim interviews.

He uses hypnosis to help witnesses relax, so that they can come to grips with traumatic situations.

In three hours, he needs to be at a meeting at Karolinska, and he's hoping to spend most of that time asleep.

He's pulled straight into deep sleep and starts dreaming that he's carrying an old, bearded man through a very small house. Simone is shouting at him from behind a closed door—when the phone rings.

Erik jumps and fumbles for the phone. His heart is beating hard from the anxiety of being yanked out of a state of deep sleep.

"Simone," he answers groggily.

"Oh hello, Simone," Nelly jokes. "Maybe it's time to give up those French cigarettes? From your voice, I could have sworn you were a man."

Erik smiles, feeling the heaviness of the sleeping pill in his head. "All right, Nelly. You got me."

Nelly Brandt is a psychologist, and Erik's closest colleague at Karolinska Hospital.

"Listen, Erik," she says, and only now does he hear the stress in her voice. "The police are at the hospital, and they're really agitated. They brought in a new patient who's in a state of shock."

Erik rubs his eyes and tries to listen to what Nelly is saying about the patient. He squints toward the window facing the street as water streams down the glass.

"We're checking his somatic status and running routine tests," she says. "Blood and urine, liver status, kidney and thyroid function."

"Good."

"Erik, the lieutenant asked for you specifically. It's my fault. I happened to let slip that you were the best."

"Flattery doesn't work on me," he says, getting to his feet unsteadily. He rubs his face with his hand, then grabs the furniture as he makes his way toward the desk.

"I hate to bother you, but this is urgent. Can you come in as soon as possible?" she asks.

"Yes, but I—"

"Great. You're a superhero. I'll tell the police you're on your way."

Beneath the desk are a pair of black socks, a taxi receipt, and a cellphone charger. As he bends over to grab the socks, the floor comes rushing up to meet him, and he almost falls but stops himself just in time.

The objects on the desk merge and divide in his double vision. The silver pens radiate harsh reflections.

He reaches for a half-empty glass of water, takes a sip, and tells himself to get his act together.

7

KAROLINSKA UNIVERSITY HOSPITAL IS ONE OF THE LARGEST in Europe, with more than fifteen thousand staff members. The Psychology Clinic is separated from the rest of the vast hospital. Though it doesn't stand out if you approach it from the street, from above, the building looks like a rock carving of a Viking ship.

The car tires crunch softly as Erik turns into the parking lot.

Nelly is on the steps waiting for him with two mugs of coffee. She's fairly tall and thin. She keeps her bleached hair neat, and her makeup is always tasteful.

Erik often sees her and her husband, Martin. Her husband is the main shareholder of Datametrix Nordic, so Nelly doesn't really need to work. But she's good at what she does, and she's confessed to Erik before that without her own career, she would get restless.

As she watches Erik's BMW pull into the parking lot, she walks over to him, a mug in each hand. She blows on one of them and takes a cautious sip before setting it on the roof of the car while opening the passenger door.

"I don't know what this is about. The police lieutenant seems pretty wound up," she says, passing him the other mug over the seat.

"Thanks."

"I explained to her that we always put our patients first," Nelly says as she gets in and closes the car door behind her. "Shit! God, sorry. Do you have any tissues? I spilled some coffee on the seat."

"Don't worry."

The smell of coffee spreads through the car, and Erik closes his eyes for a moment. "Tell me what they said."

"Nothing I haven't already told you. The bitchy—I mean, lovely—policewoman wants to speak to you directly."

"Is there anything I should know before I go inside?" he asks, opening his car door.

"I told her she could wait in your office and go through your drawers."

"Thanks for the coffee. Both mugs," he says, as they get out of the car.

Erik locks up, puts the keys in his pocket, runs a hand through his hair, and starts toward the clinic.

"Good luck!" she calls after him.

He goes inside and runs his passcard through the reader, then walks down the hallway to his office. He still feels groggy, and it occurs to him that he really needs to get the pills under control. They make him sleep too deeply. It's almost like drowning. His drugged dreams have started to feel claustrophobic. Yesterday he had a nightmare about two dogs that had grown into each other, and last week he fell asleep at the clinic and had a sexual dream about Nelly. He can't recall most of it, but he remembers that she was on her knees in front of him handing him a cold glass ball.

His thoughts dissipate when he sees the detective sitting on his office chair with her feet propped up on the trashcan. She's holding her huge stomach with one hand and a can of Coke in the other. Her brow is furrowed, and she's breathing through her half-open mouth.

Her ID badge is lying on his desk, and she gestures wearily toward it as she introduces herself: "Margot Silverman. National Crime."

"Erik Maria Bark," he says, shaking her hand.

"Thanks for coming in at such short notice," she says, moistening her lips. "We've got a traumatized witness, and everyone tells me I should have you in the room with me. We've already tried to question him four times."

"I have to point out," Erik says, "that there are five of us in our unit, and I never sit in on interviews of perpetrators or suspected perpetrators."

The light from the ceiling lamp reflects off her pale eyes. Her curly hair is trying to escape from her thick braid.

"Okay, but Björn Kern isn't a suspect. He works in London and was on a plane home when someone murdered his wife." She squeezes the Coke can, making the thin metal creak.

"Ah," Erik says.

"He got a taxi from Arlanda and found her dead," the lieutenant goes on. "We don't know exactly what he did after that. He was certainly busy. We're not sure where she was lying originally, but we found her tucked in bed in the bedroom. He cleaned up as well, wiped away the blood. He doesn't remember anything, he says, but the furniture had been moved, and the blood-soaked rug was already in the washing machine. He was found more than a kilometer from the house. A neighbor almost ran him over on the road. He was still wearing his blood-soaked suit and no shoes."

"I'll see him," Erik says. "But I must say at the outset, it would be wrong to try to force information from him."

"He has to talk," she says stubbornly, squeezing the can tighter.

"I understand your frustration, but he could enter a psychosis if you push too hard. Give him time, and he'll tell you what you need."

"You've helped the police before, haven't you?"

"Many times."

"But this time . . . this is the second murder in what looks like a series," she says.

"A series?"

Margot's face has turned gray, and the thin lines around her eyes are emphasized by the light. "We're hunting a serial killer."

"Okay, I get that, but the patient needs—"

"This murderer has entered an active phase, and he isn't going to stop of his own accord," she interrupts. "And Björn Kern is a disaster from my point of view. First he goes around and rearranges everything at the crime scene before the police get there, and now we can't get him to tell us what it looked like when he arrived."

She drops her feet to the floor, whispers to herself that they need to get going, then sits there stiff-backed, panting for breath.

"If we pressure him now, he may clam up for good," Erik says as he unlocks his cabinet and removes the case containing his video camera.

She gets to her feet, setting the can on the desk at last, picks up her badge, and walks heavily toward the door. "Obviously I realize he's gone through hell, but he's going to have to pull himself together and—"

"Yes, but it's more than that. It might actually be impossible for him to think about it at the moment," Erik replies. "Because what you've described sounds like a critical stress response, and—"

"Those are just words," she interrupts, her cheeks flushing with irritation.

"A mental trauma can be followed by an acute blockage—"

"Why? I don't believe that," she says.

"As you may know, our spatial and temporal memories are organized by the hippocampus, and that information is then conveyed to the prefrontal cortex," Erik replies patiently, pointing to his forehead. "But that all changes at times of extreme arousal and in cases of shock. When the amygdala identifies a threat, both the autonomous nervous system and what's known as the cortisol axis are activated, and—"

"I get it. Lots of stuff happens in the brain."

"The important thing is that this degree of stress means that memories aren't stored the way they usually are. They're frozen, like ice cubes, separately. Closed off."

"You're saying he's doing his best," Margot says, putting her hand on her stomach. "But Björn may have seen something that can help us stop this killer. You have to get him to calm down so he'll start talking."

"I will, but I can't tell you how long that's going to take," he replies. "I've worked in Uganda with people who've suffered the trauma of war, people whose lives have been completely shattered. You have to move slowly and use security, sleep, conversation, exercise, medication—"

"Not hypnosis?" she asks, with an involuntary smile.

"Sure, as long as no one has exaggerated expectations about the result. Sometimes gentle hypnosis can help a patient to restructure their memories so that they can be accessed."

"Right now I'd give the go-ahead for a horse to kick him in the head if that would help."

"That's a different department," Erik says drily.

"Sorry, I get impatient when I'm pregnant," she says, and he can hear how hard she's working to sound reasonable. "But I have to identify any parallels with the first murder. I need a pattern if I'm going to be able to track down this murderer, and right now I don't have a thing."

They've reached the patient's room. Two uniformed police officers are standing outside the door.

"I understand this is important to you," Erik says. "But bear in mind that he just found his wife murdered."

8

ERIK FOLLOWS MARGOT INTO THE ROOM. IT HAS BEEN FUR-
nished with two armchairs and a sofa, a low white table, two chairs,
a water cooler with plastic cups, and a garbage can.

There is a broken pot under the windowsill, and the linoleum
floor is strewn with soil.

The man is standing in the far corner, as if he were trying to get
as far away as possible.

When he sees Erik and Margot, he slides toward the sofa with
his back against the wall. He's extremely pale, and there's a hunted
look in his eyes. His blue shirt has sweat rings under the arms and
is hanging outside his pants.

"Hello, Björn," Margot says. "This is Erik. He's a doctor here."

The man peers anxiously at Erik, then moves back into the
corner.

"Hello," Erik says.

"I'm not sick."

"No, but what you've been through means that you have the
right to treatment nonetheless," Erik replies matter-of-factly.

"You don't know what I've been through," the man says, then
whispers something to himself.

"I know you haven't been given any tranquilizers," Erik says.
"But I'd like you to know that the option is there, if—"

"What the fuck do I want pills for?" he butts in. "Will pills help?
Will they make everything all right?"

"No, but—"

"Will they let me see Sanna again?" he shouts. "That's not going to happen—is it?"

"Nothing can change what happened," Erik says seriously. "But your relationship to what happened will change, regardless of whether you—"

"I don't understand what you're saying."

"I'm just trying to explain that the way you're feeling is part of a process, and I'd like to help you with that process if you'll let me."

Björn glances at him, then slips farther away along the wall.

Margot sets her little recording device on the table, then says the date and time and the names of those present in the room. "This is the fifth interview with Björn Kern," she concludes, then turns toward him as he picks at the sofa. "Björn, can you tell me in your own words—"

"About what?" he asks quickly. "About what?"

"About when you got home," Margot replies.

"What for?" he whispers.

"Because I want to know what happened and what you saw," she says curtly.

"What do you mean? I just got home, isn't that allowed?" He puts his hands over his ears and stands there panting.

Erik notes that the knuckles of both his hands are bleeding.

"What did you see?" Margot asks wearily.

"Why are you asking me that? I don't know why you're asking me. Fuck . . ." Björn shakes his head and rubs his mouth and eyes.

"I want you to feel safe here in this room," Erik says. "I know you don't think you're allowed to relax, but you are."

Björn picks at the edge of a piece of wallpaper with his fingernails, then tears off a little strip. "This is what I'm thinking," he says without looking at them. "I'm thinking I have to do it all again, but do it right this time. I have to go home and go in through the door, and then it will be right."

"What do you mean, *right*?" Erik asks, managing to catch his eye.

"I know how it sounds, but what if it's true, you don't know," he says, gesturing at them to keep quiet. "I can go in through the door, and call Sanna's name. She knows I have something for her, I always do, something from duty-free. And I take my shoes off and go inside."

He looks utterly distraught.

"There's soil on the floor," he whispers.

"Was there soil on the floor?" Margot asks.

"Shut up!" Björn yells, his voice cracking.

He walks over the soil-strewn floor, picks up the other potted plant, and throws it at the wall. The pot shatters, and soil rains down behind the sofa.

"Fucking HELL!" he gasps. He leans against the wall, and a string of saliva drops to the floor.

"Björn?"

"Fuck it, this is hopeless," he says with a sob.

"Björn," Erik says slowly. "Margot is here to find out more about what happened. That's her job. My job is to help you. I'm here for you. I'm used to seeing people who are having trouble, people who have suffered a terrible loss, who've experienced terrible things . . . things no one should have to go through, but which unfortunately are part of life for some of us."

The man doesn't respond. He just sobs quietly. His eyes are dark, bloodshot, and glassy.

"Do you want to stand over there?" Erik asks gently. "You wouldn't rather sit in the armchair?"

"I don't care."

"Nor do I."

"Good," Björn whispers, turning toward him.

"I've already mentioned it, and I know what you said, but it's my job to offer you all the help that's available. I can give you a sedative. It won't get rid of the terrible thing that's happened, but it will help calm the panic you're feeling inside."

"Can you help me?" the man whispers after a pause.

"I can help you take the first steps toward . . . toward getting through the worst of it," Erik explains quietly.

"I start to shake when I think about the front door at home . . . because I must have gone through a different door, the wrong door."

"I understand why you feel that way."

Björn moves his lips cautiously, as though they were hurting him. "Do you want me to sit down?" He glances cautiously at Erik.

"If it would make you feel more comfortable," Erik replies.

Björn sits for the first time, and Erik notices Margot looking at him, but he doesn't meet her eye.

"What happens when you walk through the wrong door?"

"I don't want to think about it," he replies.

"But you remember?"

"Can you . . . can you get rid of the panic?" the man whispers to Erik.

"That's your decision," Erik says. "But I'm happy to sit here and talk to you with Margot, or you and I could talk on our own. And we could also try hypnosis—that might help you through the worst of it."

"Hypnosis?"

"Some people find it works well," Erik replies simply.

"No." Björn smiles.

"Hypnosis is just a combination of relaxation and concentration."

Björn laughs silently with his hand over his mouth, then stands up and walks along the wall again until he reaches the corner and turns to look at Erik. "I think maybe the drugs you mentioned might be a good idea."

"Okay." Erik nods. "I can give you Stesolid—have you heard of it? It'll make you feel warm and tired but also a lot calmer."

"Okay, good." Björn slaps the wall several times with one palm, then walks over to the water cooler.

"I'll ask a nurse to bring you the pill," Erik says.

He leaves the room, confident that Björn Kern will request hypnosis soon.

9

THE GOTHIC DESIGN OF THE BUILDING AT 4 LILL-JANS PLAN differs from those around it. It has a dark facade, ornamental brickwork, bay windows, pilasters, and arches.

The curtains on the ground floor are closed.

Erik checks the address on the piece of paper, hesitates for a moment, then goes in through the large doorway. He hasn't told anyone about this.

His stomach flutters. He can hear gentle piano music in the stairwell. He looks at the time, sees he's slightly early, and returns to the front door to wait.

Back in the spring, he found a flyer advertising piano lessons in his mailbox and rather rashly booked an intensive course for his son Benjamin, who would be turning eighteen at the beginning of the summer.

It's never too late to learn to play an instrument, he thought. He himself had always dreamed of playing the piano, sitting down alone to play a melancholy nocturne by Chopin.

But the day before Benjamin's birthday, Nelly pointed out that you didn't have to be a psychologist to see that he was projecting his own dream onto his son.

Erik quickly booked a series of driving lessons instead. Benjamin was happy, and Simone thought it was a very generous gift.

He was sure he had canceled the piano lessons. But that morning he received an email reminding him not to miss the first lesson.

Erik feels ridiculously embarrassed, but he's decided to attend the first lesson himself anyway, to give it a chance.

The idea of walking away and sending a text to say that he had already canceled the lessons is whirling around his head, but he returns to the door, raises his finger, and rings the bell.

The piano music doesn't stop, but he hears someone run lightly across the floor.

A small child opens the door, a girl of about seven, with big pale eyes and tousled hair. She's wearing a polka-dot dress and is holding a toy hedgehog.

"Mommy's with a student," she says softly.

The beautiful music streams through the flat.

"I have an appointment at seven o'clock. I'm here for a piano lesson," he explains.

"Mommy says you have to start when you're little," the girl says.

"If you want to get good, but I'm not going to do that." He smiles. "I'll be happy if the piano doesn't cover its ears or scream."

The girl can't help smiling back. "Can I take your coat?" she remembers to ask.

"Can you carry it?"

He places his heavy coat in her thin arms and watches her disappear toward the closet down the hall.

A woman in her mid-thirties walks down the hallway toward him. She seems deep in thought, but perhaps she's just listening to the music.

Her hair is black and cut in a short, boyish style, and her eyes are hidden behind small round sunglasses. Her lips are pale pink, and her face appears to be completely free of makeup, yet she still looks like a French movie star.

He realizes she must be Jackie Federer, the piano teacher.

She's wearing a loose-knit black sweater, a suede skirt, and flat ballet pumps.

"Benjamin?" she asks.

"My name is Erik Maria Bark. I booked the lessons for my son, Benjamin, as a birthday present, but I never told him about the gift. I've come instead, because I'm the one who actually wants to learn how to play."

"You want to learn to play the piano?"

"Unless I'm too old," he hurries to say.

"Come in. I'm just finishing up a lesson," the woman says.

He follows her down the hallway and sees her trace the fingers of one hand along the wall as she walks. "I got Benjamin another present, obviously," he explains to her back.

She opens a door and the music gets louder. "Have a seat," she says as she sits on the edge of the sofa.

Light is streaming into the room from high windows looking out onto a leafy inner courtyard.

A teenage girl is sitting at a black piano, her back straight. She is playing an advanced piece, and her body rocks gently. She turns a page of the score, then her fingers run across the keys, and her feet press deftly on the pedals.

"Stay in time," Jackie says, her chin jutting.

The girl blushes but goes on playing. It sounds wonderful, but Erik can see that Jackie isn't happy.

He wonders if she used to be a star, a famous concert pianist whose name he should know: Jackie Federer, a diva who wears dark glasses indoors.

The piece comes to an end, its notes lingering in the air until they ebb away. They've almost vanished when the girl takes her foot off the right pedal, and the damper muffles the strings.

"Good, that sounded much better today," Jackie says.

"Thank you," the girl says, picking up her score and hurrying out.

Silence descends on the room. The large tree in the courtyard is casting swaying green shadows across the pale wooden floor.

"So you want to learn to play the piano," Jackie says, getting up from the sofa.

"I've always dreamed of learning, but I've never gotten around to it. Naturally, I have absolutely no talent at all," Erik explains quickly. "I'm completely unmusical."

"That's a shame," she says quietly.

"Yes."

"Well, we might as well give it a try." She puts her hand out to the wall.

"Mommy, I've mixed some juice," the little girl says, and comes into the room with a tray containing glasses of juice.

"Ask our guest if he's thirsty."

"Are you thirsty?"

"Thank you, that's very kind of you," Erik says, and takes a sip. "Do you play the piano as well?"

"I'm better than Mommy was at my age," the girl replies, as if that's a phrase she's heard many times.

Jackie smiles and strokes her daughter's hair and neck rather clumsily, before turning back toward him. "You've paid for twenty lessons."

"I have a tendency to go overboard," Erik admits.

"So what do you want to get out of the course?"

"If I'm honest, I fantasize about being able to play a sonata or one of Chopin's nocturnes." Erik feels himself blush. "But I know I'm going to have to start with 'Baa, Baa, Black Sheep.'"

"We can work with Chopin, but perhaps an étude instead."

"If there's a short one."

"Madeleine, can you get me Chopin? Opus twenty-five, the first étude."

The girl searches the shelf next to Jackie, pulls out a folder, and removes the score. Only when she puts it in her mother's hand does Erik realize that the teacher is blind.

10

ERIK SMILES AS HE SITS IN FRONT OF THE HIGHLY POLISHED black piano with the name C. BECHSTEIN, BERLIN stenciled in small gold lettering.

"He needs to lower the stool," the girl says.

Erik stands up and lowers the seat by spinning it a few times.

"We'll start with your right hand, but we'll pick out some notes with your left."

He looks at her fair face, with its straight nose and half-open mouth.

"Don't look at me, look at the notes and the keyboard," she says, reaching over his shoulder and putting her little finger gently on one of the black keys. A high note echoes inside the piano.

"This is E flat. We'll start with the first measure which consists of six notes, six sixteenths," she says, and plays the notes.

"Okay," Erik mutters.

"Where did I start?"

He presses the key, producing a hard note.

"Use your little finger."

"How did you know—"

"Because it's natural. Now play," she says.

He struggles through the lesson, concentrating on her instructions, stressing the first note of the six, but when he has to add a few notes with his left hand, he loses his way. A couple of times she touches his hand and tells him to relax his fingers.

"Okay, you're tired. Let's stop there," Jackie says neutrally. "You've done some good work."

She gives him notes for the next lesson, then asks the girl to show him to the door. They pass a closed door with NO ENTRY! scrawled in childish writing on a large sign.

"Is that your room?" Erik asks.

"Only Mommy's allowed in there," the child says.

"When I was little, I wouldn't even let my mommy come into my room."

"Really?"

"I drew a big skull and hung it on the door, but I think she went in anyway, because sometimes there were clean sheets on the bed."

The evening air is fresh when he steps outside. It feels like he's hardly taken a breath during the lesson. His back is so tense it hurts, and he still feels strangely embarrassed.

When he gets home, he takes a long, hot shower. Then he calls the piano teacher.

"Yes, this is Jackie."

"Hello, Erik Maria Bark here. Your new student."

"Hello," she says, curious.

"I'm calling to . . . to apologize. I wasted your whole evening and . . . well, I can see it's hopeless, it's too late for me to—"

"You did some good work, like I said," Jackie says. "Do the exercises I gave you, and I'll see you again soon."

He doesn't know what to say.

"Goodnight," she says, and ends the call.

Before he goes to bed, he puts on Chopin's Opus 25, to hear what he's aiming at. When the pianist Maurizio Pollini's bubbling notes fill the room, he can't help laughing.

11

THE SUN IS HIGH ABOVE THE TREES, AND THE BLUE AND white plastic tape is fluttering in the breeze, its shadow dancing on the tarmac.

The police officers posted at the cordon let through a black Lincoln Town Car, and it rolls slowly along Stenhammars Road as a reflection of the green gardens runs across the black paint like a forest at night.

Margot Silverman pulls over to the curb and glides smoothly to a halt behind the command vehicle, then sits for a while with her hand on the handbrake.

She's thinking about how hard they worked to try to identify Susanna Kern before time ran out, even after an hour had passed and they realized it was too late, they kept trying anyway.

She and Adam had gone down to see the exhausted IT experts and had just been told that it wasn't possible to trace the video clip when the call came in.

Shortly after two o'clock in the morning, the forensics team were at the scene, and the entire area between Bromma Kyrk Road and Lillängs Street had been cordoned off.

The task of examining the crime scene continued throughout the day as further attempts were made to question the victim's husband, with the help of psychiatrist Erik Maria Bark.

The police have knocked on doors in the neighborhood, they've checked recordings from nearby traffic cameras, and Margot has scheduled a meeting for herself and Adam with a forensics expert named Erixon.

She takes a deep breath, picks up her McDonald's bag, and gets out of the car.

Outside the cordon blocking off Stenhammars Road is a growing pile of flowers, and there are now three candles burning. A few shocked neighbors have gathered in the parish hall.

They have no suspects.

Susanna's ex-husband was playing soccer at Kristineberg Sports Club with their son when the police caught up with him. They already knew he had an alibi for the time of the murder but took him aside to tell him.

Margot has been told that after he was informed, he went back in goal and saved penalty after penalty from the boy.

This morning Margot drew up a plan for the investigation, given the absence of any witnesses or forensic results.

They're planning to track down anyone who's been institutionalized or attended a clinic for obsessive-compulsive disorder therapy in the past couple of years, paying particular attention to people convicted of sex crimes who have either been released or granted parole, and then work closely with the criminal profiling unit.

Margot crumples the paper bag while she's still chewing, then hands it to a uniformed officer. "I'm eating for five," she says.

Wearily she lifts the crime scene tape over her head, then walks heavily toward Adam, who is waiting outside the gate. "Just so you know, there's no serial killer," she says sullenly.

"So I heard," he replies, letting her go through the gate ahead of him.

"Bosses," she sighs. "What the hell are they thinking? The evening tabloids are going to speculate no matter what we say. The press is always going to dump on the police. For them, it's like shooting a fucking barrel."

"Fish in a barrel," Adam corrects her.

"We don't know what effects the media are likely to have on the perpetrator," she goes on. "He might feel exposed and become more cautious, then withdraw for a while. Or all the attention could feed his vanity and make him overconfident."

A man dressed in white protective overalls opens a can of Coca-Cola and hurries to drink it, as though there were some magic in the first bubbles. His face is shiny with sweat, his mask is tucked below his chin, and his huge stomach is straining at the seams of his overalls.

"I'm looking for Erixon," Margot says.

"Try looking for a giant marshmallow that cries if you so much as mention the numbers five and two," Erixon replies, holding out his hand.

While Margot and Adam pull on their thin protective overalls, Erixon tells them he's managed to pull a print of a rubber-soled boot, size 43, from the outside steps, but all the evidence inside the house has been ruined or contaminated thanks to the victim's husband's efforts to clean up.

"Everything's taking five times as long," he says, wiping the sweat from his cheeks with a white handkerchief. "We can't attempt the usual reconstruction, but I have a few ideas about what happened that we can talk through."

"And the body?"

"We'll take a look at Susanna, but she's been moved, and . . . well, you know."

"Put to bed," Margot says.

Erixon helps her with the zipper on her overalls, as Adam rolls up his sleeves.

"We could start a kids' show about three marshmallows," Margot says, placing both hands on her stomach.

They sign their names on the list of visitors to the crime scene, then follow Erixon to the front door.

"Ready?" he asks with sudden solemnity. "An ordinary home, an ordinary woman, all those good years—then a visitor from hell for a few short minutes."

They go inside. The protective plastic rustles, and the door closes behind them, the hinges squealing like a trapped hare. The daylight vanishes, and the sudden shift from a late-summer day to the gloom of the hallway is blinding.

They stand still as their eyes adjust.

The air is warm, and there are bloody handprints on the doorframe and around the lock and handle.

A vacuum cleaner with no nozzle is on a plastic sheet on the floor. There's a trickle of dark blood from the hose.

Adam breathes heavily through his mask, and beads of sweat break out on his forehead.

They follow Erixon across the protective boards on the floor to the kitchen. There are bloody footprints on the linoleum. They've been clumsily wiped, then stepped in again. One side of the sink is blocked with wet paper towels, and a squeegee is floating in the murky water.

"We've found prints from Björn's feet," Erixon says. "First he went around in his blood-soaked socks, then barefoot. We found his socks in the garbage can in the kitchen."

He falls silent, and they continue into the hallway that connects the kitchen with the dining and living rooms.

A crime scene changes over time and is gradually destroyed as the investigation proceeds. So as not to miss any evidence, crime scene investigators start by securing garbage cans and vehicles parked in the area, and they note specific smells and other transitory elements.

Apart from that, they conduct a general examination of the crime scene from the outside in and approach the body and the actual murder scene with caution.

Erixon leads Margot and Adam into the living room, which is bathed in sunlight. The cloying smell of blood is inescapable, but the chaos is oddly invisible because the furniture has been wiped and put back in position.

Yesterday evening Margot saw Susanna on video as she stood in this room eating ice cream with a spoon, straight from the carton.

A plane comes in to land at Bromma Airport with a thunderous roar, making the glass-fronted cabinet rattle. Margot notes that all the porcelain figures are lying down, as if they were asleep.

Flies are buzzing around a bloody mop that's been left behind the sofa. The water in the bucket is dark red, the floor streaked. It's possible to see the trail of the mop from the damp marks left on the baseboards and furniture.

"First he tried to vacuum up the blood," Erixon says. "Then, I'm not sure, but he seems to have mopped the floor, then wiped it with a dishcloth and paper towels."

"He doesn't remember anything," Margot says.

"Almost all the original bloodstain patterns have been destroyed, but he missed some here," Erixon says, pointing to a thin spatter on a strip of wallpaper.

He's used a classic technique and has stretched eight threads from the outermost marks on the wall to find the point where they converge—the point where the blood originated.

"This is one precise point. The knife goes in at an angle from above, fairly deep," Erixon says breathlessly. "And of course this is one of the first blows."

"Because she's on her feet," Margot says quietly.

"Because she's still on her feet," he confirms.

Margot looks at the cabinet with the prone porcelain figures and thinks that Susanna must have stumbled and hit it when she was trying to escape.

"This wall has been cleaned," Erixon says, showing them. "So I'm having to guess a bit now, but she was probably leaning with her back against it and slid down. She may have rolled over once and may have kicked her legs. Either way, she certainly lay here for a while with a punctured lung."

Margot bends over and sees the blood that has been expectorated across the back of the sofa, from below, possibly while Susanna coughed.

"But the blood got over here, too, didn't it?" she says, pointing. "Susanna struggled."

"And we don't know where Björn found her?" Adam asks.

"No, but we do have a large volume of blood over there," Erixon says, pointing.

"And there," Margot says, gesturing toward the window.

"Yes, she was there, but she was dragged there. She was in various different places after she died. She lay on the sofa, and . . . in the bathroom, as well as . . ."

"And now she's in the bedroom," Margot says.

12

THE WHITE LIGHT OF THE FLOODLAMPS FILLS THE BEDROOM.
Everything is illuminated: every thread, every swirling mote of
dust. A trail of blood drops runs across the pale gray carpet to the
bed, like tiny black pearls.

Margot stops just inside the door, but the others move toward
the bed. Then the rustling of their overalls stops.

"God," Adam gasps in a muffled voice.

Once again Margot thinks of the video, of Susanna walking
around, her pants dangling from one foot as she kicks them off.

She lowers her eyes and sees that her clothes have been turned
right side out and are now piled neatly on the chair.

"Margot? Are you okay?"

She meets Adam's gaze. She sees his dilated pupils, hears the
dull buzz of flies, and forces herself to look at the victim.

The covers have been pulled up under her chin.

Her face is a nothing but dark red pulp. The killer hacked, cut,
stabbed, and carved away at it.

She moves closer and sees a single eye staring crookedly at the
ceiling.

Erixon folds the covers back. They're stiff with gore; skin and
fabric have stuck together. There's a faint crunching sound as the
dried blood comes loose, and little crumbs rain down.

Adam raises a hand to his mouth.

The brutality was concentrated around her face, neck, and chest.
The dead woman is naked and smeared in blood. She's covered in

stab wounds, and Margot can see blood that spread beneath her skin.

Erixon photographs the body, and Margot points at a mottled green patch to the right of the victim's stomach.

"That's normal," Erixon says.

Her pubic hair has started to regrow around the reddish-blond tuft on her pudenda. There are no visible marks or injuries to the insides of her thighs.

Erixon takes several hundred pictures of the body, starting with her head resting on the pillow and moving all the way down to the tips of her toes.

"I'm going to have to touch you now, Susanna," he whispers, and lifts her left arm.

He turns it over and looks at the defensive wounds, cuts that indicate that she tried to fend off the attack.

With practiced gestures, he scrapes under her fingernails, the most common place to find a perpetrator's DNA. He uses a new tube for each nail, attaches a label, and makes a note on the computer on the bedside table.

Her fingers are limp, no longer seized by rigor mortis.

When he's finished with her nails, he carefully pulls a plastic bag over her hand and fastens it with tape.

"I visit ordinary people every week," Erixon murmurs. "They've all got broken glass, overturned furniture, and blood on the floor."

He walks around the bed to continue with the nails of the other hand. Just as he's about to pick it up, he stops.

"There's something in her hand," he says, reaching for his camera. "Do you see?"

Margot leans forward and looks. She can make out a dark object between the dead woman's fingers. She must have been clutching it tightly, but now that her hand has relaxed, it's visible.

Erixon picks up the woman's hand and carefully lifts the object. It's as if she still wants to hold on to it but is too tired to struggle.

His bulky frame blocks Margot's view, but then she sees it.

A tiny, broken-off porcelain deer's head.

The head is a shiny chestnut brown, and the broken surface at the bottom is as white as sugar.

Did the perpetrator or her husband put it in her hand?

Margot thinks of the glass cabinet. She's almost certain all the porcelain figures were intact, they'd just fallen over.

She steps back to get an overview of the bedroom. Erixon is next to the dead woman, photographing the little brown deer's head. Adam sits slumped on an ottoman in front of the wardrobe, looking like he's trying not to throw up.

Margot walks back out to the glass cabinet and stands for a while in front of the toppled figurines. They're all lying as if dead, but none of them is broken, none is missing its head.

Why is the victim holding a small deer's head in her hand?

13

IT'S MORNING, AND ERIK IS BUYING A CUP OF COFFEE IN THE Psychology Clinic's cafeteria. As he takes his wallet out to pay, he feels the ache in his shoulders from his piano lesson.

"It's already been paid for," the cashier says.

"Already paid for?"

"Your friend has paid for your coffee through Christmas."

"Did he say what his name was?"

"Nestor," she replies.

Erik smiles and nods, thinking he really must talk to Nestor about his overly effusive gratitude. It's Erik's job to help people. Nestor doesn't owe him anything.

He's still thinking of his former patient's friendly, cautious manner when he hears muted footsteps behind him and turns around. The pregnant lieutenant is making her way toward him, waving a shrink-wrapped sandwich in his direction.

"Björn managed to get some sleep and seems to be feeling a little better," she says breathlessly. "He wants to help us and is willing to try hypnosis."

"I've got an hour, if we can start now," Erik says, quickly drinking his coffee.

"Do you think it's going to work on him?" she asks as they head toward the treatment room.

"Hypnosis is just a way to get his brain to relax, so he can begin to sort through his memories in a less chaotic way."

"But the prosecutor's unlikely to be able to use statements made under hypnosis," she says.

"No." Erik smiles. "But it might mean Björn will be fit to testify later on, and it could definitely help move the investigation forward."

When they enter the room, Björn is standing behind an armchair, clutching its back with his hands. His eyes are dull.

"I've only seen hypnosis on television," he says in a fragile voice. "I mean, I'm not sure I really believe in it."

"Just think of hypnosis as a way to help you feel better."

"But I want her to leave," he says, looking at Margot.

"Of course," Erik says.

"Can you talk to her?"

Margot remains seated on the sofa, and there's no change in her expression.

"You'll have to go and wait outside," Erik says firmly.

Margot gestures to her stomach. "I need to sit down."

"You know where the cafeteria is," he replies.

She sighs and stands up, takes her phone out, and heads toward the door. Opening it, she turns back toward Erik. "Would you mind coming outside for a moment?" she says amiably.

"Okay." He follows her into the hallway.

"We don't have time to baby him," she whispers.

"I know you're anxious for him to talk, but I'm a doctor, and it's my job to help him."

"I have a job too," Margot says in a voice thin with irritation. "And it involves stopping a murderer. This is serious. Björn knows things that—"

"This isn't an interrogation," he interrupts. "You know that. We've already talked about it."

He watches the lieutenant fighting her own impatience. Then she nods as if she accepts his words.

"As long as it doesn't harm him," she says. "From where I'm standing . . . well, every tiny detail could be of vital importance to the investigation."

14

ERIK SHUTS THE DOOR BEHIND HIM, UNFOLDS THE STAND, and attaches the camera. Björn watches him, rubbing his forehead hard with one hand. "Do you have to film it?" he asks.

"It's just a case of documenting what I do," Erik replies. "And I'd rather not have to take notes."

"Okay," Björn says, as though he didn't listen to Erik's reply.

"You can start by lying down on the sofa." Erik goes to the window and draws the curtains.

The room fills with a pleasant half-light, and Björn lies back and shifts down a little, then closes his eyes.

Erik pulls a chair close to the sofa and sits. He can see how tense Björn is.

"Breathe slowly through your nose," Erik says. "Relax your mouth, your chin and cheeks. . . . Feel the weight of the back of your head on the pillow, feel your neck relax. You don't need to hold your head up now, because your head is resting on the pillow. . . . Your jaw muscles are relaxing, your forehead is smooth and untroubled, your eyelids are feeling heavier."

Erik takes his time and moves through the whole body, from Björn's head to his toes, then back up to his weary eyelids and the weight of his head again.

With soporific monotony, Erik slips into the induction, speaking in a soothing tone as he tries to gather his strength in advance of what is coming.

Björn's body gradually begins to relax.

"The only thing you're listening to is my voice. . . . If you hear anything else, it just makes you feel more relaxed and more focused on my words. I'm about to start counting backward, and for each number you hear, you'll relax a bit more."

Erik thinks about what's coming, what's waiting inside the house, what Björn saw when he walked in through the door: the moment the shock hit him.

"Nine hundred and twelve," he says. "Nine hundred and eleven . . ."

With each exhalation, Erik says a number, slowly and monotonously. After a while he breaks the logical sequence but continues to count down. Björn is now down at a perfect depth. The sharp frown on his brow has relaxed, and his mouth seems softer. Erik feels a curious shiver in his stomach as he sinks into hypnotic resonance, a phenomenon in which the doctor enters a sort of parallel trance while placing a patient in deep hypnosis.

"Now you're deeply relaxed. You're resting, nice and easy," Erik says slowly. "Soon you're going to revisit your memories of Friday night. When I finish counting down to zero, you will find yourself outside your house, but you're completely calm, because there's no danger. Four, three, two, one. Now you're standing in the street outside your house, the taxi is driving away, the tires are crunching."

Björn opens his eyes, but his gaze is focused inward, into his memories, and his heavy eyelids close once more.

"Are you looking at the house now?"

Björn is standing in the cool night air in front of his house. A strange glow is lighting up the sky in time with the slow rhythm of his heartbeat. The house appears to be leaning forward as the light expands and the shadows withdraw.

"It's moving," he says almost inaudibly.

"Now you're walking to the door," Erik says. "The night air is mild, there's nothing unpleasant . . ."

Björn startles as some crows fly up from a tree. They're visible against the sky, their shadows move across the grass, and then they're gone.

"You're perfectly safe," Erik says as he sees Björn's hand move anxiously over the seat of the sofa.

15

DEEP IN HIS TRANCE, BJÖRN SLOWLY APPROACHES THE DOOR. He keeps to the stone path, but something about the black shimmer of the window catches his attention.

"You've reached the door. You take your key out and put it in the lock," Erik says.

Björn carefully pushes the handle, but the door is stuck. He tries harder, and there's a sticky sound when it eventually opens.

Erik sees that Björn's brow is sweaty, and he repeats in a soothing voice that there's nothing to be scared of.

Björn tries to open his eyes and whisper something. Erik leans forward and feels his breath against his ear. "The doorstep ... something odd about it."

"Yes, this doorstep has always been odd," Erik replies calmly. "But once you've crossed it, everything will be just as it was on Friday."

Erik notices that Björn's face is covered with a sheen of sweat as his chin begins to tremble.

"No, no," he whispers, shaking his head.

Erik realizes he needs to put him in deeper hypnosis if he's to be able to enter the house.

"All you have to do now is listen to my voice," Erik says. "Because soon you'll be in an even more relaxed state, where there's nothing to be worried about. You're sinking deeper as I count: four ... you're sinking, three ... getting calmer, two ... one, and now you're completely relaxed and can see that the doorstep isn't a barrier."

Björn's face is slack. His mouth is hanging open, one corner wet with saliva. He's in a deeper state of hypnosis than Erik intended.

"If you feel ready, you can . . . cross the threshold now."

Björn doesn't want to, but he still takes a step inside. He glances along the hallway toward the kitchen. Everything looks the way it normally does. There's an advertisement from Bauhaus on the doormat, too many shoes piled up on the shoe rack, and the umbrella that always falls over does so again. His keys jangle as he sets them on the chest of drawers.

"Everything is the same as normal," he whispers. "The same as . . ."

He falls silent when he notices a strange, rolling movement from the corner of his eye. He daren't turn in that direction and stares straight ahead while something moves at the edge of his field of vision.

"There's something strange . . . off to the side. I . . ."

"What did you say?" Erik asks.

"It's moving, off to the side . . ."

"Okay, just let it go," Erik replies. "Keep going straight ahead."

Björn walks down the hall, but his eyes keep getting drawn to the side, toward the clothes hanging in the entryway. They're moving slowly in the gloom, as if a wind were blowing through the house. The sleeves of Susanna's trench coat lift in a gust, then fall back.

"Look ahead of you," Erik says.

Someone suffering mental trauma experiences a chaotic jumble of memories that press in on them from all sides. They fade away, then lurch into view, all mixed up.

All Erik can do is try to lead Björn through the rooms, toward the fundamental insight that he couldn't have prevented his wife's death.

"I'm in the kitchen now," he whispers.

"Keep going," Erik says.

Björn glances at the bag of newspapers for recycling in the hall-way. He takes a cautious step forward, looking straight ahead, but sees a kitchen drawer slide open. It rattles when it comes to a halt.

"One drawer is open," he mutters.

"Which one?"

Björn knows it's the knife drawer, and he knows he's the one opening it, because he washed a large knife several hours earlier.

"Oh, God ... I can't ... I ..."

"There's nothing to be afraid of. You're safe, and I'll be with you as you go farther in."

"I'm walking past the door to the basement, toward the living room. Susanna must have gone to bed already."

It's quiet. The television is switched off, but something's different. The furniture seems to be in the wrong places, as if a giant had picked the house up and given it a gentle shake.

"Sanna?" Björn whispers.

He reaches to the light switch. The room doesn't light up, but the glow fills the windows looking out on the garden. He can't help thinking he's being watched and feels an urge to close the curtains.

"God, oh God, oh God," he suddenly whimpers, his face trembling.

Erik realizes that Björn is there now, in the midst of his memory of the traumatic event, but he's barely describing anything, he's keeping it to himself.

Björn is getting closer. He sees himself in the black window, sees the bushes outside move in the wind, far beyond the reflections.

He's gasping, even though he's under deep hypnosis. His body tenses, and his back arches.

"What's happening?" Erik asks.

Björn stops when he sees someone with a dark gray face looking back at him in the window. Right next to the glass. He takes a step back and feels his heart pounding hard. A branch of the rosebush sways and scrapes the window ledge. He realizes that the gray face isn't outside. There's someone sitting on the floor in front of the window. He can see their reflection.

A calm voice repeats that there's nothing to be scared of.

He moves to the side and realizes it's Susanna. She's sitting on the floor in front of the window.

"Sanna?" he says softly, so as not to startle her.

He can see her shoulder, some of her hair. She's leaning back against an armchair, looking out. He approaches cautiously and feels that the floor is wet beneath his feet.

"She's sitting down," he mutters.

"She's sitting?"

Björn moves closer to the armchair by the window, and then the light in the ceiling comes on and the room is bathed in light. He knows he switched it on, but he's still scared when the bright light fills the room.

There's blood everywhere.

He's stepped in blood. There's blood splashed across the television and the sofa and up the walls, and there are smears of blood on the floor, trickling into the gaps between the wood.

She's sitting on the floor in a dark red pool. A dead woman wearing Sanna's kimono. Dust has settled on the pool of blood around her.

Erik sees Björn's face tense, and his lips turn white. As soon as Björn realizes the dead woman is his wife, Erik is planning to bring him out of the hypnosis.

"Who can you see?" he asks.

"No . . . no," he whispers.

"You know who it is," Erik says.

"Susanna," he says slowly, and opens his eyes.

"You can move back now," Erik says. "I'm going to wake you up in a moment, and—"

"There's so much blood, God, I don't want to . . . Her face, it's been destroyed, and she's sitting perfectly still, with—"

"Björn, listen to my voice, I'm going to count from—"

"She's sitting with her hand over her ear, and there's blood dripping from her elbow," he says, panting for breath.

Erik feels an icy chill, and the hairs on his arms and the back of his neck stand up. With his heart pounding, he glances toward the closed door of the treatment room and hears a cart rattle as it moves away.

"Look at your own hands," he says, trying to keep his voice

steady. "You're looking at your own hands, and you're breathing slowly. With each breath, you're feeling calmer."

"I don't want to," Björn whispers.

Erik knows he's pushing Björn too far, but he has to know the position Björn's wife was sitting in when he found her.

"Before I wake you up, we need to go deeper," he says, swallowing hard. "Beneath the house that you're in is another house, identical to this one. But down there is the only place you can see Susanna clearly. Three, two, one, and now you're there. She's sitting on the floor in the pool of blood, and you can look at her without feeling scared."

"Her face is almost gone, it's just blood," Björn says sluggishly. "And her hand is stuck to her ear . . ."

"Keep going," Erik says, glancing at the door again.

"Her hand is tangled up in . . . in the cord of her kimono."

"Björn, I'm going to bring you up now, to the house above, and the only thing you know there is that Susanna is dead and that there was nothing you could have done to save her. That's the only thing you're going to take with you when I wake you up. You're going to leave everything else behind."

16

ERIK CLOSES HIS OFFICE DOOR AND GOES OVER TO HIS DESK.
He can feel sweat on his back when he sits down. "It's nothing," he
whispers anxiously to himself.

He moves the mouse to wake his computer up, then logs in.
With his hand trembling, he pulls open the top drawer, presses
a Mogadon out of a blister pack, and swallows it without water.

He quickly signs in to the database of patients, noticing how
cold his fingers are.

He jumps when Lieutenant Margot Silverman opens the door
without knocking. She walks in and stops in front of him with her
hands clasped around her stomach.

"Björn Kern says he can't remember what you talked about."

"That's natural," Erik replies, minimizing the document.

"How did the hypnosis go?" she asks, running her hand over the
wooden elephant from Malaysia.

"He was definitely receptive."

"So you were able to hypnotize him?" She smiles.

"I'm afraid I forgot to start the camera," Erik lies. "Otherwise
I could have shown you. He went into a trance almost instantly."

"You forgot to start the camera?"

"You know this wasn't an official interview," he says, a touch
impatiently. "This was a first step toward what we call affective sta-
bilization, so that—"

"I don't give a damn about all that," she cuts him off.

"—so that you can have a functional witness later on," he concludes.

"How much later? Will he be able to say anything later today?"

"I think he's going to realize what happened fairly soon, but being able to talk about it is another matter."

"So what happened? What did he say? He must have said something, surely?"

"Yes, but—"

"No fucking oath of confidentiality bullshit now," she interrupts. "I have to know. Otherwise people will die."

Erik goes over to the window and leans on the sill. Far below a patient is smoking, thin and bent-backed in his hospital gown.

"I took him back," Erik says slowly. "Into the house. It was rather complicated, because it was very recent and full of fragments of terrible memories."

"But he saw everything? Could he see everything?"

"It was only to make him understand that he couldn't have saved her."

"But he saw the murder scene, and his wife? Did he?"

"Yes, he did," Erik replies.

"So what did he say?"

"Not much. He talked about blood . . . and the wounds to her face."

"Was she in a particular position? A posture with sexual implications?"

"He didn't say."

"Was she sitting up or lying down? How did her mouth look? Where were her hands? Was she naked? Violated?"

"He said very little," Erik replies. "It can take a long time to reach details like that."

"I swear, if he doesn't start talking, I'll take him into custody," she says loudly. "I'll drag him off to headquarters and watch him like a hawk until—"

"Margot," Erik interrupts in a friendly voice.

She looks at him with a subdued expression, nods, and breathes through her mouth. She pulls out a business card and sets it on his desk.

"We don't know who his next victim's going to be. It could be your wife. Think about that," she says, and leaves the room.

Erik feels his face relax. He walks slowly back to his desk. The floor is starting to feel soft beneath his feet. As he sits down in front of his computer, there's a knock at the door.

"Yes?"

"The charming lieutenant has left the building," Nelly says, peering around the door.

"She's only doing her job."

"I know. She really seems lovely," Nelly says ironically.

"Stop it," he says, but smiles. He rests his head on his hand.

Nelly's face turns serious, and she walks in, closing the door behind her. "What is it?" she asks. "What happened?"

"Nothing," he replies.

"Doesn't seem like nothing," she says, sitting down on the corner of his desk. Her red woolen dress crackles with static electricity against her nylon tights as she crosses her legs.

"I don't know." Erik sighs.

"You can tell me," she says gently.

Erik stands up, takes a deep breath, and looks at her. "Nelly," he says, and she can hear how vacant his voice sounds, "I need to ask you about a patient. Before you started working here, Nina Blom put together a team for a complicated research project."

"Go on," she says, regarding him with curiosity.

"I know I outlined my cases to you, but this may not have been included."

"What's the patient's name?" she asks.

"Rocky Kyrklund. Do you remember him?"

"Yes, hang on," she says tentatively.

"He was a priest."

"Exactly. I remember. You talked about him quite a bit," she says as she thinks. "You had a file of pictures from the crime scene, and—"

"You don't remember where he ended up?" he interrupts.

"It was years ago," she replies.

"He's still inside, though, isn't he?"

"We'd better hope so," she replied. "He killed people, didn't he?"

Erik nods. "A woman."

"That's right, now I remember. Her whole face was destroyed."

17

NELLY STANDS BEHIND ERIK AS HE SEARCHES THE PATIENT database on his computer. He types Rocky Kyrklund's name and discovers he was sent to Karsudden District Hospital.

"Karsudden," he says.

She brushes a strand of blond hair from her cheek and looks at him, her eyes narrowing. "Why are we talking about this patient?"

"Rocky Kyrklund's victim had been posed. She was lying on the floor with her face horribly disfigured, and her hand was around her neck. I just hypnotized Björn Kern, and . . . and he described details that were very reminiscent of the old murder."

"The one committed by the priest?"

"I don't know for sure, but Björn Kern said his wife's face had been completely destroyed, and she was sitting with her hand over her ear."

"What do the police say?"

"I don't know," Erik mutters.

"You did tell the lieutenant?"

"I didn't tell her anything," Erik says.

"You didn't?" she asks.

"Well, because it emerged while he was under hypnosis."

"But he agreed to it, didn't he?"

"I might have misheard," Erik says.

"Misheard?"

"It's just so sick. I can't think clearly anymore."

"Erik, maybe it's nothing," Nelly says, "but you have to tell the police. That's why they're here."

He walks to the window. The area where the patients stand and smoke is empty now, but he can still see the cigarette butts and candy wrappers that have been tossed on the ground, and a blue shoe cover that's been pushed into the trashcan.

"It's a long time ago, but to me . . . do you know what those weeks were like? I didn't want Rocky to be released," Erik says slowly. "The whole crime . . . it was everything. The brutality, the eyes, the hands . . ."

"I know. I read all about it," Nelly says. "I don't remember the details of your recommendation, but I know you said he was seriously dangerous and there was a severe risk of recidivism."

"What if he's out? I have to call Karsudden." Erik picks up his phone and dials the number for Simon Casillas, the chief psychiatrist there.

Nelly sits on Erik's sofa and nods at him encouragingly while he talks to the doctor.

The sun passes behind a cloud, and darkness falls across the room, as if a huge figure were standing in front of the building.

"Rocky is still in Ward D–four," Erik says. "And he's never been let out on furlough."

"Does that reassure you?"

"No," he whispers.

"Are you feeling all right?" she asks, so seriously he can't help smiling.

He sighs and puts his hands to his face, then slowly lowers them, pressing his fingertips gently against his eyelids and down his cheeks before he looks at Nelly again.

Her back is straight as she studies his face. A tiny, sharp little wrinkle has appeared between her thin eyebrows.

"Okay," Erik says. "I know this is completely wrong, but in one of the last conversations I had with Rocky, he claimed he had an alibi for the night of the murder. I didn't want him to be released simply because he'd bought himself a witness."

"What are you trying to say?" she asks with alarm.

"I never passed that information on."

"No way," she says.

"He could have been released—"

"Jesus, you can't do that!"

"I know, but he was guilty, and he would have killed again," Erik says.

"That's not our business. We're psychologists, we're not detectives, and we definitely aren't judges."

She takes a few agitated steps, then stops and shakes her head. "Fuck," she gasps. "That's insane, you're completely—"

"You're angry."

"Yes, I am angry. I mean, you know, if this got out, you'd lose your job."

"I know what I did was wrong. It's tormented me ever since. But I've still always been utterly convinced that I stopped a murderer."

"Shit," she mutters.

He picks up the business card from his desk and begins to dial the lieutenant's number.

"What are you doing?" she asks.

"I need to tell her about Rocky's alibi, and the whole business about the hand and the ear, and—"

"Go ahead," she interrupts. "But what if you were right? What if his alibi wasn't real? Then these similarities are just coincidences."

"I don't care."

"Then ask yourself what you're going to do with the rest of your life," she says. "You'll have to give up being a doctor. You'll lose your income. You might even face charges, not to mention all the scandal and gossip in the papers—"

"It's my own fault."

"Find out if the alibi checks out first. If it does, then I'll report you myself."

"Thanks." He laughs.

"I'm serious," she says.

18

ERIK LEAVES THE CAR IN FRONT OF THE GARAGE, HURRIES up the path to his dark house, and goes inside. He turns on the light in the entryway but doesn't take his coat off, just continues down the steep staircase to the basement where, in locked steel cabinets, he keeps his archive. All the written material is collected here—logbooks, personal journals, and extensive notes. The recordings of his sessions have been saved on eight external hard drives.

Erik's heart is thumping as he unlocks one of the cabinets and searches back in time for the year when his life crossed paths with that of Rocky Kyrklund.

He pulls the file out of a black box and hurries upstairs to his study. He switches the lamp on and opens the file on the desk.

It was nine years ago, and life was very different. Benjamin was still in elementary school, and he himself had just started working at the Crisis and Trauma Center with Professor Sten W. Jakobsson.

He no longer remembers the exact details, but he does know he was helping out his friend Nina Blom.

Erik remembers spending the evening in his new office, reading the material the prosecutor had sent over. The man who was to be evaluated, Rocky Kyrklund, was the vicar in the parish of Salem. He was being held in custody on suspicion of having murdered Rebecka Hansson, a forty-three-year-old woman who had attended mass and then stayed late to speak to him privately on the Sunday before she was murdered.

The murder had been extremely aggressive, fueled by hatred. The victim's face and arms had been destroyed. She was found lying on the linoleum floor of her bathroom, with her right hand around her neck.

There was fairly persuasive forensic evidence. Rocky had sent her a number of threatening text messages, his fingerprints and strands of his hair were found in her home, and traces of Rebecka's blood were found on his shoes.

An arrest warrant was issued, and he was picked up seven months later in conjunction with a serious traffic accident on a highway in Brunnby. He had stolen a car at Finsta and was heading for the airport at Arlanda.

In the accident, Rocky suffered serious brain damage, which led to epileptic seizures in his frontal and temporal lobes.

He would suffer recurrent bouts of memory loss, involuntary action, and epilepsy for the rest of his life.

When Erik met Rocky, his face was crisscrossed with red scars from the accident, his arm was in a cast, and his hair had just started to grow back after several operations. Rocky was a large man with a booming voice. He was almost six and a half feet tall, broad-shouldered, and had big hands and a thick neck.

Sometimes he would faint, falling off his chair, knocking over the flimsy table holding drinking glasses and a jug of water. But sometimes his epileptic attacks were almost invisible. He just seemed a bit subdued and distant, and afterward he couldn't remember what they had been talking about.

Erik and Rocky got along fairly well. The priest was undeniably charismatic. He somehow managed to give the impression he was speaking straight from the heart.

Erik leafs through the private journal in which he made notes during their conversations. The various subjects can be traced from one session to the next.

Rocky had neither admitted nor denied the murder; he said he couldn't remember Rebecka Hansson at all, and he couldn't explain why his fingerprints had been found in her home or how her blood came to be on his shoes.

During the best of their conversations, Rocky would circle his small islands of memories and perhaps discern a bit more.

Once he said he and Rebecka Hansson had had intercourse in the sacristy, albeit it was interrupted. He could remember details, such as the rough rug they had been lying on—an old gift from the young women of the parish. Rebecka had begun to menstruate, leaving a small bloodstain—like a virgin, he said.

In their following conversations, he couldn't remember any of this.

The conclusion of the examination was that the crime had been committed under the influence of severe mental disturbance. The team believed that Rocky suffered from a grandiose, narcissistic personality disorder with elements of paranoia.

Erik leafs past a circled note, "paying for sex + drug abuse," in the journal, followed by some ideas for medication.

Naturally he shouldn't have had an opinion on the matter of guilt, but as time passed, he became convinced that Rocky was guilty and that his mental disorder constituted a serious risk to the public.

During one of their last sessions, Rocky was talking about a ceremony to mark the end of the school year in a church decked out with spring greenery, when he suddenly said he hadn't murdered Rebecka Hansson.

"I remember everything now. I have an alibi for that entire evening," he said.

He wrote down the name Olivia, and an address, then gave the sheet of paper to Erik. They continued talking, and Rocky began to speak in broken fragments, then fell completely silent, looked at Erik, and suffered a severe epileptic attack. Afterward Rocky didn't remember anything, he didn't even recognize Erik, just kept whispering about wanting heroin, saying he could kill a child for thirty grams.

Erik never took Rocky's alibi seriously. At best it was a lie; at worst Rocky could have bribed or threatened someone to support the alibi.

Erik threw away the scrap of paper, and Rocky Kyrklund was found guilty and sentenced to secure psychiatric care.

And nine years later a woman is murdered in Bromma in a way reminiscent of Rebecka Hansson's murder, Erik thinks, closing the file.

Aggressive violence directed at the face, neck, and chest.

But on the other hand, murders of this kind aren't altogether unusual. They can be triggered by anything from the jealousy of an ex-husband, aggression linked to Rohypnol and anabolic steroids, so-called honor killings, or a pimp making an example of a prostitute trying to break away from him.

The only concrete connection is that Susanna Kern was left at the scene of the murder with her hand covering her ear, just like Rebecka Hansson was found on the floor with her hand around her own neck.

Perhaps Susanna Kern merely got tangled up in the belt of her kimono during the struggle.

The parallels certainly aren't unambiguous, but they are there, and they're forcing Erik to do something he should have done a long time ago.

He lays the file in his desk drawer and looks up the number of chief psychiatrist Simon Casillas at Karsudden Hospital once more.

"Casillas," the man answers in a voice like dried leather.

"Erik Maria Bark from Karolinska."

"Hello again."

"It's been a long time, but I was wondering if I might come in soon for a visit."

"A visit?"

The sound of a squash court is audible in the background, a ball hitting the wall, the squeak of shoes.

"I'm taking part in a research project for the Osher Center at the institute that requires us to follow up on old patients, right across the spectrum ... which means I'm going to have to interview Rocky Kyrklund." Erik babbles a bit more about the research project, then ends the conversation and slowly puts his phone down on the desk. He watches the little screen turn black as it slips into dormancy.

The room is perfectly still. His leather seat creaks like a boat on a mooring. Through the open window he can hear the hiss of an evening shower approach across the gardens.

He bends forward and rests his elbows on the desk, leans his head on his hands, and asks himself what on earth he's doing. What did I just say? he thinks.

This could be a crazy idea, he knows that. But he also knows he has no choice. If Rocky's alibi was genuine, then he must be released, even if that would mean a media frenzy and a miscarriage of justice.

Erik skims through the logbook. There are no notes about an alibi, but toward the end, one page has been torn out. He leafs forward, then stops. From that last session with Rocky, there's a faint note in pencil that Erik doesn't remember. In the middle of the page, it says "a priest with dirty clothes." The remainder of the book is blank.

19

SAGA BAUER IS DRIVING SLOWLY THROUGH KAROLINSKA Institute's vast campus. As she approaches 5 Retzius Road, she turns into the deserted parking lot and stops in front of the empty building.

She's tired. She's not wearing any makeup, hasn't washed her hair, and is dressed in baggy clothes, but still, most people would probably say she was the most beautiful person they had ever seen.

Recently there's been something hungry and hunted about her appearance: the bright blue of her eyes makes her creamy white skin look translucent.

On the floor in front of the passenger seat is a green duffel bag containing underwear, a bulletproof vest, and five cartridges of ammunition: .45 ACP, hollow-tipped.

Saga has been on sick leave from her job with the Security Police for more than a year, and she hasn't visited the boxing club at all.

The pathology lab is closed, and all the lights in the redbrick building seem to be off, but a white Jaguar with a damaged front bumper is parked on the path right in front of the entrance.

Saga leans to the side, opens the glove compartment, takes out the glass jar, and leaves the car. The air is mild and smells like freshly mown grass. She feels her Glock 21 bouncing under her left arm, and she can hear a faint sloshing sound from the jar as she walks.

Saga has to squeeze by the flowerbed to get past Nils "The Needle" Åhlén's car. The thorns of the wild rose make a scratching sound as they let go of her pants. The branches sway, and a few rose petals drift to the ground.

The front door has been propped open with a rolled-up leaflet.

She's been here enough times to find her way. The grit on the poorly cleaned floor crunches as she heads down the hallway toward the swinging door.

She can't help smiling when she looks at the jar, and the cloudy liquid, the particles circling.

The memory flashes through her, and her free hand goes involuntarily to one of the scars he left on her face, the deep cut just below her eyebrow.

Sometimes she thinks he must have seen something special in her, that that was why he spared her life, and sometimes she thinks he simply considered death too easy—he wanted her to live with the lies he had made her believe, in the hell he had created for her.

She'll never know.

The only thing she knows for certain is that he chose not to kill her, and she chose to kill him.

She thinks of the darkness and the deep snow as she walks down the empty hallway.

"I hit him," she whispers to herself.

She licks her lips and in her mind's eye sees herself firing and hitting him in the neck, arm, and chest.

"Three shots to the chest."

She changed her magazine and shot him again when he'd fallen into the rapids. She held the flare up and saw the cloud of blood spread out around him. She ran along the bank, shooting at the dark object, and she kept firing even though the body had been carried away by the current.

I know I killed him, she thinks.

But they never found his body. The police sent divers under the ice and checked both banks with sniffer dogs.

Outside the office is a neat metal sign that reads: NILS ÅHLÉN, PROFESSOR OF FORENSIC MEDICINE.

The door is open, and the slight figure is sitting at his spotlessly clean desk reading the newspaper, a pair of latex gloves on his hands. He's wearing a white polo shirt under his white coat, and his aviator sunglasses flash as he looks up. "You're tired, Saga," he says amiably.

"A little."

"Beautiful, though."

"No."

He puts the newspaper down, pulls off the gloves, and notices the quizzical look in her eyes.

"To keep ink from getting on my fingers," he says, as though it were obvious.

Saga doesn't answer, just sets the jar down in front of him. The object moves slowly in the alcohol, through a cloud of wispy particles. A swollen and half-rotten index finger.

"So you think that this finger belonged to . . ."

"Jurek Walter," Saga says curtly.

"How did you get it?" The Needle asks.

He picks up the jar and holds it to the light. The finger falls against the inside of the glass as if it were pointing at him.

"I've spent more than a year looking."

To start with, Saga Bauer borrowed sniffer dogs and walked up and down both banks of the river, from Bergasjön all the way to Hysingsvik on the Baltic coast. She followed the shoreline, combed the beaches, studied the currents of Norrfjärden all the way down to Västerfladen, and made her way out to every island, talking to anyone who went fishing in the area.

"Go on," The Needle says.

She looks up and meets his relaxed gaze. His latex gloves are lying on the desk, inside out, in two little heaps. One is quivering slightly, either from a draft or from the rubber contracting.

"This morning I was walking along the beach out on Högmarsö," she explains. "I've been there before, but I gave it another try. The terrain on the north side is pretty tricky, a lot of forest on the cliffs at the headland."

She thinks of the old man walking toward her from the other direction with an armful of silver-gray driftwood.

"You're quiet again."

"Sorry. I bumped into a retired churchwarden. He said he'd seen me the last time I was there and asked what I was looking for."

Saga went with him to the inhabited part of the island. Less than forty people live there. The warden's house is tucked behind the white chapel and its freestanding bell tower.

"He said he found a dead body on the shore toward the end of April."

"A whole body?" The Needle asks in a low voice.

"No, just the torso and one arm."

"No head?"

"No one can live without a torso," she says, and she can hear how feverish she sounds.

"No," The Needle replies.

"The warden said the body must have been in the water all winter, because it was badly swollen and very heavy."

"They look terrible," The Needle said.

"He brought it back through the forest in his wheelbarrow, and laid it on the floor of the toolshed behind the chapel. But the smell drove his dog crazy, so he had to take it to the old crematorium."

"He cremated it?"

She nods. The crematorium had been abandoned for decades, but in the middle of the overgrown foundations was a sooty brick oven with a chimney. The warden used to burn trash in the oven, so he knew it worked.

"Why didn't he call the police?" The Needle asked.

Saga thinks of the way the churchwarden's house stank of fried food and old clothes. His neck was streaked with dirt, and the bottles of home brew in the fridge had dirty marks from his fingers.

"He had a still at home . . . I don't know. But he did take a few pictures with his phone in case the police showed up and started asking questions. And he kept the finger at the bottom of his fridge."

"Do you have the pictures?"

"Yes," she says, and pulls out her phone. "It must be him. Look at the gunshot wounds."

The Needle examines the first picture. On the bare cement floor of the toolshed lay a bloated, marbled torso with just one arm. The skin had split across the chest and slipped down. There were four ragged gunshot holes on the body. The water had made a black mark on the pale gray floor—a shadow that got narrower toward the drain.

"That is good, very good," The Needle says, handing her phone back.

There is a tense look in his eyes as he gets to his feet and picks up the glass jar from the desk, and he looks at her as if he were about to say something else but walks out of the room instead.

20

SAGA FOLLOWS THE NEEDLE DOWN A DARK HALLWAY INTO the closest pathology lab. The chilly fluorescent lights in the ceiling flicker a few times before settling and lighting up the white-tiled walls. Beside one of the metal tables is a desk with a computer and a large bottle of Trocadero.

The room smells like disinfectant and damp. A bright yellow hose is attached to one of the faucets, and a trickle of water runs from it toward the drain in the floor.

The Needle walks straight over to the long, plastic-covered postmortem table.

He pulls over a chair for Saga, then places the glass jar on the slab.

She watches him put on protective overalls, a mask, and latex gloves. Then he stops and stands very still in front of the jar, like an old person disappearing into a memory. Saga is on the verge of saying something when The Needle takes a deep breath.

"The right finger of a body found in brackish water, preserved in strong alcohol at a temperature of forty-six degrees for four months," he says to himself.

He photographs the jar from various angles, then unscrews the lid bearing the words BOB RASPBERRY JAM.

Using a pair of steel tweezers, he removes the finger, lets it drip for a while, then places it on the table. The nail has come off and is still lying in the murky liquid. The nauseating smell of rotten seawater and decaying flesh spreads through the room.

"The finger was definitely removed from the body long after death," he says to Saga. "With a knife or perhaps a pair of pliers or shears."

The Needle is breathing through his nose audibly as he carefully rolls the finger over so he can photograph it from every angle.

"We can get a good fingerprint from this," he says seriously.

Saga has backed away and is standing with her hand over her mouth, watching as The Needle picks up the dead finger and holds it against a print scanner.

The machine bleeps when the print has been scanned.

The tissue is swollen and pudgy, but the fingerprint that appears in the little screen is still very clear. Saga stares at the oval containing a labyrinth of swirls.

The room is full of suppressed anticipation.

The Needle takes off his protective clothing and logs into the computer, hooks up the scanner, and clicks on the icon with the text LIVESCAN.

"I have a private AFIS system," he says as he clicks another icon and types in a new password.

Saga sees him search for "Walter," then bring up Jurek's record. The sharp reproductions of the thumb and fingerprints from both hands were made in ink at the time of his arrest.

Saga tries to control her breathing.

Sweat is trickling down her sides from her armpits.

The Needle whispers something to himself and drags the best image from LiveScan across to the search box of the AFIS system, then clicks the button saying ANALYSIS AND COMPARISON and immediately gets a result.

"What's happening?" Saga swallows hard.

Reflections of the fluorescent lights slide across his glasses. She sees his hand shake as he points at the screen.

"The details of the initial level are rather vague. Mostly just patterns," The Needle explains, and clears his throat quickly. "The second level are so-called Galton details. You can see the length of the papillary lines and the way they relate to each other. The differences are only the result of tissue breakdown. And the third level, that's primarily concerned with the layout of pores—there the match is perfect."

"Do you mean we've found Jurek?" she whispers.

"I'll send the DNA to the National Forensics Lab in Linköping, but purely as a formality," he replies with a nervous smile. "You've found him. There's no doubt it's him. It's over."

"Good," she says, feeling hot tears well up in her eyes. Her initial relief gives way to fear, and an almost empty feeling in the pit of her stomach.

"You've said all along that you were sure you killed Jurek. Why was it so important to find his body?" The Needle asks.

"I couldn't try to find Joona before I'd found it," she replies, rubbing her cheeks with her hand to wipe the tears away.

"Joona's dead," The Needle says.

"Yes." She smiles.

Joona's jacket and wallet were found in the possession of a homeless man who hung around Strömparterren. Saga's watched the video of the interview plenty of times. The homeless man identified himself as Constantine the First. He usually climbed aboard one of the fishing boats and slept outside a heating vent.

He had a big beard and dirty fingers, cracked lips and a wary look in his eyes. He sat in the interview room, and in a rattling voice he told them about the big Finn who told him to keep his distance, before taking his jacket off and swimming out into the water. He watched him swim out toward Strömbron until he reached the fast-flowing current and disappeared.

"You don't believe he's dead?" The Needle asks.

"Several years ago he called me. He wanted me to find out some information about a woman in Helsinki, in secret," Saga says. "At the time I thought the woman had something to do with the case at Birgittagården."

"What did you find out about her?"

"She was seriously ill, in the hospital for an operation. Her name was Laura Sandin," Saga says, holding The Needle's gaze. "But she was really . . . really Summa Linna, his wife, wasn't she?"

"Yes." He nods.

"I tried to get ahold of Laura to tell her that Joona was dead," Saga explains. "Laura had been in a cancer hospice for palliative care, but two days after Joona's suicide, she was discharged to spend her last days at home. But neither Laura nor her daughter is at their address on Elisabet Street."

"Really?" The Needle's thin nostrils turn pale.

"They aren't anywhere," Saga says, taking a step toward him.

"That's good to hear."

"I think Joona arranged his suicide so he could go and pick up his wife and daughter and go into hiding with them."

The Needle's eyes are red, and his mouth is twitching slightly when he speaks: "Joona was the only person who believed that Jurek's reach extended beyond the isolation unit, and as usual, he was right. If we hadn't done this, Jurek would have killed Summa and Lumi, just like he killed Disa."

"Nils, I need to find Joona and tell him that Jurek Walter is dead," Saga says. "He needs to know that the body's been found."

She puts her hand on his arm and sees his shoulders slump when he makes his mind up.

"I don't know where they are," he eventually says. "But if Summa is dying, as you say . . . I know where you could try looking."

"Where?"

"Go to the Nordic Museum," he says thickly, as if he were worried about changing his mind. "There's a small bridal crown, a Sámi bridal crown made of woven roots. Look at it carefully."

"Thanks."

"Good luck," The Needle says seriously, then hesitates. "No one wants to hug a pathologist, but . . ."

Saga hugs him hard, then leaves the room and hurries along the hallway.

21

SAGA PARKS IN FRONT OF THE STEPS TO THE NORDIC MUSEUM, drinks a sip of cold coffee from the 7-Eleven mug, and looks at the people around her, all dressed for summer. She's taking in her surroundings for the first time: adults and children tired from the sun or long picnics, or excited and expectant on their way to the amusement park or a restaurant.

She's barely noticed the summer passing her by. Since Joona disappeared, she has withdrawn from the world, searching for Jurek's body.

Now it's time to bring it to an end.

Saga gets out of the car and goes up the steps.

She walks in through the imposing entrance, buys a ticket, picks up a plan of the museum, and continues into the entrance hall.

She makes her way to the section that houses Sámi handicrafts. A few visitors are studying the glass cabinets containing jewelry, knives with reindeer horn handles, cultural artifacts, and clothes.

She stops in front of a display featuring a bridal crown. This must be the one The Needle meant. It's a beautiful piece of work, made of woven birch root, with points like the fingers of two interlaced hands.

Saga looks at the small lock on the case and sees that it would be easy to pick, but the cabinet is alarmed, and there's a risk that a guard would arrive before she had time to get the crown.

An elderly woman stops next to her and says something in Italian to a man pushing a stroller a short distance away.

The man speaks to the guard and is helped toward the elevators. A girl with straight fair hair is looking at the ceremonial Sámi costumes.

There's a crackle of Velcro as Saga pulls her tiny dagger out from its sheath below her left armpit. She carefully slides the tip in next to the lock on the glass door and jerks it. The door shatters, and the splinters fall to the floor as an alarm goes off.

The girl gazes at Saga in astonishment as she calmly puts the knife away, opens the door, and removes the bridal crown.

It seems smaller outside the case and weighs practically nothing. Saga stares at it as the alarm blares.

The Needle told her Summa's mother wove the crown for her own wedding, and that Summa had worn it for hers, then donated it to the museum of handicrafts in Luleå.

Saga sees the guard hurrying back and carefully turns the crown over in her hands, looks inside it, and sees that someone has burned "Nattavaara 1968" into it with a brand. She puts the crown back in the case and closes the shattered door.

She knew there was some sort of family connection to Nattavaara and guesses that that's where Joona is at the moment.

Saga feels her heart swell at the thought of being able to tell Joona that it's all over.

The guard's cheeks are flushed. He stops five meters away and points at her with his radio without managing to get a word out.

22

THE TRAIN PULLS OUT OF STOCKHOLM CENTRAL STATION, rocking noisily as it rolls away from the dirty platform. To the left, big white boats are gliding along on Karlbergssjön, while to the right is a concrete wall covered in badly painted-over graffiti.

Since all the sleeping cars were booked, Saga had to take an ordinary seat. She shows her ticket to the conductor, then eats a sandwich with her eyes fixed outside the window. As the train passes Uppsala, she takes off her military boots, folds her jacket around her pistol, and uses that as a pillow.

The train journey to Nattavaara, more than a thousand kilometers away, will take almost twelve hours.

The train rumbles on through the night. Lights pass by outside like tiny stars, fewer and fewer the farther north they get. Warm air streams from the scorching-hot radiator by the panel beside her seat.

As it gets later, the night outside the window turns into solid darkness.

She closes her eyes and thinks about what Nils told her. When Joona and his partner Samuel Mendel caught Jurek Walter many years ago, Jurek announced his plan for revenge before he was isolated in the secure unit at the Löwenströmska Hospital. Samuel thought it was an empty threat, but somehow Jurek managed to reach out from his cell and snatch Samuel's wife and two sons.

Joona realized the threat was serious. With The Needle's help, he arranged for his wife and little daughter to "die" in a car accident.

Summa and Lumi were given new identities and had no further contact with Joona. As long as Jurek was alive, there was a risk that his threat might be real. In hindsight, Joona saved them from a terrible death by sacrificing their life together.

But Saga can free Joona now. Jurek Walter is dead. His remains have been found and identified.

At the thought, an almost-erotic shiver runs through her body. She leans back in her seat, shuts her eyes, and falls asleep. For the first time in a long time, she sleeps deeply.

When she wakes up, the train is standing still, and chilly morning air is streaming into the carriage. She sits up and sees that she is now in Boden. She has been asleep for almost ten hours and needs to change trains for the last part of the journey to Nattavaara.

She puts her boots on, tucks her gun in its holster, and gets off the train. She buys a large cup of coffee at the station, then returns to the platform. A group of young men in military fatigues and green berets get on a train heading in the other direction. A black locomotive with a red undercarriage approaches with a squeal of brakes. The train stops and wheezes slowly at the deserted platform. Saga is the only person who gets on the train to Gällivare, and she has the carriage to herself.

The journey to Nattavaara is supposed to take less than an hour. Saga drinks her coffee, washes her face, and then sits watching the landscape go past, vast stretches of forest with the occasional red cottage.

Her plan is to go to the village shop or parish hall and ask about people who have moved in recently—there can't be that many.

It's almost eleven in the morning when she steps onto the platform. The station is little more than a shack with a sign on its roof. In the weeds in front of it is a bench with peeling paint and rusting armrests.

Saga starts to walk along the road through the dark green, whispering forest. There's no sign of anyone, but occasionally she hears dogs barking.

The road surface is uneven and cracked from frost.

She continues over a bridge that stretches across the valley of the Pikku Venetjoki, then hears the sound of an engine behind her. An old Volkswagen pickup is heading toward her, and she waves to stop it.

A suntanned man in his seventies, wearing a gray sweater, winds down his window and nods in greeting. Beside him sits a woman of the same age, in a padded green vest and pink-framed glasses.

"Hello," Saga says. "Do you live in Nattavaara?"

"We're just passing through," he replies.

"We're from Sarvisvaara . . . another metropolis," the woman says.

"Do you know where the grocery store is?"

"It closed last year," the old man says, picking at the wheel. "But we have a new shop now."

"That's good." Saga smiles.

"It's not a shop," the old woman says.

"I call it a shop," he mutters.

"But that's wrong," she says. "It's a service point."

"Then I'd better stop doing my shopping there." He sighs.

"Where's the service point?" Saga asks.

"In the same building as the old shop," the woman replies with a wink. "Jump up on the back."

"She's not a high jumper," the man retorts.

Saga climbs up onto the wheel, grabs hold of the edge of the pickup, swings herself over, then sits down with her back to the cab.

During the drive, she hears the old couple continue to argue, to the extent that the pickup almost drives into the ditch at one point. The bumper thuds, and grit flies up under the vehicle, which is surrounded by a cloud of dust.

They drive into the village and stop in front of a large red building with an ice cream sign out front. The shop also serves as the post office and the national lottery, as well as a pickup point for prescriptions and supplies from the state-owned alcohol monopoly.

Saga clambers down, thanks the pair for the lift, and goes up the steps. A little bell on the door rings as she walks in.

She finds a bag of dill-flavored potato chips, then goes over to the young man at the counter.

"I'm looking for a friend who moved here just over a year ago," she says without further elaboration.

"Here?" he asks, then stares at her for a while before lowering his eyes.

"A tall man with his wife and daughter."

"Ah," he says, blushing.

"Do they still live here?"

"Just follow the Lompolovaara Road," he says, pointing. "Up to the bend at Silmäjärvi."

Saga leaves the shop and heads in the direction he indicated. Tractor tires have furrowed the ground, and the curb is virtually nonexistent. There's a beer can in the grass. The wind in the trees sounds like a distant sea.

She eats some of the chips as she walks, then puts the rest in her bag and wipes her hands on her pants.

Saga has walked six kilometers by the time she sees a rust-red house at a point where the road bends around a broad mountain lake. There's no car in sight, but there's smoke coming out of the chimney. The house is surrounded by tall meadow grass.

She stops and hears insects in the ditch.

A man comes out of the house. She watches his figure move through the trees.

It's Joona.

It's him, but he's lost weight, and he's leaning on a walking stick. He has a curly blond beard and strands of hair are sticking out from his woolly black hat.

Saga walks toward him. The grit crunches beneath her boots.

She sees Joona stop beside a woodshed, lean his stick against the wall, pick up an ax and split a large log. Then he picks up another one and splits that, then rests for a moment before starting again.

She doesn't call out because she knows he's already seen her, probably long before she saw him.

He's wearing moss-green fleece beneath a bomber jacket made of coarse leather. The folds have cracked, and the sheepskin lining of the collar has turned yellow.

She walks over and stops five meters from him.

He stretches his back, turns around, and looks at her with those gray eyes of his. "You shouldn't have come," he says quietly.

"Jurek's dead," she says breathlessly.

"Yes," he replies, and picks up a new log and places it on the chopping block.

"I found his body," Saga says.

His swing goes wrong, the ax catches, and he loses his grip. He stands for a while with his head lowered. Saga looks down into the large wood basket and sees a sawed-off shotgun taped to one side of it.

23

JOONA LEADS HER THROUGH A DARK ENTRANCE HALL. HE doesn't say anything but holds a door open and ushers her into a little kitchen with copper saucepans on the walls.

An elk-hunting rifle with telescopic sights is hanging under the windowsill, and there are at least thirty boxes of ammunition on the floor.

The sun is shining through the drawn curtains. On the table is a coffeepot and two cups.

"Summa died last spring," he explains.

"I'm so sorry," she murmurs.

He sets the wood basket down on the floor and slowly straightens his back. There's a faint smell of smoke in the kitchen, and she can hear the pine logs crackling behind the closed hatch of the iron stove.

"So you found the body?" he says.

"I wouldn't have come otherwise," she replies seriously. "Call The Needle if you want confirmation."

"I believe you," he says.

"Call him anyway."

He shakes his head but doesn't say anything, then, leaning on the drain board, he makes his way to the other door, nudges it open, and says something in Finnish into the gloom.

"This is my daughter, Lumi," Joona says as a girl comes into the kitchen.

"Hello," Saga says.

Lumi has straight brown hair and a friendly, curious smile, but her eyes are as gray as Joona's. She's tall and thin, dressed in a simple blue cotton shirt and a pair of faded jeans.

"Are you hungry?" Joona asks.

"Yes," Saga replies.

"Sit down."

She takes a chair, and Joona gets out bread, butter, and cheese, then chops tomatoes, olives, and peppers. Lumi heats some water and grinds coffee beans in a hand mill. Saga looks at the dimly lit room behind them and sees a sofa and a stack of books on a table. Hanging from an IV stand is a night-vision scope and a mount, allowing it to be attached to a rifle for nocturnal hunting.

"Where was he?" Joona asks.

"He drifted ashore on Högmarsö," Saga replies.

"Who?" Lumi asks, glancing at the control panel for some twenty motion detectors that's attached to the wall beneath the spice rack.

"Jurek Walter," Joona says, cracking twelve eggs into the frying pan.

"I found his body," Saga says.

"So he's dead?" she asks lightly.

"Lumi, can you take over for a minute?" Joona says, then leaves the kitchen. His heavy steps echo from the hallway, and then the front door closes.

Lumi gets some dried basil and rubs it between her palms.

"Dad says he had to leave me and Mom." She tries to keep her voice steady. "He says Jurek Walter would have killed us if we'd had any contact with him at all."

"He did the right thing. He saved your lives—there was no other way," Saga says.

Lumi nods and turns toward the stove. A few tears drip onto the black metal range in front of her.

Lumi wipes her face, lowers the heat, and then carefully turns the omelette with a spatula.

Through the closed curtains, Saga can see Joona standing out on the road with a phone pressed to his ear. She knows he's talking to The Needle. He's frowning, and his jaw muscles are tense.

Lumi turns off the stove and sets the table as she looks at Saga curiously. "I know you're not going out with Dad," the girl says after a while. "He told me about Disa."

"We used to work together." Saga smiles.

"You don't look like a police officer."

"Security Police," Saga says curtly.

"You don't look like one of them either." She laughs, sitting down opposite Saga. "But if you're from the Security Police, then you must be Saga Bauer."

"Yes."

"Dig in," Lumi says. "It'll get cold."

Saga thanks her, helps herself to some omelette, bread, and cheese, and pours coffee for the two of them.

"How is Joona?" she asks.

"Yesterday I'd probably have said not good," Lumi says. "He's freezing most of the time and hardly sleeps. He keeps watch over me, makes himself stay awake. I don't know how he does it."

"He's very stubborn," Saga says.

"Is he?"

They laugh.

"You know, I didn't have my dad for so many years," the girl says, and her eyes grow moist. "I barely remembered him. I mean, nothing can make up for that, but we've spent more than a year sitting and talking. Every day, for hours . . . I've told him about me and Mom, what we did and how we were. And he's talked about himself. There can't be many people who've talked so much with their dad."

"Not me, that's for sure," Saga says.

Lumi stands up when a motion sensor reacts to Joona's approach. She switches the alarm off, and then they hear the front door open, followed by footsteps in the hall.

Joona comes into the kitchen, puts his walking stick down, leans against the table, then sinks into a chair.

"The Needle is certain," he says, helping himself to some food.

"We're even now," Saga says, looking him in the eye. "I don't care what you think, we're even. I killed him, and I found the body."

"You never owed me anything." Joona leans forward slightly, his arms wrapped around his body, taking small mouthfuls of food.

Lumi wraps a thick blanket around his shoulders, then sits back down.

"Lumi's going to study in Paris," Joona says, smiling at his daughter.

"We don't know that," Lumi says quickly.

A smile flits across her pale face. Saga sees Joona's hands shake as he picks up his cup and drinks some coffee.

"I'm cooking venison fillet tonight," he says.

"My train leaves in two hours," Saga says.

"With chanterelles and cream," he adds.

She smiles. "I have to go."

24

ERIK ARRIVES EARLY FOR HIS PIANO LESSON AND STANDS ON the road opposite 4 Lill-Jans Plan. The ground-floor curtains are open, and he can see straight into Jackie Federer's apartment. She's in the kitchen. She runs her hand along the wall-mounted cupboards, takes out a glass, then holds her finger under the faucet. She's wearing a black skirt and an unbuttoned blouse. He walks across the street for a better view, gets closer to the window, and can now see that her wet hair has dripped down the back of her silk blouse. She drinks the water, wipes her mouth, then turns around.

Erik stretches and catches a glimpse of her stomach and navel through the opening of her unbuttoned shirt. A woman with a stroller stops on the sidewalk and stares at him, and he suddenly realizes how he must look. He hurries in through the entrance. He stands in the darkness outside her door, then pushes the bell.

Since the hypnosis session, he has been thinking that Rocky's alibi may well have been genuine, and has had to double his nightly dose of Stilnoct in order to get any sleep. The earliest he has been able to schedule a visit to Karsudden Hospital is first thing tomorrow morning.

When Jackie opens the door, her blouse is buttoned. She smiles at him, and the light in the stairwell reflects off her dark glasses.

"I'm a little early," he says.

"Erik." She smiles. "Welcome."

They go inside, and he sees that her daughter has pinned up a drawing of a skull under the NO ENTRY sign.

He follows Jackie along the hallway, watching her right hand trace the wall, and it strikes him that she seems to move without fear. Her shiny blouse is hanging outside her black skirt, across the small of her back.

As her hand reaches the doorframe, she switches the light on and heads out across the living room floor until she reaches the rug, where she stops and turns toward him.

"Let's hear what you can do," she says, gesturing toward the piano.

He sits down, opens the score, and brushes his hair from his forehead. He puts his right thumb on the right key and spreads his fingers.

"Opus Twenty-five," he says with jokey solemnity.

He starts to play the notes that Jackie gave him for homework. Even though she's told him not to, he can't help looking at his hands the whole time.

"It must be awful for you to have to listen to this," he says. "I mean, if you're used to beautiful music."

"I think you've done very well," she replies.

"Can you get music scores in Braille? You must be able to?" he asks.

"Louis Braille was a musician, so that happened fairly naturally. But in the end you have to memorize everything anyway, because of course you need both hands when you're playing," she explains.

He puts his fingers on the keys and takes a deep breath. Then the doorbell rings.

"Sorry, let me get that." Jackie stands up.

Erik watches her go out into the hall and open the door. Her daughter is outside, next to a tall woman in gym clothes.

"How was the match?" Jackie asks.

"One-one," the girl replies. "Anna scored our goal."

"But it was your pass," the woman says kindly.

"Thanks for bringing Maddy home," Jackie says.

"My pleasure. On the way, we talked about not having to be

the best at everything, and that maybe she could be a bit more confident."

Erik doesn't hear Jackie's reply, but the door closes, and then Jackie kneels in front of her daughter and feels her hair and face gently.

"So you're going to have to be a bit more confident," she says softly.

She returns to Erik and apologizes for the interruption. Then she sits down and explains what he should do next.

Erik struggles to get his hands to work independently of each other and feels his back start to sweat.

After a while, the little girl comes into the room. She's changed into a casual dress and sits down on the floor to listen.

Erik tries to play the section but gets the fourth bar wrong. He starts over but makes the same mistake and laughs at his own failure.

"What's so funny?" Jackie asks.

"Just that I'm playing like an old robot," Erik replies.

"My hedgehog makes mistakes as well," Madeleine says consolingly, holding up her stuffed toy.

"My left hand is the worst," Erik says. "It's as if my fingers don't want to hit the right things."

Madeleine blinks but manages to keep a straight face.

"Keys, I mean," Erik says quickly. "Maybe your hedgehog says 'things,' but I say 'keys.'"

The girl looks down with a broad grin.

Jackie gets up from her chair. "Let's give you a break from playing," she says to Erik. "We'll run through a bit of music theory before we end the lesson."

"I'll load the dishwasher," the girl says.

"Maddy, you know it's bedtime soon—you should start getting ready."

The girl leaves, and Erik and Jackie sit down at the table. Erik picks up the jug and pours two glasses of water. It feels impossible not to sneak glances at Jackie as she explains the G clef, F clef, and different overtones. Her blouse is creased at the waist, and her face is thoughtful. He can make out her simple bra and her breasts beneath the silk.

He feels a nervous temptation at being able to look at her without her knowing.

He carefully shifts position so he can see between her thighs and catch a glimpse of her plain white underwear.

His heart beats faster as she parts her legs slightly. He has a feeling she knows she's being watched.

She takes a sip of water.

Her open eyes are only just visible behind her dark glasses.

He looks between her thighs again and leans a little closer, but the next moment she crosses her legs and sets the glass down.

Jackie smiles and says she imagines he works as a professor or a priest. Erik replies that the truth is somewhere in between and tells her about his work at the Psychology Clinic, and his research into hypnosis, then falls silent.

She gathers together the various sheets of music theory, taps them on the table to neaten them, then sets them down in front of him.

"Can I ask you something?" Erik asks.

"Yes," she says simply.

"You turn your face toward me when you talk. Does that come naturally, or do you have to learn that?"

"It's a concession to what sighted people find pleasant," she answers honestly.

"That's what I thought," Erik says.

"Like switching the light on when you enter a room to alert sighted people that you're there."

She stops speaking, and her slender fingers trace the rim of her glass.

"Sorry, I'm being horribly rude, asking about these things."

"Most people with impaired vision prefer not to talk about it. And I understand that," Jackie says. "We'd all rather be seen as individuals and all. But I think it's better to talk."

"Good."

He looks at her soft pink lipstick, the curve of her cheekbones, her boyish haircut, and the green-tinted vein pulsing in her neck.

"Isn't it odd, being able to hypnotize other people and see into their secret, private thoughts?" she asks.

"It's not like I'm spying on them."

"Isn't it?"

25

THE BRIGHT SKY REFLECTS OFF THE CELLOPHANE COVERING the pack of cigarettes on the seat beside Erik as he slowly drives past a sign saying that access is prohibited and that all visits must be announced in advance.

Karsudden District Hospital is the largest secure psychiatric facility in Sweden, with room for one hundred and thirty criminals, all of whom have been sentenced to treatment rather than prison because of mental illness.

His stomach is churning with anxiety. Soon he will be seeing Rocky Kyrklund, to ask him about his supposed alibi.

If it's genuine, then Rocky is innocent. The murder of Susanna Kern could be connected to that of Rebecka Hansson, and it would be no coincidence that Susanna was found with her hand strapped to her ear. Then Erik would have to tell the police everything.

I'm not guaranteed to lose my job, he tells himself. That will depend on whether the police decide to pass the case on to a prosecutor.

In front of the entrance to the main building is a sign showing a camera with a line across it. Yet this place is full of surveillance cameras, Erik thinks.

He picks up the cigarettes and starts to walk toward the white building. A snail's trail shimmers across the path in front of the reception area. In the sharp sunlight inside the doors, the dust is clearly visible as it drifts toward the battered furniture and worn floor.

Erik shows his ID, is given a name badge, and gets no farther than the magazine rack next to the waiting area before a man with blond highlights in his hair comes in.

"Erik Bark?"

"Yes," Erik replies.

The man stretches his lips into a semblance of a smile and introduces himself as Otto. There's something exhausted about the man's face, a sadness that's impossible to hide.

"Casillas would have liked to be here himself, but . . ."

"I understand, don't worry," Erik says, and feels his face flush as he thinks of his lies.

They head out, and the man explains that he's an orderly and has worked at Karsudden for years.

"We'll go the long way around. No one likes the tunnels," Otto mutters as they head outside.

"Do you know Rocky Kyrklund?" Erik asks.

"He was here when I started." Otto gestures toward the high fences and dismal brown buildings.

"What do you make of him?"

"A lot of people are scared of Kyrklund," he replies.

They go in through Entrance D and over to a locker room, where Erik has to leave his loose possessions.

"Can I take the cigarettes with me?" he asks.

Otto nods. "They'll probably come in handy."

The orderly puts Erik's keys, pen, phone, and wallet in a plastic bag, seals it, and hands him a receipt.

Then he unlocks a heavy door that leads to another door with a coded lock. They pass through and walk down a hallway with a gray linoleum floor and security doors leading to small rooms with beds in them.

The air is heavy with disinfectant and stale cigarette smoke.

From one room comes the sound of a porn film. The door is open, and Erik sees a fat man lean forward on a plastic chair and spit on the floor.

They go through another airlock and find themselves in a shadowy exercise yard. Six-meter-high fences link two brick buildings, forming a cage around a yellowing patch of grass edged with concrete paths.

A skinny man in his twenties is sitting on a park bench, his face tense. Two orderlies are talking over by one of the brick walls, and at the far end a heavyset man is standing facing the fence.

"Do you want me to come with you?" Otto asks.

"No need."

The former priest is facing the high fence, smoking. His eyes are roaming across the grass of the parkland toward the leafy trees. By his feet is a mug of instant coffee.

Erik walks along the path, which is littered with cigarette butts and discarded plugs of chewing tobacco. Dust from the path swirls around his legs, and he knows Rocky can hear him approaching.

"Rocky?" he says.

"Who wants to know?"

"My name is Erik Maria Bark."

Rocky lets go of the fence and turns around. He's tall, and his shoulders are even broader than Erik remembers. He has a full beard, specked with gray, and combed-back hair. His eyes are green, and his face radiates a chilly pride. He's wearing a pilled camouflage-green sweater with worn elbows. His sturdy arms are hanging by his sides, a cigarette clasped between his fingers.

"The chief psychiatrist said you liked Camels," Erik says, attempting to give him the cigarettes.

Rocky juts his chin out and looks down at him. He doesn't reply and makes no move to accept the gift.

"I don't know if you remember me," Erik says. "I was involved in your trial nine years ago, I was part of the group that conducted the psychological assessment."

"What conclusion did you reach?" Rocky says in a dark voice.

"That you needed neurological and psychiatric treatment," Erik replies calmly.

Rocky flicks his glowing cigarette at Erik. It hits him in the chest and falls to the ground. A few sparks fly out.

"Go in peace," Rocky says, then purses his lips.

Erik stubs the cigarette out and sees that two orderlies are approaching across the grass. "What's going on here?" one of them asks as they stop.

"It was an accident," Erik says.

The men stay for a few moments, but neither Erik nor Rocky says anything. In the end, the guards go back to their coffee.

"You lied to them," Rocky says.

"I do that sometimes," Erik replies.

Rocky's face remains impassive, but there's a flicker of interest in his eyes now.

"Have you received neurological and psychiatric treatment?" Erik asks. "You have a right to it. I'm a doctor. Do you want me to look at your notes and rehabilitation plan?"

Rocky shakes his head slowly.

"You've been here a long time, but you've never applied for parole."

"Why would I do that?"

"Don't you want to get out?"

"I accept my punishment," Rocky says in his deep voice.

"You had trouble remembering back then. Is that still the case?" Erik asks.

"Yes."

"But I remember our conversations, and sometimes it sounded like you thought you were innocent."

"Naturally. I surrounded myself with lies in an attempt to escape. They crawled all over me like a swarm of bees, and I tried to avoid responsibility by blaming someone else."

"Who?"

"That doesn't matter. I was guilty, but I let the lies crawl all over me."

Erik bends over and puts the cigarettes at Rocky's feet, then takes a step back. "Do you want to talk about the person you wanted to blame?" he asks.

"I don't remember the specifics, but I know I thought of him as a preacher—an unclean preacher."

The priest falls silent and turns back toward the fence. Erik goes and stands next to him and looks out at the trees. "What was his name?"

"I can't remember names anymore, I don't even remember their faces, scattered like ashes."

"You called him a preacher—was he a colleague of yours?"

Rocky's fingers clutch the fence, and his chest rises and falls as he breathes. "I only remember that I was scared. That was probably why I tried to blame him."

"You were scared of him? What had he done? Why were you—"

"Rocky? Rocky!" says a patient who has walked up behind them. "Look what I got for you!"

They turn around and see the skinny man holding out a jam biscuit in a napkin.

"Eat it yourself," Rocky says.

"I don't want to," the other inmate says eagerly. "I'm a sinner, God and His angels hate me, and—"

"Shut up!" Rocky roars.

"What have I done? Why are you—"

Rocky takes hold of the man by the chin, looks him in the eyes, then spits in his face. The man loses his balance when Rocky lets go, and the biscuit falls to the ground.

The guards approach across the grass again.

"What if someone came forward and gave you an alibi?" Erik says quickly.

Rocky's green eyes stare into his without blinking. "Then they'd be lying."

"Are you sure about that? You don't remember anything from—"

"I don't remember an alibi because there wasn't one," Rocky interrupts.

"But you do remember your colleague. What if he was the one who murdered Rebecka?"

"I murdered Rebecka Hansson," Rocky says.

"Do you remember that?"

"Yes."

"Do you know anyone named Olivia?"

Rocky shakes his head, then looks toward the approaching guards and raises his chin.

"What about before you ended up here?"

"No."

The guards push Rocky up against the fence, force him to the ground, and put handcuffs on him.

"Don't hurt him!" the other patient cries.

The larger of the guards puts his knee on Rocky's back while the other one holds his baton to his throat.

"Don't hurt him," the other patient sobs.

As Erik follows one of the guards away from Ward D, he smiles to himself. There is no alibi. Rocky killed Rebecka Hansson, and there's no connection between the murders.

Out in the parking lot, he stops and takes several deep breaths as he looks up past the trees at the bright sky. A feeling of liberation is spreading through his body. A long-standing burden has been lifted from his shoulders.

26

NILS "THE NEEDLE" ÅHLÉN, PROFESSOR OF FORENSIC MEDI-
cine, pulls in and parks his white Jaguar across a couple of parking
spaces.

National Crime wants him to take a look at two homicides.

Both bodies have already been through postmortems. The
Needle has read the reports. They're beyond reproach, far more
thorough than is strictly necessary. Even so, the head of the investigation has asked him to take a second look. They're still fumbling
in the dark and want him to try to identify any subtle similarities,
signatures, or messages.

Margot Silverman believes she's dealing with a narcissistic serial
killer and thinks the murderer is trying to communicate.

The Needle leaves his car and breathes in the morning air.
There's almost no wind today, and the sun is shining.

There's something next to the entrance. At first The Needle
thinks someone's dumped something behind the railing of the little
concrete steps, but then he sees it's a human being. A bearded man
is asleep on the asphalt, his back against the cement foundations
of the brick wall. He's wrapped in a blanket, and his forehead is
resting against his tucked-up knees.

It's a warm morning, and The Needle hopes the man is left to
sleep in peace. He adjusts his aviator sunglasses and walks toward
the door but stops when he notices the man's clean hands and the
white scar running across his right knuckles.

"Joona?" he asks gently.

Joona raises his head and looks at him, as though he were just waiting to be addressed.

Nils stares at his old friend. Joona has lost a lot of weight and is sporting a thick, fair beard. His pale face is gray, there are dark rings under his eyes, and his hair is long and messy.

"I want to see the finger," he says.

"I should have guessed." The Needle smiles. "How are you?"

Joona grabs the railing and pulls himself up, then picks up his bag and walking stick.

"Did you fly or drive down?" The Needle asks.

Joona peers at the lamp above the door. At the bottom of the glass under the bulb is a small heap of dead insects.

After Saga's visit, Joona went with his daughter Lumi to visit Summa's grave in Purnu. Then they walked down to a little sandy beach and talked about the future.

He knew what she wanted to do, without her having to say anything.

In order for Lumi not to lose her place at the Paris College of Art, she had to be there to enroll in two days' time. Joona arranged for her to live with a friend's sister in the Eighth Arrondissement. They didn't have time to make too many other arrangements, but he gave Lumi enough money to get by.

And a lot of useful tips about close combat and automatic weapons.

He drove her to the airport, and it took a lot for him to keep from breaking down. She gave him a hug and whispered that she loved him.

"Or did you catch the train?" The Needle asks patiently.

He returned to the house in Nattavaara, dismantled the alarm system, locked the weapons in the basement, and packed a backpack. Once he'd turned the water off and shut the house up, he walked to the railway station and caught the train to Gällivare, made his way to the airport, and flew to Arlanda, then caught the bus in to Stockholm. He covered the last five kilometers to the campus of Karolinska Institute on foot.

"I walked," he replies, without noticing the look of surprise on The Needle's face.

Joona waits with one hand on the black iron railing as The Needle unlocks the blue door. They walk together down the hallway with its muted colors and worn floor.

Joona can't walk quickly with his stick.

They pass the door to the bathroom and are approaching a window with a large potted plant that seems to consist mainly of roots. Dandelion seeds drift through the air in the sunshine outside. Something moves unexpectedly out there. Joona's instinct is to duck down and draw his gun, but he forces himself to walk over to the window instead. An old woman is standing on the pavement, waiting for a dog that's running back and forth among the dandelions.

"How are you?" The Needle asks.

"I don't know."

Joona is trembling, and he goes into the bathroom, leans over the sink, and drinks some water directly from the tap. He straightens up and dries his face with a paper towel, then goes back out into the hallway.

"Joona, I have the finger in the locked cabinet in the pathology lab, but I'm meeting Margot Silverman in half an hour. You can wait in my room instead if you don't feel up to it—"

"I'm fine," Joona interrupts.

27

THE NEEDLE OPENS THE DOOR TO THE LAB AND HOLDS IT
for Joona. Together they walk into the bright room with its shimmering white tiles. Joona sets his backpack down by the wall.

A cloying stench of decay lingers over the room in spite of the whirring fans. There are two bodies on the postmortem tables. The more recent one is covered, and blood is slowly trickling down the stainless steel gutter.

They go over to the desk with the computer, and Joona waits patiently as The Needle unlocks a heavy door.

"Sit down," he says as he puts the glass jar on the table.

He pulls a folder out of a box, opens it, and places the test results from the crime lab, the ID documents, the fingerprint analysis, and enlargements of the images from Saga's phone in front of Joona.

Joona sits down and stares at the jar. After a few seconds, he picks it up, holds it up to the light, examines it closely, and nods.

"I've kept everything here because I had a feeling you'd show up," The Needle says. "But like I said on the phone, you'll see that it all checks out. The old man who found the body cut the finger off, as you can see from the angle of the cut, and that happened long after death, just as he explained to Saga."

Joona carefully reads the report from the laboratory. They built up a DNA profile based on thirty STR regions. The match was one hundred percent, thus confirming the results of the fingerprint analysis.

Not even identical twins have the same fingerprints.

Joona lays out the photographs of the mutilated body in front of him and examines the entry wounds.

He leans back and closes his burning eyelids.

Everything checks out.

The angles of the shots are just as Saga described. The size and constitution of the body, the size of the hand, the DNA, the fingerprint.

"It's him," The Needle says quietly.

"Yes," Joona whispers.

"What are you going to do now?" The Needle asks.

"Nothing."

"You've been declared dead," Nils says. "There was a witness to your suicide, a homeless man who—"

"Yes, yes," Joona cuts in. "I'll work it out."

"Your apartment was sold when your estate was settled," The Needle explains. "They got almost seven million kroner for it. The money went to charity."

"Good," Joona says bluntly.

"How has Lumi taken everything?"

Joona looks over at the window, watching the slanting light and the shadows of the dirt on the glass. "Lumi? She's in Paris," he replies.

"I mean, how did she deal with you coming back after so many years? How has she dealt with the loss of her mother, and . . ."

Joona stops listening as memories unfold. More than a year ago he made his way in secret to Finland. He thinks about the afternoon when he arrived at the gloomy Radiotherapy and Cancer Clinic in Helsinki to find Summa. She could still make her way around with a walker at the time. He can remember exactly how the light fell in the foyer, reflecting off the floor, the windows and the pale woodwork, as well as the row of wheelchairs. They walked slowly past the unstaffed cloakroom and the candy machine and emerged into the fresh winter air.

The Needle's phone buzzes, and he pushes his sunglasses onto his nose and reads the text message.

"Margot's here. I'll go and let her in," he says, heading toward the door.

Summa had chosen to have palliative care in her apartment on Elisabet Street, but Joona took her and Lumi to her grandmother's house in Nattavaara, where they had six happy months together. After the years of chemotherapy, radiation, cortisone, and blood transfusions, all that was left was pain relief. She had morphine patches that lasted for three days and took another 80 milligrams of OxyNorm every day.

Summa loved the house and the countryside around it, the air and light that streamed into the bedroom. Her family was together at last. She grew thinner, lost her appetite, and lost all the hair on her body. Her skin became as soft as a baby's.

Toward the end, she weighed almost nothing, and her whole body hurt. But she still liked it when Joona carried her around and sat her on his lap so they could kiss.

28

JOONA SITS MOTIONLESS, STARING AT THE GLASS JAR CON-
taining the amputated finger. The particles in the liquid have sunk
to the bottom.

He really is dead.

Joona smiles to himself as he repeats the sentence in his head.

Jurek Walter is dead.

He disappears into memories of his staged suicide and is still
sitting there when Margot Silverman and The Needle come into
the pathology lab.

"Joona Linna. Everyone said you were dead," Margot says with
a smile. "Can I ask what the hell actually happened?"

Joona meets her gaze, thinking about every step he was forced
to take over the past fourteen years.

Margot stands still, staring into Joona's eyes as Nils removes the
protective covering from his sterilized tools.

"I came back," Joona replies in a deep Finnish accent.

"Too late," Margot says. "I already got your job and your office."

"You're a good detective," he replies.

"Not good enough, according to Nils," she says breezily.

"I just said you should let Joona look at the case," The Needle
mutters, stretching the latex gloves before putting them on.

While Nils begins his external inspection of Maria Carlsson's
body, Margot tries to explain the case to Joona. She recounts all
the details about the tights and the quality of the video, but she
doesn't get the response or the follow-up questions she has been

expecting, and after a while she starts to worry that he may not even be listening.

"According to the victim's calendar, she was about to go to a drawing class," Margot says, glancing at Joona. "We checked, and it's true enough, but there's a small 'h' at the bottom of the page of the calendar that we don't understand."

The legendary lieutenant has aged. His blond beard is thick, and his matted hair is hanging down over his ears, curling at the back of his neck, over the padded collar of his jacket.

"The videos suggest narcissism, obviously," she goes on, sitting down on a stainless steel stool with her legs wide apart.

Joona is thinking about the perpetrator watching the woman through the window. He can come as close as he wants, but there's still a pane of glass between them. It's intimate, but he's still shut out.

"He wants to communicate something," Margot says. "He wants to make a point . . . or compete, match his strength against the police, because he feels so damn strong and smart while the police are still miles behind him. And that feeling of invincibility means he's going to kill again."

Joona looks over at the first victim, and his eye is caught by her white hand, resting beside her hip, cupped like a small bowl, like a mussel shell.

He stands up with effort, using the stick for support, thinking that something attracted the perpetrator to Maria Carlsson, made him cross his boundary as an observer.

"And that's why," Margot goes on. "That strong sense of superiority is why I think there could be some sort of signature that we haven't seen."

She trails off when Joona walks away from her, heading toward the postmortem table. He stops in front of the body. His heavy leather bomber jacket is open, its sheepskin lining visible. As he leans over the body, his holster and Colt Combat come into view.

She stands up and notices that the child in her belly has woken. It falls asleep when she moves around and wakes if she sits or lies down. She holds one hand to her stomach as she walks over to Joona.

He's looking closely at the victim's ravaged face. It's like he doesn't believe she's dead, as if he wants to feel her moist breath against his mouth.

"What are you thinking?" Margot asks.

"Sometimes I think our idea of justice is still in its infancy," Joona replies without taking his eyes from the dead woman.

"Okay," she says.

"So what does that make the law?" he asks.

"I could give you an answer, but I'm guessing you have a different one in mind."

Joona straightens up. He's thinking that the law chases justice the way Lumi used to chase fireflies when she was little.

Nils follows the original postmortem as he conducts his own. The usual purpose of an external examination is to describe visible injuries, such as swellings, discoloration, scraped skin, bleeding, scratches, and cuts. But this time he is searching for something that could have been overlooked between two observations, something beyond the obvious.

"Most of the stab wounds aren't fatal, and the killer never intended them to be," he says to Margot and Joona. "If they were, they wouldn't have been aimed at her face."

"Hatred is stronger than the desire to kill," Margot says.

"He wanted to destroy her face." The Needle nods.

"Or change it," Margot says.

"Why is her mouth gaping like that?" Joona asks.

"Her jaw is broken," The Needle says. "There are traces of her own saliva on her fingers."

"Was there anything in her mouth or throat?" Joona asks.

"Nothing."

Joona is thinking about the perpetrator standing outside filming her as she puts on her tights. At that point, he is an observer who needs, or at least accepts, the boundary presented by the thin glass of the window.

But something lures him over that boundary, he repeats to himself, as he borrows The Needle's thin flashlight. He shines it into the dead woman's mouth. Her saliva has dried up, and her throat is pale. There's no sign of anything in her throat. Her tongue has retracted, and the inside of her cheeks are dark.

In the middle of her tongue, at its thickest part, is a tiny hole from a piece of jewelry. It could almost be part of the natural fold of the tongue, but Joona is sure her tongue was pierced.

He goes over and looks at the first report and reads the description of the mouth and stomach.

"What are you looking for?" The Needle asks.

The only notes under points 22 and 23 are the injuries to the lips, teeth, and gums, and at point 62 it says the tongue and hyoid bone are undamaged. But there's no mention of the hole.

Joona continues reading, but there's no mention of any item of jewelry being found in the stomach or gut.

"I want to see the video," he says.

29

MARGOT SIGNS JOONA IN AS HER GUEST, AND HE HAS TO PUT on a visitor's badge before they pass through the security doors.

"There are going to be a lot of people who want to see you," Margot says as they walk toward the elevators.

"I don't have time," he says, taking his badge off and throwing it in a trashcan.

"It's probably a good idea to prepare yourself for shaking a few hands. Can you handle that?"

Joona thinks of the mines he laid out behind the house in Nattavaara. He made them out of ammonium nitrate and nitromethane, so he had a stable secondary explosive substance. He had already armed two mines with three grams of pentaerythritol tetranitrate as a detonator, and he was on his way back to the outhouse to make the third detonator when the entire bag of PETN exploded. The heavy door was blown off and knocked his right leg out of its socket.

The pain had been like a flock of blackbirds, heavy jackdaws landing on his body and covering the ground where he lay. They rose again, as though they'd been blown away, when Lumi ran over to him and held his hand in hers.

"At least I still have my hands," he says.

"That makes it easier."

Margot holds the elevator door open and waits for him to catch up. "I don't know what you think you're going to see on the video," she says.

He follows her in.

"You seem pretty weird," she says with a smile, "but I think I like that."

When they emerge from the elevator, the hallway is already full of their colleagues. Everyone comes out of their offices.

Joona doesn't look anyone in the eye, doesn't smile back at anyone, and doesn't answer anyone's questions. He knows what he looks like: his beard is long and his hair scruffy, and he's limping and leaning on his walking stick.

No one seems to know how to handle his return; they want to see him, but they seem afraid to approach.

Someone's holding a stack of papers, someone else a mug of coffee. These are people he saw every day for years. He walks past Benny Rubin, who's eating a banana with a neutral expression on his face.

"I'll leave as soon as I see the video," Joona tells Margot as he passes the doorway of his old office.

"We're working in room eight twenty-two," Margot says, pointing down the hallway.

Joona stops to catch his breath for a moment. His injured leg hurts, and he presses the stick into the floor to give his knee a break.

"What dumpster did you get him from?" Petter Näslund says with a grin.

"Idiot," Margot says.

The head of National Crime, Carlos Eliasson, comes toward Joona. His reading glasses are swinging on a chain around his neck.

"Joona," he says warmly.

"Carlos," Joona replies.

They shake hands, and patchy applause breaks out in the hallway.

"I didn't believe it when they said you were in the building," Carlos says, unable to contain his smile. "I mean—I can hardly take this in."

"I just want to look at something," Joona says, trying to walk on.

"Come and see me afterward, and we'll talk about the future."

"What's there to say?" Joona says, and walks away.

His work feels distant now, even further away than his childhood. There's nothing for me to come back to, he thinks.

He wouldn't be here now if the first victim's hand hadn't been cupped like a little bowl by her hip.

That made a small spark begin to smolder inside him.

Her slender fingers could have been Lumi's. A deep-seated curiosity woke up inside him, and he suddenly felt compelled to get closer to the body.

"We need you here," Magdalena Ronander says as they shake hands.

It's no longer his job, but when he was confronted with the first victim, he felt a connection that he'd like to be able to control. Maybe he can give Margot a hand early on, just until she gets her bearings.

Joona stumbles as pain shoots down his leg.

"I put a note up on the intranet to let people know you were coming," Margot says as they stop outside room 822.

Anja Larsson, Joona's old assistant, is standing in the doorway of her office. Her face is red. Her chin starts to quiver, and tears well up in her eyes as he stops in front of her.

"I've missed you, Anja," he says.

"Have you?"

Joona nods and looks her in the eye. His pale gray eyes have a dull shimmer, as if he had a fever.

"Everyone said you were dead, that you . . . But I couldn't believe that. I didn't want to, I—I suppose I always thought you were too stubborn to die." She smiles as tears run down her cheeks.

"It just wasn't my time," he replies.

The hallway starts to empty as everyone returns to their offices; they've already seen enough of the fallen hero.

"You look . . ." Anja trails off, wiping her nose on the sleeve of her blouse.

"I know," he says simply.

She pats his cheek. "You'd better go, Joona. They're waiting for you."

30

JOONA ENTERS THE OPERATIONS ROOM AND CLOSES THE door behind him. On the long wall is a huge map of Stockholm with the crime scenes marked on it. Next to the map, pictures from the crime scenes have been taped up: footprints, bodies, bloodspatter patterns. There's a large photograph of the porcelain deer's head, with its reddish brown glazed fur and eyes like black onyx. Joona looks at the copy of Maria Carlsson's Filofax. The day she was murdered she had written, "class 7:00 pm—graph paper, pencils, ink," and underneath she had scribbled the letter "h."

On another wall, they've tried to map the victims' profiles. They've begun to identify family connections and other relationships. Their movements—workplaces, friends, supermarkets, gyms, classes, buses, cafés—have been marked with pins.

Adam Youssef walks over to Joona, shakes his hand, then pins a picture of a kitchen knife on the wall.

"They just confirmed that this knife was the murder weapon. Björn Kern washed it and put it back in the drawer. But we had a number of stab wounds through the sternum, so it was fairly easy to reconstruct the type of blade we were looking for, and it turned out there were still tiny traces of blood on it."

Youssef catches his breath, scratches his head hard a couple of times, then moves on to the enlargement of the deer's head.

"The porcelain figure is made of Meissen china," he says, letting his finger linger over the animal's glistening black eye. "But the rest of the deer wasn't at the crime scene. Björn Kern hasn't been able to give any sort of coherent statement yet, so we don't know if he was the one who put it in her hand."

Joona stops and looks at the photograph of Maria Carlsson's body. The dead woman is sitting propped up against a radiator under a window, wearing a pair of tights.

He reads the report from the examination of the crime scene. There's no mention of any tongue stud or similar item of jewelry being found in her home.

Adam shoots a questioning glance at Margot behind Joona's back.

"He wants to look at the Maria Carlsson video," she says.

"Okay. What for?"

She smiles. "We missed something."

"Probably." He laughs and scratches his neck.

"You can borrow my computer," Margot says amiably.

Joona thanks her and sits down on her chair, adjusts the media player to full-screen, and starts the clip. Just as Margot has described, it shows a thirty-year-old woman, filmed in secret through her bedroom window, as she pulls on a pair of black tights.

He sees her face, completely unaware: her downturned eyes and the calm set of her mouth, which then switches to something approaching lethargy. Her hair is hanging around her face—it looks like she just washed it. She's wearing a black bra and is trying to get her tights to sit properly.

There's a lamp with a translucent white shade and an alabaster base in the window, and her shadow moves across the chest of drawers and the flowery wallpaper. She slips her hand between her thighs and tries to pull the thin nylon material up toward her crotch. Joona can see her breathing through her mouth as the video ends.

"Did you see what you were looking for?" Adam asks, leaning over his shoulder.

Joona remains seated in front of the screen, then plays the video again, watches her struggle with her tights, then freezes the picture after thirty-five seconds and clicks to advance it frame by frame.

"We did that too," Adam says, stifling a belch.

Joona moves closer to the screen and watches Maria Carlsson as she moves very slowly, breathing with her mouth open. Her eyes blink, and her long lashes cast shadows across her cheeks. Her right hand sinks weightlessly between her thighs to her crotch.

"We can't do this," Adam says to Margot. "We've got work to do."

"Give him a chance," she replies.

Maria Carlsson turns jerkily toward the camera, and the gray shadow crosses her face. Her lips part, the light from the lamp in the window shines on her face, making her eyes glow, and there's a shimmer in her mouth. Then the video ends.

Behind Joona, Adam and Margot have started to talk about investigating the people in Maria's drawing class; they've already tried to find out if any of their names begin with "H," but haven't had success so far.

Joona moves the cursor and plays the last five seconds again. The light plays across her hair, her ear, and her cheeks, making her eyes shine, and then her mouth flashes.

He enlarges the image as far as he can without causing too much blurring, then shifts the enlarged area so it covers her mouth and studies the last few frames again. Her parted lips fill the screen, light shines in, and the pink tip of her tongue becomes visible. He clicks to advance the image, frame by frame. The curve of her tongue comes into view, becomes lighter, and in the next shot it looks like a white sun fills her entire mouth. The sun contracts. And in the penultimate frame the glow has shrunk to a white dot on a gray pea.

"He took the jewelry," Joona says.

The two detectives stop talking and turn to look at him and the computer screen. It takes a few moments for them to interpret the enlarged image: the pink tongue and the hazy stud.

"Okay, we missed the fact that her tongue was pierced," Adam says in a rasping voice.

Margot, standing with her legs apart and her hands around her stomach, looks at Joona as he gets up. "You saw that she had a hole in her tongue and wanted to watch the video to see if the stud was there," she says, picking up her phone.

"I just thought her mouth was important," Joona says. "Her jaw was broken, and she had her own saliva on her hand."

"Impressive," Margot says. "I'll request an enlargement from forensics right away."

Joona stands still, staring at the pictures and maps on the wall as Margot speaks into the phone.

"We're collaborating with the BKA," Margot explains once she's hung up. "The Germans are way out in front when it comes to this kind of thing, all forms of image enhancement. Have you met Stefan Ott? Handsome guy, curly hair. He developed his own programs, which J-lab—"

"Okay, so we have an item of jewelry on the video," Adam says, thinking out loud. "The degree of violence is aggressive, fueled by hatred, probably jealousy, and—"

Margot's inbox bleeps, and she opens the email and clicks on the image so that it fills the whole screen.

In order to improve the contrast of the stud itself, the image enhancement software has changed all the colors. Maria Carlsson's tongue and cheeks are blue now, and the stud is clearly visible.

"Saturn," Margot whispers.

At the end of the stud piercing Maria's tongue is a silver sphere with a ring around its equator, just like the planet Saturn.

"That's not an 'h,'" Joona says.

They turn and see that he's looking at the photograph of Maria's planner where it says "class 7:00 pm—graph paper, pencils, ink," then on the line below, the letter "h."

"That's the symbol for Saturn," he says. "It represents a scythe or sickle. That's why it's slightly crooked, and sometimes it's crossed at the top."

"Saturn . . . the planet. The Roman god," Margot says.

31

JOONA AND MARGOT ARE STANDING BAREFOOT, LOOKING through a pane of glass. The room inside is warm and damp.

"I've tested for allergens, and it turns out I'm allergic to mindfulness," she says.

About thirty perspiring women are moving with mechanical symmetry on their yoga mats to the strains of Indian music.

Margot got five officers to search Maria Carlsson's Internet activity once more: her email, Facebook, and Instagram accounts. The stud in her tongue is visible in only a few pictures and is mentioned only by one of her friends on Facebook before all communication between them ceased: "You gotta lick it before we kick it. I wanna get my tongue pierced too."

The woman who posted that was Linda Bergman, and she was a Bikram yoga instructor in the center of Stockholm. She and Maria had been in very regular contact for six months before she suddenly unfriended Maria.

Linda Bergman emerges from the staff room dressed in jeans and a gray sweater. She's tan and looks like she quickly showered and put on some makeup.

"Linda? I'm Margot Silverman," Margot says, shaking the woman's hand.

"You didn't say what this was about, and I can honestly say that I have absolutely no idea," she says.

They walk along the sidewalk in the direction of Norra Bantorget while Margot tries to get Linda to relax by asking about Bikram.

"It's a form of hatha yoga, but it takes place in a room with high humidity, at a temperature of a hundred and four degrees," Linda explains.

They enter the former playground in front of the old Norra Latin School. The spherical fountain shimmers silvery white, and the wind keeps scattering showers of tiny droplets.

"The founder's name is Bikram Choudhury," she continues. "He created a series of twenty-six positions that are the best I've ever tried."

"Let's sit down," Margot says, holding her stomach.

They sit on an empty park bench.

"You used to be friends with Maria Carlsson on Facebook," Joona says, drawing a deep vertical line in the path, raising a little cloud of dust.

"What happened?" she asks warily.

"Why did you unfriend her?"

"Because we no longer have anything to do with each other."

"But you seem to have been in very close contact for several months," Margot says.

"She came to a few classes, and we started talking, and . . ."

Linda trails off, and her gaze flits anxiously from Margot to Joona.

"What did you talk about?" Margot asks.

"Can I ask if I'm suspected of something?"

"You're not," Joona says.

"You knew Maria had a piercing, a tongue stud?" Margot goes on.

"Yes," Linda says, giving a slightly embarrassed smile.

"Did she have several different studs?"

"No."

"Do you remember what hers looked like?"

"Yes."

Linda stares at the old school building and the play of the shadows under the trees for a moment before replying: "It had a tiny model of Saturn at the top."

"A tiny model of Saturn," Margot repeats very gently. "What does that mean?"

"I don't know," Linda says blankly.

"Does it have something to do with astrology?"

Linda looks over at the trees again and kicks the ground.

"Do you know where she got it? It doesn't seem to be for sale anywhere."

"I don't understand where this is going," Linda says. "I have another class soon, and—"

"Maria Carlsson's dead," Margot interrupts, with quiet seriousness. "She was murdered last week."

"Murdered? She was murdered?"

"Yes, she was found on—"

"Why are you telling me?" Linda interrupts, and stands up.

"Please sit down," Margot says.

"Maria's dead?" Linda sinks onto the bench, her eyes drift off toward the fountain, and she starts to cry. "But I . . . I . . ."

She shakes her head and hides her face in her hands.

"Did you give her the stud?" Joona asks.

"Why the hell do you keep talking about that tongue stud?" she snaps. "Find the killer instead. This is completely sick!"

"Did you give her the stud?" Joona repeats, drawing a short line across the first one.

"No, I didn't." She wipes tears from her cheeks. "She got it from a guy."

"Do you know the name of the guy?" Margot asks.

"I don't want to get involved," she whispers.

"We respect that." Margot nods.

Linda looks at her with bloodshot eyes and purses her lips.

"His name is Filip Cronstedt," she says.

"Do you know where he lives?"

"No."

"Was Maria going out with him?"

Linda doesn't answer, just stares down at the ground as the tears begin to fall again. Joona adds the last curve to the symbol with his walking stick and leans back.

"Why did she have a model of Saturn on her tongue stud?" Margot asks carefully. "What does it mean?"

"I don't know. Because it looked nice," she says weakly.

"In Maria's calendar there's a symbol written in ten different places. It's the old symbol for Saturn," Margot says, and points to the ground.

32

LINDA'S CHEEKS TURN RED AS SHE LOOKS AT THE SYMBOL drawn in the grit in front of Joona's feet. The wind has already begun to erase the stylized scythe. She says nothing, but her forehead is shiny with sweat.

"Sorry, but I'm expecting a phone call," Joona says, and stands up with the help of his stick.

Margot watches him limp off toward the steps and pull out his phone. He's left them alone so she can create a more intimate atmosphere.

"Linda," she says, "I'm going to find out what all this is about sooner or later, but I'd rather you told me."

The young woman has dark gray sweat marks under her arms now, and she slowly brushes the hair from her face.

"It's just that it's personal." She licks her lips.

"I appreciate that."

"They call it saturnalia," Linda says, looking down at the ground.

"Is that some sort of role-play?" Margot asks gently.

"No, it's an orgy," Linda replies as steadily as she can.

"Group sex?"

"Yes, although group sex sounds like . . . I don't know, it's not like some sort of tragic old swingers' club." She smiles, embarrassed.

"You seem to know what you're talking about," Margot says.

"I went with Maria a few times," she replies, shaking her head almost imperceptibly. "I'm single, there was nothing weird.

You didn't have to sleep with everyone just because you were there."

"But isn't that the point?"

"I don't have any regrets about trying it, but it's not exactly something I'm proud of either."

"Tell me about the saturnalias," Margot asks.

"I don't know what to say." Linda crosses her legs. "I was carried along by Maria's—I don't know, completely open attitude about sex. Well, I thought I was, anyway."

"Were you in love with her?"

"I did it for my own sake," Linda says, without answering the question. "To try something new, no obligation, to just let go and allow it to mean nothing but sex."

"I get it." Margot smiles gently.

"The first time," Linda says, giving Margot a dark look, "your whole body just shakes. You think, *I can't be doing this.* Several men at the same time . . . and there are a ton of drugs, and you have sex with other girls, and it goes on for hours. It's crazy."

She looks over toward Joona and brushes sweat from her top lip with her forefinger.

"But you stopped going," Margot says.

"I'm not like Maria. I wanted to be with her, and I tried doing it her way. And after a while, I felt different, and brave and everything. But after the third time, I started to think a whole lot of things . . . it wasn't like I regretted it. More like, *Okay, why am I doing this? I don't have to feel ashamed, I'm allowed to do it—but why?*"

"That's a good question."

"It was my decision to go, but it sort of wasn't on my terms. I think I felt a little exploited."

"Was that why you stopped?"

Linda rubs the end of her nose and lowers her voice.

"Someone filmed one of the saturnalias. You're not supposed to do that, no phones. Maria called and told me. She was really angry, but it just made me worried. I felt like I was going to be sick. The clip was on a porn site for amateur videos, it was shaky and dark, but I could still see myself, and that wasn't exactly a great feeling, I can tell you."

A few drops from the fountain reach them, and Linda turns away from the hazy sphere and shakes her head.

"I can't believe she's dead," she whispers.

"These saturnalias—how are they arranged?"

"It's two guys from Östermalm, Filip and someone named Eugene. It probably started out as parties with a lot of cocaine and Ecstasy. And then there was spice, monkey dust, Spanish fly, and all the rest . . . and now it's been going on for at least two or three years. There are maybe a couple of saturnalias every month. Exclusive, invite only."

"Always on Saturdays?"

"You know where the English word *Saturday* comes from?" Linda replies.

Margot nods, and Linda kicks at the ground again. "I'd just like to say that I never took any drugs," she says.

"Good for you," Margot says neutrally.

"I drank too much champagne instead." She smiles.

"Where do they take place?"

"When I was involved, they had a suite at the Birger Jarl Hotel. All I remember is really weird, psychedelic rooms."

"Tell me about the stud Maria had in her tongue."

"Filip and Eugene gave studs to all the girls who belonged to the inner circle."

"Did Maria want to leave as well? Do you know?"

"I don't think so. Well, I—" She stops and gathers her hair over one shoulder.

"What were you going to say?"

"Just that Filip fell in love with her, he wanted to see her on her own, didn't want her sleeping with other men. She just laughed. That was what she was like, Maria."

Margot pulls out a photograph of Susanna Kern.

"Do you recognize this woman? Take a good look."

Linda studies Susanna Kern's smiling face, her warm, light brown eyes and glossy hair, and shakes her head.

"No," she replies.

"Was she at the saturnalias?"

"I don't recognize her," Linda says, getting to her feet.

Margot remains seated on the bench. They still haven't found a connection between the victims. They're dealing with a serial killer who stalks his victims, but they have no idea where he finds them or how he chooses them.

33

MADELEINE FEDERER IS WALKING ALONG A PATH THAT CUTS diagonally across Humlegården. After school she went to St. Jacob's Church with her mother. Jackie takes all the extra work she can get as an organist so they can get by financially.

Now Madeleine is walking next to her, talking and keeping an eye on the path even though she knows her mom doesn't need help.

Her mother walks with one foot nudging the edge of the grass, so she can feel the plants against her leg and listen to the stick tapping the path at the same time.

A compressor starts to rumble outside the Royal Library, and she can hear the whine of powerful drills. The noise makes her mother lose her bearings, and Madeleine takes her arm.

They pass the playground with the spiral slide she used to love when she was younger. It smelled so good, like plastic and warm sand.

When they reach the street, her mother thanks her for her help, and they walk toward the pedestrian crossing.

Madeleine can hear how the tapping of the stick against the stone pavement sounds harder than it did on the road, but she can't tell how the sound changes when they pass a pole close to the edge of the road.

"It's just a momentary gap in the noise of the cars," her mother explains, and stops.

As usual, she puts the tip of her stick over the edge of the pavement so she'll be prepared to navigate the curb when the cars stop and the ticking sound from the walk sign starts up.

They cross and walk in front of a large yellow building, where her mother turns toward an open garage door and clicks her tongue. A lot of people with visual impairments do this to listen to the echo and so identify potential hazards.

Once they're home, Jackie closes the door, locks it, and puts on the security chain. Madeleine hangs up her coat and watches her mom go into the living room without switching on the light and set her music scores on the table.

Madeleine goes to her room, says hello to Hoggy, and just has time to change into more comfortable clothes before she hears her mother's voice.

"Maddy?" she calls from her bedroom.

When Madeleine enters the brightly lit room, she sees her mother in just her underwear, trying to close the curtains in front of the window. Just outside the window a pink child's bicycle is lying on the grass. The curtain is caught in the door of the wardrobe, and her mother runs her fingers down the fabric and manages to pull it free before she turns around.

"Did you turn the light on in here?" she asks.

"No."

"I mean this morning."

"I don't think so," she replies.

"You need to make sure we don't leave any lights on when we go out."

"Sorry," she says, although she really doesn't think she did it.

Her mom reaches for the blue robe on the bed. Her hands fumble and locate it up near the pillow.

"Maybe Hoggy got scared of the dark and came in and turned the light on."

"Maybe," she says.

Her mom turns the flimsy robe the right way around, puts it on, then kneels and cups Madeleine's face with both her hands.

"Are you the prettiest girl in the world? You are, I know you are."

"Don't you have any students today, Mom?"

"Only Erik."

"Aren't you going to put some clothes on?"

"Thanks for the suggestion." She wraps the silk gown around her body.

"Put the silvery skirt on. That's nice."

"You'll have to help me find something."

Her mother has a color reader but always asks Madeleine if her clothes look right, if the colors match.

"Should I go and get the mail?"

"Bring it to the kitchen."

Madeleine walks through the hall, where she can smell damp earth and stinging nettles as she picks the mail up from the floor in front of the door. Her mother is already sitting at the kitchen table when she comes in and stops next to her.

"Are there any love letters?" Jackie asks, as she always does.

"There's . . . an advertisement from a realtor."

"Throw it away. Throw all the ads away. Anything else?"

"A reminder about the phone bill."

"Nice."

"And . . . a letter from my school."

"What do they have to say?" Jackie asks.

Madeleine opens the envelope and reads the letter, which has been sent to all parents. Someone has been writing curse words on the hallway walls and in the bathroom. The principal asks parents and guardians to talk to their children about the matter, and tell them how much it costs to clean it up and reduces the money available for maintenance of the playground.

"Do you know who's doing it?" her mother asks.

"No, but I've seen the graffiti. It's really stupid. Really childish."

Her mother gets up and starts to take cherry tomatoes, crème fraiche, and asparagus out of the fridge.

"I like Erik," Madeleine says.

"Even though he called the keys 'things'?" her mom asks, filling a large saucepan with water for pasta.

"He said he played like an old robot." Madeleine giggles.

"Which is absolutely true."

Madeleine can't help smiling, and sees her mom smile as she switches the hotplate on.

"A handsome little robot," Madeleine goes on. "Can't I keep him? My very own little robot. He could sleep in the doll's bed."

"Is he really handsome?"

"I don't know," she replies, thinking of his kind face. "I think so. He looks a little like one of those actors everyone keeps talking about."

Her mother shakes her head but looks happy as she adds salt to the water.

34

ERIK SEEMS PLEASED WITH HIMSELF THAT HE CAN PLAY ALL the way to the eighteenth bar with his right hand, even though his left hand can manage only six. Jackie smiles to herself for a few seconds but decides not to give him any praise. Instead she asks if he's been practicing the way she told him to.

"As often as I can," he assures her.

"Can I hear?"

"I've been practicing, but it doesn't sound right."

"There's nothing wrong with making mistakes," Jackie points out.

"But you won't want me as a student if I can't play well."

"Erik, there's no danger of—"

"And I really love being here," he goes on.

"That's nice to hear, but if you're going to learn how to play, you have to . . ."

Jackie trails off in the middle of the sentence and blushes, before raising her chin again.

"Are you flirting with me?" she asks with a skeptical smile.

"Am I?" He laughs.

"Okay," she says seriously.

"I'll try playing the piece I practiced, if you promise not to laugh."

"What will happen if I laugh?" she asks.

"That will just prove you have a sense of humor."

She smiles broadly just as Madeleine comes in, dressed in her nightgown and a pair of slippers.

"Goodnight, Erik," she says.

He smiles. "Goodnight, Madeleine."

Jackie gets up and follows her daughter to her bedroom. Erik watches them go and has just put his left hand on the keys when he sees that Madeleine has forgotten her stuffed hedgehog on the armchair.

He picks it up and goes after them, turning right into the hallway. The door of the girl's room is ajar, and the light is on. He can see Madeleine's back, and Jackie turning back the covers.

"Maddy," he says, opening the door. "You forgot—"

He gets no further before the door slams into his face, and he bounces back. Madeleine is screaming hysterically and slams the door again. Erik tumbles backward into the wall of the hallway and puts his hand to his nose as the blood starts to flow.

Madeleine is still screaming in her room, and he hears something fall to the floor and break.

He goes into the bathroom, puts the hedgehog down, and squeezes his nose. He hears Jackie calming the girl down.

After a while Jackie knocks softly on the bathroom door. "Are you okay? I don't understand what—"

"Tell her I'm sorry," Erik interrupts. "I forgot the sign. I just wanted to give her her hedgehog."

"She was asking where it was."

"It's on the cabinet in here," Erik says, opening the door. "I didn't want to get blood on it."

"Are you bleeding?"

"Just a slight nosebleed."

Jackie takes the hedgehog and goes to her daughter while Erik rinses his face. He returns to the piano as Jackie comes out again.

"Sorry," she says, holding her hands out. "I don't understand what got into her."

"Don't worry. She's wonderful," Erik says.

Jackie nods. "Yes, she really is."

"My son is eighteen, and he's still never switched the dishwasher on. But now he's living with his mother, and she's a bit tougher than I am."

They fall silent. Jackie is in the middle of the room. She can smell Erik, his clean clothes and the warm wood from his after-shave. Her face is somber as she wraps her knitted cardigan more tightly around herself, as if she were cold.

"Would you like a glass of wine?" she asks.

35

ERIK AND JACKIE ARE SITTING ACROSS FROM EACH OTHER AT the kitchen table. She's taken out wine, glasses, and bread.

"Do you always wear dark glasses?" he asks.

"My eyes are light sensitive. I can't see anything, but light makes them hurt," she says.

"It's almost completely dark in here," he says. "Only the little lamp behind the curtain is on."

"Do you want to see my eyes?"

"Yes," he confesses.

She takes a small bite of bread and chews slowly, as if she were thinking about it.

"Have you always been blind?" he asks.

"I had retinitis pigmentosa when I was born. I could see fairly well for the first few years, but I was completely blind by the time I was five."

"You didn't get any treatment?"

"Just Vitamin A, but . . ."

She stops speaking, then takes off her dark glasses. Her eyes are the same sad, bright blue as her daughter's.

"You have beautiful eyes," he says softly.

It feels strange that they aren't staring at each other, even though he's looking into her eyes. She smiles and almost closes them.

"Can you get scared of the dark if you're blind?" he asks.

"In the dark the blind man is king," she says. "But you get scared of hurting yourself, of getting lost."

"That makes sense."

"And earlier today I somehow got it into my head that someone was looking at me through my bedroom window," she says with a short laugh.

"Really?"

"You know, windows are strange things for blind people. A window is just like a wall, a cool, smooth wall. I mean, I know most people can see straight through a window. So I've learned to close the curtains, but at the same time you don't always remember."

"I'm looking at you now. Does it feel uncomfortable to have someone watching you?"

"It's—it's not without its challenges," she says, with a brief smile.

"You don't have any help? What about Madeleine's father?"

"Maddy's father was . . . it wasn't good."

"In what way?" Erik asks.

"He was . . . damaged. I found out later that he'd tried to get psychiatric help but was turned down."

"That's a shame," Erik says.

"It was for us."

She shakes her head and takes a sip of wine, wipes a drop from her lip, and sets the glass back on the table.

"There are different ways of being blind," she goes on. "He was my professor at the music college, and I didn't realize how unwell he was until I got pregnant. He started saying it wasn't his child, calling me all sorts of horrible things. He wanted to force me to have an abortion, said he fantasized about pushing me in front of an underground train."

"You should have reported him."

"Yes, but I was too afraid."

"What happened?"

"One day I put Maddy in her stroller and walked to my sister's in Uppsala."

"You walked there?"

"I was just glad it was over," Jackie says. "But for Maddy . . . obviously, it's impossible for anyone to know how much longing a child can live with. How much fantasizing and magical thinking a child can manage, to explain why her dad never gets in touch."

"All these absent fathers . . ."

"When Maddy was almost four and was able to answer the phone, she picked up once when he called. She was delighted. He promised to come on her birthday, and bring a puppy, and . . ."

Her lips begin to tremble, and she falls silent. Erik pours them both some more wine and puts her hand to the glass, feeling her warmth.

"But you're not an absent father?" she says.

"No, I'm not. But when Benjamin was little, I had a problem with prescription drugs, and things got pretty bad," he replies honestly.

"And his mother?"

"Simone and I were married for almost twenty years."

"Why did you split up?"

"She met a Danish architect. I don't blame her, I actually like John. And I'm genuinely happy for her."

"I don't believe that." She smiles.

He laughs. "Sometimes you just have to pretend you're grown up and do what you're supposed to, say the things that grown-ups say."

He thinks about Simone, and the backward ceremony where they gave their rings back to each other, retracted their vows, and then at the party afterward had a divorce cake and a last dance.

"Have you met anyone else?" Jackie asks quietly.

"I've had a few relationships since the divorce," he admits. "I met a woman at the gym, and—"

"You go to the gym?"

"You should see my muscles," he jokes.

"Who was she?"

"Her name was Maria. Nothing came of it. She was probably a little too adventurous for me."

"But you've never slept with your professor?"

"No." Erik laughs. "Almost, though. I did end up in bed with a colleague of mine."

"Oops."

"No, it was okay, actually. We were drunk, I was divorced and felt abandoned. She told me she and her husband were taking a break, so it wasn't a big deal."

"What about patients?"

"Occasionally you find them attractive," Erik says honestly. "That's unavoidable. Therapy is an extremely intimate situation. But attraction and seduction are merely a way for the patient to avoid thinking about anything painful."

He thinks of how Sandra used to stop in the middle of a sentence and feel her beautiful, intelligent face with her fingertips as tears welled up in her forest-green eyes. She wanted him to hold her, and when he did, she dissolved in his arms, as though they were making love.

He doesn't know if Sandra's actions were premeditated, but he still asked a colleague to take her on afterward. Sandra had already met her, and it seemed like the natural solution.

"So who are you seeing at the moment?" Jackie says.

Erik looks at her smile, at the shape of her face in the soft light, at her short dark hair and white neck. The worries about Rocky Kyrklund that have been consuming him lately suddenly feel very far away.

"I don't know how serious it is, but . . . well, we've only met a few times," he says. "But I feel happy whenever I'm with her."

"That's good," Jackie mumbles, blushing.

She picks up another piece of bread.

"When I'm with her, I never want to go home. And I already like her daughter, and I'm also learning to play the piano like a robot." He puts his hand on hers.

"You have soft hands," she says with a big smile.

He strokes her hands, wrists, and lower arms, slides his fingers up to her face, following her skin. He leans forward and kisses her gently on the mouth, several times.

She smiles as she waits to be kissed again, and when they kiss, they open their mouths and feel each other's tongues, tentatively, breathing tremulously, when the doorbell suddenly rings.

They both startle and sit perfectly still, holding their breath.

The bell rings again.

Jackie hurries to get up, and Erik does the same, but when she opens the door, there's no one there. The stairwell is completely dark.

"Mommy!" Madeleine calls from her room. "Mommy!"

Jackie reaches out and touches Erik's face.

"You should probably go now," she whispers.

36

AN OLD WOMAN WITH PLASTIC BAGS WRAPPED OVER HER clothes casts an anxious glance at Joona as he wobbles unsteadily beside her in the line of homeless people.

He tried to get some rest on the green line of the subway, then met a Roma man who offered him somewhere to sleep. He's been lying on the floor of a trailer out in Huddinge, wrapped in a blanket, with his eyes closed, waiting for sleep, but his thoughts won't leave him alone.

He hasn't eaten or slept since Lumi left. He gave her all his money, keeping only enough to cover the journey to see The Needle.

Lack of sleep means his migraines are more and more frequent. The pain is like a burning needle behind one eye, and his hip is getting even worse.

An Iranian man with friendly eyes is patiently pouring coffee for the hungry and giving them sandwiches.

Joona is so hungry, he can no longer feel it in his stomach. Instead it feels like a weight that makes his legs weak. When he's handed his coffee and sandwich, he feels like he's going to faint. He moves to one side, unwraps the bread, takes a bite, and swallows it, but his stomach starts to cramp, trying to reject the food. He puts his hand over his mouth and turns his back on the others. Dizziness forces him to his knees. He spills his coffee on the ground, takes another bite, coughs, and spits it out. Sweat breaks out on his forehead.

"How are you doing?" the Iranian man says.

"I haven't eaten anything for a while," he replies.

"A busy man." The Iranian smiles gently.

"Yes," Joona says, coughing again.

"Just let me know if you need help."

"Thanks, but I'm fine," Joona mutters, then limps away.

"At one o'clock, the soup kitchen in St. Clara Church opens," the man calls after him. "Come by—you could use a place to sit down and get warm."

Joona crosses the bridge toward City Hall, feeds the sandwich to the swans, and walks heavily up the long slope of Hantverkar Street. He stops and rests for a while, fingering the little stone in his pocket, then continues toward the fire station before turning into Kronoberg Park. The foliage high above is drenched in sunlight, but the grass beneath the trees is shady, a soft moss green.

Joona walks slowly up the hill, opens the gate, and enters the old Jewish Cemetery.

"I'm sorry I look like this," he says, putting the stone down on Samuel Mendel's family grave.

Joona pushes a candy wrapper away with his stick and tells his former partner that Jurek Walter is dead at last. Then he stands in silence, listening to the wind through the trees and the sounds of children in the nearby playground.

"I've seen the evidence," he whispers, patting the headstone before he leaves.

Margot has asked Joona to attend an unofficial meeting today. He thinks she's probably trying to be nice to him, letting him play at being a detective for a while.

On his way down toward Fleming Street, Joona thinks about the orgies Maria Carlsson attended.

Saturnalias, carnivals, drunken binges—they've always been part of human life. Every breath takes us closer to death, and we console ourselves with work and routines, but every so often we have to turn our lives upside down, if only to prove to ourselves that we are free.

Maria Carlsson had evidently been planning to attend a saturnalia the day she was murdered. It's impossible to say if the orgies link the victims, but on her calendar Susanna Kern had circled the same July Saturday.

FILIP CRONSTEDT AND EUGENE CASSEL ARE JOINT OWNERS of Croca Communication Ltd., which grossed ninety-five million euros last year.

Neither of them has visited the office on Sibylle Street in the past six months, and they haven't attended a board meeting in a very long time. The managing director has been in touch with Eugene, most recently just last week, but he hasn't heard from Filip since the beginning of the year.

Linda Bergman says she was still in contact with Maria Carlsson when Filip suddenly withdrew from the saturnalias.

But the orgies have gone on, attended by both Maria and Eugene.

There seem to be a number of regular participants who attend every time, while a limited number of new people are invited on a trial basis.

According to Linda, passcards for the hotel suite double as entrance tickets.

The investigative team have little expectation of finding Filip at the hotel, but they're relatively confident that Eugene will be there. According to Maria Carlsson's planner, there's an orgy planned for next Saturday, and another one in three weeks' time. These two dates may be their only hope of finding Eugene and tracing Filip.

37

ADAM, MARGOT, AND JOONA ARE SITTING AT A BAR. A SOCCER match is playing on the television. Margot is eating a large hamburger and drinking water. Adam and Joona are both drinking black coffee.

"Filip doesn't seem to have left Sweden," Adam says, arranging some printouts on the table. "He's here, but he's not registered as living here, and he doesn't appear to have been in any of the homes owned by the company."

Filip Cronstedt's face looks up at them from the table. The photograph shows a man in his forties with back-combed blond hair and pale eyebrows. He looks like a friendly, considerate banker. His furrowed brow and the set of his cheeks and chin suggest hard living, but that only makes him look more sympathetic.

"I don't know if I believe that he killed Maria Carlsson," Adam adds, pointing a finger at the picture. "It doesn't make sense. I mean, he doesn't have a history of violence. He has no criminal record—he's never even been suspected of anything. And there's no mention of him in Social Service records."

"He can afford good lawyers," Margot says.

"Yes, but even so," Adam says.

A woman is dragging a fifty-liter barrel of beer across the floor. A family with three young girls walk past the scratched window overlooking Tule Street.

"All we know is that Filip Cronstedt started to get jealous," Margot says, putting some French fries in her mouth. "He wanted

Maria to stop going to the saturnalias, but she kept going. And now she's dead, and that stud in her tongue is missing."

"Yes, but—"

"I'm thinking," she goes on, "I'm thinking that he became obsessed with Maria Carlsson, on the sidelines watching her at the orgies. So far, so good—but is he a serial killer?"

"Or a spree killer," Adam says. "We only have two murders, and that's not enough to—"

"We're hunting a serial killer," she interrupts.

"It doesn't really matter," Joona says. "But Margot's right, because . . ."

He shuts his eyes as his migraine flares up behind his eye, and he raises his hand slowly to his head. While the pain subsides, he sits absolutely still and tries to remember what he was going to say about spree killers. The term refers to a murderer who has killed at least two people in different places, with barely any time between them. A spree killer doesn't have the serial killer's lifelong, sexualized attitude toward murder, but commits his murders as a direct response to a crisis.

"Okay," Adam says after a while.

"It's still too early to say anything about Filip," Margot says with her mouth full. "It could be him, I think that's a possibility, but—"

"In that case, the orgies form part of his fantasy about killing," Joona says, opening his eyes.

"We'll move forward with what we have," Margot declares. "This evening is the only time we know where Eugene Cassel is going to be. And if anyone can tell us where Filip is, it's Cassel."

"Mind you, we can't just storm into a private orgy." Adam grins.

"Only one of us needs to go in, find Eugene, and talk to him," Margot says, then takes a large bite of her hamburger.

"You can't work out in the field," Adam says. "You're pregnant."

"Does it show?" she asks as she chews.

"Okay, what the hell, I'll do it," Adam says.

"This isn't a raid," Margot says. "There's no obvious threat. We'll call it a meeting with an anonymous informant. Then we don't need to run it past management beforehand."

Adam sighs and leans back. "So this means I have to be in a room with a bunch of . . ." He trails off, staring into space with glazed eyes, then shakes his head.

"Obviously it's a little tricky, approaching people in a situation like that, but what can we do?" Margot says.

"I don't get it. What kind of person would want to go to an orgy?"

"I don't know. I haven't had group sex for at least ten years." Margot dips some fries into ketchup.

Adam stares at her openmouthed as she chews, a slight smile on her face. She wipes her fingers on a napkin and then looks up at him.

"I was joking," she says with a grin. "I'm a nice girl, I promise, but I was involved in a raid on a swingers' club when I worked in Helsingborg. As I recall, it was mostly just men in their sixties, with big bellies and skinny legs—"

"Enough," Adam says, slumping down in his chair.

"I'll give your wife a call tomorrow and ask what time you got home."

"Fine," Adam sighs, then grins.

"Think of it as a job, nothing more," Joona says. "The other people are irrelevant. You just go straight in and talk to Eugene, get him to tell you where Filip is, and arrest him as soon as you're sure you have the information."

"Arrest him?"

"To stop him from warning Filip," Joona says, looking Adam in the eye.

"If you find out anything about Filip," Margot says, "then—"

"Then I'll call you," Adam fills in.

"No, I'll be asleep." She puts the last of the food in her mouth. "If you find out anything, hand it over to the rapid response team."

The two men remain seated at the table after Margot leaves. A few elderly patrons get up from their table and go outside to smoke.

"Where are you staying?" Adam looks at Joona.

"There's a campsite on the outskirts of Huddinge."

"The Roma?"

Joona doesn't reply, just takes a sip of coffee and looks out the window.

"I looked you up," Adam says. "I saw that . . . the year before you were injured, you taught the Special Operations unit in military Krav Maga. Sorry, but looking at you now, it's hard to believe you were a paratrooper."

38

THE PSYCHEDELIC ROOM AT THE BIRGER JARL HOTEL IS ACTU-
ally known as the Retro Room and can be booked just like any
other room.

The hotel underwent a complete renovation in 2000. All the
rooms were gutted, and the decor was completely changed. Once
the workmen left, it turned out that room 247 had been forgotten.

The room has somehow been ignored during every refurbish-
ment since the hotel was built in 1974.

It's still intact, like a small time capsule from a bygone age.

In 2013 a murder was committed at the hotel, after a sofa in
room 247 was changed. Of course there was no real connection
between the two events, but now the staff refuse to make any
adjustments to the layout of the room.

Adam has been sitting in his car for five hours, watching the
entrance to the hotel. Joona has been outside, wrapped in his blanket, holding out a cup with some coins in it.

Thirty-five guests have gone in during that time, but no Eugene.

Farther down the street, a gray-haired waiter is squatting down
outside an Italian restaurant, smoking.

When the church bells slowly strike eleven o'clock, Joona limps
over to the car. "You'd better go in," he says to Adam.

"Can't you come with me?"

"I'll wait here," Joona says.

Adam drums his thumbs on the steering wheel.

"Okay," he says, and rubs his chin a few times.

"Take it easy in there," Joona says. "Just because they're there doesn't make them criminals. You're likely to see a lot of drugs, but ignore that. You should intervene only if you see signs of forced sexual activity, or if there's anyone underage."

Adam nods and feels his stomach flutter as he gets out of the car and walks into the hotel.

The softly curved reception desk is empty except for a man talking on the phone.

Adam goes over to the desk and shows his ID. He gets a passcard and continues toward the elevators. The Retro Room is at the end of the hallway, and on the door handle is a floppy plastic sign saying DO NOT DISTURB.

Adam hesitates, then lowers the zipper on his black leather jacket. His white T-shirt is tucked inside his black jeans, and his Sig Sauer is in a holster beneath his left armpit.

All he has to do is go in, nice and calmly, he tells himself. Find Eugene, take him to one side, and ask his questions.

Adam clears his throat and runs the card through the reader. The lock clicks, and a little green light comes on. He opens the door, walks into a dark hallway, and shuts the door behind him.

He can hear music and muffled voices, and a bed creaking.

The light is weak, but it isn't completely dark. He looks around. He's in a small lobby where people have left their clothes.

A blond woman with a boyish haircut comes out of the bathroom and blinks at him in the darkness. She's wearing nothing but a pair of skimpy black silk panties, and she's so beautiful, his heart starts to beat faster.

She has traces of white powder stuck in the lip gloss at one corner of her mouth. She looks at Adam; her big black pupils are surrounded by a narrow ring of ice blue. She licks her lips and says something he doesn't hear, before going back into the bedroom.

He follows her, unable to stop himself staring at her naked glistening back.

Inside the dimly lit room, there's a sweet, smoky smell.

Adam stops and looks over at the bed, then looks away again

immediately. He shuffles sideways along the wall, passing a naked man with a glass of champagne in his hand, then stops.

No one has reacted to his presence.

A woman pushes past, her eyes focused on the floor. The wallpaper is pink and wavy, the carpet brown with a starburst pattern. There are no lamps on, but the light of the city outside reaches around the curtains, spreading across the ceiling.

The whole room is heavy with the smell of excited people. Wherever Adam looks, he can see glistening genitals, open mouths, breasts, tongues, buttocks.

Apart from the music, there's very little sound. The people having sex are concentrating on that, intent on their own or their partner's pleasure. Others are resting, watching the orgy with a hand between their legs.

His pulse thuds in his ears, and he can feel himself blushing.

He needs to try to find Eugene.

Adam passes a beautiful woman in her thirties. He can't help looking at her. She's wearing a batik blouse and is sitting on the desk with her eyes closed. Her exposed crotch looks like polished marble, with a line drawn on it in pink chalk.

None of it is as desperate or grubby as he imagined. It's more introverted, more self-aware.

He walks around the bed, wondering if this is all simply part of these people's trendy lifestyle.

He's the same age as most of them, but he's here to do his job, then go home to his wife, no doubt to remember forever what he has seen. He knows already that he won't be able to talk to her about it—not seriously. He'll end up joking or turning it into something disgusting.

He tells himself the people around him are spoiled, that he feels sorry for them, but that isn't true, not right then.

A pang of envy runs through him.

39

ADAM WALKS THROUGH THE OPEN DOOR TO THE NEXT ROOM. The wallpaper is darker here, with big, bold patterns, like pale green crystals.

The music is louder, too. Two naked men have put an orange plastic armchair on top of the bed. A woman with straight black hair is sitting on the chair, laughing as the others rock the mattress. More men join in, and someone grabs her feet as she laughs louder.

The woman with the boyish haircut is kneeling in front of a glass-topped table, dabbing at the remains of some white powder and rubbing her finger on her gums.

Adam steps aside and almost steps on a large tube of lubricant on the floor. Dust and strands of hair are stuck in the goo that's spilled out.

In the window are ten glasses full of champagne. Drops of condensation are running down the stems and forming small puddles on the marble sill.

Farther into the room, Adam reaches a windowless hallway containing closets and a suitcase rack. The bathroom door is half open. A naked woman is sitting slumped on the lid of the toilet, her stomach folded and one arm tensed.

"Are you all right?" Adam asks softly.

She lifts her head and looks at him. Her eyes are dark and moist, and he gets a strong feeling that he should leave the hotel.

"Help me," she whispers.

"How are you feeling?"

"I can't stand up," she mumbles.

A slim man comes toward them from the bedroom and stops in the doorway. His erect penis sways as he moves. "Is Paula here?" he asks.

He looks at them through half-closed eyes, then disappears the way he came.

"Help me up," the woman says, breathing through her mouth.

Adam takes her hand and pulls her to her feet. He backs away, and she stumbles out of the bathroom, managing to pull a towel down. Only now does he notice that she has a dildo strapped around her hips. She falls toward him and puts her hand around his neck.

The woman's breath smells like alcohol, and the dildo slips between his thighs. Her legs begin to give out, and he holds her up, feeling her heavy breasts against his body.

"Can you stand?"

"I don't know if this thing is on right," she mutters against his neck. "Can you check the strap at the back?"

She turns around and leans one hand against the wall, knocking against a plastic brown wall clock and making its cover rattle.

"Have you seen Eugene?" Adam asks.

The black leather strap between her buttocks is twisted, and she feels along it with tired fingers.

"It's twisted," Adam says.

He doesn't know what to do, hesitates, then tries to help her. He twists the strap twice but notices that it's tangled farther down as well.

Her skin is hot and sweaty. He's trembling and can feel how cold his fingers are as he follows the strap down between her buttocks.

A naked man pushes past and weaves into the bathroom. He urinates without closing the door or so much as glancing at them.

Adam can't help noticing that the leather strap between her legs is wet and slippery. She stumbles again and leans her cheek against the wall, as the plastic clock sways on its hook.

A woman in the next room is whimpering. Two men move

through the hallway, and then he sees the beautiful woman with the boyish haircut in the doorway. She's no longer wearing her underwear. She's walking slowly toward the next room when she catches sight of him. She raises her champagne glass toward him in a toast, and he sees pale lip prints on the rim.

The woman in front of him leans her shoulder against the wall, then slides down onto the floor and rests her cheek on the carpet.

The woman with the boyish haircut comes over to Adam. Her neck looks flushed, and she leans into him, pressing her forehead to his chest, then looks up at him with a smile.

Adam can't help himself. He kisses her, and she responds, and he can feel her tongue stud against his tongue.

It's wrong, and he already knows that he's going to regret it, but all he wants right now is to have sex with her.

The woman on the floor mutters something about falling over and pulls at his leg, making him sway.

When the woman with the boyish haircut unzips his pants, a wave of icy fear runs through him.

This is too easy, too tempting, he thinks.

But his hands are touching her breasts, and they're warm and tense and powdered with something rough and glittery.

He's never seen such a beautiful woman.

He picks her up, pushes her back against the wall, and slides inside. Angst and lust spin through him. He groans and sees her mouth open, and Saturn sparkles on her tongue. Her body billows, and her breasts quiver with his thrusts. She's smiling, eyes closed, but she makes no noise, and she doesn't really seem interested in what's happening. Maybe she's too drugged.

Two women come into the hallway and watch them for a while before moving on.

The woman with the dildo is on her feet. She's behind him, and her hands are suddenly under his T-shirt, caressing his waist and back. He tries to pull away. He doesn't know if she's felt his gun, but she suddenly stops, moves away from him, mutters something, and lurches into the bedroom.

Adam knows his cover may have been blown, but he can't stop now. The woman says something to his neck, and he can smell raspberries. She puts her hand on his chest, trying to get him to slow down, but he moves it away and pushes her hard against the wall.

40

WHEN ADAM ENTERS THE THIRD ROOM, HE IMMEDIATELY sees Eugene Cassel. He's wearing a black top hat but nothing else. Five people are having sex with each other on the large bed. The shade of a table lamp is hanging askew and shaking in time with their movements. Eugene is on his knees behind a woman on all fours.

Her pearl necklace is swinging between her breasts.

The woman with the strap-on dildo comes staggering into the room after Adam. He watches her sit down on the edge of the bed, almost fall, then sit up again. Another woman grabs the dildo, says something, and laughs. She replies, then coughs into her elbow.

"What did you say?"

"Tra-la-la-laa." She smiles.

"Okay."

"The cops are here, tra-la-laa," she repeats, and coughs again.

Eugene hears her words and stops, sits down on the bed, puts an arm on the woman's backside, and then turns to look at Adam.

"This is a private party," he says with a look of disappointment.

"Is there somewhere we can talk in private?" Adam shows his police ID.

"Leave your card, and I'll get my lawyers to call you on Monday," Eugene says, getting up from the bed.

Eugene is about forty, probably the oldest person in the suite. His naked, hairless body is in good shape, despite his protruding stomach. His erection has subsided. Beneath the rim of his hat, a gold ring sparkles in his eyebrow, and his pupils are dilated.

"I need to find Filip Cronstedt," Adam says.

"Good luck." Eugene raises his hat slightly. "He isn't here, but I can give you a clue: follow the white rabbit."

"Listen," Adam says, "we can leave the hotel nice and quietly, but if I have to, I'll put handcuffs on you in here and drag you all the way to the car."

A woman with shimmering white skin, her reddish brown hair in two braids over her breasts, enters the room and comes over to Eugene.

"Should I order some food?" she says, putting a joint to her lips.

"Still hungry?" he asks flirtatiously.

She nods and smiles, then exhales a narrow plume of smoke and walks off toward the phone beside the bed.

"Okay, I'm going to have to arrest you according to chapter twenty-four, paragraph seven of the penal code," Adam says.

"It's not my fault you went to a bad school and ended up having to join the police," Eugene says sternly. "The world's unfair, and—"

"You know Maria Carlsson, don't you?" Adam butts in.

"I love her," Eugene replies slowly.

"Give her a kiss." Adam pulls out a picture from the crime scene.

In the sharp light of the flash, the dead woman's ravaged face, gaping mouth, and broken jaw are brutally visible.

Eugene whimpers, staggers backward, and knocks over a table lamp. Its brown ceramic base shatters.

41

EUGENE PUTS HIS CLOTHES ON, AND ADAM CALLS FOR A patrol car. They walk down the hotel hallway together.

"I'm really sorry. I'm shocked. Just tell me what I can do. I want to help, as a point of honor . . . but I have to speak to my lawyer first."

Eugene has washed his face, but his cheeks are white and shiny with sweat.

"I need to find Filip," Adam says.

"He didn't do this," Eugene says instantly.

"Filip isn't at any of his usual addresses. Where is he?"

"He's not doing too well." Eugene scratches his forehead with his hat. "Look, I'm not going to spread shit about Filip, but the way things are right now, I really don't want anything to do with him. I've tried to get him to seek help, but—"

"Help with what?" Adam says.

The elevator door opens, and they step aside to let a woman in an orange trench coat get out before going in.

"He's been taking a little too much." Eugene smiles, waving his hand toward his temple.

"Is he an addict?"

"Yes, but the problem with taking too much bath salts . . . it doesn't work. You just get fucking paranoid, and then you get the wrong kind of high and end up feeling so bad you want to die."

"Does it make you aggressive?" Adam asks as they step out of the elevator onto the ground floor.

"I mean, you're terrified all the time, but sort of ultrafocused at the same time. You think too quickly, don't sleep at all. The last time I met Filip, he was completely fucking manic, said he was on thousands of satellite pictures on Google, kept going on about Saturn being forced to eat his own children. He couldn't stand still, he kept ranting, waving this little knife around. He cut my hand and yelled that I should be grateful. And then he cut himself, right across the arm. He was dripping with blood when he ran off into the subway."

They pass the lobby and walk out the doors onto Tule Street at the very moment a patrol car pulls up.

"Right now I just need to know where I can find him," Adam repeats, stopping Eugene.

"Fine. I feel like a traitor, but he said they couldn't see him at the storage warehouse."

"Storage warehouse?"

"He rents a shitload of storage over on Vanadis Road, you know, that self-storage place. I think he's got more than half the units there."

Two uniformed officers come over. One of them leads Eugene to the backseat of the car while the other listens to Adam.

"Take him to the custody negotiation room," Adam says. "Make sure he doesn't call anyone. Buy us some time. Once his lawyer shows up, we won't be able to hold him."

42

JOONA IGNORES THE RED LIGHT AND TURNS LEFT ONTO ODEN Street, driving fast.

A homeless woman with two overloaded shopping carts is asleep outside the 7-Eleven.

Adam tells Joona that Filip has been overdosing on several different varieties of bath salts for a while now, and that Eugene thinks he's entered a paranoid psychosis.

The drug has caused a number of deaths recently and was referred to in the evening tabloids as the "cannibal drug" after a man who'd taken it tried to eat a homeless man's face.

"We don't have much time," Adam says tensely. "They won't be able to hold Eugene for long. He'll be out soon, and I think he's likely to warn Filip."

Joona passes a taxi, pulls in front of it, then swerves into the oncoming lanes and turns onto Vanadis Road.

The bumper thuds as he drives up onto the sidewalk and stops in front of a pale mocha-colored building with red garage doors.

In central Stockholm, the storage companies have had to make do with existing basements so they don't change the visible appearance of the city. Huge areas of small, locked rooms spread out just below the ground, like old catacombs beneath the city.

Joona and Adam get out of the car and head over to the closed office looking out over the little parking lot. In the gloom through the window, they can make out flat stacks of moving boxes, a reception desk, and a large security monitor on the wall.

"I want to look at a map of the storage warehouse, and I want to look at those cameras," Joona says.

"It's closed. We're going to have to go through a prosecutor," Adam replies.

Joona nods, tapping his walking stick against the edge of the pavement and thinking about how it feels to sink through broken ice. It's when you warm up that you start to freeze. He picks up a heavy stone and throws it through the window. There's a loud crash as the glass shatters, and a red light begins to flash over on the reception desk.

"The alarm will go off at their security company," Adam says feebly.

Joona pushes some loose splinters from the window frame with his stick, then goes inside. Adam looks around, then follows him.

There's a map hanging on the wall, showing a grid system of wide and narrow hallways.

Every unit is numbered, and they're arranged in blocks. A list of staff codes for the stores is neatly posted alongside.

Joona sits down at the computer. The hallways between the storage blocks are monitored by security cameras. Twenty-five small squares cover the screen. All the cameras are filming windowless darkness. It's night, and the lights have all been switched off.

"See if you can find a list of customers," Adam says.

Joona minimizes the security cameras and tries to open various programs but can't get anywhere. Everything other than the cameras requires a password.

He quickly returns to the cameras and enlarges the first square and stares at the gray-black stillness. Then the next one. The camera is filming nothing but darkness. Adam shuffles nervously behind him. He examines the map on the wall.

Everything is quiet.

The third camera is pointed toward an emergency exit. A green sign above the door casts an algaelike glow across the flecked cement floor and corrugated metal walls.

There's some trash outside one of the storerooms, and the

underwater lighting from the emergency exit illuminates an abandoned dolly.

Joona glances at the map on the wall again and locates the emergency exit, then figures out where the camera is mounted. Everything is still quiet. Numbing exhaustion washes over him like a wave, forcing him to close his eyes for a couple of seconds.

The darkness on the computer screen is monotonous. Some of the cameras register light from coded locks but nothing else.

"Dark," Adam says.

"Yes," Joona says, enlarging the fourteenth square.

He's just about to close it when there's a flicker in the bottom corner.

"Hang on," he says.

Adam leans forward and peers at the dark image. There's nothing in sight, everything is still, but then the little light in the corner flashes again.

"What was that?" Adam whispers, leaning closer to the screen.

The little light flashes again. It's faint but manages to light up a small area of the floor, revealing the pattern of the cement.

Joona clicks to enlarge the next camera image, then the next, and waits a while, but they show only blackness. He looks at the overview, all twenty-five cameras at the same time. Number fourteen flickers again, but the others remain lifeless.

"The source of the light should be here, or here." Joona points at the map. "But it's not covered by one single camera, which makes no sense."

"Where are we?" Adam asks, looking at the map.

"Camera fourteen must be at the far end of hallway C," Joona says.

He enlarges the images one by one. All is black and still, but suddenly he stops.

"Did you see something?" Adam asks.

They both stare at the static black image.

"That's what I mean," Joona replies. "Where's the green light? This is the camera pointing at the emergency exit."

"Try that one," Adam says, pointing. "That should pick up the light from the lock leading to the next section."

Joona quickly enlarges the image. Also completely black. The door and lock can't be seen at all.

There's something wrong with the camera. There seem to be an awful lot of faulty cameras down there.

"There's a huge area missing, encompassing a number of cameras," he says, looking at Adam.

"Where?"

"This whole upper area, along hallways C, D, and E. That's maybe fifty storerooms." Joona looks back at the image from camera fourteen again.

The faint light flickers across the uneven floor and remains on for a moment. He can just make out the bottom of the metal doors before the light goes off, then comes on again.

"That light's an emergency signal," Joona says, getting up from the chair. "Further down the hallway, where the cameras aren't working, someone is flashing a light. Three quick flashes followed by three longer ones, then three short ones again. It's the international SOS signal."

43

THE AUTOMATIC GARAGE DOOR CLANGS SHUT BEHIND THEM.
The pain in his hip from walking down the slope makes Joona
break into a sweat. His heavy pistol is swinging against his ribs, and
the sound of his walking stick echoes in the narrow tunnel leading
down to the storage area.

"We ought to call for backup." Adam draws his Sig Sauer.

He pulls out the magazine, checks that it's full, pushes it back
in, and feeds the first bullet into the chamber.

"There's no time, but I can go in on my own," Joona says.

"I was thinking of telling you to wait outside. You're not a police
officer anymore, and I can't take responsibility for you," Adam
explains.

They emerge into an underground garage, with metal doors
leading to the storage area. Large ventilation pipes run across the
ceiling.

"I can usually manage," Joona says.

He pulls out his large-caliber pistol. It's a Colt Combat, with
new sights and an improved trigger coil. He's filed one side of the
rosewood grip so that the gun sits snugly in his left hand.

Adam walks over to the keypad to the coded lock and pulls out
the list of staff codes. The little screen casts a blue light over his
hand and up across the white concrete wall.

"Stay behind me," he whispers, then opens the door.

They go inside, closing the steel door carefully behind them, and head along a dark passage. The monotonous gray metal walls, covered by storage unit doors, stretch off into the darkness.

They're approaching a wider hallway that, according to the map, runs the entire length of the basement.

They move across the cement floor. The only sound is Adam's breathing and the faint tapping of Joona's stick.

Adam, walking ahead, slows down when he reaches the junction with the main hallway. His right shoulder rubs against the metal wall. He stops, then swings around the corner quickly with his pistol raised.

There's a buzzing sound as the ceiling lights come on ten meters away. Adam lowers his gun and tries to breathe through his nose.

The barrel of his pistol is moving slightly in time with his raised pulse.

The sudden light makes Joona's migraine flare behind his eye, and he has to lean against the wall for a moment before following Adam.

The lights in the main hallways seem to have been activated by motion sensors.

Joona looks up at one of the security cameras. The dark lens shimmers.

The pipes running across the ceiling tick, but otherwise the basement is completely quiet.

They reach a side passage and turn left, walk past rows of sealed storerooms, and pass two shabby sofas as the lights go out behind them.

"We should be reaching his area soon," Adam whispers.

Indirect light from an electronic lock some way ahead makes the storerooms seem to bulge out into the hallway.

Adam pauses to listen.

There's a drumming, rattling sound somewhere. They can both hear something hard knocking against metal.

Then everything falls silent again.

They wait several seconds before continuing to move into the darkness.

There's a sudden scraping sound, then a metallic noise far in the distance. Joona points up at a camera in the ceiling: the lens has been covered with duct tape.

Adam stops before he reaches the next hallway, wipes his right palm on his trousers, gives his hand a shake, then takes a firm grip of his gun again. He notices that some gold glitter from the woman in the hotel room is stuck to the sleeve of his jacket, and he glances at Joona. Then he focuses and rounds the corner.

The ceiling clicks and ticks along the hallway as the lights come on in quick succession.

The walls, floor, and ceiling are bathed in sharp light, but beyond the lights, there's nothing but blackness. Even though the hallway runs another fifty meters or so, only the first ten are visible.

"Stop," Joona says behind Adam.

They both stand completely still. A drop of sweat falls from the tip of Adam's nose. Joona leans on his stick, feeling strangely dizzy.

The brittle knocking sound starts up again in the distance, a high-frequency metallic buzz.

The lights in the main hallway go out because the sensors can't detect any movement. The two men stand motionless, staring into the darkness. Up ahead there's a faint glow across the floor, from one of the side passages.

The light vanishes, then returns in the same sequence: three longer flashes, followed by three short ones.

The strange drumming sound echoes again, followed by something hitting a metal wall. It's much closer now.

"What do we do?" Adam whispers.

Joona doesn't have time to answer before the ceiling lights at the very far end of the main hallway come on.

A young woman is standing in the middle of the passageway, swaying. She's wearing nothing but a pair of dirty sweatpants and a worn padded jacket. Her feet are bare, and her hair is matted.

Her waist is tied with thick steel wire, which snakes off into the side passage next to her. Whenever she takes a step forward, the wire makes a metallic rattling sound against the walls behind her.

Her right arm is moving strangely, twitching and then moving away from her. There's a black band around her wrist, and it looks like someone's tugging the band.

She steps toward them. Her arm sinks, and then there's a large shadow behind her. A huge dog with a bloody ear appears at her side. Its black leash hangs limply in her hand and leads behind her to the dog's neck.

The huge dog is a Great Dane. It is as tall as her chest and must weigh twice as much as she does.

The dog moves nervously, twitching its head.

The woman says something, then drops the leash onto the ground. The dog leaps forward and picks up speed rapidly in the hallway. The huge animal is getting closer to Joona and Adam with powerful, silent movements. Its muscles ripple across its back and loins as the lights come on, section by section.

They move back and raise their guns just as the lights go off at the far end of the hallway.

The young woman is no longer visible.

The sounds of the animal's claws and its panting breath are getting louder.

They run into a side passage, past padlocks that shimmer in the light from the main hallway. But fifteen meters in, their way is blocked by a barricade of furniture and cardboard boxes.

Now they can hear barking from another direction.

A sharp pain flares behind Joona's eye. It's as if a hot knife is being pushed into his head, and when it gets pulled out again, he can't see for a few seconds.

The pain of his migraine almost makes him drop his gun.

Coming around the corner, the dog slides on the cement floor, then catches sight of them and speeds up again.

Joona raises his pistol and blinks hard in an effort to see straight, but the sight on the barrel is trembling too much.

It's too dark, but he fires anyway. The sound of the shot echoes off the metal walls and concrete. The bullet misses and ricochets between the walls.

The dog is approaching with powerful bounds.

Joona blinks and can just make it out as a series of flickering images: pointed ears and shimmering muscles, shoulders, and strong thighs. His walking stick clatters to the floor as he rests his shoulder against the corrugated metal door and takes aim again.

"Joona!" Adam cries.

The sights quiver and slip past the beast's head. He squeezes the trigger. The sight slides down toward its dark torso, and the shot rings out as the bullet slams into the dog's chest just beneath its throat. The recoil sends Joona staggering backward. He tries to keep his balance and throws his arm out, hitting the door with the barrel of the pistol.

The dog's legs buckle. Its heavy body thuds to the floor, momentum carrying it forward. It slides across the cement floor and hits Joona's legs. He sinks to one knee and lets out a gasp, his vision flaring.

The dog's legs are still twitching as Joona gets to his feet and picks up his stick.

Some distance away Adam is clambering over the barricade of old furniture, rolled-up carpets, and boxes. He gets tangled up in a bicycle and falls over the other side, hitting his head against a metal door.

In front of Joona is an overturned bed that's been pushed against one wall. He shoves it over across the rest of the barricade and squeezes through the gap between it and the wall. He sees Adam get to his feet just as the second dog launches itself at him.

44

ADAM CRIES OUT IN PAIN AS JOONA PUSHES HIS WAY through the gap between the bed and the wall. He hears something made of glass break under the pressure. The lights in the main hallway go out, but Joona can still see that the huge dog has clamped its jaws around Adam's lower arm. It's pulling hard, snarling as its claws scrabble on the cement floor.

Adam is gasping and trying to hit the animal.

Joona can't fire into the darkness, so he tries to force his way over to them. A lamp with a broken shade catches on his clothes.

The dog isn't letting go of Adam's arm. They crash into the metal wall, blood from Adam's arm running from its locked jaws.

The dog makes a sudden downward jerk, and when Adam stumbles forward, it lets go and snaps at his neck. It misses and only catches part of his jacket collar. It rips the fabric and tries to bite again. Adam throws himself back and kicks. The dog bites his foot and tugs him closer.

Joona stumbles out onto the floor, knocking over a box of books. He runs over with his pistol raised, but the dog suddenly lets go and disappears.

"Big dogs," Joona says, leaning on his stick.

Adam picks his pistol up off the floor and gets to his feet.

Joona shuts his weary eyes for a moment and can't help feeling like he might be about to break.

They move toward the next major hallway. The lights go on ahead of them, and the clicking sound is back.

"There," Adam says.

They catch a glimpse of someone disappearing into a side passage and hear clattering metal wire vibrating against the walls.

"Did you see? Was it the same woman?"

"I don't think so," Joona replies, noticing how pale and sweaty Adam's face is. "How are you doing?"

Adam doesn't answer, just shakes the blood running down the back of his hand onto the floor. His lower arm is injured, but his leather jacket protected it from serious damage.

They stick to the right-hand side of the hallway in order to be able to see into the side passage on the left.

A young woman is standing in the hallway, swaying. She's not the same one as before. Her white jeans and checkered shirt are much dirtier.

"He said you'd come," she mumbles in a brittle voice.

"We're police officers," Adam says.

She staggers and fumbles for a little dog whistle attached to a cord around her neck.

"Don't do it," Adam says when he sees the second large dog get closer, crouching low with its ears folded down.

She's been crying. Her makeup has run down her face, and her hair is hanging in messy clumps.

There's blood around the waist of her shirt.

She rolls the dog whistle between her fingers, then puts it to her lips.

Adam raises his pistol, takes aim, and shoots the dog in the forehead. It collapses to the floor, and the echo fades away.

She smiles at them through cracked lips, then staggers backward when someone tugs on the metal wire around her waist.

"We saw an SOS signal," Adam says.

"I'm smart, aren't I?" she says wearily.

She moves back along the hallway, the metal wire still pulling her, clattering against the walls and floor.

"How many of you are there down here?" Adam asks as they follow her.

They step over the dog and the pool of dark blood spreading out across the floor.

"Where are you going?"

She doesn't answer, and they continue around a corner. Farther along the dimly lit hallway is a faint light. They pass an open storeroom, and in the gloom they can see a mattress on the floor, boxes, some old skis, and stacks of canned food.

Someone tugs harder on the wire, and the young woman keeps stumbling on. She opens the next door and staggers into the storeroom.

Light shines out, and her shadow sways across the doors and smooth walls.

There's a growing stench of rotting garbage.

Joona and Adam follow her with their pistols pointed at the floor. The light is coming from a pocket flashlight hanging from the ceiling, illuminating part of the large storeroom. Among a mass of moving crates and picture frames stands an emaciated man dressed in an unbuttoned mink coat.

It's Filip Cronstedt.

Joona and Adam raise their guns.

He's filthy and has white froth at the corners of his mouth. His bare chest is covered with blood from a patchwork of cuts.

The woman in the worn padded jacket is sitting on a box in front of him, eating mushrooms from a jar with her fingers.

Filip hasn't seen them yet. He's carefully winding the retracted wire around a huge spindle. Then he scratches his neck and pulls the woman in the checkered shirt closer without looking up.

"Filip," she whispers.

"I need you on guard, Sophia. I don't want to have to lock you up, but I've told you before, you can only have the light on when the door is closed."

"Filip Cronstedt?" Adam says loudly.

45

FILIP LOOKS UP AND STARES AT ADAM WITH TIRED EYES AND dilated pupils.

"I'm the hat maker," he says quietly.

Sweat is running down Joona's back, and he can't hold his pistol up any longer.

The flashlight hanging from the ceiling sways in a gust of air, sliding the shadows around the walls. Its light reflects off a large floor mirror.

Joona moves to one side, blinks, and sees in the mirror that there's a knife sticking out of the box in front of Filip.

"We need to talk to you," Adam says, moving forward cautiously.

"How many videos are you in every day?" Filip asks, staring at the floor. "Where does it all go? What decisions does it lead to?"

"We can talk about that if you let the girls go."

"I don't give a shit about Snowden and optic nerves," he says slowly, pointing at the ceiling.

"Just let the girls go, and—"

"This isn't Prism or XKeyscore or Echelon," he interrupts more loudly. "This is way fucking bigger than that."

Joona puts his pistol back in its holster and walks slowly toward the woman whose name is evidently Sophia. The last of his strength is draining away, the way icy water makes everything sluggish.

Filip's hand is getting closer to the knife sticking out of the box.

Sophia falters, and the wire rattles softly.

"Saturn ate his children," Filip goes on, then sniggers. "I mean, the NSA is much bigger. And we're their children."

Joona manages to see him put his hand on the knife, before his vision flares again and he has to put his hand against the wall to keep himself from falling.

Little dots float before his eyes as he loosens the coarse wire around Sophia's waist. He has to rest his forehead against her shoulder for a while before going on. He can hear her shallow breathing.

Without showing any outward signs of anxiety, he unwinds the wire some twenty revolutions before she's free.

"Are there more of you down here?" he asks in a subdued voice as he leads her out of the storeroom.

"Just me and my sister," she replies.

"We're going to get you out. What's your sister's name?"

"Carola."

The metal wire unravels on the cement floor with a scraping sound.

Filip tugs at the knife, making the side of the box bulge before he loses his grip.

"We're here now, but who ends up in Guantánamo? You don't know, do you?" he says without looking at them.

"Carola," Joona says in a normal tone of voice, "could you come over here, please?"

Sophia's sister puts the lid back on the jar of mushrooms and shakes her head without looking up.

"Carola, come here," Sophia says.

She sits picking at the jar, as Filip looks at her and scratches his neck.

"Come on." Joona feels his gun rubbing against his chest.

"Eugene is with them, you know, GCHQ . . . the NSA. Same thing. I've been so badly fucking deceived, for years. Everyone's naked, everyone's having fun . . . but how can you protect yourself if you're completely naked, if everyone can film you from the fucking back?"

The flashlight spins around, and dark shadows cross their faces and shoulders.

"Sophia wants you to come over here," Joona says.

Carola looks up and smiles at her sister. Sophia brushes tears from her cheeks and holds out her hand.

"Can we go home now?" Carola whispers, and stands up at last.

She's about to start walking when Filip grabs her by the hair and pulls her back, tugs the knife from the box, and holds it to her throat.

"Hang on, hang on, take it easy now," Adam calls. "Look, I'm putting my gun down."

"Go to hell!" Filip screams and stabs the knife into his forehead before putting it to Carola's throat again.

"Do something!" Sophia whimpers.

Blood from the wound in Filip's forehead trickles through an eyebrow and drips onto his cheek.

"I know you're just trying to protect her," Joona says calmly.

"Yes, but you—"

"Listen to me," Adam interrupts, breathing quickly. "You need to put the knife down."

Sophia is sobbing with her hand over her mouth.

Filip grins at Adam. "I know where you're from," he says, and presses the knife harder against Carola's neck.

"Put the knife down now," Adam shouts, moving sideways to get a clear line of fire.

Filip watches Adam and licks his lips nervously. The room is gloomy, but blood is clearly running down the blade.

"Filip, you're hurting her," Joona says, trying to conquer his dizziness. "You don't have to do that. We're no threat to you."

"Shut up!"

"We're just here to—"

"Shut up!"

"We're here to ask about Maria Carlsson," Joona concludes.

"Maria? My Maria?" he says in a low voice. "Why . . . ?"

Joona nods, thinking that he could shoot Filip in the shoulder and disarm him, then finally lie down on the floor. He's waited too long. He can hardly see anything now, through the burning pain behind his eyes.

"Look, I'm taking my gun out and giving it to you." Joona carefully draws his Colt.

Filip stares at him with bloodshot eyes.

"Maria said the NSA have started creeping about in her garden," he explains. "I went over and saw for myself, a skinny man in a yellow oilskin raincoat, like the Lofoten fishermen when I was little. He was filming her through the window, and . . ."

Joona wipes some blood from his nose, and then his head explodes and his legs give out.

Sophia screams when he slumps to his side, falls onto his back, and lies with his eyelids quivering.

She goes over to him and kneels. A bubbling, pulsing sensation behind one eye makes him hold his breath. Before it goes completely dark, he feels her pull the pistol from his hand.

She stands up, straightens her back, takes a few shallow panting breaths, then aims at Filip.

"Let my sister go!" she says sharply. "Just let her go!"

"Put the gun down," Adam says shakily, and moves between them. "I'm a police officer. You need to trust me."

"Get out of the way!" she yells. "Filip's not going to let her go!"

"Don't do anything stupid," Adam says, holding out his hand.

"Don't touch me—I'll shoot!" She's clutching the pistol with both hands, but the barrel is still shaking.

"Give me the gun and—"

There's a deafening explosion as the pistol goes off. The bullet grazes Adam's torso and hits Filip in the top of his arm.

The knife falls to the floor, and Filip stares at Sophia in astonishment as blood seeps through his fingers.

"Get out of the way!" she shouts again.

Adam lurches to the side and feels warm blood pulsing out beneath his clothes. Sophia fires again and hits Filip right in the chest. Blood spatters the boxes behind him and across the glass of the mirror. The empty cartridge falls to the ground with a tinkling sound.

Carola, still standing there with her head bowed, slowly raises her hand to her neck. Sophia lowers the gun and stares blankly at Filip, who slumps to the floor, leaning back against a box.

He picks listlessly at the wound in his chest as blood pumps out, and his eyes flit wildly as he tries to say something.

46

ON HIS WAY TO HIS PIANO LESSON, ERIK STOPS AT THE ICA supermarket next to the Globe. He knows Madeleine loves popcorn, so he's thinking of buying a few bags. As he walks through the shop, he catches sight of a former patient, Nestor, in the dairy section. The tall, slim man is dressed in pressed khakis and a gray sweater over a white shirt. He looks the same as he always does with his thin, clean-shaven face and small head with its white hair parted on the side.

Nestor has seen him and smiles in surprise, but Erik just waves from a distance and continues shopping.

He picks up some popcorn and is on his way to the checkout when he sees a popcorn machine on special offer. He knows he has a tendency to go overboard, but it doesn't weigh much and isn't particularly expensive.

When he emerges into the parking lot with his bags of corn and the popcorn machine, he catches sight of Nestor again. The tall man is waiting at the pedestrian crossing, on his way to the subway. He has six full bags of shopping beside him. They're so heavy, he can carry them only a few meters at a time.

Erik opens the trunk of his car and puts the box inside. He's sure Nestor hasn't seen him. The shy man is muttering to himself as he picks up the bags, shuffles a few meters, then sets them down again.

Nestor is standing blowing into his thin hands as Erik goes over to him.

"That looks heavy," he says.

"Erik? No, it's f-fine." Nestor smiles.

"Where do you live? I'll give you a ride."

"I don't want to be a nuisance," he whispers.

"You're not." Erik picks up four of the bags.

As Nestor gets into the car beside him, he repeats that he could have managed. Erik replies that he knows that and pulls slowly from his parking space.

"Thanks for the coffee, but you shouldn't be buying things for me," Erik says.

"You saved m-my life," Nestor replies.

Erik recalls how Nestor's psychotic breakdown happened when his dog had to be put down three years ago.

At the time when Nestor was assigned to him as a patient, Erik read the notes from the hospital where Nestor had been admitted. He used to talk to dead people: a gray lady who brushed dandruff from her hair, and a mean old man who twisted his arms in different directions.

During Erik's conversations with him, it emerged that Nestor was fixated upon his dog's death. He talked a lot about the syringe being stuck in his right front paw, and how the fluid had been injected. The dog shook, and urine spread across the bench as its muscles relaxed. He felt he had been tricked by the vet and the vet's wife.

Nestor responded well to treatment, but when he tried to cut down his daily dose of Risperdal, he began hearing strange voices again.

Erik was never sure if he'd actually managed to hypnotize Nestor—he may have belonged to the small group who weren't receptive—but during those relaxed sessions in the dimly lit treatment room, they did at least begin to get a grip on things.

Nestor had grown up with his mother, his younger brother, and a black Lab. When he was seven, his five-year-old brother became seriously ill with a lung infection, which exacerbated his already bad asthma. The boys' mother told Nestor that his brother would die unless they had the dog put down. Nestor took the dog to Söderbysjön and drowned it in a hockey trunk full of stones.

But his brother died anyway.

In Nestor's mind, the two events became intertwined. He had always suffered from the belief that he drowned his brother in a trunk, and he had no memory of the dog.

They worked on his anger with his mother's damaging manipulation, and after a month, he finally let go of the idea of his own guilt and the notion that his mother could sometimes control his actions from beyond the grave.

Nestor is living normally again now. He doesn't need to take any medication and is incredibly grateful to Erik.

They pass St. Mark's Church in Björkhagen and pull up outside 53 Axvalls Road.

Nestor unbuckles his seatbelt, and Erik helps him carry his food to the door of his ground-floor apartment.

"Thanks for everything," the former patient says tremulously. "I have ice cream and time to—"

"I need to get going," Erik says.

"But I have to give you s-something," Nestor says, opening the door.

"Nestor, I have to get to an appointment."

"Walk across the dead without a s-sound. Walk across the dead and hear their murmuring resound."

"I don't have time for riddles now," Erik says, walking out the door of the building.

"Leaves!" Nestor calls after him.

47

JACKIE AND MADELEINE ARE SITTING TOGETHER ON THE sofa eating popcorn while Erik tries to play his étude.

Madeleine says he's very good every time he makes a mistake. She's tired, and her yawns are getting bigger and bigger.

Jackie tries to explain the eighth rests and the rhythmic pattern. She gets up and puts her right hand on top of his.

She asks him to start from the twenty-second bar with his left hand, then stops speaking abruptly, goes back to her daughter, and listens to her breathing.

"Could you carry her to bed?" she asks. "My elbow isn't up to it."

Erik gets up from the piano and picks the child up. Jackie walks ahead of them, opens the door to the girl's room, turns the light out, and pulls the covers back for Erik.

Erik carefully lays Madeleine down on her bed and brushes the hair from her face.

Jackie tucks her daughter in and kisses her cheek, whispers something in her ear, and turns on the little pink nightlight on the bedside table.

Only now does Erik see that the walls of the child's bedroom are covered in curses and obscenities.

Some of the words are written in childish scribble in chalk, misspelled, whereas others are written in more confident handwriting. Erik presumes Madeleine has been doing this for several years. Her mother is the only person unable to see it.

"What is it?" Jackie says, noticing his silence.

"Nothing." He closes the door gently behind himself and Jackie.

As they walk down the hall, Erik wonders if he should tell Jackie about what he saw or just let it go.

"Should I leave?" Erik asks.

"I don't know," Jackie replies.

She holds out her hands and feels his face, stroking his cheeks and chin.

"I'm going to get some water," she says hoarsely, then goes into the kitchen and opens a cabinet.

He stands close to her, filling the glass and passing it to her. She drinks, and then he kisses her cool mouth before she has time to wipe her chin.

They embrace, she stands on tiptoe, and they kiss each other deeply, foreheads bumping.

Erik's hands slide over her back and hips. The fabric of her skirt rustles like thin paper.

She pulls away slightly, turns her face, and puts one hand on his chest.

"We don't have to," he says to her.

She shakes her head and puts her hand behind his neck again, pulls him to her, kisses his neck, and fumbles with the buttons of his pants, then stops herself.

"Are the curtains closed?" she whispers.

"Yes."

She goes to the door and listens for any sound in the hallway, then closes it carefully.

"Maybe we shouldn't do this here. Not now."

"Okay," he says.

She stands with her back to the drain board, one hand on the counter, her mouth half open.

"Can you see me?" she asks, taking her dark glasses off.

"Yes," Erik replies.

Her clothes are disordered, her blouse hangs outside her skirt, and her short hair is messed up.

"Sorry, I'm being difficult."

"There's no rush," Erik mumbles, and walks up to her, grabs her shoulders, and kisses her again.

"Let's take our clothes off. Shall we?" she whispers.

They get undressed in the kitchen, and Jackie starts talking slowly about a radio report she heard about the persecution of Christians in Iraq.

"Now France is offering asylum to them all." She smiles.

He unbuttons his pants and looks at her as she lays item after item on the chair and undoes her bra.

Completely naked, Erik goes and stands beside her, thinking that he feels oddly natural. He doesn't even try to hold his stomach in.

Jackie's teeth glisten in the faint light as she pulls her underwear down, wriggles her legs, and lets it fall.

"I'm not a shy person," she says.

Her nipples are pale brown, and in the darkness she looks luminous. A marbled network of veins is faintly visible beneath her pale skin. Her dark pubic hair makes her inner thighs look fragile.

Erik takes her outstretched hand and kisses her. She backs into the chair and sits down. He leans forward, kisses her on the lips again, then kneels and kisses her breasts and stomach. He pulls her carefully to the edge of the chair and parts her legs. Her folded clothes fall to the floor.

She's already wet and tastes like warm sugar to Erik. Her thighs quiver against his cheeks, and her breathing grows heavier.

The salt shaker topples over on the table and rolls in a semicircle.

She holds his head between her legs, gasping faster, the chair slides backward, and she slips gently onto the floor with a smile.

"I'm not sure I'm good at relationships," she says, resting the back of her head uncomfortably against the seat of the chair.

"I'm just a student," he whispers.

She rolls over onto her stomach and crawls under the table. He follows her and grabs hold of her butt just as she rolls onto her back.

She pulls him gently to her, between her thighs, hears him hit his head on the table, and feels the heat of his bare skin against hers.

Jackie grips his back firmly and gasps for breath as he slowly slides into her and then pauses.

"Don't stop," she whispers.

Her heart is pounding, and the torrent of thoughts within her finally falls silent. She moves her hips, presses herself toward him, and feels the silky heat from her crotch.

The hard floor disappears behind her, her thighs tremble and stretch, and Erik moves faster. She tenses her buttocks and toes and whimpers against his shoulder as her orgasm pulsates through her body.

ERIK WAKES UP IN THE DARKNESS TO GENTLE PIANO MUSIC. It sounds strangely muted, like a piano buried under the ground. At first he thinks he's dreaming. He reaches out his hand but can't feel Jackie. Moonlight filters through the fabric of the curtains, casting long strange shadows across the room. With a shiver, he creeps out of bed and goes out into the living room. Jackie is sitting naked on the piano stool. She's placed a thin blanket over the piano to muffle the sound.

Through the gloom, he sees her body swaying gently. In the darkness, her elegant hands look like they're floating through water. Her bare feet move over the brass pedals. She is sitting on the edge of the stool, and he can see her slender waist and the shadowy groove down the center of her upright back.

"*Nam et si ambulavero in medio umbrae mortis,*" she murmurs to herself.

He thinks she knows he's there, but she still plays to the end of the piece before turning toward him.

"The neighbors have complained," she says. "But I need to learn a fairly hard piece for a wedding tomorrow."

"It sounded wonderful."

"Go back to bed," she whispers.

He returns to the bed and is just about to fall asleep when he finds himself thinking of Björn Kern. The police still don't know that the dead woman was sitting with her hand to her ear. The thought snaps Erik awake when he realizes that he could be hindering the police investigation.

After an hour, the music falls silent, and Jackie comes back to the bedroom. It's already light outside by the time he falls asleep again.

IN THE MORNING, THE BED IS EMPTY. ERIK GOES TO THE bathroom, showers, then gets dressed. When he emerges, he can hear Jackie and Madeleine in the kitchen.

He walks in and gets a cup of coffee. Madeleine is eating cereal with milk and fresh raspberries.

Jackie explains that she has to be in Adolf Fredrik Church in a little while to rehearse for the wedding.

As soon as she leaves the kitchen to get changed, Madeleine puts her spoon down and turns toward Erik.

"Mom says you carried me to bed," she says.

"She asked me to help her."

"Was it dark in my room?" she asks, looking at him with bottomless eyes.

"I didn't say anything to your mom. It would be better coming from you."

The girl shakes her head, and tears run down her cheeks.

"It's not as bad as you think," Erik says gently.

"Mom will be really sad." She hiccups.

"It'll be all right. But you should talk to your mother if there's something on your mind."

"I don't know why I did it. I don't know why I have to ruin everything," she sobs.

"You don't."

"Yes I do, and I can't get rid of that," she says, wiping her cheeks.

"I did much worse things when I was your age."

"No," she sobs.

"Maddy, listen, now," he says. "We can . . . why don't you and I paint your walls?"

"Can you do that?"

"Yes."

She nods at him with a trembling chin, several times.

"What color would you like?"

"Blue . . . blue, like Mom's nightgown." She smiles.

"Is that light blue?"

"What are you talking about?" Jackie asks.

She's standing in the doorway, already dressed in her black skirt and jacket, a pale pink blouse, round sunglasses, and pink lipstick.

"Maddy thinks it's time to repaint her room, and I said I'd be happy to help."

"Okay," Jackie says, with a slightly bemused expression.

48

MARGOT SEES ADAM WAITING FOR HER IN THE UNDER-
ground garage of police headquarters. His T-shirt is bulging
because of the bandage around his chest. She walks toward him
but has to stop when the baby kicks.

Another colleague approaches from the other direction, and she
hears him say something appreciative to Adam before he crosses
to the elevator.

Adam has a five o'clock shadow, and his face looks weary and
brittle in the harsh lighting.

Behind him she can see people cataloguing the vast amount of
material. The plastic-covered trestle tables are covered with objects
seized from Filip Cronstedt's storage locker, lined up and numbered, ready for analysis. On the first table lies a gilded bedstead,
a wooden crate containing starched, folded linen, battered books,
and three pairs of sneakers.

"How are you feeling?" Margot asks.

"It's nothing," he replies, putting his hand to his ribs. "My mind's
spinning, though. I keep reliving it. I'd be dead if she'd angled the
gun just a tiny bit more, three millimeters to the left."

"You should never have gone down there without backup."

"I made the decision to go in, but I don't think I really appreci-
ated the state Joona was in. He collapsed on the floor and dropped
his gun."

"He shouldn't have been there."

"It was a fuck-up." He nods. "There's going to be an internal inquiry, obviously, since I was shot."

Margot looks at one of the items pulled from the storage locker—a faded school poster of the female anatomy. The eyes have been colored in with blue chalk.

"But without Joona, we'd never have caught Filip," she says.

"I caught Filip. Joona was lying on the floor."

The harsh glare from the fluorescent lights and magnifying lamps reflects off the plastic between the objects on the tables. Margot stops next to three video cameras with crushed lenses.

"Is anyone trying to match Filip's cameras with the videos of the victims?" she asks.

"I presume so."

"But you haven't found the tongue stud or the rest of the deer?"

"Give it time." Adam smiles. "This is just the material from the storage locker. There's no rush. The important thing is that it's over. We got him."

They pass a pile of hand-painted tin soldiers, and Margot can't help thinking that the rest of the little porcelain deer and the Saturn stud should be here.

"How sure are we that it's him?" she asks.

"Filip's in the operating room at Karolinska, but as soon as he can talk, we'll get a confession."

"Do you have anyone on guard there?" she asks.

"He was shot in the chest, and one lung is wrecked, so I hardly think that's necessary."

"Do it anyway."

There are about twenty Polaroids of young women with bare chests in a small plastic folder.

"If it will calm you down, I'll do it as soon as I get upstairs," Adam replies.

"I spoke to Joona in the hospital. He seems to think Filip didn't commit the murders, and—"

"What the fuck?" Adam interrupts with an irritated smile. "I let Joona come with me because I felt sorry for him—that was a mistake I'm not going to repeat. We can't let him play at being a detective."

"I agree," she says quickly.

"He messed up, and he's not coming anywhere near this investigation again."

"I'm just trying to say, this feels too easy." Margot walks between the tables.

"Filip was on the point of confessing when he was shot. He said he'd been creeping around outside Maria Carlsson's windows." Adam turns to her with a grin. "He has no alibi for the evenings of the murders. He's extremely violent, paranoid, and completely obsessed with cameras and surveillance—"

"I know, but—"

"He'd locked himself away with two women. You should have been there—he had them tied up with steel wire."

Even though Adam is hollow-eyed and exhausted, there's an underlying fire in his eyes, and his cheeks are flushed.

He stops and catches his breath, leaning his knuckles on the nearest table with his eyes closed.

The events of the night before come back to him like a heavy pendulum. He thinks about the ringing in his ears after the last shot, and the blood trickling down his side and under the waist of his jeans, before he managed to disarm Sophia.

He thinks of the huge dog that tried to rip him apart, and the orgy in the Birger Jarl Hotel, the unprotected sex he had with an unknown woman.

Tears well up in his eyes as he thinks about how little control he has, how little he knows himself.

He suddenly feels an intense desire to go home and be with his wife, to curl up in his warm bed behind Katryna, to smell her hand cream and see her ugly bed socks and the moles on her back that look almost like the Big Dipper.

Margot walks past an old-fashioned gramophone and stops in front of some jewelry on a piece of cardboard. She gets out a pen and pokes through the tarnished silver rings, brooches, broken chains, and crucifixes. She picks up a heart-shaped charm with her pen just as her cellphone rings.

Margot lets the heart fall back onto the cardboard and answers.

Something in her voice makes Adam turn toward her.

Margot will always remember this moment, the way they were standing in the bright light among Filip's possessions, and how for a few seconds her heartbeat drowned out absolutely everything else.

"What is it?" Adam says.

She stares at him. She can't talk, her throat is so dry, and she realizes her jaw is trembling.

"A video," she hisses. "We've received another video."

49

ADAM RUNS DOWN THE HALLWAY AHEAD OF MARGOT. FILIP Cronstedt was sedated early that morning, when he was brought into the emergency room, and he has been kept like that ever since.

The real killer is still on the loose.

Margot follows Adam into their office and sees the treetops of Kronoberg Park in the pale sunlight through the small windows.

"Do we have a copy?"

"Looks like it," he replies.

Margot is gasping for breath as she sinks into a chair next to the computer while Adam cues up the video file. The base of her spine is aching, and she leans back, her shirt riding up over her bulging stomach.

"The video has been online for two minutes," he whispers.

The camera is moving quickly through the outer fringes of a bird cherry. The leaves obscure the view for a moment, then a bedroom window appears on the screen, with condensation along the bottom.

The garden is shady, but the white sky shimmers in the windowsill.

The camera moves backward when a woman dressed in her underwear comes into the room. She hangs a white towel with old hair dye stains over the back of a chair, then stops and leans one hand against the wall.

"One minute left," Adam says.

The room fills with soft light from a lamp in the ceiling. They can make out fingerprints on the mirror, and a slightly tilted framed poster from the Picasso exhibition at Moderna Museet.

The camera moves to one side, and they can both see a reddish brown porcelain deer on the bedside table.

"The deer," Margot says, leaning toward the screen as her braid falls over her shoulder.

The deer's head that Susanna Kern was clutching in her hand must have come from an ornament exactly like that one.

The woman in the bedroom holds one hand to her mouth, walking slowly over to the bedside table. She opens the drawer and takes something out of it. Her face is more visible in the glow of the bedside lamp. She has pale eyebrows and a straight nose, but her eyes are hidden behind the reflection in her dark-framed glasses, and her mouth is relaxed. Her bra is red and worn, and her underwear is white, with some sort of sanitary pad in it. She rubs something over one of her thighs and then takes out a small white stick and presses it into her muscle.

"What's she doing?" Adam asks.

"That's an insulin injection."

The woman holds a swab against her thigh and screws her eyes shut for a moment, then opens them. She leans forward to put the syringe back in the drawer and knocks the little deer over. Small fragments fly up in the sharp lighting, as the head snaps off and falls to the floor.

"What the hell is this?" Adam whispers.

Looking weary, the woman bends over and picks up the porcelain head. She puts it on the bedside table, then goes around the bed toward the steamed-up window. Something makes her stop and peer out, searching the darkness beyond.

The camera moves slowly backward, and some leaves brush over the lens.

The woman looks worried. She pulls the blinds down, but they end up crooked. She pulls the cord and lets them fall again, then gives up. Through the damaged blinds, she can be seen turning back toward the room and scratching her right buttock before the video suddenly comes to an end.

"Okay, I know I'm a little tired," Adam says unsteadily, and stands up. "But this is crazy—isn't it?"

"It is totally fucking insane." Margot rubs her face.

"So what do we do? Watch the video again?"

Margot's phone buzzes on the desk. She sees that it's someone from the forensics team.

"What do you have?" Margot says as soon she answers.

"Same thing. Impossible to trace either the video or the link."

"So we're waiting for someone to find the body," Margot says, and ends the call.

"She's maybe five foot six, weighs less than one hundred thirty-five pounds," Adam says. "Her hair is probably dark blond when it's dry."

"She has type-one diabetes, went to see the Picasso exhibition last autumn, is single, and regularly dyes her hair," Margot adds in a monotone.

"Broken blinds," Adam says. "There's not much to go on." After a few minutes, he prints out a large color photo that illuminates the woman's face.

He goes over to the wall and pins it up as high as he can.

"Victim number three," he says weakly.

50

SANDRA LUNDGREN LEAVES THE BEDROOM, AND A SHIVER
runs down her spine, as if someone were watching her.

She tightens the belt of her robe, which is so long it reaches the
floor. Her medication leaves her feeling drowsy for most of the day.
She goes into the kitchen, opens the fridge, takes out the rest of the
chocolate cake, and puts it on the counter.

She adjusts her glasses, and her robe falls open again, uncov-
ering her stomach and sagging underwear. She shivers, pulls the
wide-bladed knife from the block, cuts a small slice of cake, and
puts it in her mouth without bothering to get a spoon or plate.

She's started using Stefan's striped robe even though it makes
her feel sad. But she likes the way it weighs upon her breasts, its
drooping shoulders, the threads hanging off the sleeves.

Beside the candleholder on the drop-leaf table is the letter
from Södertörn University. She looks at it again, even though she's
already read it thirty times. She'd been on the wait-list for creative
writing. Her mom had helped her fill in the application. Back then
she didn't feel up to doing it herself, but her mother knew how
much it would mean to her if she got into the program.

She cried in the spring when she was told she didn't get in.
That was probably a bit of an overreaction. Nothing had really
changed, after all. She would just stay in the career counseling
program instead.

She doesn't know how long the letter had been lying there with all the old mail on the floor—she might never have seen it if she hadn't gotten a welcome email from the admissions director.

She decides to phone her mom and tell her the news.

Sandra glances out the window and sees two men walking toward Vinterviken on the other side of the road. She lives on the ground floor and still hasn't gotten used to the fact that people sometimes stop and look right in through her windows.

The wooden floor in the hallway creaks. She thinks it sounds like an adult trying to creep quietly.

Sandra punches in the number as she sits down on one of the kitchen chairs.

"Hi, Mom, it's me," she says.

"Hello, darling, I was just going to call you. Have you thought any more about this evening?"

"What?"

"About coming over for dinner."

"Oh yes. . . . I don't think I feel up to it."

"You still have to eat, you know. I could come and pick you up in the car. I'll give you a ride both ways."

Sandra suddenly hears something rustling and looks over toward the dark hallway, with the hanging coats and piles of shoes.

"Will you let me do that? Darling?"

"Okay," she whispers, looking at the letter in her hand.

"What would you like?"

"I don't know."

"Shall I do beef *à la* Rydberg? You usually like that, you know, cubes of steak and—"

"Okay, Mom," she interrupts, and goes into the bathroom.

The blister pack of Prozac is on the edge of the sink. The green and white capsules shimmer in their plastic rows.

Sandra looks at her own reflection in the mirror. The bathroom door is open behind her, and she can see out into the entryway. It looks like there's someone standing there. Her heart skips a beat, even though she knows it's just her black raincoat.

"The three musketeers went out for lunch today . . ."

Sandra leaves the bathroom, half listening as her mother tells her that she and her sisters went out to the Waxholms Hotel and had fried Baltic herring with mashed potatoes and lingonberry jam, melted butter, and nice cold beer.

"How is Malin?" Sandra asks.

"She's amazing," her mother replies. "I don't know how she manages to be so positive all the time. She just had her last session of radiation and feels pretty good. It makes you glad you live in Sweden. She'd never have been able to pay for the treatment on her own."

"Is there anything else they can do now?"

"Karolina thinks we should all move to Jamaica and sit around smoking weed and eating good food until the money runs out."

"I'll come with you," Sandra says, smiling.

"I'll let her know." Her mom laughs.

The phone feels warm and sticky against her cheek. Sandra moves it to her other ear and walks to the bedroom but stops suddenly. She stares at the window. The big plum tree is moving through the broken blinds.

"I took a look at the list of required reading for your fourth term," her mom says. "It's all about the politics of the job market."

"Yes," Sandra says weakly.

She isn't sure why she doesn't just tell her mom about her place at Södertörn.

Slowly she forces herself to look away from the window and catches sight of herself in the mirror. Her robe has fallen open again. She stands there in her underwear, looking at her pale skin, rounded breasts, smooth stomach, and the long, pink scar across her right thigh.

She and Stefan had rented a cottage in Åre over the Easter holiday. She was driving and Stefan was asleep as they got close to Östersund. It was dark, and the box of skis on the roof was making a lot of noise. They had been stuck behind a logging truck for several kilometers while driving through the black fir forest. The wide rear tires of the swaying trailer churned up masses of snow from the edge of the road. She pulled to the left to overtake it, then saw the lights of an oncoming bus and pulled in again.

After the bus, there were three cars, then nothing. Sandra pulled out again and accelerated. They had just reached a long downward slope, and the timber truck was going faster. She sat beside the huge trailer, clutching the wheel with both hands and felt the car lurch in the wind turbulence.

Sandra accelerated a bit too hard trying to get past, and her wheels slid in the ridge of snow in the middle of the road. She lost control of the car and ended up underneath the truck. They got stuck and were dragged along, the metal screeching and shaking. She had blood in her eyes but saw the huge wheels thud into the side of the car. The metal gave way and crumpled on top of Stefan. There was a whirlwind of glass, and the truck jackknifed as the driver braked and the trailer lurched forward with a screech.

She was alive, but Stefan was dead. She had seen the photographs and read what little had been reported about the event that had thrown her life off course.

"Are you taking your pills like you should?" her mom asks gently, and Sandra realizes that she must have stopped talking.

"Mom, I can't talk now," she says.

"But you'll come tonight?" her mom says quickly, unable to conceal her concern.

"I don't know." Sandra is sitting on the bed and screwing her eyes shut as tight as she can.

"It would be lovely if you did. I'll come and get you, and if you change your mind, I can take you back whenever you want."

"We'll talk later," Sandra says, and ends the call. She sets the phone down on the bedside table, next to her blood sugar monitor.

Outside the window, the bushes are swaying.

Sandra takes off the robe and lays it on the bed, pulls on her jeans, and opens the chest of drawers. The little deer figurine is lying next to the pile of neatly folded clothes. Its head is missing. She takes off her glasses and pulls on a clean T-shirt. Once again she feels like she's being watched and glances at the broken blinds, the shadowy garden, the leaves moving in the wind.

She hears a thud from the entryway and jumps. It's probably just more ads, despite the sign on the door. She picks up the phone to call her mom back and apologize, and to explain that she is happy but being happy dredges up a lot of sadness too.

She goes into the kitchen again, looks at the letter on the table, and walks over to the counter to cut herself another slice of cake, but the knife isn't there.

She thinks her medication has made her confused, that she must have put the knife down in the bathroom or bedroom, when someone dressed in yellow comes at her with long strides.

Sandra just stands still. This can't be happening.

She doesn't say a word, just holds her left hand up to protect herself.

The knife comes from above and hits her in the chest. Her legs collapse and the knife is jerked out as she falls backward and sits down hard on the floor. She hits her head against the table, dislodging the candle from its holder, and it rolls over the edge.

Sandra feels hot blood pulsing down over her stomach. She has a terrible pain deep inside her chest. It feels like her heart is shaking.

Sandra just sits, unable to move, unable to understand, until she feels a blow to her head and falls backward. Everything becomes dark and warm. She can hear burbling water, then feels a burning pain in her lungs. She comes around and starts coughing up blood, stares up at the ceiling for a few seconds, and feels the blade of the knife inside her chest.

It all goes quiet. It's like she's wading out into warm water. A silver-gray river that flows gently into the night.

51

THE POLICE HAVE HAD THE THIRD VIDEO FOR ONLY EIGHTY minutes when the emergency call center receives a phone call from a woman who says her daughter has been murdered.

At four forty-five Margot parks her Lincoln Town Car in front of the fluttering police tape at the scene.

The policeman who went inside to see if the victim could be saved is sitting on the steps next door. His face is gray, and his eyes have a dark look. A paramedic puts a blanket around his shoulders and checks his blood pressure as Adam talks to him. The woman who found her daughter is in the hospital with her sister. Margot makes a mental note to go and talk to her later, once the tranquilizers have softened the pain and shock.

While Margot was driving to Hägersten, she'd called Joona at the hospital to tell him about the third murder. He sounded very tired but listened carefully to everything she told him, and for some strange reason that made her feel calmer.

Margot passes the inner cordon and enters the communal hallway. Floodlights illuminate the stairwell, reflecting off the glass covering the list of residents' names.

Margot pulls on some shoe protectors and passes the crime scene officers.

She stops in the harsh glare of the floodlights. The metal lamps click as they heat up. The smell of warm blood and urine is overpowering and acrid. A crime scene officer is filming the room. On the linoleum floor sits a woman with an utterly ravaged face, her chest split open. Her glasses have fallen into the pool of blood beside her.

She's lying with her hand over her left breast. Her soft skin shimmers pearly white beneath her blood-blackened hand.

She was evidently placed in that position after death.

Margot stands for a few moments looking at the scene.

They know far too little about the second murder, but this one seems to follow the pattern of the first exactly. The level of brutality is inconceivable and appears to have extended far beyond the moment of death.

Once the fury of the attack subsided, the killer arranged the body before leaving.

In the first case, the victim's fingers were inserted into her mouth, and this time her hand is covering her breast.

Margot steps aside to make way for one of the officers, who is laying boards on the floor.

With her hand on her protruding stomach, she moves into the bedroom and looks down into the open drawer at the porcelain deer, chestnut brown except for the break where the head should be. After a while, she returns to the victim.

She stares once again at the carefully staged arrangement of the hand on her chest, and a thought flits through her head.

There's something she recognizes.

Margot stands for a while and thinks, then leaves the apartment and goes to her car. She starts the engine and holds one hand on the wheel and the other on her stomach, moving it down to counter the baby's rapid movements with her fingertips, the small nudges from the other side, the beginning of life.

She tries to make herself more comfortable, but the steering wheel presses against her stomach.

What is it I can't quite remember? she thinks. It could have been five years ago, in a different police district, but she definitely read something.

Something about the hands, or the deer.

She knows she won't sleep tonight if she doesn't work out what it is.

She turns into Polhems Street and pulls up on the roadside.

Her phone rings, and she sees the picture of Jenny in her cowboy hat from Tucson on the screen.

"Hey there," Margot answers.

"Evening, officer," Jenny says flirtatiously. "I have a crime to report."

"Well, if it's urgent you should call 112," she says, parking more neatly. "But otherwise—"

"This is a crime against public decency," Jenny interjects.

"Can you be a bit more specific?" Margot opens the car door.

"If you come here, I can show you . . ."

Margot has to take the phone from her ear as she gets out of the car and locks it.

"Sorry, what did you say?"

"I just called to find out where you've been," Jenny says in a different tone.

"I'm on Kungsholmen. I have to—"

"You don't have time. You need to come home right away," she cuts in.

"What happened?"

"Seriously, Margot? You're hopeless. For God's sake, you were the one who picked Sunday. They'll all be here any minute—"

"Don't be mad at me. I just can't let go of this case—"

"You're not coming?" Jenny interrupts. "Is that what you're saying?"

"I thought it was next weekend," Margot replies.

"How the hell could you think that?"

Margot had completely forgotten about dinner with her family. The idea was for her and Jenny to thank everyone for their support during the Pride festival. Everyone had marched with banners saying PROUD PARENTS AND FAMILIES.

"You'll just have to explain that I'll be a little late," she says, ten meters from the entrance to police headquarters.

"Look, this isn't okay," Jenny says, then takes a deep breath. "You're really letting me down. I know this is a big career opportunity for you, and I'm happy to support you, but—"

"You said you'd be okay with this."

"But you're working all the goddamn time, and—"

"I have to," Margot interrupts.

She walks to the entrance as a colleague comes out and unlocks the heavy chain around the rear wheel of a motorbike.

"Fine," Jenny says quietly.

"I'll be home as soon as—"

Margot stops when she realizes Jenny has hung up on her. She continues into the lobby and toward the elevators.

Maria Carlsson, the first victim, had her hand in her mouth, Margot thinks again.

That wasn't enough for her to discern a pattern. But when she saw Sandra Lundgren lying with her hand over one breast, she had a fleeting sense of a connection.

She walks along the empty hallway to her office, closes the door behind her, sits down at the computer, and searches for crimes where the bodies have been staged.

She can hear sirens.

She kicks off her shoes as she clicks through the results. She doesn't find any similarity to her murders in any of the cases. Her stomach feels tight, and she takes off her belt.

She expands the search to cover the entire country, and when the list of results appears, she knows she's found what she was looking for.

A murder in Salem.

The victim was found with her hand around her own neck.

She had been arranged like that after she died.

The Södertälje Police District had conducted the preliminary investigation.

As she read, she remembered more details. A lot had been leaked to the press. An extreme level of brutality had been focused primarily on the victim's face and upper body.

The dead woman had been found in her bathroom with her hand around her own throat.

The victim's name was Rebecka Hansson. She had been wearing pajama bottoms and a sweater, and according to the postmortem, she had not been sexually assaulted.

Margot's heart is pounding as she reads the information about Rocky Kyrklund, a priest. An arrest warrant was issued for him, and he was subsequently apprehended in connection with a traffic accident. The forensic evidence against him was compelling. Rocky Kyrklund underwent a forensic psychiatric examination and was consigned to Karsudden District Hospital.

I've found the murderer, Margot thinks, and her hand is trembling as she calls Karsudden Hospital.

When she learns that Rocky Kyrklund is locked up and has never been let out, she demands an immediate meeting with the head of security.

TWO HOURS LATER MARGOT IS SITTING IN THE OFFICE OF the head of security, Neil Lindegren, in the gleaming white main building, discussing the security arrangements for Section D–4.

Neil is a heavyset man with a fleshy forehead and neat, stubby hands. He leans back in his chair as he explains the secure perimeter fences, the alarm system, the airlock, and the passcards.

"That all sounds very good," Margot says when Neil finishes. "But the question is, could Rocky Kyrklund have managed to get out anyway?"

"You're welcome to meet him, if that would make you feel any better," he says with a smile.

"You're absolutely sure you'd have noticed if he escaped and came back the same day?"

"No one's escaped," Neil says.

"But hypothetically," Margot goes on. "If he got out immediately after you did your round at eight o'clock last night—when would he have to be back today in order for his absence not to be noticed?"

Neil's smile fades, and his hands fall to his lap.

"Today is Sunday," he says slowly. "He wouldn't need to be back until five o'clock, but you know . . . the doors are locked and alarmed, and the whole area is covered by surveillance cameras."

52

ON A LARGE MONITOR, THIRTY SQUARES SHOW WHAT THE facility's security cameras are picking up.

A technician in his sixties shows Margot the system of security and motion-activated cameras, their locations, and the laser and infrared barriers.

Recordings are stored for a maximum of thirty days.

"This is Section D–4," he says, pointing. "The hallway, day room, exercise yard, fence, outside of the fence, outside of the building. And these show the park and the driveway."

The monitor shows an image of the hospital as it was at five o'clock that morning. The static glow from the lamps makes the park look strangely lifeless. The clock in the corner of the screen moves on, but everything remains perfectly still.

When the man speeds up the replay, a few trees appear to move in the wind. The late-night security guard walks along the hallway and disappears into the staff room.

Suddenly the technician stops the tape and points at an area of grass that spreads out like a patch of gray water. Margot leans forward and sees a number of dark shapes against the bushes and trees.

The technician enlarges the image and plays the footage. Three deer appear in the glow of a lamp. They walk across the grass, all stop at once, standing still with their necks craned, then bound away.

He shrinks the image and fast-forwards again. Daylight arrives, and the transparent shadows grow sharper as the sun rises.

Cars arrive, and staff go inside and spread out through the hallways and tunnels.

The technician stops the recording to show the night staff leaving. Margot watches the morning round in the various sections in silence.

There's very little activity, given that it's Sunday. There's no sign of Rocky Kyrklund among the patients who have opted to go into the exercise yard.

They keep fast-forwarding, stopping occasionally to look more closely at anyone in the hallways, but everything seems calm as the hours tick by.

"And there you are," the technician says with a smile.

He enlarges one square to show her struggling to get out of her car, and her wrap dress slips open, revealing her pink underwear.

"Whoops," she mumbles.

Margot sees herself walk across the parking lot with her big leather bag over her shoulder, her hands around her stomach. She goes around the corner of the building and disappears from view, but the next camera picks her up outside the entrance. At the same time, she is visible from another angle on a camera above the reception desk in the lobby.

"I disappeared for a few seconds as I went around the corner of the building," she says.

"No," he says.

"It felt like it," she insists.

He goes back to the image of her getting out of her car, flashing her underwear, follows her across the parking lot, and stops the recording as she walks around the corner of the building and disappears from that screen.

"We have a camera here that should . . ."

He enlarges another square, showing the end of the building, and lots of leaves but not her. He plays the footage slowly, and she comes into view outside the entrance.

"Okay, you're gone for a few seconds," he eventually says. "There are always going to be tiny gaps in the system."

"Could someone exploit them to escape?"

The technician leans back, and the wad of chewing tobacco beneath his lip slips down over one of his teeth as he shakes his head.

"Not even theoretically," he says firmly.

"How sure are you?"

"Pretty much one hundred percent," he replies.

"Okay," Margot says. She gets up laboriously from her chair and thanks him for his help.

If Rocky couldn't have escaped, she's going to have to think again. The murder he committed has to be linked to the recent killings.

There are no coincidences on that level.

The priest must have had someone helping him, an apprentice on the outside, she thinks. Unless they're dealing with a completely independent copycat, or someone with whom Rocky Kyrklund has been communicating.

The technician leads her back through the deserted hallways to Neil Lindegren's office. The head of security is talking to a woman in a white coat when Margot walks in.

"I need to talk to Rocky Kyrklund," she says.

"But he may not even be able to remember what he's been doing today," Neil says, gesturing toward the doctor.

"Kyrklund has a serious neurological injury," the doctor explains. "His memories only come back to him as tiny fragments, and sometimes he does things without being aware of them at all."

"Is he dangerous?"

"He would already be getting prepared for rehabilitation back into society if he'd shown any indication that he wanted that," Neil says.

"He doesn't want to get out—is that what you're saying?" Margot asks.

"We start socializing most of our inmates fairly early," the doctor says. "They get a chance to meet people outside the hospital, and they have supervised excursions, but he mostly keeps to himself and won't accept visitors. He never calls anyone, writes no letters, and doesn't use the Internet."

"Does he talk to the other patients?"

"Sometimes, as I understand it," Neil replies.

"I need to know which patients have been discharged from Section D–4 during the time he's been there," she says, sitting down.

She looks around Neil's tidy office while he searches his computer. He has no photographs on display, no books or ornaments.

"Did you find anything?" she asks, and can hear how anxious she sounds.

Neil turns the screen to show her.

"Not much," he says. "That section has a very low turnover of patients. There are a few who have been moved to other psychiatric institutions, but we've only had two inmates discharged in the time Rocky has been here."

"Two in nine years?"

"That's normal," the doctor says.

Margot opens her leather bag, takes out her notebook, and writes the names down.

"Now I want to see Rocky Kyrklund," she says.

53

TWO GUARDS WITH PANIC BUTTONS, BATONS, AND TASERS
on their belts accompany Margot through the airlocks and into the
hallway where Rocky Kyrklund's section is located.

He's sitting on the bunk in his room watching a Formula One
race on the television fixed to the wall.

The shimmering cars move around the track like dragonflies,
with their bursts of speed and metallic colors.

"My name is Margot Silverman. I'm a detective with National
Crime," she explains, leaning against his desk chair.

"Adam fucked Eve, and then she got pregnant and gave birth to
Cain," Rocky says, looking at her stomach.

"I've come here from Stockholm to talk to you."

"You're not observing the day of rest," Rocky states, then looks
back at the television.

"Are you?" She pulls the chair out and sits down. "What have
you done today?"

His face is calm. His nose looks like it was broken at some
point, his cheeks are covered by a gray beard, and there are folds
in his thick neck.

"Have you been out today?" She waits a moment before going
on. "You haven't been out in the exercise yard, but perhaps there
are other ways of getting out."

Rocky Kyrklund shows no reaction. His eyes are following the
cars on the screen. One of the guards by the door shifts his weight,
and the keys on his belt jangle.

"Who have you been in contact with on the outside?" she asks. "Friends, relatives, other patients?"

The engines roar from the television. They sound like chainsaws cutting through dry wood.

Margot looks at his stockinged feet—the worn heels and the clumsy darning of one sock.

"I've been told you don't see any visitors?"

Rocky doesn't answer. His stomach rises and falls evenly under his denim shirt. One hand is resting between his legs, and he's leaning back against two pillows.

"But you do have personal contact with the staff? Some of them have worked here for many years. You must have gotten to know each other. Right?"

Rocky Kyrklund remains silent.

On the television, a Ferrari driver comes into the pits at speed. Before his car has even stopped, the crew are ready to change his tires.

"You have your meals with patients from other sections, and you share the exercise yard. Who do you like the most? If you had to say a name?"

A Bible with about sixty bookmarks made of red thread is lying on the bedside table next to a dirty milk glass. Light filtered by the trees comes through the vertical bars on the window.

Margot shifts position uncomfortably on the chair and takes the notebook with the names of the two discharged patients out of her bag.

"Do you remember Jens Ramberg? Marek Semiovic?" she asks. "You do, don't you?"

One car collides with another and spins around in a cloud of smoke while parts of it fly across the track.

"Do you have any memory of what you were doing earlier today?"

She waits awhile, then stands up again as the accident is replayed on the screen, its glow reflecting off Rocky's face and chest.

The guards don't meet her gaze as they leave the room together. Rocky doesn't even seem to notice her departure.

As she walks back toward the parking lot, she can feel the technician watching her on one of the thirty cameras.

Before she drives away, she sits in the car and reads through the material about the murder of Rebecka Hansson. Rocky Kyrklund must be involved in the new murders in some way.

Margot sees that Erik Maria Bark was part of the team that conducted the psychiatric evaluation of Kyrklund. Their conclusions, which formed the basis of the sentence, were based on long conversations between Erik and Rocky. Erik evidently managed to gain his trust.

54

ADAM YOUSSEF IS SITTING IN HIS CAR NEXT TO HIS WIFE, Katryna. She's massaging her hands, and the smell of her hand cream is spreading through the car. It's starting to get dark, and the traffic on Valhalla Road is fairly light. They've been to the Dramatic Institute to watch her brother Fuad in a play about the band The Cure. Adam stops at a red light and looks at Katryna. She's plucked her eyebrows a little too much, and her face looks rather cruel. She hasn't said a word since they got in the car.

"What are you thinking about?" he asks.

She shrugs.

He looks at her nails. She's painted them in such a way that the color shifts from violet to pink at their tips. He should say something nice about them.

"Katryna," he says. "What is it?"

She looks him in the eye with a seriousness that scares him.

"I don't want the baby," she explains.

"You don't?"

She shakes her head, and the red light disappears from her face. He turns back toward the traffic light. It's green, but he can't bring himself to drive on.

"I'm not sure I want children at all," she whispers.

He swallows. A car honks a couple of times before passing on the right, and then the light turns red again. He looks at the button for his hazard lights but can't be bothered to press it.

"But you just got pregnant," he says helplessly. "Can't you wait, see if you change your mind?"

"I already made an appointment. I'm getting an abortion next week."

"Do you want me to come with you?"

"There's no need."

He stares at the cars driving across the junction in front of them, then at some black birds flying overhead in a wide arc in front of Stockholm's Olympic Stadium.

He's losing her. It's already happening.

The light turns green, and he presses his foot onto the accelerator.

Recently he's been trying to show her every day that he loves her. They love each other, after all, they really do. Or at least he thought they did. Is she telling the truth when she says she goes out with her co-workers at Sephora every Thursday night? She never talks about it, and he realizes he hasn't been interested enough to ask or to offer to go along.

"Look, Katryna, I can change. I'm trying to—" He stops midsentence when his phone rings.

Katryna picks it up from the pocket by the gearshift and turns it over. "It's your boss."

Adam lets out a sigh and glances away from the traffic at her. They stare at each other for a second before Katryna accepts the call and puts the phone to his ear.

"Hello?" he says weakly.

"It's the same deer," Margot says.

The broken edge of the deer in Sandra's room has been matched with the little head found in Susanna Kern's hand.

"It seemed completely insane when we saw it on the video," Margot says, sounding like she's panting. "But all it means is that the murders are planned long before they take place, that someone records the victims and then waits—possibly for weeks."

"But why?" Adam asks, his hand sweating on the wheel.

The murders are following each other like a string of pearls, a rosary, he thinks. The order of death is ordained long before the killer strikes. That should give us time, but it doesn't, because the murderer only uploads the videos when it's too late for us to locate the woman.

"I've found some similarities with an old case," Margot says.

"What did you say?"

"Are you listening?"

"Yes. Sorry."

He looks at Katryna's face, turned away from him, as Margot tells him about the old murder in Salem, about the priest who was found guilty, about Rebecka Hansson's ravaged face and the way her body was arranged.

She checked the security arrangements at Karsudden, she explains, and it seems impossible that anyone could have got out without being discovered.

"So he must have an accomplice, a disciple . . . unless it's a copycat."

"Okay," Adam says hesitantly.

"Do you think I'm making too much of this?"

"Maybe," he says.

"Even if I am, right now it doesn't matter. You'll see what I mean when you take a look."

"Do you want us to go and talk to the priest?" Adam asks.

"I'm on my way back from there now."

"Weren't you and Jenny supposed to be having some big dinner today?"

"That's next weekend," she says curtly.

"What did he say?"

"Nothing. He didn't even look at me," she says. "It appears I'm completely devoid of interest."

"Nice," Adam says.

"That seems to be par for the course with him," she says. "That was why they brought Erik Maria Bark in, to help conduct the forensic psychiatric examination. He gets people to talk."

"Not our witness," Adam points out.

"The entire investigation was practically based on his conversations with Kyrklund," Margot explains. "It's a huge amount of material. We're going to have to get people to examine every last detail."

"How long's that going to take?"

"That's why I'm on my way to see Bark now," Margot says.

"Now?"

"Well, I'm already in the car, so—"

"So am I." Adam laughs. "But I'm certainly not planning on—"

"Well, it would be great to have you there," she interrupts.

55

ERIK IS SITTING IN HIS CHAIR WITH A COPY OF A PSYCHIAT-ric journal in his lap, thinking about dinner at Nelly and Martin's. They invite him over fairly often to their huge modernist house with its curved windows and its terrace that looks like the bridge of an old yacht.

After dinner this time, Martin took off his tie and led them through the house clutching a glass of Calvados. In his study, he had a small oil painting he had just been given by his aunt in West-phalia. It was of a gloomy-looking angel. Nelly thought it was awful and tried to offer it to Erik. Martin said he agreed with her, but Erik declined because it was obvious that Martin wanted to keep it.

Then Martin had to take a call from Sydney, so Erik and Nelly went to the game room. Nelly poured more wine, despite the fact that she was already fairly drunk. Her eyes were moist, and she was leaning against the raised edge of the table.

"Martin looks at porn," she slurred.

"Why do you think that?" Erik asked, rolling a ball across the green felt.

"I don't care. It's nothing perverse."

"Does it make you jealous?"

"Not jealous, but . . . I don't know, you should see the women. They're young and beautiful, and they do things I'd never dare try." She reached out and touched his lips.

"Talk to him."

"Is youth the only thing that counts?" she drawled.

"Not to me."

"What does matter, then? What do you want? What does any man really want?" She was swaying slightly.

He helped her to her bedroom.

When Nelly called him to discuss two Iranian patients, he thanked her for dinner. She just laughed and said he should be grateful she didn't get too drunk and embarrassing.

Now Erik leans back in his armchair and thinks about the bottle of champagne in the fridge that he opened earlier, all alone. He sealed it, and it would taste just as good if he were to have a glass now.

That would get rid of my headache, he thinks, as he sees car headlights sweep in, through the large glass window.

With a short sigh, he gets up and goes to open the door. He watches Margot struggle out of her car and wave to him, and then another car pulls into the drive.

A younger man with short dark hair hurries over to Margot and exchanges a few words with her. Behind them is a beautiful young woman with clear eyes and a serious face.

Erik shakes hands with Margot and the young man, whom she introduces as a colleague working on the murder investigation with her.

The young woman hesitates in the doorway. Her black coat is shiny with rain, and she looks frozen.

"I didn't have time to take my wife home," Adam explains, looking unexpectedly awkward. "This is Katryna."

"Adam didn't want me to wait in the car," she says softly.

"You're more than welcome to come in," Erik says, shaking her hand.

"Thank you."

"What wonderful fingernails," he says, holding on to her hand to look at them for a few seconds.

She smiles in surprise, and her dark eyes warm up instantly.

Erik invites them to take their coats off, then steps onto the porch to close the front door. The gentle rain is dripping rhythmically through the leaves of the lilac. The road is shimmering under the streetlights, and suddenly he imagines he can see the silhouette of a tall figure in his own garden. He switches the outside light on, thinking it must have been the scrawny juniper next to the wheelbarrow.

Erik shuts the door and shows them into the library, where Katryna stops, looking a little embarrassed.

"I'm probably not supposed to overhear your conversation," she says.

"You can sit here if you want," Erik says, pulling a folio off the shelf. "I don't know about you, but I'm a bit addicted to Caravaggio."

He sets the art book down on the table, then shows the detectives into his study. Adam closes the door behind them.

"We found a third victim today," Margot says at once.

"A third victim," Erik repeats.

"We were expecting it, but it's still a blow."

She looks down toward her stomach, and the corners of her mouth twitch slightly, possibly from exhaustion. A deep frown on her forehead stretches down between her eyebrows.

"What can I help you with?" Erik asks neutrally.

"Do you know a man called Rocky Kyrklund?" Margot asks, looking up at him.

"Should I?"

"You should know that he was sentenced to psychiatric care after an evaluation nine years ago."

"Okay," Erik says gently.

As soon as she mentioned Rocky's name, it occurred to him that she might know everything.

"You were part of the team," Margot explains.

"I'm part of many teams," Erik says.

He's spent hours conjuring up different scenarios in which he's confronted with what happened, then imagining possible reactions and answers that won't incriminate him but also won't technically be lies.

"And we have reason to believe he confided in you."

"I don't remember that, but—"

"He'd murdered a woman in Salem in a way that's reminiscent

of the murders that I'm currently investigating," Margot says without further elaboration.

"If he's been released and is killing again, then something has gone very wrong with the parole process," Erik replies, just as he had planned.

"He hasn't been released. He's still in Karsudden, and he hasn't left the facility at all," she says. "I just went out there and spoke to the head of security."

56

MARGOT OPENS HER LEATHER BAG AND HANDS ERIK A COPY of the verdict and the psychiatric evaluation. He sits down opposite Adam at the little octagonal table, leafs through the material, nods, and looks up.

"Yes, I remember him."

"We think he has an apprentice, a disciple. Maybe a copycat."

"That's possible. If the similarities are that strong . . . well, I can't offer an opinion."

Margot shakes her wrist to get her watch in the right place. "I spoke to him today," she says. "I asked him a lot of questions, but he just sat there in silence on his bed, staring at the television."

"He suffered serious brain damage," Erik says, gesturing toward the old evaluation.

"He could hear and understand everything I said. He just didn't want to answer." Margot smiles.

"It's often rather difficult to start when you're dealing with this sort of patient."

She leans forward, so that her stomach ends up resting on her thighs. "Can you help us?"

"How?"

"Talk to him. He trusted you before, and you know him."

Erik's heart rate starts to increase. He can't show any emotion, so he slowly clasps his hands together to stop them from shaking.

They're probably going to find the tape recordings of the sessions in which Rocky talks about his alibi, he thinks.

But because Rocky is guilty, Erik can always say that he didn't take the idea of an alibi seriously.

"What do you want to know?"

"We want to know who he may have been working with."

Erik nods, thinking he'll be free at last after this. He'll no longer have to carry the burden of knowledge that he can't off-load. He can tell them about the person Rocky blamed, whether or not Rocky just sits there in silence. He could even hypnotize Björn Kern again and then tell them about the hand clasped to Susanna's ear.

"Naturally, this is rather outside my usual brief," he begins.

"Of course we'd pay."

"That's not what I meant. I need to know the parameters of the task, so I know what to say to the institute."

Margot nods, with her lips half open, as though she were about to say something, but decides against it.

"And I need to know what to say to the patient," Erik goes on. "I mean, am I allowed to let him know that you think his former associate has started killing again?"

Margot waves her hand. Erik notes that her colleague seems to have stiffened slightly as he sits there with his arms folded.

"We'll have to see if we have any negotiating room," Margot says. "We don't know yet, of course, but you might be able to offer him supervised excursions outside the hospital."

She stops speaking abruptly, as if she's run out of breath. Her hand goes to her stomach. Her thin wedding ring sits tightly around her swollen finger.

"What did you say to him today?" Erik asks.

"I asked which people he had the most contact with."

"Does he know why you were asking?"

"No. He didn't react at all to anything I said."

"He has epileptic activity in his brain that affects his memory, and according to his diagnosis, he suffers from a narcissistic, para-noid disorder. But all the evidence suggests that he's intelligent," Erik says.

He falls silent.

"What are you thinking?" Margot asks.

"I'd like the authority to be able to tell him why I'm asking him these questions."

"To tell him about the serial killer?"

"He'll probably figure out that I'm lying otherwise."

"Margot," Adam says. "I have to—"

"What?"

He looks troubled as he lowers his voice. "This is police work," he says.

"We don't have a choice," she says curtly.

"I just think you're going too far," Adam says.

"Am I?"

"First you get Joona Linna mixed up in this, and now you're going to let a hypnotist do police work."

"Joona Linna?" Erik asks.

"I'm not talking to you," Adam says.

"He's back," Margot says.

"Where?"

"*Back* probably isn't the right word," Adam says. "He's living with the Roma out in Huddinge. He's an alcoholic, and—"

"We don't know that," she interrupts.

"Oh right, Joona's the best," Adam says.

Margot meets Erik's quizzical gaze.

"Joona fainted and ended up in the emergency room at St. Göran's," she says.

"When?" Erik asks, getting to his feet.

"Yesterday."

Erik immediately picks up his phone and dials a colleague in the hospital's intensive care unit and waits as the call goes through.

"When can you talk to Rocky?" Margot asks, standing up.

"I'll head out there first thing tomorrow," Erik says as his colleague answers the phone.

57

AFTER A SHORT CONVERSATION WITH THE DOCTOR AT St. Göran's Hospital, Erik accompanies the two detectives to the door. Katryna and Adam don't look at each other as they walk out, and Erik gets the distinct impression they've had an argument.

The three of them leave the house and are swallowed up by the darkness as soon as they move beyond the door. Erik hears their footsteps on the gravel path leading to the driveway, and they come into view again when the insides of their cars light up. He returns to his study and sees that the fax from the hospital has arrived. The patient's name and ID number have been redacted.

The report says Joona arrived by ambulance after a priority-one call from the emergency command center. Erik glances through the records.

He was suffering from malnutrition, fever, confusion, and poor circulation.

The triage nurse made the right call from the available evidence when she suspected he was suffering from blood poisoning.

After checking his blood gases and lactic acid, she took him to the ICU.

Because of his fluctuating vital signs, Joona Linna was placed in a room under close supervision and attached to a monitor.

While they were waiting for the results of his blood analysis, they gave him broad-spectrum antibiotics and a colloid solution to help his circulation and fluid balance.

But Joona disappeared before completing the full course of antibiotics.

He hadn't given an address.

Erik leaves his study and picks up his jacket in the hall. He doesn't bother to switch the lights off.

It's no longer raining. The night air is cool, and the car windows are covered with condensation. He turns the windshield wipers on and drives off as soon as he can see through the glass.

It's close to midnight, and the streets are almost empty. Beyond the yellow glow of the streetlamps, the late-summer night is as dark as heavy velvet.

He drives into an industrial area with high fences, then emerges into a small grove.

There never used to be any beggars in Sweden, but over the past few years, migrants from the EU have become visible in Swedish towns and cities. They've come here to plead for help, on their knees in the snow outside supermarkets, with outstretched hands and empty paper cups.

It's struck Erik several times that modern Swedes have reacted with unexpected generosity to this change.

There are faint lights between the trees. He slows down and drives toward them, turning onto a gravel track, and the tiny monkey attached to his ignition key bounces up and down.

In a clearing he can see sheets flapping on a rope strung between two trees. Lengths of plywood have been nailed together and covered with tarps and plastic.

Erik turns around and parks at the edge of the grove. He locks the doors and walks from the car into the trees.

The air smells like potatoes and liquid gas. Four battered trailers are standing in a row, with crooked wooden shacks between them. Smoke is rising from a buckled oil drum, and glowing embers drift up, spreading the stench of burning plastic.

Joona is here somewhere, Erik thinks. He has blood poisoning and is going to die unless he gets the right antibiotics very soon. No other person on the planet has done as much for Erik as the tall detective.

A woman with a shawl over her head gives him a wary look and hurries away as he draws close to her.

He approaches the first trailer and knocks on the door. On a beautiful rug beneath it stand five shabby pairs of sneakers of various sizes.

"Joona?" Erik says loudly, and knocks again.

The trailer sways slightly, and then an old man with eyes clouded by cataracts opens the door. Behind him sits a child on a mattress. On the floor, a woman is asleep, fully dressed in a woolen hat and a winter coat.

"Joona," Erik says in a subdued voice.

A heavyset man in a padded tunic suddenly appears behind him and asks what he wants in broken Swedish.

"I'm looking for a friend of mine," Erik says. "His name is Joona Linna."

"We don't want problems," the man says anxiously.

"I'll ask someone else." Erik walks over to the second trailer and knocks on the door. It's covered with circular scorch marks, as if people had stubbed cigarettes out on it.

A young woman in glasses cautiously opens it. She's wearing a thick sweater and baggy sweatpants with damp knees.

"I'm looking for a sick friend," Erik says.

"Next house," she whispers with a frightened look.

A child has come over and pokes at Erik with a plastic crocodile.

Erik steps across two crutches lying on the ground and walks up to the third trailer. The windows are broken and covered with pieces of cardboard.

In the darkness between the trees, an unshaven, tired-looking man is smoking a cigarette.

Erik knocks on the door and opens it when there's no answer. In the glow of a clock radio he sees his friend. Joona is lying on a damp mattress, using a folded blanket as a pillow. An elderly woman in an old-fashioned quilted jacket is sitting beside him, trying to get him to drink some water from a spoon.

"Joona," Erik says softly.

The floor creaks as he climbs into the trailer, sloshing a plastic bucket full of water. The carpet on the floor is wet from the rain, and there's a strong smell of damp and cigarette smoke. Scraps of bluish gray cloth cover the cardboard-patched windows. As Erik moves farther inside, he sees a crucifix on the wall.

Joona's face is emaciated, covered by a gray beard, and his chest seems unnaturally sunken. His gaze is so unfocused that Erik isn't sure if he's actually conscious.

"I'm going to give you an injection before we leave," Erik says, putting his bag down on the floor.

Joona barely reacts when Erik pulls his sleeve up, wipes the crook of his arm with a swab, looks for a vein, and then injects a mixture of benzylpenicillin and aminoglycoside.

"Can you get up?" he asks as he puts a bandage where he stuck the needle.

Joona lifts his head slightly and coughs. Erik helps him get up on one knee. A tin can rolls across the floor. Joona coughs again, points at the woman, and tries to say something.

"I can't hear," Erik says.

"Crina needs to be paid," Joona hisses, and stands. "She's . . . helped me."

Erik nods, takes his wallet out, and gives the woman a five-hundred-kronor note. She nods in return and smiles with her lips closed.

Erik opens the door and helps Joona down the steps. A bald man in a crumpled suit holds the trailer door open for them from the outside.

"Thanks," Erik says.

A blond man in a black, shiny jacket is approaching from the other direction. He's hiding something behind his back.

Beside the next trailer is a third man holding a soot-stained saucepan. He's wearing jeans and a denim vest, and his bare arms are dark with tattoos.

"You have a nice car," he calls out with a grin.

Erik and Joona walk toward the road, but the blond man blocks their path.

"We need some rent," he says.

"I already paid," Erik says.

The bald man shouts into the trailer, and the old woman comes to the door and holds up the money she has just been given. The man snatches the note, says something angrily, then spits at her.

"We have to collect rent from everyone here," the blond man explains, showing the length of metal pipe in his hand.

Erik mutters something noncommittal in agreement, thinking it would be best just to try to get to the car, when Joona stops.

"Give the money back to her," he says, pointing at the bald man.

"I own the trailers," the blond man says. "I own all this, every mattress, every single fucking saucepan."

"I'm not talking to you," Joona says, and coughs into the crook of his arm.

"It's not worth it," Erik whispers, his heart pounding.

"For fuck's sake, we have a deal with them," the tattooed man shouts.

"Erik, get in the car," Joona says, and limps over to the men.

"It costs more now," the blond man says.

"I have a little more money," Erik says, taking his wallet out.

"Don't do it," Joona says.

Erik gives a few more notes to the blond man.

"That's not enough," he says.

"Give it all back," Joona tells the blond man feebly.

"It's only money," Erik says quickly, and pulls out the last couple of notes.

"Not to Crina," Joona says.

"Run home and hide before we change our minds." The blond man grins, pointing at them with the metal pipe.

58

JOONA STANDS STILL WITH HIS ARMS WRAPPED AROUND HIM, leaning forward slightly. He sees the blond man change his grip on the pipe and move to the side. The bald man takes off his jacket and hangs it over a plastic chair.

Joona slowly raises his head and looks the bald man in the eyes.

"Give the money back to Crina," he repeats.

The bald man grins with surprise and steps sideways into the darkness. There is a click as he unfolds a switchblade.

"I'm going to hurt you if you don't drop the knife on the ground now," Joona says in his melancholic Finnish accent, and takes a step forward.

The bald man crouches and moves aside, holding the knife in a classic hammer grip, then reaches forward and takes a few trial stabs.

"Be careful," Joona says, coughing gently. The knife is sharp and glimmers in the weak light. Joona watches it with his eyes and tries to read the man's irregular movements.

"Do you want to die?" the man grunts.

"I may look slow," Joona says, "but I'm going to take that knife and break your arm at the elbow. And if you don't stop after that, I'll puncture your right lung."

"Stab the Finn!" the blond man shouts. "Stab the fucking Finn."

"And I'll deal with you next, once I have the knife," Joona says, stumbling into a rusty bicycle.

The bald man unexpectedly swings the knife to the side, and the blade catches Joona across the back of his hand, which starts to bleed.

The blond man backs away with a forced smile.

Joona wipes the blood from his hand on his pants. The bald man shouts something to the blond one. A baby starts crying in one of the trailers.

The blond man moves in behind Joona's back. Joona notices but is too weak to move.

When Joona glances over his shoulder, the bald man mounts an attack. He aims low, toward Joona's kidneys. The white blade jabs forward like a lizard's tongue.

It happens fast, but everything is still there in muscle memory. Joona doesn't think as he deflects the knife, grabs the man's hand, and closes his fingers over his cold knuckles.

Joona bends the man's wrist, puts his other hand under his elbow, and jerks upward.

When the man's arm breaks, there's a cracking sound, like standing on a twig. The man sinks to his knees, screaming, and bends double on the ground.

"Behind you!" Erik shouts.

Joona turns. Suddenly giddy, he stumbles into a pool of water, but manages to keep his balance.

He spins the knife between his fingers, changes his grip, and hides it behind his body as he approaches the blond man.

"Leave me the fuck alone!" the man shouts, swiping at the air with the pipe.

Joona goes straight in, takes a blow on his shoulder, cuts the man across the forehead, and rams his lower arm up into the man's armpit, knocking his arm out of its socket as the pipe falls to the ground.

The blond man gasps as he clutches the top of his arm. He moves backward but can't see anything because of the blood running into his eyes. He stumbles over a pile of wood and stays down, lying on his back.

The man with the saucepan has disappeared into the darkness behind the camp. Joona walks over, leans down, and takes the money from both men, panting as he does so.

He knocks on the door of the trailer, leaning against the frame to stop himself from falling. Erik runs over and holds him up when he staggers.

"Give the money to Crina," Joona says, and sits down on the step.

Erik opens the trailer door, sees the woman in the gloom at the far end, and shows her where he hides the money under her carpet.

Joona slips down onto the grass with his head resting against one of the concrete blocks holding the trailer up.

The tattooed man comes back around the first trailer. He's holding a shotgun and is approaching with long strides.

Erik realizes Joona is in no condition to run, so he crawls beneath the trailer and tries to pull him in behind him.

"Try to help," he whispers.

Joona kicks his legs and slowly slides in. The grit rustles against his jacket, and they can hear steps nearby.

They hear the man with the gun open the trailer door and shout at the old woman. The floor above them thunders as he goes inside.

"Come on," Erik says, crawling farther in. He hits his head on a cable tray.

Joona shuffles after him but catches his jacket on a strut. Erik emerges on the other side of the trailer and hides among some nettles.

Beneath the trailer Joona watches as the tattooed man steps down onto the ground.

They hear voices, and suddenly the man bends down, puts his hands on the ground, and stares right at Joona as he lies under the trailer.

"Get them!" the blond man shouts.

Joona tries to pull himself free, and the seams of his jacket start to tear. The tattooed man begins to walk around the trailer, through the rough undergrowth.

Erik slips hurriedly back underneath, crawls over to Joona, and frees his jacket.

They roll sideways, crawl between the concrete blocks, emerge into the weeds, toss aside a rusty sheet of tin, and take cover beside a shack.

The tattooed man comes around the trailer, slipping on the wet ground. He raises his gun and takes aim.

Erik pulls Joona out of his line of fire.

The man follows them with his gun raised. They crouch beside a kitchen sink mounted between two trees.

The gun goes off, and a stack of dishes on the drain board explodes. Broken shards rain down on them.

There's shouting, and voices echo through the trees. Erik leads Joona behind the shack. The tattooed man follows them, the broken dishes crunching beneath his feet. The gun clicks as he expels the cartridge and feeds in a new one.

Erik can feel his legs shaking as he pulls Joona after him into the forest.

They hurry across the uneven ground, pushing through tight thickets of pine scrub and getting caught on branches.

Joona's back is wet with sweat. His hip is burning, and he's lost all feeling in one foot.

Erik is holding him firmly by the arm as they move through the edge of the woods toward the car. Between the trees, they can see the flickering light of pocket flashlights, and a dozen migrants arguing after disarming the tattooed man with the gun.

Joona has to rest for a while before he and Erik cross the road to the car.

His legs give out, and he all but falls into the passenger seat and closes his eyes, coughing so badly it makes his lungs burn.

Erik runs around the car, gets in, and locks the doors, as there's a sudden thud on the windshield. The blond man with the blood-smeared face is lit up by the headlights. He's holding a heavy branch and raises it as Erik starts the engine and puts his foot down. The front wheel spins on the shoulder, and grit and small stones fly up beneath the car.

There's another crash, and the side mirror comes loose. It dangles from its wires as they lurch back onto the road. They can already hear the sound of emergency vehicles beyond the patch of woodland.

59

ERIK TAKES A DOUBLE DOSE OF PILLS THAT NIGHT SO HE CAN sleep, but he still wakes up early and gets out of bed at first light. He thought he had hung a blue shirt over the back of the chair the night before, but now he can't find it, and he has to get another one from his wardrobe.

Joona is still asleep in the guestroom when he leaves the house, performs a makeshift repair on the side mirror with some duct tape, and drives away.

As Erik passes a horse trailer, he thinks about how he helped put Joona to bed in the guestroom. The towel ended up covered in blood as he cleaned the knife wound to the Finn's hand and taped the edges of the cut together. Joona was awake the whole time, looking at him calmly. Erik gave him an intramuscular tetanus injection and some more penicillin, got him to drink a glass of water, and then examined the injury to his hip. The old wound had caused a lot of internal bleeding, which had run down into his leg beneath the skin. Nothing was broken. Erik injected some cortisone into the muscle just above his hip and tucked him in.

On his way back from Karsudden Hospital, he needs to stop at a pharmacy and pick up some topiramate for Joona's migraines.

The roads are quiet, and it's still early in the morning as he drives past Katrineholm and approaches the large institution.

Casillas is standing on the steps outside reception, tapping his pipe against the railing. He holds out his hand to greet Erik as he approaches along the path.

"We've conducted neurological examinations," he explains as they head toward the gloomy brick buildings. "They've ruled out surgery. They say the damage to his brain tissue is permanent. He can function, but he just has to accept the blackouts and erratic memory."

After checking in to Section D–4, they are met by a female staff member with laugh lines around her eyes.

"Rocky Kyrklund is waiting for you in the calm room," she says, shaking hands with Erik.

No matter what happens during this meeting, Erik will tell Margot about the unclean preacher, the man Rocky tried to blame nine years ago.

They stop, and Casillas explains to the guard that she should wait outside the calm room and then escort Erik to the exit when he's finished.

Erik pushes the bead curtain aside and goes in. Rocky is sitting in the middle of one of the sofas with his arms stretched out along the back of it, as if he's been crucified. There's a mug of coffee and a cinnamon bun on the low table in front of him. Gentle classical music is playing from two loudspeakers.

Rocky scratches the back of his head against the wall, then looks at Erik with a completely relaxed expression.

"No cigarettes today?" he says after a while.

"I can arrange that," Erik replies.

"Get me a pack of Mogadon instead," Rocky says, tucking his hair behind his ears.

"Mogadon?"

"Then Jesus will forgive you for your sins."

"I can have a word with your doctor if—"

"You're on something, aren't you?" Rocky interrupts. "Mogadon? Rohypnol?"

Erik reaches into his inside pocket and gives him a whole blister pack.

Rocky presses one pill out and swallows it without drinking anything.

"Last time I was here, I asked you about someone, a colleague of yours," Erik says, sitting down in an armchair.

"I don't have any colleagues," Rocky says darkly. "Because God lost me somewhere along the way, and he never came back to look for me."

He moves his white plastic mug and picks up a piece of sugar on his index finger.

"Do you have any memory of having an accomplice in the murder?"

"Why are you asking?" Rocky wonders.

"We talked about it last time."

"Did I say I had an accomplice?"

"Yes," Erik lies.

Rocky closes his eyes and nods slowly.

"You know . . . I can't trust my memory," he says, and opens his eyes. "I can wake up in the middle of the night and remember a day twenty years ago and write it all down. Then when I read what I wrote a week later, it feels like I made it all up, like it never happened. And of course I don't really know. It's the same with my short-term memory. Half of my days disappear. I take my medicine, play pool, talk to some idiots, eat lunch, then it's all gone."

"You still haven't told me if you had an accomplice when you murdered Rebecka."

"I don't give a damn about that. You tell me you were here, but I've never met you before—"

"I think you remember that I was here."

"Do you?"

"And I think you lie sometimes," Erik says.

"Are you saying I tell lies?"

"Just now you referred to the cigarettes I gave you last time."

"I wanted to see if you were keeping up," Rocky says with a smile.

"So what do you remember?"

"Why should I tell you?" He takes a sip of coffee, then licks his lips.

"Your accomplice has started murdering on his own."

"Serves you right, in that case," Rocky mutters, and suddenly starts to shake.

The mug falls from his hand, spilling the last of the coffee across the floor, and his chin trembles. His eyes roll backward, his eyelids close and twitch. The epileptic attack lasts just a few seconds. Then he straightens, wipes his mouth and looks up, apparently unaware of what just happened.

"You told me before about a preacher," Erik says.

"I was alone when I murdered Rebecka Hansson," Rocky says in a low voice.

"So who's the unclean preacher?"

"What difference does it make?"

"Just tell me the truth."

"What do I get out of it?"

"What do you want?"

"I want pure heroin." Rocky looks Erik in the eye.

"You can get permission to go out if you help," Erik says.

"I don't remember. Anyway, it's all gone. This is pointless."

Erik leans forward in the soft armchair. "I can help you remember," he says after a pause.

"No one can help me."

"Not in a neurological sense, but I can help you remember what happened."

"How?" he asks.

"I can hypnotize you."

Rocky leans his head back against the wall. His eyes are half closed, and his mouth is slightly pursed.

"There's nothing to be worried about. Hypnosis is merely a way of accessing another level of consciousness through deep relaxation."

"I read that journal, *Cortex*, and I remember a long article about neuropsychology and hypnosis," Rocky says, waving his hand.

60

THEY HAVE MOVED TO ROCKY'S ROOM, WITH THE DOOR closed and the lighting dimmed. The weak lamplight reflects off a *Playboy* calendar. Erik has set up his tripod, attached the video camera, and adjusted the angle and exposure. He has made sure the microphone is pointing in the right direction.

A small red dot indicates the camera is recording.

Kyrklund is sitting on a chair. His broad shoulders are relaxed, rounded like a bear's. His head is drooping. He slid into deep relaxation very quickly, and he responded well to the induction.

The difficult part isn't performing the act of hypnosis but finding the right level and placing the patient in a state where the brain is as relaxed as possible, yet still able to distinguish between real memories and dreams.

Erik, standing just behind Rocky, slowly counts backward as he prepares Rocky to examine his memories.

"Two hundred and twelve," Erik says in a monotone. "Two hundred and eleven . . . you will soon find yourself outside Rebecka Hansson's house."

Erik recognizes he's entering a state of hypnotic resonance. He knows he has to be careful, especially with a volatile patient like Rocky. It's vital that he manage to differentiate between his real-life self and his observing self.

The observing self, in Erik's own personal trance, is always underwater. That's become his internal image of hypnotic immersion.

While his patients are led through their memories, Erik sinks into a warm sea, past steep cliffs and coral.

By holding this image, Erik can remain utterly present in the patient's experience, yet still maintain a protective distance.

"Eighty-eight, eighty-seven, eighty-six," Erik goes on in a somnolent tone. "The only thing that exists is my voice and your desire to listen to it. With each number, you're sinking deeper and deeper into relaxation . . . eighty-five, eighty-four . . . There's nothing dangerous here, nothing to be worried about."

As Erik counts down, he feels himself sinking through pink water with Rocky Kyrklund. They're following the chain of an anchor. The rusty links are covered in stringy algae. Above them, on the silvery surface, is the hull of a large ship with motionless propellers.

They drift lower.

Rocky's eyes are closed, and small air bubbles are rising from his beard. His arms are by his sides, but the water passing them makes his clothes sway.

"Fifty-one, fifty, forty-nine . . ."

Erik sees the top of a vast underwater mountain, gray-black, like a heap of ash, sticking out of the violet darkness.

Rocky raises his face and tries to look, but only the whites of his eyes are visible. His mouth opens, and his eyes close again. His hair is drifting above his head as bubbles emerge from his nostrils.

"Eleven, ten, nine . . . You will be able to remember all your real memories of Rebecka Hansson when I say so."

As Erik sinks through the water, he simultaneously observes Rocky on the chair in his room. A string of saliva is hanging from his mouth, and the seams of his white vest are coming loose under his arms.

"Three, two, one . . . Now you open your eyes and can see Rebecka Hansson the way she was when you last saw her."

Rocky is standing in front of him on top of the underwater mountain, his clothes moving in the gentle current, his hair floating like slow flames above his head. He opens his mouth, and large bubbles stream out and float up in front of his face.

"Tell me what you can see," Erik says.

"I see her. . . . I'm in the garden at the back of the house. Through the patio door, I see her sitting on the sofa watching television. Her knitting needles are moving, and a ball of blue wool is slowly unraveling beside her hip. She's said she doesn't want to see me, but I think she'll open her legs anyway."

"What's happening?"

"I knock on the glass door. She takes her glasses off and lets me in. She says she has to go to bed because she's working in the morning, but that I can spend the night if I want."

Erik doesn't interrupt, just waits for the next segment of memories, waits for the images to join up.

"I sit down on the sofa and touch her necklace. There's an old knitting pattern in a women's magazine on the floor. . . . Rebecka sets her knitting down on the table, and I slip a hand between her thighs. She pulls away, says she doesn't want to, but I pull her nightgown up again . . ."

Rocky is breathing heavily.

"She resists, but I know she's changed her mind, I can see it in her eyes, she wants this now. . . . I kiss her, and put my hand between her legs."

He's smiling to himself on the chair, then turns serious.

"She says we should go to her bedroom, and I put a finger in her mouth, and she sucks it, and . . . outside."

Rocky stops himself and just stares, his eyes wide open.

"There's someone outside! I can see a face. There's someone at the window."

"Outside the house?" Erik asks.

"It was a face. I go over to the glass door, but I can't see anything . . . just darkness, and the room reflected in the glass. And then I see someone standing behind me. I spin around, ready to lash out, but it's only Rebecka. She gets scared and tells me to leave. . . . She means it, so I go into the entryway and take all the money she has in her bag, and . . ."

He falls silent, breathing more heavily, and the energy in the room changes, slowly becomes more dangerous.

"Rocky, I want you to stay with Rebecka," Erik says. "It's the same evening, you're at home with her, and—"

"I've gone to the Zone," Rocky interrupts in a slurred voice.

"Later that evening, you mean?"

"I ignore the strippers on the main stage," he whispers. "I ignore the dealers, because what I'm looking for . . ."

"Do you go back to Rebecka's?"

"No, we sit in the disabled toilet so we can be alone."

"Who are you talking about?"

"My girlfriend . . . the woman I love. Tina, who . . . She gives me a blowjob without a condom, she doesn't care. She's in a hurry now, she's sweating all over."

Erik wonders if he should bring the patient out of hypnosis. He can feel Rocky moving too quickly through his memories, and he no longer knows if it's possible to keep him at the right level.

"Tina coughs over the sink and looks at me in the mirror with fear in her eyes. I know she's not doing well, but . . ."

"Is Tina your accomplice?" Erik looks at Rocky's open face.

"For fuck's sake, they owe me a hundred thousand, I'll be getting it next week," he mutters. "But right now I can only afford . . . shitty brown shoe scrapings, have to dissolve it in acid so I can shoot up."

Rocky shakes his head anxiously and breathes unevenly through his nose.

"There's no danger here," Erik says as calmly as he can. "You're quite safe, you can talk about everything that happens."

Rocky's body relaxes again, but his face is lined and sweaty.

"I sit there and let her have the spoon. I'm not getting a kick anymore, but I feel great and start to nod off. I see her tie a cable as a tourniquet around her arm. . . . The cable's getting all tangled, and she can't fix it. I'm too out of it to help her. I hear her ask for help with a sob in her voice . . ."

Rocky whimpers slightly, and the atmosphere seems to contract to a single dark pinprick.

"What's happening now?" Erik asks.

"The door opens," Rocky replies. "Some bastard has picked the lock. I shut my eyes. I have to rest, but I know it's the preacher, the preacher's found me . . ."

"How do you know that?"

"I can tell because of the filthy smell of an old smack junkie. It's withdrawal, it smells metallic, like fish guts."

Rocky shakes his head again. His breathing is getting too quick, and Erik thinks he should start to bring him out of his hypnosis but holds back.

"What's happening?" he whispers.

"I open my eyes, and the preacher looks like a fucking wreck," he says. "Hepatitis, probably, completely yellow eyes. . . . The preacher snorts back some snot, then starts to speak in a really high voice."

Rocky is breathing shallowly, turning in his chair and moaning in anguish between his words.

"The preacher goes over to Tina. She's shot up but can't get the cable loose. . . . Dear God in heaven, have mercy on my soul, dear God in heaven . . ."

"Rocky, I'm going to start to wake you up, and—"

"The preacher's holding a machete, and it sounds like when you stick a shovel into mud—"

Rocky starts to retch. He's panting heavily now but goes on talking.

"The preacher chops her arm off at the shoulder, loosens the tourniquet, and drinks . . ."

"Listen to my voice now."

"And drinks the blood from her arm . . . while Tina lies bleeding to death on the floor. . . . Dear God in heaven . . . Dear God—"

"Three, two, one . . . Now you're above the disabled toilet, you're high above it, and nothing you can see is going to hurt you . . ."

"Dear God," Rocky sobs, hanging his head.

"You're still in a state of deep relaxation, and you're going to tell me how much of what you've just said to me was a dream. You've taken drugs and have been having nightmares. You're looking down at yourself on the toilet floor. What's really going on?"

"I don't know," Rocky says slowly.

"Who is he?"

"The preacher's face is covered in blood . . . shows me a Polaroid picture of Rebecka . . . just like Tina the week before, and . . ."

His hoarse voice disappears, but his mouth keeps moving for a while until it stops. He leans his big head to one side and looks straight through Erik with empty eyes.

"I didn't hear you," Erik says.

"It's my fault. . . . I should pluck out my eye, for it has offended me, it would be better to pluck my eye out than this."

Rocky tries to stand up, but Erik holds him down with a gentle hand on his shoulder and feels the big body vibrate, trembling with fear.

"You're in a state of deep relaxation," Erik says, sweat trickling down his back. "But before you wake up, I want you to look straight at the preacher and . . . tell me what you see."

"I'm lying on the floor. I can see boots. . . . I can smell blood, and I shut my eyes."

"Go back a little."

"I can't do any more," Rocky says, and starts to come out of his hypnosis.

"Stay there, just for a second. There's no danger, you're relaxed, you're telling me about the first time you saw the unclean preacher."

"It's in the church."

He opens his eyes for a moment, then shuts them again and mutters something inaudible.

"Tell me about the church," Erik says. "What's happening?"

"I don't know," Rocky gasps. "It's not a sermon . . ."

"What can you see?"

"He's wearing makeup over his stubble, and his arms are so fucking riddled with holes that—"

Rocky tries to stand up, but his chair falls over, and he collapses and hits the back of his head on the floor.

61

ROCKY ROLLS ONTO HIS SIDE, AND ERIK HELPS HIM TO HIS feet. He stretches his back, rubs his mouth with his hand, then pushes Erik away and goes over to the window.

"Do you remember anything from when you were hypnotized?" Erik asks, picking the chair up off the floor.

Rocky turns around and looks at him through narrowed eyes. "Was I entertaining?"

"You talked a lot about the preacher. You do know what his real name is, don't you?"

Rocky purses his lips and slowly shakes his head. "No."

"I think you do, and I don't understand why you're protecting him."

"The preacher is just a scapegoat, a—"

"Give me a name, then," Erik persists.

"I can't remember," Rocky says.

"A place, then. Where is he? Where's the Zone?"

Sunlight from behind shines through his beard onto his furrowed cheeks.

"Was this the first time you've hypnotized me?" Rocky asks.

"I've never hypnotized you before."

"As far as I'm concerned, the evaluation was a waste of time," Rocky says without listening. "But I liked talking to you."

"You remember that? It's almost ten years ago."

"I remember your brown corduroy jacket that must have been pretty damn retro even then. We used to sit on opposite sides of a table . . . particleboard, with a birch veneer, you can tell by the smell. Paper cups of water, Dictaphone, notebook . . . and my head was really hurting again. I needed morphine, but I wanted to tell you about my alibi first."

"I don't remember that," Erik says, taking a step back.

Rocky picks at the window between the bars. "I wrote down Olivia's address, but that was never mentioned in court."

"But you confessed to murdering—"

"Just tell me what happened to my alibi," he interrupts.

"I didn't really take it seriously."

Rocky turns around, walks closer, hunches up slightly, and lowers his head, as if to see Erik better. "So you never mentioned it to my defense lawyer?"

Erik glances over his shoulder and can see that the guard outside the door has disappeared.

Rocky shoves the chairs between them out of the way with his foot.

"I don't remember being given an address," Erik says quickly. "But if I was, I'm sure I would have handed it to your defense team."

"You threw it away—didn't you?" Rocky says darkly, and steps closer.

"Calm down." Erik moves toward the door.

"You sentenced me to this!" Rocky shouts. "It was you! You were the one who did this to me!"

Erik has his back to the door and raises his hands to hold Rocky off, but he doesn't stand a chance of defending himself. Rocky just brushes his arms aside and punches him in the chest with his fist. The blow feels like a sledgehammer. All the air goes out of his lungs, and he can't breathe. The next punch strikes exactly the same place, and Erik's head slams back against the door with a dull thud.

He is struggling to stay upright. The zipper on his jacket catches on the textured wallpaper as he moves sideways to get away. He raises a hand to fend Rocky off, coughs, and tries to breathe.

"Do you want me to look into your alibi?" he hisses.

"Liar!" Rocky roars, grabbing Erik by the chin and pressing his mouth closed.

Rocky pulls him toward him and hits the side of his head so hard that his vision goes black. Erik staggers to one side with the force of the blow, falls over the plastic chair, and careens into the metal bed-frame with a force that makes his back crack. He pulls the covers off the bed as he slides down onto the floor, his cheek burning.

"That's enough, now," Erik gasps, shuffling backward.

"Shut up," Rocky yells, shoving the plastic chair aside.

As he leans forward, Erik kicks out at him and hits him in the chest. Rocky catches his foot, and Erik kicks out with the other one. His shoe comes off, and Rocky stumbles back just as the guard comes in holding a Taser.

"Stand against the wall, Rocky! Hands behind your head, feet wide apart."

Erik gets slowly to his feet and adjusts his clothes. He picks up the covers from the floor with trembling hands and puts them back on the bed. "It might look a bit odd," he gasps, tasting blood in his mouth. "But I had a cramp in my leg, and Rocky was helping me take my shoes off."

The guard stares at him. "A cramp?"

"It feels better already."

Rocky is standing quietly to the side with his fingers laced behind his neck. The back of his white vest is wet with sweat.

"What do you have to say, Rocky?"

He lowers his hands and turns around slowly, scratches his beard, and nods. "I was helping the doctor with his shoe," he says gruffly.

"We did shout, but no one heard," Erik explains. "I tried lying down on the bed, but slipped off onto the floor."

"Is it feeling better now?" Rocky asks, picking Erik's shoe up from the floor.

"Much better, thanks."

The guard stands there holding the Taser, looks at them, then nods, although something obviously isn't right. "The visit's over," he says.

"If you can just tell me Olivia's last name, I can find her," Erik says, meeting Rocky's gaze.

"Her name is Olivia Toreby," he says simply.

Erik leaves with the guard, follows him along the hallway, and sees that Casillas is talking to the head of section in the day room.

"Did it go okay?" Casillas calls.

Erik stops in the doorway, his cheek still stinging from the force of the blow. "I have to say, you've done a remarkable job with the patient," he replies.

"Thanks." Casillas smiles. "I'm pretty sure he'd have been released if he'd applied for parole, but he doesn't seem to think he's done his penance yet."

Erik gets out his phone and dials Margot's number to tell her about Olivia Toreby.

62

JOONA OPENS HIS EYES AND LOOKS UP AT THE WHITE CEIL-
ing. Daylight is filtering into the room around the edges of the dark
blue blinds. The window is open slightly, and fresh air is streaming
in, cooling the clean sheets.

There are blackbirds singing in the garden.

He looks at the alarm clock and sees that he has slept for thirteen hours. Erik has left him a phone, and on the bedside table are
two pink capsules and three pills on top of a note saying, "Eat us
now, drink a ton of water, and take a look in the fridge."

Joona swallows the drugs, empties the glass of water, then
groans as he stands up. But he can at least bear to put some weight
on his leg. The pain is still there, but it's much less severe. The nausea and pain in his stomach have vanished as though they never
existed.

He goes over to the window and looks out at the apple trees as
he dials Lumi's number.

"It's Dad," Joona says, feeling his heart tighten.

"Dad?"

"How are you doing? Do you like Paris?"

"It's a little bigger than Nattavaara," his daughter replies in a
voice that could be Summa's.

"How's college?"

"I'm still finding it confusing sometimes, but overall I think it's
pretty good."

Joona makes sure she has everything she needs, and Lumi tells him to shave off his beard and join the police force again, and then they end the call.

Erik has left him a pair of black sweatpants and a white T-shirt. The clothes are too small—the pants flutter around his calves, and the T-shirt is tight across his chest. By the bed is a pair of white slippers, the kind you get in hotels.

Joona thinks about how mysteries are only mysteries until you have discounted all the impossibilities.

When he was in the hospital, Margot told him the videos had been recorded long before the murders took place.

Maria Carlsson owned nothing but black underwear, but the seams of the tights she was wearing when she died were different from the ones in the video. The spoon found in the carton of ice cream in Susanna Kern's home wasn't the same one that was in the video, and the postmortem will probably show that Sandra Lundgren hadn't injected herself with insulin in her thigh on the day she was murdered.

Classic stalking. The women have been watched and their behavior mapped over a long period.

Joona leans against the walls as he walks through the house toward the kitchen. He tells himself that he'll call the police in Huddinge and follow up the previous day's events as soon as he gets something to eat.

He drinks some more water, puts coffee on, and looks in the fridge, where he finds half a pizza and a yogurt.

On the kitchen table, next to Erik's empty coffee cup, are print-outs relating to an almost-ten-year-old case that was tried in Södertälje District Court.

Joona eats the cold pizza as he reads the verdict, the postmortem analysis, and the entire investigation report.

The old murder has striking similarities to the recent ones.

The vicar of Salem parish, Rocky Kyrklund, was arrested and convicted of the murder of a woman named Rebecka Hansson.

Joona was pretty out of it yesterday when Erik was taking care of him, but he can remember what Erik said. Margot had asked him to go and talk to a guy who had been sentenced to psychiatric care. She wanted Erik to find out if he had any accomplices or disciples.

She must have meant Rocky Kyrklund.

Margot's thinking along the right lines, Joona thinks, bracing his arms on the table as he gets up again. He walks barefoot into the backyard and sits down on the cushionless couch swing. Then he walks over to the shed.

On one end is a water-damaged dartboard. Joona opens the door and gets out the cushions for the couch swing. He goes back to the shed to close the door but stops and looks at the neat arrangement of DIY tools and gardening implements on the wall.

In the cul-de-sac at the end of the road, an ice cream truck starts to play its jingle. Joona picks up an old knife with a red wooden handle and tests its weight, then takes down a smaller knife in a plastic sleeve, walks out, and shuts the door behind him.

He sets the smaller knife on the ground beside the swing, then stands in the middle of the lawn and weighs the other knife in his right hand. He changes his grip, trying to find some sort of balance, a sense of lightness, then puts the knife down by his hip and stretches out the other arm, feeling it tug at his wound.

Cautiously he tries to perform a kata against two opponents with the knife. He doesn't follow through on all the elements, but his legs still feel frustratingly heavy when he finishes.

Joona twists his body and moves his legs in the reverse order, leaving his first attacker's torso unguarded. He performs a diagonal cut, starting at the bottom, blocks the second attacker's hand, and diverts the force of the assault as his knife moves downward, then glides out of danger.

He repeats the pattern of movements, slowly, perfectly balanced. His hip hurts, but his level of concentration is the same as before.

The different elements of the kata are complicated only because they don't come naturally, but against untrained opponents they can be extremely effective. In nine coordinated movements, attackers are disarmed and rendered harmless. It works like a trap—if anyone chooses to attack, the trap is sprung.

Katas and shadowboxing can never replace sparring and real-life combat, but they get the body used to the movements and, by repetition, train the body to think that certain movements belong together.

Joona rolls his shoulders, finds his balance, strikes out a few times, follows through with his elbow, then repeats the kata, faster this time. He performs the vertical cut, deflects the imaginary attack, and changes grip but drops the knife in the grass.

He stops and straightens his back. Listens to the birdsong and the wind in the trees. He takes some deep breaths, bends over, picks up the knife, blows some grass off it, and finds its center of gravity. Then he takes the knife in his right hand and throws it past the hammock at the dartboard, which wobbles. The old darts come loose and fall off into the grass.

Someone claps softly, and he turns around and sees a woman in the garden. She's tall and blond and is watching him with a smile.

63

THE WOMAN LOOKING AT JOONA HAS A SELF-AWARE BUT relaxed posture, reminiscent of a mannequin. Her arms are slender, and her hands are very freckly. She's wearing only a little makeup and is blushing slightly.

Joona bends down and picks up the second knife from the ground, weighs it in his hand, then throws it over his shoulder toward the dartboard. It ends up in the branches of the weeping birch and falls to the grass next to the shed. She claps again and walks over to him, smiling.

"Joona Linna?" she asks.

"It's not easy to tell with a beard like this, but I think so," he replies.

"Erik said you were confined to bed, and—"

The porch door opens, and Erik comes out into the yard with a worried look. "You should be careful with that hip until we've had it X-rayed."

"It's fine," Joona says.

"I gave him cortisone in—"

"So you said," the smiling woman interrupts, "and it seems to have worked."

"This is Nelly," Erik says. "She's a colleague—one of the best psychologists in the country for traumatized children."

"I wouldn't go that far," she says, shaking Joona's hand.

"How do you feel?" Erik asks.

"Fine," he replies quietly.

"The penicillin will really kick in tomorrow, and you should feel much stronger," Erik says.

Joona groans as he lowers himself onto the couch swing. The others sit down beside him, and they swing together gently. The springs creak, and the cushions give off a damp, musty smell.

"Did you read the notes on the investigation?" Erik asks after a while.

"Yes," Joona says, glancing at him.

"I went and talked to Rocky this morning. He's had terrible problems with his memory since the accident, but he was willing to try hypnosis."

"You hypnotized him?" Joona asks with interest.

"I wasn't sure if it would work, given the amount of damage to his brain tissue and his epileptic attacks."

"But he was receptive?" Joona leans his head back and looks up at the sky.

"Yes, but it wasn't easy working out which of the memories were real. Rocky did a lot of drugs in those days, and some of the things he said under hypnosis—which should have been memories—sounded more like nightmares, or delirium."

"God, that sounds difficult," Nelly says, stretching her ankles.

Erik stands up, making the couch swing move again.

"I was really only going to ask about the murder of Rebecka Hansson to find out if he had an accomplice," he says. "But under hypnosis, Rocky sounded like he was completely innocent."

"In what way?" Joona asks.

"He kept returning to a man he calls the preacher. The unclean preacher."

"That's a little creepy," Nelly says.

"And now all of a sudden, he remembers that he has an alibi for the night of the murder," Erik says in a low voice.

"He said that under hypnosis?" Joona asks.

"No. He was awake then."

"Is there anyone who can confirm the alibi?"

"Her name is Olivia Toreby. He remembered it at the time, but he's probably forgotten it," Erik says, looking away.

"Interesting," Nelly says.

"It's worth checking out anyway," Erik says.

"Did you speak to Margot about this?" Joona asks.

"Of course."

"Psychologists lead, one-nothing," Nelly says.

Erik sits down beside her again, and they spend a little while swinging, drifting off to the slow creaking of the metal springs, the birdsong, and the sounds of children playing in a nearby garden.

Then Erik's phone buzzes on the cushion. It's Margot.

Joona takes the call. "I presume you've checked criminal records and the police database?"

"Good to hear you're feeling better," Margot's rough voice says.

"The murderer may have done time or been out of the country for all these years," Joona goes on. "I have pretty good contacts with Europol, and—"

"Joona, I can't discuss the investigation with you," she interrupts.

"No, but I was just trying to say that nine years is one hell of a long cooling-off period for a—"

"I understand what you mean, but Rocky Kyrklund's alibi doesn't hold up."

"You found her?"

"Olivia Toreby had no idea what we were talking about. She was living in Jönköping at the time, and we can't find any connection between her and Rocky Kyrklund."

"So you still think he had an apprentice? That he's mixed up in the murders?"

"That's why I'm calling Erik," Margot says. "I want him to go back and ask Rocky properly about accomplices."

"Here he is." Joona hands over the phone.

While Erik is talking to Margot, Joona picks up the knives and takes them back to the shed. He rests against the handle of a lawn-mower for a moment. There's a small wasps' nest up by the roof.

When he comes out again, Erik is no longer on the phone and has stretched out next to Nelly.

"Do you ever call witnesses to ask about alibis?" Erik asks him.

"It depends," Joona replies.

"I just mean . . . you don't know if people are ready to get involved," Erik says. "You don't know if people tell the truth when the police call them so many years later."

"No," Joona says.

"I need to talk to her if I'm going to be able to go back to Rocky and look him in the eye," Erik says.

64

JOONA WANTS TO GO WITH ERIK TO TALK TO OLIVIA TOREBY but accepts that it is too soon. Erik gives him some more penicillin, another cortisone injection in his hip, and makes sure he takes 50 milligrams of topiramate to forestall further migraines.

Nelly gets in the passenger seat, and as Erik drives off, he glances in the rearview mirror and sees Joona on the swing again.

"Should I drive you home?" Erik asks.

"Didn't you say she lived in Jönköping?"

"Apparently she moved to Eskilstuna five years ago."

"That's only an hour away, isn't it?"

"Yes."

"Martin said he'd be working late today," says Nelly. "I don't want to have to sit in the house alone with all those windows. I keep getting the feeling someone's spying on me."

"You think someone might be watching you?"

"No." She laughs. "I'm just scared of the dark."

They head down Enskede Road toward Södertälje and sit in silence as they pass a long, gray noise-proof fence.

"You said you were sure the priest was guilty," Nelly says after a while, looking at him.

"He said so himself. He said he'd killed Rebecka. But after hypnosis, he suddenly remembered."

"Remembered what, though? Suddenly remembered a woman who could confirm his alibi?" she asks skeptically.

"He remembered telling me about the alibi."

"Shit," she says. "What happened? Was he angry?"

"He punched me in the chest a couple of times."

"You had a fight? Are you hurt?"

"No."

"Can I see?" She reaches over and pulls his shirt up.

He holds the wheel with his left hand as he fends her off with the right. "We'll end up in the ditch." He laughs.

She loosens her seatbelt and turns in her seat so she can see his bruised chest.

"God, look at you." She leans close to him. "What the hell did he do?"

She kisses Erik's neck, then quickly on the mouth, before he turns his face away.

"Sorry," she says.

"I can't, Nelly."

"I know. I didn't mean . . . it's just that I sometimes think about that night we had together."

"We were both very drunk," Erik reminds her.

"I don't regret a thing." Her face is right next to his.

"Neither do I," he replies.

They drive along the E20 for a while in silence. Two emergency vehicles race past with their sirens blaring. Nelly picks up her purse, folds down the sun visor to use the mirror, and touches up her lipstick.

"Sometimes I think about how things could have turned out differently, in another universe."

"All the lives we haven't lived," Erik says.

"This must mean I'm getting old."

"The tiniest choice closes a thousand doors and opens a thousand more," Erik says. "I ignored an alibi, and nine years later that omission catches up with me."

"You behaved like an idiot," Nelly says, leaning back. "You've put me in an impossible situation. Personally I don't believe in that alibi, but if this woman confirms it, then I should report you. I don't want to do it, but as a doctor—"

"I know," Erik interrupts.

"Because of your lie, Rocky's been locked up and medicated for nine years."

"Please, Nelly," he says. "I'm sorry, but I can't handle this conversation right now. I'm not going to ask you for anything. You can do whatever you think is right."

"The right thing would be to report you."

"So go ahead."

"But it would be a lot easier if you weren't so cute when you get angry." She smiles.

"Maybe I need therapy."

"You need medication." She pulls a pack of Mogadon from her bag and presses out two capsules. She takes one and gives Erik the other.

"Thanks," he murmurs, tips his head back, and swallows.

65

WHEN ERIK PARKS THE CAR NEXT TO THE SCHOOL WHERE Olivia Toreby teaches, Nelly hesitates, her hand on the door handle.

"Do you want me to come?" she asks.

"I don't know . . . no, maybe it would be better if you wait here."

"So you can work your charm?" She smiles.

"I'll try."

"I'll stay here with your sweetheart." She points at the little monkey in the pink skirt, hanging from the ignition key.

Erik walks across the playground and asks a janitor for Olivia Toreby. He points her out.

Olivia is in her fifties, a thin woman with a pale, worn face. She's standing with her arms folded, watching the children on the jungle gym. Now and then one of them calls out to her or runs over wanting help with something.

"Olivia? My name's Erik Maria Bark, and I'm a doctor." He hands her his card.

"A doctor," she repeats, putting the card in her pocket.

"I need to talk to you about Rocky Kyrklund."

Her thin face hardens for a moment, then reverts to neutral. "The police again," she says simply.

"I've spoken to Rocky, and he—"

"I've already said that I don't know anyone by that name," she interrupts.

"I know," he says patiently. "But he talked about you."

"I have no idea how he managed to get my name."

She notices some children with jump ropes around their necks, playing horses, and hurries over and puts the ropes around their waists instead.

"I have work to do," she says when she returns to Erik.

"Just give me a few minutes."

"Sorry, I have to get home and write evaluations for twenty-two children." She starts toward the school building.

"I believe Rocky Kyrklund was convicted of a murder he didn't commit," Erik says, hurrying after her.

"I'm sorry to hear that, but—"

"He was a priest, but he was also addicted to heroin. He exploited the people around him."

She stops in the shade in front of the steps and turns toward Erik. "He was utterly ruthless," she says tonelessly.

"So I understand," Erik replies. "But he doesn't deserve to be convicted of a murder he didn't commit."

Olivia's graying hair falls over her forehead, and she blows it away. "Will anything bad happen to me if I lied to the police before?"

"Only if you lied under oath in a court."

"Okay," she says, her thin mouth quivering nervously.

They sit on the steps. Olivia looks down at her sneakers, picks something off her jeans, and clears her throat.

"I was a different person then, and I don't want to get mixed up in it all again," she says quietly. "But it's true, I did know him."

"He says you can give him an alibi."

"I can," she admits, swallowing hard.

"Are you sure?"

She nods. Her chin trembles, and she looks down again.

"It's been nine years," Erik says.

She tries to swallow the lump in her throat, rubs her top lip, then looks up at him with shiny eyes and swallows hard once more.

"We were in the rectory in Rönninge . . . that's where he lived," she says unevenly.

"We're talking about the evening of April fifteenth," Erik reminds her.

"Yes," she replies, brushing tears from her cheeks.

"How can you remember that?"

Her mouth quivers, and she bites her bottom lip to pull herself together. "We were on a bender together," she whispers. "We started on the Friday, and . . . it was at its worst on Sunday night."

"You're sure about the dates?"

She nods and loses control of her voice. "My little boy died in his crib on the fifteenth. I found him the next day. It was sudden infant death syndrome—that's what the doctors said. It wasn't my fault, but if he'd been with me, it might not have happened."

"I'm sorry to—"

"Oh, God," she sobs, and gets to her feet.

Olivia turns her back to the playground, wraps her arms tightly around herself, and forces herself to quiet down, to stop her grief from pouring out. Erik tries to give her a handkerchief, but she doesn't see it. She takes a few trembling breaths and wipes more tears away.

"For years after that, I just wanted to die," she says, swallowing hard again. "But I've never touched drugs since, and I haven't had sex with anyone. I can never get pregnant again, I don't have the right, I . . . he took everything from me. I hate him for getting me to try heroin. I hate him for everything."

A ball rolls under the bench, and a child comes running over to get it. Erik hands Olivia his handkerchief.

"Don't worry, Marcus," she says warmly to the little boy, who's looking at her with the ball under his arm. "I just need to blow my nose."

The boy nods and runs off.

Erik thinks about Rocky's erratic memory. At various moments during his years at Karsudden, he must have known he had been wrongly convicted because of Erik's betrayal.

"Olivia," Erik says, "I appreciate that this isn't easy, but are you prepared to swear under oath that you were with Rocky when the murder took place?"

"Yes," she says, looking him in the eye.

66

BEFORE THE PAINT DRIES COMPLETELY, ERIK AND MADELEINE carefully pull the masking tape from the baseboards and from the door and window frames, fold up the stiff protective paper, and pull the plastic off the furniture stacked in the middle of the room. Although he's taken two tranquilizers, he still feels overwhelmed whenever he thinks about the priest who has been locked up for longer than Madeleine has been alive, because of his lie.

They continue cleaning up until the pizza delivery guy rings the bell. Madeleine holds Erik's hand as they go out to open the door.

"How does it look?" Jackie asks when they come into the kitchen.

"Great," Madeleine says, looking up at Erik.

Outside in the street, rain is falling through the thin sunlight, and the day feels pleasantly slow, like one from childhood. Erik cuts the pizza and puts slices on their plates.

"Robots eat pizza," Madeleine says happily.

Her face is totally relaxed. She's so relieved that she sings a song from the Disney film *Frozen*, even though Jackie tells her several times not to sing at the dinner table.

"Clever robot," Madeleine keeps saying to Erik.

"But what if he gets rusty?" Jackie says, smiling as she feels something against her foot.

"He won't," the little girl says.

"Maddy, what's this?"

Jackie is carefully shaking a blister pack of Morfin Meda. It must have fallen out of Erik's jacket as it hung over the back of the chair.

"That's mine," he says. "It's just some headache pills." He takes the pack from her and puts it in his pocket.

"Erik," Jackie says, "can I ask you for a favor? Maddy has a game on Wednesday, and I'm playing at the evening service in Hässelby Church. I don't like to ask, but Rosita, who usually brings Maddy home, has been ill all week."

"You'd like me to pick her up?"

"I can walk on my own, Mom. It's only at Östermalm," Madeleine says quickly.

"You're certainly not walking on your own," Jackie snaps.

"I'll pick her up," Erik says.

"It's a dangerous road," Jackie says seriously.

"Lidingö Road and Valhalla Road are completely crazy," Erik agrees.

"She's got her own key, and you don't have to stay if you can't. I'll be back by eight."

"I might have time to watch the match," Erik says hopefully to Madeleine.

"Erik, I'm incredibly grateful, and I promise I won't ask again."

"Don't say that. I'm happy to help."

Jackie whispers a silent thank you to him.

Just as he gets up to clear the table, his cellphone buzzes in his shirt pocket. It's Casillas, from Karsudden District Hospital. After his meeting with Olivia Toreby, Erik called him to discuss the chances of Rocky Kyrklund being allowed on excursions outside the hospital and beginning his rehabilitation.

"I've spoken to the court," Casillas tells him. "And you won't be surprised to hear that you and I are in complete agreement."

"That's great," Erik says.

"The big problem is that Rocky refuses to sign. He says he murdered a woman and doesn't deserve to be free."

"I can talk to him," Erik volunteers quickly.

"It's just that there's not much time if it's going to be considered at the next quarterly meeting."

———

AN HOUR AND A HALF LATER ERIK PASSES THROUGH THE security doors of Section D–4, is led down the hallway, and goes out into the fenced exercise yard.

He approaches the high fence where Rocky is standing. On the other side of the fence is a low hedge. The bushes press against the fence as if they want to get inside the yard.

Rocky Kyrklund squints at him in the hazy sunshine.

"No nice pills today, doctor?"

"No."

A man shouts something at Rocky from a distance, but Rocky ignores him.

"I've spoken to Olivia Toreby," Erik begins.

"Who's she?"

"We talked about her last time . . . and she confirms your alibi."

"My alibi for what?"

"For the murder of Rebecka Hansson."

"Good." Rocky smiles, running his huge hand through his steel-gray hair.

"She was addicted to heroin at the time, and I don't think her evidence would have affected the verdict against you, but I wanted you to know that it all seems to prove that you're innocent."

"This is really happening?" he says skeptically.

"Yes."

"An alibi," Rocky repeats to himself.

"Olivia Toreby is living a different life these days, and she's sure of what she says. You were together at the time of the murder."

Rocky focuses his eyes on Erik's. "So I didn't murder Rebecka Hansson?" he says quietly.

"I don't think so," Erik replies without looking away.

"How sure is she?" Rocky's jaw muscles are tensing.

"She's sure, because you were high on the night of the murder, and it was the same night her son died of sudden infant death syndrome."

Rocky nods and stares straight up at the sky.

"Her son's death certificate confirms the date," Erik concludes.

"So all this crap has been for nothing." Rocky takes a crumpled pack of cigarettes from his pocket.

"She was a drug addict, and I don't think the court would have believed her testimony at the time," Erik repeats.

"I might still have ended up here, but I'd have felt completely different if I'd known . . ."

The air currents between the buildings are picking up dust and loose particles in the sunlit park. A man walks toward them across the yard, then passes them, whispering to himself. His face is covered in clumsy tattoos and seems puffy from medication.

"It's time for you to give your consent to the application for parole."

"Maybe."

"What are you going to do when you get out?" Erik asks.

"What do you think?" Rocky smiles, pulling a half-smoked cigarette from the pack.

"I don't know," Erik says.

"I'm going to fall to my knees and thank God," he says sarcastically.

"You'll be free, but your alibi also means something else that I need to talk to you about."

"I knew you weren't here just to deliver good news."

"The reason I've been coming here is that the police are hunting a serial killer whose methods are reminiscent of those used in Rebecka Hansson's murder."

"Say that again?"

67

ROCKY CLENCHES HIS TEETH AND LEANS BACK AGAINST THE fence, so the light shining through the links changes.

"The police are hunting a serial killer," Erik repeats. "And the murders are reminiscent of that of Rebecka Hansson."

"I'm still trying to take in the fact that I'm innocent," Rocky says loudly. "I'm still trying to understand that I haven't killed a person."

"I know."

"I've been living with a fucking killer for nine years now." He points to his own heart.

"Rocky?" an approaching guard calls.

"Isn't a person allowed to be happy?"

"What's going on?" the guard asks, stopping in front of them. "Are you going back inside?"

"Do you know I've been wrongly convicted?"

"Then we're back to one hundred percent innocent here at Karsudden," the guard says, and goes in.

Rocky watches him with a smile and puts his cigarette pack back in his pocket. "Tell me why I should help the police," he says, cupping his hands around a match.

"Innocent people are dying."

"That's debatable," he mutters.

"The real murderer was responsible for you ending up in here," Erik says. "You understand? He did this to you, no one else."

Rocky inhales the smoke and wipes the corners of his mouth

with his big, nicotine-stained thumb. Erik looks at his worn face and deep-set eyes.

"You could end up getting a pardon in the appeals court," Erik says tentatively. "And maybe the church can find a place for you again."

Rocky smokes for a while, then flicks the cigarette toward another patient, who thanks him and picks it up off the ground.

"What could I do for the police?" he asks.

"You might be a witness," Erik says. "It's possible you knew the perpetrator. From what you've said, it sounds like he could be a colleague of yours."

"How do you mean?"

"You've spoken about a preacher." Erik watches Rocky closely. "An unclean preacher who could have been a heroin addict like you."

The priest seems lost in thought. A prison service van is visible in the distance, driving along the road between the tree trunks.

"I don't remember that," Rocky says slowly.

"You seemed scared of him."

"The only people you're scared of are the dealers. Some are completely crazy. There was one whose mouth was full of gold teeth. . . . I remember him because he loved the fact that I was a priest, so I always had to do a bunch of crap. Money wasn't enough, he wanted me on my knees, denying the existence of God, before he would let me buy smack, that sort of thing."

"What was his name?"

Rocky shakes his head and shrugs. "It's gone," he says in a low voice.

"Could 'the Preacher' have been the name you gave the dealer?"

"No idea. . . . But I used to feel like I was being stalked in those days. Presumably it was a symptom of withdrawal, but you know . . . once when I was supposed to pick up some new vestments . . . it was morning, and the light was coming in through the christening window. There were a thousand colors on the altar rail, and along the aisle . . ."

Rocky trails off.

"What happened?"

"What?"

"You were talking about the church."

"Yes, the vestments had been dumped in front of the side altar. Someone had pissed on them, and it had run all over the floor, in the cracks around the flagstones."

"It sounds like you had an enemy," Erik says.

"I used to think people were creeping around outside the rectory at night. I would turn the lights off, but I never saw anyone. But once I did find big tracks in the snow outside the bedroom window."

"Did you have an enemy who—"

"What do you think?" Rocky asks impatiently. "I knew a thousand idiots, and practically all of them would have killed their own brothers or sisters to score. I'd smuggled a bunch of amphetamines from Vilnius and was waiting for the money."

"Yes, but this is a serial killer," Erik persists. "The motive isn't money or drugs."

Rocky's pale green eyes stare at him. "I might have met the murderer, like you say. But how am I supposed to know? You're not telling me anything. Give me a detail—it might trigger my memory."

"I'm not involved in the investigation."

"But you know more than I do," Rocky says.

"I know that one of the victims was named Susanna Kern. Before she got married, she was Susanna Ericsson."

"I don't remember anyone with that name," the priest replies.

"She was stabbed in—in the chest, neck, and face."

"Like they said I did to Rebecka," Rocky says.

"And the body was arranged so that her hand was covering her ear," Erik goes on.

"And the others?"

"I don't know."

"Well, I can't help unless I know more," he says. "My memory has to have something to latch on to."

"I understand, but I don't—"

"What were the other victims' names?"

"I don't have access to the investigation," Erik concludes.

"So what the hell are you doing here?" Rocky roars, and marches off across the grass.

68

IT'S FIVE O'CLOCK WHEN ERIK WALKS DOWN THE HALLWAY at the psychiatric clinic with a cup of coffee. A tall figure stands very still against the ribbed glass of the stairwell. As he pulls out his keys and stops outside his door, he realizes it's his former patient, Nestor.

"Are you waiting for me?" Erik asks, walking over to him.

"Thanks for the ride."

"You've already thanked me."

The thin hand moving across his chest stops. "I just wanted to s-say I'm thinking of getting another d-dog," he says in a low voice.

"That's great, but you know, you don't have to tell me."

"I know." Nestor blushes slightly. "But I was here anyway, check-ing M-Mother's grave, so . . ."

"How did that go?"

"Would it be p-possible to b-bury her any deeper, do you think?"

He falls silent and takes a step back as Nelly enters the hallway. She waves to Erik, but when she sees he's busy, she stops outside her own office and rummages for her keys in her bag.

"We can make an appointment for you to come and talk, if you want," Erik says, glancing at his door.

"There's n-no need, it's just—" Nestor says. "A d-dog is a big step for me, so . . ."

"You're better now. You can do whatever you want."

"I know how I w-was when I came to you. I . . . you can ask me for anything, Erik."

"Thanks."

"You n-need to go," Nestor says.

"Yes."

"I walked and walked and suddenly it c-came to me," Nestor says with unexpected intensity. "I bent down and—"

"No riddles now," Erik interrupts.

"No, sorry," the tall man says, and walks off.

Erik checks his watch. He has a few minutes before he's due to meet Margot, and he might have time for a quick word with Nelly before then. He goes to her office and knocks on the open door.

Nelly's already sitting at her computer with her reading glasses on. She's wearing a white blouse with black polka dots that ties at the neck, and a tight burgundy skirt.

"What did Nestor want?" she asks without looking up from the screen.

"He's going to get a dog and wanted to talk about it."

"Maybe he needs to cut the cord."

"He's sweet," Erik says.

"I'm n-not so s-sure," Nelly says.

Erik can't help smiling as he walks over to the window and tells her that her idea for restructuring the group therapy is working well.

"Thanks. I feel good about it," she says, taking her glasses off.

"I have a meeting soon with Margot, but . . ."

She smiles. "Wish I could join you."

"Nelly, I just wanted to say that you were right before. There are always problems once you start telling lies."

"Can we do this later?" she asks.

"I want you to know that I'm going to do all I can to get Rocky out of Karsudden as soon as possible, and—"

"Listen, Erik, I'm not going to report you. But this whole thing has really upset me."

"I'm so sorry," he says, heading for the door.

As he leaves Nelly's room, he sees Margot and her colleague waiting outside his own door. They follow him into a meeting room, which has a glass wall facing the hallway and new chairs that smell like plastic. Erik opens the window to let some air in and invites them to sit down. Margot fills a mug from the water cooler, drinks, then refills it.

"Well, you know that Olivia Toreby has changed her mind," he begins.

"Rocky remembers a nine-year-old alibi but not a single damn thing we can actually use," Margot says, sitting down heavily.

"You wanted me to ask him about an accomplice, but we've ended up with something completely different. Rocky was wrongly convicted, and—"

"What if he's just faking his memory loss?" she says.

"He isn't, but—"

"He's involved. He's mixed up in this somehow."

"If I could just continue." Erik runs his hand over the surface of the table. "The real murderer was never caught and has suddenly started killing again. Both in conversation and under hypnosis, Rocky keeps coming back to a preacher who—"

"A priest?" Adam says.

"A preacher who there's good reason to take seriously, in light of the alibi."

"But you have no name, no location."

"It takes time to find a way through the chaos, but under hypnosis he described how the preacher killed a woman by chopping her arm off. The problem is, I'm not completely sure how much of that is genuine memory."

"But you believe there's some truth in it?" Adam leans forward.

"He's mentioned the preacher several times, even when he's not hypnotized."

"But nothing about the murder?"

"Rocky says he's prepared to help the police if he can—at least, he was prepared to do so earlier. I'm trying to help him remember, but I don't know anything about the investigation."

"Everything is strictly confidential," Margot explains.

"If you want his help," Erik says, "then you're going to have to go and see him and give him some details: names, locations, things that could trigger his memory."

"It's probably best if you continue to talk to him," she says.

"I can do that, but—"

"What do you need to make progress?" Margot says.

"That's your decision."

"We're still trying to hold the media at bay, although our press officer doesn't think that's sustainable," Adam says.

"It's just that . . . we have no idea how the serial killer will react to publicity," Margot says. "He might simply vanish, or—"

"So we need to move fast," Adam says.

"You can have some pictures of the victims to show Rocky," she says. "We have a criminal profile, and I can tell you about his modus operandi and specific characteristics."

"Will you be including any fake information?"

"Of course," she says.

"As long as I know," Erik says.

Margot takes a deep breath, then begins to describe the killer's methods and choice of victim.

"So far it's been women who are alone in their homes," she says. "First he films them through a window. Then he plans his attack. And then, once he's decided to murder them . . ."

"He sends the video to us," Adam says heavily. "The killer finds his murder weapon at the scene and always leaves it behind."

He leans over, takes three photographs out of his case, and sets them on the table, picture side down.

"As soon as you've shown these to Rocky, we need you to destroy them."

Erik looks at the backs of the photos, which are inscribed with the names of the victims: Maria Carlsson, Susanna Kern, Sandra Lundgren.

"Sandra Lundgren?" Erik turns the picture over and gasps.

"What is it?" Margot asks.

"She's a patient of ours. . . . God—she's dead?"

"You knew her?"

69

ERIK'S MOUTH IS COMPLETELY DRY AS HE STARES AT THE large color photograph. It's a recent picture, and he can see that Sandra is struggling to look happy. The light is reflecting off her glasses, but her green eyes are visible. Her dark blond hair is slightly longer than he remembers it, settling on her shoulders.

"God," he repeats. "She was in a car accident. Her boyfriend was killed, and . . . we were a bit late starting her treatment. She was very badly depressed, survivor's guilt, kept having panic attacks . . ."

"She was your patient?" Margot says slowly.

"At first. But one of my colleagues took over."

"Why?"

He forces himself to tear his eyes from Sandra Lundgren's symmetrical face and looks up at Margot again.

"That often happens," he tries to explain. "Different doctors work with the patient for different stages of the treatment."

He turns over the next photograph, and his heart rate speeds up when he sees Maria Carlsson. He recognizes her, too. Before he met Jackie, he had a brief fling with Maria. She used to go to his gym. They walked to the bus stop together, went to the movies, and slept together once. He remembers her pierced tongue and the hoarse laugh he found so attractive.

A sudden lump in his throat makes it hard for him to breathe. If he hadn't taken a Mogadon earlier, he wouldn't be able to hide how upset he is now.

"I—I think I've seen her, too, at the gym. . . . This is starting to feel a little creepy," he says, trying to smile at Margot.

"Which gym do you go to?" Adam takes out a notebook.

"SATS, on Mäster Samuels Street," he replies, and swallows hard, but the lump of anxiety keeps growing.

Adam looks at him blankly. "And you'd seen her there?" he says, pointing at the picture of Maria Carlsson.

"I have a good memory for faces," Erik says hollowly.

"It's a small world," Margot says without taking her eyes off him.

"Have you met Susanna Kern as well?" Adam asks, reaching for the last photograph.

"No." Erik laughs nervously.

But when Adam turns the picture over, he's sure he's seen her somewhere. He doesn't know where.

Erik shakes his head and tries to make sense of this.

"Are you sure?" Adam holds up the photograph of the smiling woman.

"Yes," Erik replies.

Erik takes the picture from Adam and looks at Susanna's face. His mind races and the room shrinks around him.

He realizes that he's on the verge of a panic attack. His mouth is dry, and he puts both hands in his lap to stop them shaking.

"Tell me about . . . about the profile," Erik says in a voice that seems to belong to someone else.

He forces himself to sit still while they explain that the profile suggests the perpetrator is divorced, with a relatively high socio-economic status.

He tries to concentrate on what they're saying, but his thoughts are scattered. How is this possible? He had a brief affair with Maria Carlsson, Sandra Lundgren was his patient, and he knows he's met Susanna Kern.

Three pictures of three women he's met.

It's like a recurring nightmare. What does he recognize in this terrible situation? He can't figure it out. Across the table, Margot picks up her cellphone. Adam walks to the window, where someone's left a coffee cup.

Suddenly Erik realizes that the feeling of similarity has to do with Rocky.

Rocky described how the unclean preacher had shown him pictures of Tina and Rebecka.

Rocky had blamed himself, bellowing with pain and repeating words from the Bible: *I should pluck out my eye, for it has offended me.*

And now Erik has lied to the police again. It feels impossible to say that he'd met all three of them.

When Erik feels he can control his voice and body, he stands up. "I have an appointment with a patient," he says.

"When can you talk to Rocky next?" Margot asks.

"Tomorrow, I think."

"Don't forget the pictures," Adam reminds him, passing them to him.

As Erik reaches out to take the photographs from Adam, he sways slightly. It strikes him that he's the mirror image of Rocky. All of a sudden he feels like a condemned man, and for a moment he sees himself gazing out through the six-meter-high fence surrounding the exercise yard at Karsudden.

70

JOONA IS PRACTICING HIS KNIFE TECHNIQUES AND HIS FIST and elbow strikes, as well as jumping rope, weight training, and running. His hip ached after his five-kilometer run, and he had to walk the last stretch. He's still a long way from his old fitness level, but he's getting stronger all the time.

It's seven o'clock when Erik's BMW turns into the drive. Joona puts the meat in the oven and pours two glasses of Pomerol as the front door closes and he hears keys being put on the chest of drawers.

Joona takes the glasses to the library, pushes the door open with his foot, and walks in.

Erik's jacket is on the floor. He's in his study, searching through the papers on his desk.

"Food will be ready in forty minutes," Joona says.

"Great," Erik murmurs, glancing up with a harried look. "You've shaved. Good."

"It felt like it was time."

"How are you?" Erik asks, switching his computer on.

"I feel better," Joona says, walking farther into the room.

"How's your hip?" Erik says, looking at the screen.

"I've done some exercise, and I'm—"

"I just had a meeting with Margot and Adam," Erik interrupts, looking Joona in the eye. "I'm not prone to paranoia, but I've met all three of the victims. It's crazy, and I don't understand it, but that can't be a coincidence—can it?"

"How do you know—"

"What are the chances of that?" Erik stares at Joona.

"How do you know the victims?" Joona prompts, setting the glasses of wine on the desk.

"It feels like this is directed at me."

"Sit down," Joona says gently.

"Sorry, I'm just—I'm shocked." Erik sinks into his chair and takes a deep breath.

"How do you know the victims?" Joona asks for the third time.

"I had a brief fling with Maria Carlsson earlier this summer. Sandra Lundgren was a patient at the clinic. And I recognize Susanna Kern—I've met her, but I don't know where."

"What does Margot say?"

"Well, I was so surprised, I didn't say anything about Susanna Kern, but I'm going to, obviously."

His phone rings, making Erik jump.

"It's work," he mutters. While clicking to reject the call, he drops the phone.

"And I couldn't tell her I'd slept with Maria," he goes on, picking up his phone. "I just said we went to the same gym."

"Anything else?"

"I said Sandra had been a patient of mine. . . . I still don't think this is relevant"—he smiles, scratching his forehead—"but I'll say it anyway. It's not unusual for patients to try to seduce their therapist. There's an intense connection, that's only natural, but in this instance the patient went so far that I passed her on to Nelly."

"But nothing happened between you?"

"No."

Erik's hand is shaking as he picks up the wineglass, raises it to his lips, and takes several large gulps.

"Could it be a disgruntled patient?"

"I don't think so. I no longer work with dangerous patients."

"But when you were doing research on—"

"That was fifteen years ago," he says.

"How far back do your records go?"

"I archive everything."

"Can you go through it?"

"Only if I know what to look for."

"Some sort of parallel, a connection, anything—stalking, violence directed at the face, the arrangement of bodies. And probably someone who collects trophies of some sort."

Erik stands and paces back and forth across his study. He runs his hand through his hair and mutters to himself, "This is crazy. It's completely sick."

"Sit down and tell me what—"

"I don't want to sit down," Erik snaps. "I have to—"

"Listen," Joona says. "I have to know as much as possible, and to be honest, you look like you need to sit down."

Erik reaches for his glass, drinks on his feet, then pulls a pack of pills from his inside pocket. He presses a couple out and washes them down with more wine.

"Shit," he sighs.

"You're taking pills again?" Joona looks at him with sharp gray eyes.

"I'm keeping an eye on it. It's fine."

"Okay," Joona says hesitantly.

Erik sits down on his desk chair, wipes his forehead, and tries to slow his breathing.

"I can't get my thoughts together," he mutters. "I've been trying to figure out if Rocky had an accomplice or an apprentice."

"What do you think?"

"I'm not sure. Hypnotizing Rocky was unusually complex. I managed to get past his organic amnesia, only to end up in a world of heroin highs and delirium."

"What happened?"

"I don't really know how to interpret it," Erik says unsteadily. "But today when I was sitting there with Margot and Adam and realized that I'd met all three victims, when I saw the photographs . . . I started to think back to the hypnosis."

"I'm listening," Joona says, sipping his wine.

Erik screws his eyes up as he tries to describe what happened. "Rocky was in a state of deep hypnosis when he said the preacher had shown him a picture of a woman he later killed in front of Rocky's eyes . . . and then the preacher showed him a picture of Rebecka Hansson. I could have sworn that was just a nightmare."

"But it's the same killer," Joona says. "The preacher is back. It's the same pattern."

Erik's face has turned gray. "In that case, I'm playing Rocky's role this time," he whispers.

"Did Rocky have relationships with the two women?"

"Yes."

"Call Simone immediately," Joona says seriously.

Erik picks up his phone, clears his throat, then stands up anxiously.

"Simone," the familiar voice says in his ear.

"Simone, it's Erik."

"What happened? You sound upset."

"I need to ask you for a favor. Are Benjamin and John there?"

"Yes, but why—"

"I think I have a patient who's stalking me, and I don't want you and Benjamin to be at home alone until this is sorted out."

"What happened?"

"I can't tell you."

"Are you in danger?"

"I don't want to take any risks. Please, just do as I say."

"Okay, I'll try to bear it in mind," Simone says.

"Promise me."

"You're scaring me, Erik."

"Good," he replies.

71

IN THE KITCHEN, ERIK RECOUNTS EVERYTHING ROCKY SAID about the unclean preacher—that he wore makeup over his stubble, was a heroin addict, and showed Rocky pictures—while Joona puts the food on the table.

He's roasted lamb with root vegetables and garlic. He scatters some herbs over the dish, then pours more wine into their glasses.

"Thank you for this," Erik says, taking his seat.

"You know . . . Summa's last months," Joona begins, looking up at him. "We had half a year together, the whole family. That wouldn't have been possible without you, Erik, without the medication you prescribed for her and everything. I knew I could trust you, and I'll never forget that."

They clink glasses, drink, and then chat about how they first met but are soon back on the subject of Rocky and the photographs.

"Margot needs to take the preacher seriously," Erik says.

"She will," Joona assures him. "The profilers have come up with a—"

"I've seen it."

"I'm not involved in the case, but Anja told me they've done a first sweep. She started with the parish of Salem, then nearby parishes and congregations." Joona pushes the serving dish toward Erik. "Roman Catholic, Assyrian, Russian and Greek Orthodox . . . the Scientologists, Mission Church, Salvation Army, Jehovah's Witnesses, Latter-day Saints, Methodists, Pentecostalists. And now they're expanding the search to look at all the priests in the country who work with drug addicts, in prisons, institutions, and hospitals."

Erik's hands have almost stopped shaking, but he's moving slowly, as if he doesn't quite trust himself as he takes some food.

"How many names are on the list?" he asks, pushing the dish back to Joona.

"More than four hundred already. But if you can get Rocky to remember the preacher's name . . . even a first name, a description, a parish, then—"

"It's just so difficult," Erik interrupts. "His brain damage and addiction . . ."

"Why don't we talk about this tomorrow?" Joona says, and starts to eat.

"His memory follows its own patterns," Erik says, cutting his meat.

"But he seems to remember much better under hypnosis."

"Yes, although the line between his nightmares and memories seems to become pretty thin."

"Some of what he told you has to be based on real memories," Joona says.

"It should all be real, in theory," Erik points out. "It's just that it sounds psychotic."

"If Rocky agrees to be hypnotized again, do it at once. Try to get concrete details, like names and places."

"I can do that. I know I can."

"If you can, I'll be able to stop this serial killer," Joona says.

"I'll drive out there first thing tomorrow morning," Erik says.

They eat in silence. The glazed root vegetables lend an earthy sweetness to the acidity of the red-currant sauce, the salad is dressed with balsamic vinegar and truffle oil, and the lamb, slightly pink, is spiced with coarsely ground black pepper.

"You really do look much better already," Erik says as Joona helps himself to more food. "It only took six injections of penicillin and a little bit of cortisone."

He trails off when his phone rings in his pocket. It's Margot.

"Yes, Erik here."

"Is Joona there?" she asks shakily.

"What happened?"

"Rocky Kyrklund has escaped."

Erik passes the phone to Joona, then covers his face with his hands, trying to gather his thoughts.

Margot tells Joona that the chief psychiatrist at Karsudden decided Rocky should begin his rehabilitation as soon as possible.

Rocky was supposed to try ordering food at the Pizzeria Primavera on Stor Street in Katrineholm. Two guards were seated at another table a short distance away, so as not to put him off. Rocky ate his pizza, drank a large glass of water, and ordered coffee. Then he went into the bathroom and climbed out the window.

Some youngsters saw him running along the railway line toward the forest, but since then there has been no sign of him.

"We're not making a public appeal," Margot says. "The administrative court has already decided he's eligible to apply for parole, so Karsudden is taking care of this themselves."

"How?" Joona asks.

"By not doing a thing," she replies. "I've spoken to the chief, and he's so relaxed I almost nodded off. Apparently it's not uncommon for patients to run away the first chance they get. They almost always come back of their own accord when they realize how much things have changed, that their friends, apartment, wife are all gone."

Joona ends the call and meets Erik's tired gaze.

"I was the one who recommended he be let out on supervised excursions," Erik says, running his hand through his hair. "But he'll come back. They almost always do."

"We don't have time to sit and wait," Joona says. "We have to find him and get him to talk before the preacher kills again."

"He doesn't have any family, and he's never mentioned any friends. And the rectory isn't there anymore."

"Couldn't he hide in the church itself or somewhere nearby?"

"I'm pretty sure he'll try to make his way to a place called the Zone. That was where he used to get heroin, and it sounded like he thought someone there owed him money."

"I don't know about this Zone," Joona says.

"It sounds like a place to score hard drugs. A fairly large place. There's a stage and a lot of prostitutes."

"I'll find out where it is," Joona says, rising.

"Thanks for dinner."

"There's ice cream for dessert," Joona says, heading toward the entryway.

Erik starts to clear the table, but exhaustion gets the better of him, and he staggers off to the library. His silver glasses case is no longer beside the stack of books on the smoking table. He shudders and turns to look out the window, which is rattling on its latch. It's still light out but will soon be dark, he thinks as he sinks into the leather armchair and closes his eyes.

He needs to pull himself together if he's going to figure out what's happening to him.

Without opening his eyes, he pops a sleeping pill from the pack on the table, holds it in his sweaty palm for a moment, then puts it in his mouth.

Milky stillness settles over his thoughts, and he feels sleep rising like a heavy wave—when the phone rings. He can't focus his eyes enough to see who's calling and almost drops the phone, but somehow he catches it and puts it to his ear.

"Hello?" he says hoarsely.

"You won't forget Maddy, will you?"

"What?"

"Erik, what's wrong?" Jackie asks seriously.

"Nothing, I was just sitting . . . and . . ." He loses his train of thought and clears his throat instead.

"You're picking Maddy up—but you knew that?"

"Of course, no problem. It's on the calendar."

"Thanks," she says warmly.

"I've been practicing," he slurs, and shuts his eyes.

"Call me if there's a problem, and I'll come. They'll have to make do without an organist. Promise you'll call me."

72

JOONA IS IN ERIK'S CAR, DRIVING TOWARD THE CENTER OF
Stockholm while he waits for Anja to call him back. He's nearly in
the tunnels beneath Södermalm when his phone lights up.

He can hear Anja's fingernails tapping at her keyboard as she
tells him she hasn't managed to find anything yet.

"The Zone isn't in our register. It never has been," she says,
sounding resigned.

"Maybe its real name is something different?"

"I've tried the border control agency, the security section, IT,
and Surveillance. I've started asking questions on a bunch of really
nice online forums and sex websites."

"Can you get hold of Milan?" he asks.

"I'd rather not," Anja replies bluntly.

The car windows sigh as Joona heads into the tunnel.

"We have to find Rocky Kyrklund," he says, unsure if the connection has been lost.

"Wait outside the front door," she says distantly. "I'll come down
and . . ."

Then silence, and Joona thinks about everything Erik told him.

Ten minutes later he parks atop the steep hill leading to the
park and walks down to the entrance of the National Police
Headquarters.

Through the glass wall at the entrance, he sees Margot making
her way with heavy steps and joins her in walking down Bergs
Street.

"I happened to hear that Anja has arranged a meeting between you and Milan," Margot says.

"You'll have to keep your distance."

They pass the solid facade of the Kronoberg swimming pool and the heavy metal gate to the prison.

"When can I have my pistol back?" Joona says.

"I'm not even allowed to talk to you," she points out.

As they pass the oldest parts of police headquarters, Margot tells him Björn Kern has started to talk. Apparently his hypnosis had the effect Erik was hoping for.

"Björn says his wife was sitting on the floor with her hand over her ear when he found her."

"The same pattern." Joona nods.

"We still have nothing but the murders themselves and the recurring modus operandi. We've gathered a hell of a lot of questions but no answers."

They cut across Rådhusparken. Joona is limping a bit, and Margot holds both hands around her big stomach.

"The act of filming them through windows is central," Joona says after a while.

"What are you thinking? I'm not getting anywhere," she admits, glancing sideways at him.

The trees shimmer with damp, their crown of leaves turning yellow.

Joona is thinking the murderer is a voyeur, a stalker who gets to know his victims, and chooses to capture a recurring moment in their lives in his videos.

"And the hands," he mutters.

"Yes, what the hell is going on with the hands?"

"I don't know," he replies, thinking that the hands are used to mark different places on the body.

It wasn't Filip Cronstedt who took the Saturn tongue stud from Maria. It was the murderer, the person Filip had caught a glimpse of in the garden, filming in the rain.

Maybe the tongue stud was the reason the preacher attacked, the trigger that prompted him to cross the boundary.

They walk past a 7-Eleven. The tabloids are offering a test to check if your boss is a psychopath.

Joona thinks the preacher kills the woman, takes her jewelry, and marks the place he took it with the victim's hand in order to let the police know why. It's a sort of mocking accusation, like the one hung on Jesus's cross.

Rebecka Hansson was found sitting with her hand around her neck, Maria Carlsson with her hand in her mouth, Susanna Kern with her hand over her ear, and Sandra Lundgren with her hand over her breast.

"He's taken something from each and every one of them. It could be jewelry, or it could be something else," he says.

"But why?" Margot asks.

"Because they've broken the rules."

"Joona, I know you do things your own way," Margot says. "But off the record, we need all the help we can get at this point. If you do track Rocky down and find anything out, it would be nice if you shared the information."

"I'll call you privately," he replies after a brief pause.

"I don't care how you go about it," she says. "But I'd really like to stop this fucking killer before we have any more victims, and preferably without losing my job."

As they cross Fleming Street and approach the location for his meeting, he tells her to wait.

"Keep your distance," he repeats.

"Who the hell is this Milan, anyway?"

Milan has steered clear of police headquarters for the past six years. The only time Joona has seen him was on surveillance camera footage. He was in the background of a mafia showdown, acting strangely and then shooting a man in the back.

Milan Plašil works for the drug squad, usually on long-term surveillance and infiltration jobs, and he has the largest network of informants in all of Stockholm.

"He's pretty smart," Joona replies.

There are rumors that he has a child with a woman in the Bosnian mafia, but no one really knows. Milan has become a shadowy figure, always living in the liminal world of the infiltrator, always keeping his own hidden agenda, a stranger to everyone.

"It might look like he's unarmed, but he's probably got a Beretta Nano strapped around his ankle," Joona says.

"Why are you telling me this?"

"Because he'd sacrifice us if we posed a risk to his undercover work."

"Should I be worried?" Margot wonders.

"Milan's kind of unusual. It's best not to get too close," Joona repeats.

He leaves her on the other side of the street, then continues alone, past the imposing buildings to the end of the bridge, then down the steps to the place where addicts usually hang out.

The air is thick with the smell of stale urine, and the ground is covered with cigarette butts and the remnants of a broken green-glass bottle.

The bridge's steel arches are covered with spikes to stop pigeons from landing, but the entire foundation is still hidden beneath a thick layer of droppings.

A shadow approaches along the walkway. Joona realizes it's Milan, leans his walking stick against the wall, and waits for him to climb to the landing.

Milan Plašil is thirty years old, with a shaved head and dark canine eyes. He's thin as a teenager and dressed in a shiny black tracksuit and expensive sneakers.

"I've heard about you, Joona Linna," Milan says, glancing down toward the water.

"I need to find a place called the Zone."

"You usually carry a forty-five."

"Colt Combat."

"She can't stand up there." Milan nods up the steps.

Joona sighs when he realizes Margot has followed him.

"Margot? Come down!" he calls.

She looks over the railing, hesitates, then comes down the steps with her hand on the rail.

"The Zone," Milan repeats.

"It's existed for more than ten years, somewhere probably south of Stockholm, but we don't know for sure."

"You can stop there," Milan says to Margot when she has almost reached the landing.

"It's a place where you can buy hard drugs and sex," Joona says.

"If I say something, I want a kiss on the lips." Milan smiles.

"Okay," Joona says.

"Her too. She needs to do it, too."

"What?" Margot asks, peering at them.

"I want a kiss," Milan says, pointing at his lips.

"No." She laughs.

"Then you have to look at my cock," he says seriously, and pulls his pants and underwear down.

"Sweet," she says without batting an eyelid.

"Shit, I'm only messing with you. I get it—you're National Crime, aren't you?"

"Yes."

"Armed?" He pulls his pants back up.

"Glock."

Milan laughs silently and looks down at the walkway. A swarm of tiny insects is hovering in the air by the side of the steps.

"The only place that matches your description at all used to be out in Barkarby," he says, glancing at Joona. "Club Noir—that was its name. But it's gone now. This is neither the country nor the time for big brothels. These days it's usually an apartment with a couple of girls from Eastern Europe, all business done on the Internet, a lot of links in the chain, no one's ever guilty of a fucking thing."

"But this place did exist?" Joona says.

"Before my time. It's not there anymore. It can't be. No one ever mentions it."

"Who do we ask?"

Milan turns toward him. A faint shadow of a mustache makes

his lips look even thinner. His small black eyes are set deep, close together.

"Me," he replies. "If it's possible to buy heroin there, I'd know about it, unless it's a tiny Russian enclave."

"So where do people buy heroin?" Margot asks.

73

ERIK HAS HAD A TERRIBLE HEADACHE FOR TWO DAYS. HE'S spent the morning reading Rainer Maria Rilke's poetry while a morose man tunes the grand piano that's just been brought in through the patio doors.

Erik looks up as Joona emerges from the study. He's changed into a tracksuit and disappears when the doorbell rings.

"Erik bought a grand piano," an excited girl's voice says.

"You must be Madeleine," Joona says.

Erik puts his book down when he hears their voices and quickly goes into the bathroom and rinses his face. His hands are shaking, and he feels a pang of angst as he looks into his own bloodshot eyes. He thinks of the three photographs and the smell of plastic in the meeting room, of Sandra's green eyes and Maria's generous smile.

When he enters the living room, Jackie and Madeleine are already in front of the piano, whispering and giggling.

Jackie folds her white stick away and puts her hand on her daughter's shoulder. "Are you trying to impress me?" she asks.

"It's really, really lovely," Madeleine says.

"Try it," Erik says shakily.

"Has it been tuned after the move?" Jackie asks.

"That was part of the deal," he replies.

Madeleine sits down on the stool and starts playing one of Satie's nocturnes. She moves her fingers softly, and her little body is upright and focused. When she finishes the last note, she turns around with a big smile.

Erik applauds and can almost feel tears welling up in his eyes. "Wonderful. How can you be so good?"

"It's going to need to be tuned again fairly soon," Jackie says.

"Okay."

She smiles and runs her fingers over the shiny black of the closed lid. Her hand looks like it's made out of stone in the reflection in the varnish.

"But it sounds very nice."

"Good," Erik says.

Madeleine tugs at his arm. "Now I want to hear the robot play," she says.

"No," Erik protests.

"Yes!" Both Madeleine and Jackie laugh.

"You've set a very high standard," Erik mumbles, and sits down.

He puts his fingers on the keys, feels himself shaking, and stops before he even starts. "I mean, Maddy, I'm so impressed," he says.

"You're good too," she says.

"Are you this good at soccer?"

"No."

"I bet you are," he says warmly. "I was thinking of coming early, so I have time to see you score a goal tomorrow."

The girl's face stiffens and she looks upset.

"What?" Jackie asks.

"When I pick Maddy up after her match," Erik replies.

Jackie's face goes pale and turns hard. "That was yesterday," she says heavily.

"Mom, I—I can do it myself . . ."

"Did you walk on your own?" Jackie asks.

"I don't understand," Erik says. "I thought—"

"Be quiet," she interrupts. "Maddy, did Erik not show up after the match?"

"It was fine, Mom," the little girl says, and starts to cry.

Erik merely sits there with his hands hanging, feeling his headache throb. He suddenly feels sick.

"I'm so sorry," he says quietly. "I don't understand how—"

"You promised me!"

"Mom, stop," Madeleine cries.

"Jackie, I've had such a ridiculous amount to—"

"I don't care!" she yells. "I don't want to hear it!"

"Stop shouting," Madeleine sobs.

Erik kneels in front of her and looks her in the eye. "Maddy, I thought it was tomorrow. I got it wrong."

"It's okay—"

"Don't talk to him!" Jackie snaps.

"Please, I just want to—"

"I knew it," she says, and her dark glasses flash angrily. "Those pills—they weren't aspirin, were they?"

"I'm a doctor," Erik tries to explain, standing up. "I know what I'm doing."

"Right," Jackie mutters, as she pulls Madeleine toward the door.

"But this time it—"

She walks into a table that had to be moved to make room for the piano. A vase of dried flowers falls and breaks into three large pieces.

"Mom, you broke—"

"I don't care," Jackie snaps.

Madeleine looks scared as she follows her mother, crying and hiccuping.

"Jackie, wait," Erik pleads, trying to follow them. "I'm having some trouble with my pills. I don't know how it happened, but—"

"Do you think I care? Am I supposed to feel sorry for you now? Because you take drugs and put my daughter in danger? I can't trust you. You must see that, surely. I don't want you anywhere near her."

"I'll call a taxi," Erik says heavily.

"Mom, it wasn't his fault. Please, Mom—"

Jackie doesn't answer. Tears are streaming down her cheeks as she leads her daughter outside.

"I'm sorry. I ruin everything," Madeleine sobs.

74

WHERE MÄSTER SAMUELS STREET CROSSES MALMSKILLNADS Street, the tall buildings form a wind tunnel. Dust and garbage swirl restlessly around the little bronze statue of a girl whose downturned eyes have been surrounded by prostitutes for more than three decades.

Erik has come with Joona so he'll be close at hand if they find Rocky. He's sitting in the Mozzarella restaurant and has just ordered a cup of coffee.

He's already called Jackie and left two messages for her, trying to explain that there might be a patient stalking him.

He takes a sip of coffee and sees his worried face reflected in the street window. He can't understand how he's managed to mess this up. Being alone after Simone left hadn't scared him, but then he'd been given another chance. Cupid had crept to the edge of his cloud and fired another arrow his way.

He gets out his phone, looks at the time, then calls Jackie again. When her recorded voice asks him to leave a message, he closes his eyes and speaks:

"Jackie . . . I'm so very sorry. I've already said that, but people do make mistakes. I'm not going to make any excuses, but I'm here. I'll wait for you. I'll practice my étude. And I'm prepared to do whatever it takes to make you start trusting me again."

He sets his phone down on the table.

Outside Joona stops next to two women in front of a blank concrete wall. Leaning on his walking stick, he tries to strike up a conversation with them, but when they realize he isn't a customer, they turn their backs on him and begin talking to each other in low voices.

"Do you know somewhere called the Zone?" he asks. "I'll pay well if you can tell me where it is."

They start to walk off, and Joona limps after them, trying to explain that the Zone might be called something else.

He stops and turns in the opposite direction. Farther ahead, close to the Kungs Street towers, a thin woman climbs into a white van.

Joona passes some scaffolding and sees a pile of discarded latex gloves and condoms next to the wall.

A woman in her forties is sitting in the next doorway. Her hair is pulled up into a messy ponytail, and she's wrapped in a thick jacket. She's wearing a pair of stained red shorts, and her bare legs are covered in scabs.

"Excuse me," Joona says.

"I'm going," the woman slurs.

She stands up in the resigned manner of someone who is used to being moved on. Her coat falls open, revealing her cropped T-shirt.

"Liza?" Joona says.

Her eyes are watery, and her face is wrinkled and tired. "They told me you were dead," she says.

"I came back."

"You came back." She laughs hoarsely. "Doesn't everyone?" She rubs her eyes hard, smearing her makeup.

"Your son?" Joona says, leaning on his stick. "He was with a foster family, and you were going to start seeing him again."

"Are you disappointed in me?" She turns her face away.

"I just thought you'd packed this in," he replies.

"So did I, but what the hell." She takes a few unsteady steps, then stops and leans on an overflowing trashcan.

"Can I get you a coffee and a cheese roll?" Joona asks.

Liza shakes her head.

"You have to eat, don't you?"

She blows some strands of hair from her face. "Just tell me what you want to know."

"Do you know a place called the Zone? It sounds like a lot of girls work there. It's Russian, it's existed for ten years or so, and you can get heroin fairly easily there."

"There used to be a place out in Barkarby—what the fuck was it called?"

"Club Noir. That's gone now."

A flock of sparrows takes off from the trees.

"There's the massage parlor out in Solna, but . . ."

"That's too small," Joona says.

"Try the Internet," she suggests.

"Thanks, I'll do that," he says, and starts to walk off.

"Most men are okay," she mutters.

Joona stops and looks at her again. She's standing unsteadily with her hands on the trashcan, licking her lips.

"Do you know where Peter Dahlin hangs out these days?" he asks.

"In hell, I hope."

"I know . . . but if he hasn't gotten there yet?"

She bends over and starts scratching her leg. "I heard he'd moved back to his mom's place in the Fältöversten building, over at Karlaplan," she says, staring at her nails.

75

ERIK PULLS UP IN THE PARKING LOT BENEATH THE SHOPPING center at Fältöversten, and as they walk toward the elevators, Joona explains that he's technically not allowed to be there.

"There's a restraining order against me," he says, and his smile makes Erik shiver.

On the sixth floor, they walk along a dull hallway with names on mailboxes, dusty doormats, strollers, and sneakers.

Joona rings the bell on a door bearing an ornate brass sign with the name Dahlin.

After a while, a woman in her twenties opens the door. There's a frightened look in her eyes, she has bad skin, and her hair is in old-fashioned rollers.

"Is Peter watching television?" Joona asks, walking in.

Erik follows him and closes the front door. He looks around the drab entry with floral embroidery on the walls, as well as color photographs of an old woman with two cats in her lap.

Joona pushes a door open with his walking stick, walks straight into the living room, and stops in front of an older man sitting on a brown leather sofa with two tabby cats. He's wearing thick glasses, a white shirt, and a red tie, and his wavy hair has been combed over a bald patch in the middle of his head.

An old episode of *Columbo* is on television. Peter Falk puts his hands in the pockets of his crumpled raincoat and smiles to himself.

The man on the sofa glances at Joona, pulls a cat treat from a dusty bag, throws it on the floor, and then smells his fingers.

The two cats jump down onto the floor without much enthusiasm and sniff the treat. The young woman limps to the kitchen and squeezes out a dishcloth.

"Did you do your usual?" Joona asks.

"You don't know anything," Peter Dahlin says nasally.

"Does she have any idea that this is only the beginning?"

Peter Dahlin smiles at him, but the corners of his eyes are twitching nervously. "I've undergone voluntary sterilization, you know that," he says. "My conviction was overturned, I was awarded damages, and you're not allowed to come anywhere near me."

"I'll leave as soon as you answer my question."

"I'll be reporting this," he says, scratching his groin.

"I need to find a place called the Zone."

"Good luck."

"Peter, you've been to all the places people aren't supposed to go, and—"

"I'm so very, very bad," the man says sarcastically.

The girl in the kitchen puts her hand against her stomach and closes her eyes for a moment.

"She's not wearing any underwear." Peter puts his feet up on the end of the sofa. "They're soaking in vinegar under the bed."

"Erik," Joona says, "get her out of here. Explain to her that we're with the police. She might need to see a doctor."

"I'll find another one," Peter says nonchalantly.

Erik leads the girl into the entryway. Holding her hand to her stomach, she sways as she pulls her boots on and picks up her bag.

Before they've even closed the door, Joona grabs one of Peter's ankles and starts walking toward the kitchen.

The older man manages to grab the arm of the sofa, which moves with him, pulling the Persian carpet. "Let go of me, you're not allowed—"

The sofa catches on the threshold of the kitchen, and Peter slides over the armrest and groans loudly as he hits the floor. Joona drags him across the linoleum kitchen floor. There's a clatter of cats' paws as they scuttle away. Peter tries to grab a leg of the table but can't quite reach.

Joona leans his stick in the corner, opens the door to the balcony, and drags Peter out onto the green plastic grass before letting go.

"What are you playing at? I don't know anything, and you're not—"

Joona grabs him and heaves him over the railing, and he thuds into the outside of the red balcony screen. He doesn't let go until he sees that Peter is holding on tightly.

"I'm slipping, I'm slipping!" Peter cries. His knuckles are turning white and his glasses tumble to the ground far below.

"Tell me where the Zone is."

"I've never heard of it," he gasps.

"A large place, could be Russian . . . with prostitutes, a stage, plenty of drugs circulating."

"I don't know," Peter sobs. "You have to believe me!"

"Then I'm leaving." Joona turns away.

"Okay, I've heard the name, Joona! I can't hold on any longer. I don't know where it is, I don't know anything."

Joona looks at him, then pulls him back over the railing. Peter's whole body is shaking as he tries to get into the kitchen.

"That's not enough," Joona says, pushing him back toward the railing.

"A few years ago . . . there was a girl. She mentioned some guys from Volgograd," he says quickly, moving along the railing to the wall. "It wasn't a brothel, it sounded more like a ring . . . you know, tough as hell, everyone watching one another."

"Where was it?"

"I have no idea, I swear," he whispers. "I'd tell you if I knew."

"Where can I find the woman who told you about it?"

"It was in a bar in Bangkok. She'd spent a few years in Stockholm. I don't know what her name is."

Joona returns to the kitchen.

Peter Dahlin follows him and closes the door to the balcony.

"You can't just do this," he says, pulling himself together and wiping his tears with a paper towel. "You'll get sacked, and—"

"I'm not a police officer anymore," Joona says, picking up his stick from the corner. "So I have plenty of time to keep an eye on you."

"What do you mean, keep an eye on me? What do you want?"

"If you do as I say, you'll be fine," Joona replies, turning his stick over in his hands.

"What do you want me to do?" Peter Dahlin asks.

"As soon as you've been to the hospital, you go to the police and . . ."

"Why would I be going to the hospital?"

Joona hits Peter Dahlin across the face with his stick. He staggers backward, clutching both hands to his nose, stumbles into a chair, falls onto his back, and hits his head on the floor so hard that blood splatters the cat food in the bowls.

"When you've been to the hospital, you go to the police and confess to all the assaults," Joona says, pushing the walking stick onto the pit of his throat. "Mirjam was fourteen years old when she killed herself. Anna-Lena lost her ovaries. Liza got caught in prostitution, and the girl who was here just now—"

"Okay!" Peter cries. "Okay!"

76

ERIK DRIVES THE YOUNG WOMAN TO A GYNECOLOGIST HE knows at Sophia Hospital, then picks Joona up from Valhalla Road.

"Now we know the Zone exists," Joona says as he gets in the car. "But it seems to be a Russian setup where you buy membership by contributing to their illegal activities."

"And that way you're bound to keep quiet," Erik says, drumming his fingers on the wheel. "That's why no one knows anything."

"We'll never be able to track it down, and it would take several years to infiltrate."

Joona looks at his phone and sees that The Needle has called him three times in the last hour.

"Now we have only one lead to follow if we're going to find the Zone," Joona says. "And that's the woman Rocky called Tina."

"But she's not alive anymore—is she?"

"She not in the database, so no one's been murdered that way in Sweden," he replies. "Having an arm chopped off isn't the kind of thing that's likely to get missed."

"Maybe it was just a nightmare?"

"Do you believe that?" Joona asks.

"No."

"Okay, then let's go see The Needle."

———

THE CHIEF PATHOLOGIST'S OFFICE HAS A NUMBER OF LEC-
ture rooms, but only one room for the display of bodies. The hall
is reminiscent of an anatomy theater. The room is circular, with
banks of seating rising higher and higher around the small stage
with the autopsy table on it.

From the lobby they can hear The Needle's sharp voice through
the closed doors as he finishes a lecture. They go in as quietly as
they can and sit down.

Nils is dressed in his white coat and is standing beside the
blackened body of a man who froze to death.

"And out of everything I've said today, there's one particular
thing that you must never forget," The Needle says in conclusion.
"A human being isn't dead until it's both dead and warm."

He puts a gloved hand on the chest of the corpse and gives a
bow as the medical students applaud.

Joona and Erik wait until the students have left the room before
going down to the lectern. The corpse is giving off a strong smell
of yeast and decay.

"I've checked our records," The Needle says, "but there's no mention of that sort of injury. I've been through the databases covering
violent crime, accidents, and suicide. She doesn't exist."

"But you also looked for me when I was gone," Joona says.

"So the obvious answer is that the body hasn't been found," The
Needle mutters, taking off his glasses and polishing them.

"Of course, but—"

"Some are never found," Nils interrupts. "Some are found many
years later, and some are found but never identified. We try dental
records and DNA and keep the bodies for a couple of years. Our
pathologists are good, but even they have to bury a few unidentified bodies each year."

"The injuries would still be recorded, though, wouldn't they?"
Joona persists.

The Needle has a strange glint in his eye as he lowers his voice.

"I've thought of another possibility," he says. "There used to
be a group of pathologists who collaborated with certain detec-

tives. They were known as the 'Tax Savers,' and they believed they could identify in advance the cases that were never going to lead anywhere."

"You never told me about that," Joona says.

"It was back in the eighties. The Tax Savers didn't want Swedish taxpayers to be burdened with the cost of pointless police investigations and hopeless attempts to identify bodies. It wasn't a major scandal, though a few people got pissed off, and the group was dissolved. But when you described Tina as a heroin addict, a prostitute, possibly a victim of human trafficking . . ."

"You were wondering if the Tax Savers still exist?" Joona asks.

"There would have been no paperwork," Nils says. "No investigation, no Interpol. The body would have been buried as an unknown, and the resources would have been used elsewhere."

"But Tina would still be in the database of the National Board of Forensic Medicine," Erik says.

"Try looking for an unidentified body, natural cause of death, illness," The Needle says.

"Who do I talk to?" Joona asks.

"Talk to Johan in forensic genetics, mention my name," he says. "Or I could give him a call, since we're here."

He scrolls through his contacts, then puts his phone to his ear.

"Hello, this is Professor Nils Åhlén. I . . . no, thank you, it was very enjoyable. Just offbeat enough, I'd say."

The Needle circles the body twice as he talks. When he ends the call, he stands in silence for a moment. His mouth twitches slightly. The empty benches spread out around them like the growth rings of a huge tree.

"There's only one unknown woman from Stockholm who matches Tina's age during the period in question," The Needle says eventually. "Either it's her, or her body was never found."

"So could it be her?" Erik asks.

"The death certificate says heart attack. There's a reference to another file, but that file doesn't exist."

"There's no description of the body?"

"Obviously they kept a DNA sample, fingerprints, dental records," The Needle replies.

"Where is she now?" Joona asks.

"She's in Skogskyrkogården, buried among the trees of the Forest Cemetery," The Needle says. "No name, grave number 32 2 53 332."

77

SKOGSKYRKOGÅRDEN IS A UNESCO WORLD HERITAGE SITE south of Stockholm that holds more than one hundred thousand graves. Erik and Joona walk along the well-tended paths, past the Woodland Chapel, and notice the yellow roses in front of Greta Garbo's red headstone.

Block number 53 is located farther away, close to the fence facing Gamla Tyresö Road. The cemetery workers have unloaded a backhoe from a truck and have already dug out the earth above the coffin. The grass is lying alongside the heap of soil, a tangle of fibrous roots and plump worms.

The Needle and his assistant Frippe are approaching from the other direction, and the four of them greet each other in subdued voices. Frippe has gotten a haircut, and his face looks a little rounder, but he's still wearing the same studded belt and washed-out T-shirt with a black Hammerfell logo that Joona's always seen him in.

The cab of the backhoe rotates gently and the hydraulics hiss as the scoop sinks and moves forward, carefully scraping the soil from the lid of the coffin.

As usual, The Needle is giving Frippe a short lecture, this time about how ammonia, hydrogen sulfide, and hydrocarbons are released when proteins and carbohydrates break down. "The final stage of the decomposition process leaves the skeleton entirely exposed."

Nils signals to the backhoe operator to back away. Clumps of clay soil fall from the blade of the scoop. He slides down into the grave with his hand on the edge. The lid of the coffin has given way under the weight of the soil.

He scrapes around the edge of the coffin with a shovel, then brushes it clean with his hands, inserts the blade of the shovel under the lid, and tries to pry it open, but the particleboard snaps. There's no strength left in it. It's like wet cardboard.

The Needle whispers something to himself, tosses the shovel aside, and slowly starts removing it, piece by piece, with his hands. He passes the pieces to Frippe, until the contents of the grave are entirely uncovered.

The skeleton in the coffin isn't unpleasant. It just looks defenseless. It looks small, almost like a child's, but The Needle assures them that it belonged to a grown woman.

"Five foot five," he murmurs.

She was buried in a T-shirt and briefs. The fabric is clinging to the skeleton. The curve of the rib cage is intact, but the material has sunk into the pelvis.

An image of a cobalt-blue angel is still visible on the T-shirt.

Frippe walks around the grave taking photographs from every angle. The Needle has taken out a small brush that he uses to remove soil and fragments of particleboard from the skeleton.

"The left arm has been chopped off close to the shoulder," The Needle declares.

"We've found the nightmare," Joona says in a low voice.

They watch The Needle carefully turn the skull. The jaw has come loose, but otherwise the cranium is in one piece.

"Deep incisions across the front of the cranium," The Needle says. "Forehead, zygomatic bone, cheekbone, upper jaw. The incisions continue across the collarbone and sternum."

"The preacher's back," Erik says with an ominous feeling in the pit of his stomach.

The Needle continues brushing soil from the body. Next to the hip bone, he finds a wristwatch with a scratched face. The leather strap is gone, turned to gray dust.

"Looks like a man's watch," he says, picking it up and turning it over.

The back is inscribed with Cyrillic letters. The Needle takes out his phone and photographs the lettering.

"I'll send this to Maria at the Slavic Institute," he mutters.

78

JOONA'S JUST GOTTEN ANOTHER CORTISONE INJECTION, AND is in Erik's backyard practicing combat techniques with a long wooden pole.

The Needle is trying to track down the colleague who signed Tina's death certificate while they wait for the translation of the engraving on the watch, to find out if it can help them.

Erik is sitting at the grand piano, watching his friend's repetitive pattern of blocks and attacks as shadows cross the thin linen curtain.

Like Chinese shadow theater, he thinks, then looks down at the piano keys in front of him.

He was planning to practice his étude but can't bring himself to try. His mind is too unfocused. He still hasn't reached Jackie, and Nelly called him from work an hour ago to ask if she could come over.

Slowly he puts his little finger on a key and strikes it, making the first note echo as his phone rings.

"Erik Maria Bark," he answers.

"Hello," a high voice says. "My name is Madeleine Federer, and—"

"Maddy?" Erik gasps. "How are you?"

"Fine," she whispers. "I borrowed Rosita's phone. . . . I just wanted to say it was nice when you were here with us."

"I loved spending time with you and your mom," Erik says.

"Mom misses you, but she's silly and pretends that—"

"You need to listen to her, and—"

"*Maddy*," someone calls in the background, "*what are you doing with my phone?*"

"Sorry I ruined everything," the girl says quickly, then the call ends.

Erik slips off his piano stool and just sits on the floor with his hands over his face. After a while, he lies back and stares up at the ceiling, thinking that it's time to get a grip and stop taking pills.

He's used to helping patients move on.

When everything is at its darkest, it can only get brighter, he says to himself.

He gets up with a sigh, rinses his face, then sits down on the steps outside the glass door.

Joona groans as he turns around, strikes low with the stick, then jabs behind him before he stops and looks at Erik.

His face is wet with sweat, his muscles are pumped with blood, and he's breathing hard but isn't exactly out of breath.

"Did you have time to look into your old patients?"

"I've found a few who were the children of priests," Erik says. He hears a car pull up and stop at the front of the house.

"Give their names to Margot."

"But I just started going through the archive," he says.

Nelly walks around the house and comes over to them. She's wearing a fitted riding jacket and tight black pants. "We're supposed to be at Rachel Yehuda's lecture," she says, sitting down next to Erik.

"Is that today?"

Joona's phone rings, and he walks toward the shed before answering.

It strikes Erik that Nelly seems tired and subdued. The thin skin below her eyes is gray and she's frowning. "You seem worried," he says.

She just shakes her head and looks wearily at him.

"Do you think my mouth is ugly?" she asks. "Your lips get thinner as you get older. And Martin—he's very sensitive when it comes to mouths."

"So how does Martin look, then? Hasn't he aged at all?"

"Don't laugh, but I'm thinking of having surgery. I'm not ready to get older. I don't want anyone to think he's sleeping with me out of pity."

"You're beautiful, Nelly."

"I'm not fishing for compliments. It's just that's not the way it feels, not anymore." She stops speaking, and her chin trembles.

"What happened?"

"Nothing." She gently rubs beneath her eyes before looking up.

"You need to talk to Martin about the porn if it's upsetting you."

"It's not that," she says.

Joona has finished his call and is heading toward them with his phone. "The Slavic Institute has managed to decipher the lettering on that watch. It's Belarusian, apparently."

"What does it say?" Erik asks.

"'In honor of Andrej Kaliov's great achievements, Military Faculty, Yanka Kupala University.'"

They follow Joona into the study. He's able to track the name down in less than five minutes through Interpol. The unit for international police cooperation puts him through to the office of the National Central Bureau in Minsk.

He finds out that there's no indication that Andrej Kaliov disappeared, but a woman by the name of Natalia Kaliova from Gomel has been reported missing.

In British-accented English, the woman on the phone explains that Natalia—the woman Rocky called Tina—is believed to have been a victim of human trafficking.

"Her family say that a friend of hers called from Sweden and encouraged her to go there via Finland, without a residence permit."

"Is that everything?" Joona asks.

"You could try talking to her sister," the woman says.

"Her sister?"

"Her younger sister went to Sweden to look for her and is evidently still there. It says here that she calls us regularly to find out if there's any news."

"What's the sister's name?"

"Irina Kaliova."

79

THE CENTRAL KITCHEN ON KUNGSHOLMEN IN STOCKHOLM smells like boiled potatoes. The cooks are working by the stoves, dressed in protective white clothing and hairnets. The sound of a slicing machine echoes off the tiled walls and metal countertops.

Erik has asked Nelly to go with them to meet Irina Kaliova. It could be useful to have a female psychologist on hand when the woman finds out that her sister was a victim of sex trafficking before she was murdered.

Irina is dressed like all the others, in a hairnet and white coat. She's standing by a row of huge saucepans hanging from hooks. She concentrates on a display panel, then taps a command and pulls a lever to tip one of the pans.

"Irina?" Joona asks.

She lifts her head and looks inquisitively at the three strangers. Her cheeks are red, and her forehead is sweaty from the steam rising from the boiling water, and a strand of loose hair is hanging over her brow.

"Do you speak Swedish?"

"Yes," she says, and continues working.

"We're from National Crime."

"I have a residence permit," she says quickly. "Everything's in my locker, my passport and all my documents."

"Is there somewhere we could go and talk?"

"I need to ask my boss first."

"We've already spoken to him," Joona says.

Irina says something to one of the women, who smiles back. She puts her hairnet in her pocket, then leads them through the noisy kitchen, past a row of food carts, and into a small staff room with a sink full of unwashed mugs. There are six chairs around a table with a bowl of apples at its center.

"I thought I was about to get fired," she says with a nervous smile.

"Can we sit down?" Joona asks.

Irina nods and sits on one of the chairs. She has a pretty, round face, like a fourteen-year-old. Joona looks at her slender shoulders in her white coat and finds himself thinking of her sister's white skeleton in the grave.

Natalia used the name Tina as a prostitute, and she was murdered and buried like garbage because she was alone and had no papers and no one to help her. She was used up by Sweden and afterward wasn't even worth the cost of a proper identification.

There's nothing more difficult than having to inform a relative about a death. There's no way to get used to the pain you inflict, to the way all the color drains from their faces. Any attempt to be sociable, to laugh and joke, vanishes.

Irina gathers some crumbs on the table with a trembling hand. Hope and fear flit across her face.

"I'm afraid we have bad news," Joona says. "Your sister Natalia is dead. Her remains have just been found."

"Now?" she asks hollowly.

"She's been dead for nine years."

"I don't understand."

"The body has just been discovered."

"In Sweden? I looked for her. I don't understand."

"She had been buried but couldn't be identified before. That's why it's taken so long."

The small hands keep moving the crumbs, then slip onto her lap.

"How did it happen?" she asks, her eyes wide open and empty.

"We're not sure yet," Erik replies.

"Her heart was always . . . she didn't want to worry us, but sometimes it would just stop beating, it felt like an eternity before it . . ." Irina's chin begins to tremble. She hides her mouth with her hand, looks down, and swallows hard.

"Do you have anyone to talk to after work?" Nelly asks.

"What?" She quickly wipes the tears from her cheeks and swallows again. "Okay," she says, more focused. "What do I have to do? Do I have to pay anything?"

"You don't have to do anything. We'd just like to ask a few questions," Joona says. "Would that be okay?"

She nods and picks at the crumbs on the table again. They hear a metallic sound from the kitchen, and someone tries the door.

"Did you have any contact with your sister while she was in Sweden?"

Irina shakes her head. Her mouth moves slightly, then she looks up. "I was the only person who knew she was heading to Stockholm, but I promised not to say anything. I was young, I didn't understand. She was very stern with me, said she wanted to surprise Mom with her first wages. Nothing ever came, but I spoke to her on the telephone once. She just said that everything would be all right."

Irina falls silent and appears to drift off in thought.

"Did she say where she was living?"

"We don't have any brothers," she replies. "Dad died when we were little. I don't remember him, but Natalia did. And after Natalia left, there was just me and Mom. . . . Mom missed her so much, she used to cry and worry about her weak heart, and said she just knew something terrible had happened. So I thought if I could find my sister and bring her back home, everything would be fine. Mom didn't want me to leave, and she was alone when she died."

"I'm so sorry," Joona says.

"Thank you. Well, now I know Natalia is dead." Irina gets to her feet. "I suppose I suspected as much, but now I know."

"Do you know where she was living?"

"No."

She takes a step toward the door, clearly eager to get away from the whole situation.

"Please sit down for a moment," Erik asks.

"I need to get back to work."

"Irina," Joona says with a dark resonance that makes the young woman listen, "your sister was murdered."

"No, I just told you, her heart—"

Irina's coat catches on the back of the chair, dragging it with her. As the truth sinks in, she loses control of her face. Her cheeks turn white, her lips quiver, and her pupils dilate. "No," she whimpers.

She leans back against the counter, shakes her head, and fumbles across the front of the fridge for something to hold on to.

Nelly tries to calm her, but she pulls free. "Irina, you need to—"

"God, no, not Natalia!" she cries. "She promised—" She grabs the handle of the fridge, and the door swings open as she falls, dislodging a shelf full of ketchup and jam.

Nelly hurries over to her and holds her slender shoulders.

"*Nie maja siastra*," she gasps. "*Nie maja siastra.*"

She curls up in Nelly's lap and holds her hand over her mouth as she cries, screaming into her palm and shaking uncontrollably.

After a while she calms down and sits up, but she's still breathing unevenly and sobbing. She wipes her tears and clears her throat weakly, trying to control her breathing.

"Did someone hurt her?" she asks raggedly. "Did they hit her? Did they hit Natalia?"

Her face contorts as she tries to hold her tears back, but they run down her cheeks.

Joona takes some napkins from a pack on the counter and hands them to her, then pulls a chair over and sits in front of her. "If you know anything at all, it's very important that you tell us," he says.

"What could I know?" she says, confused.

"We're just trying to find the person who did this." Nelly brushes the hair from Irina's face.

"You spoke to your sister on the phone," Joona goes on. "Did she tell you where she lived or what her job was?"

"There are men who trick girls from poor countries, who say they're going to get good jobs, but Natalia was smart, she said it wasn't anything like that, that it was real. She promised me. But I've been to the furniture factory. No one there had heard of Natalia, *durnaja dziaŭtjynka*. They're not employing anyone, haven't done so for years."

Her eyes are red from crying, and tiny red spots have appeared on the fair skin of her forehead.

"What's the name of the factory?" Erik asks.

"Sofa Zone," she says. "It's out in Högdalen."

Nelly remains on the floor with Irina, stroking her head and promising to stay with her as long as she wants. Erik exchanges a glance with Nelly, then walks back out through the noisy kitchen with Joona.

80

MARGOT IS SITTING IN FRONT OF A COMPUTER IN THE INVES-
tigation room, looking at Erik's video of Rocky's hypnosis again.

His large head droops forward as he describes his visit to the
Zone in a languid voice. He talks about the dealers and strippers
and the fact that he thought he could collect some money there.

As Margot listens, her eyes drift along the walls of the room to
a large map. There the victims' patterns of movement are marked
in three different colors. Every place, every street where they could
have come into contact with the preacher is marked with a pin.

On the screen, Rocky shakes his head as he says the preacher
smells like fish guts.

Margot sees the pin marking Rebecka Hansson's home in
Salem.

Serial killers usually stick to their home turf, but in this case
the locations are spread out across the most densely populated
metropolitan district in Scandinavia.

"*The preacher snorts back some snot, then starts to speak in a really
high voice,*" Rocky says, breathing unevenly.

Margot shudders and watches the big man squirm on his chair
and howl with angst as he describes the way the preacher cuts the
woman's arm off.

"*It sounds like when you stick a shovel into mud . . .*"

After the discovery out in Skogskyrkogården, no one doubts
that the unclean preacher is the serial killer they're all looking for.

She knows Joona persuaded The Needle to order the body exhumed. It would have been much easier if she could work with Joona openly, but Benny Rubin and Petter Näslund are backing Adam up, resisting his involvement.

Margot doesn't have the authority to let Joona join the investigation, but she's sure as hell not going to stop him from conducting his own inquiries.

Rocky shakes his head and his shadow moves across the glossy *Playboy* pinup on the wall behind him.

"*The preacher chops her arm off at the shoulder,*" Rocky gasps, "*loosens the tourniquet, and drinks.*"

"*Listen to my voice now,*" Erik says.

"*And drinks the blood from her arm . . . while Tina lies bleeding to death on the floor . . . Dear God in heaven . . . Dear God . . .*"

Inside Margot's womb, the baby moves so violently that she has to lean back and close her eyes for a moment.

The investigation is proceeding, but no one really believes it's going to prevent another murder.

The police have knocked on doors and questioned hundreds of neighbors. They've examined footage from all the surveillance and traffic cameras around the crime scenes.

Unless Rocky returns to Karsudden Hospital soon, so Erik can question him, they'll have to make a public appeal for information about him.

Margot switches off the video. She has a strong feeling she's being watched. She gets up and closes the curtains over the window looking out onto the park.

She opens her bag and takes out her compact. She examines herself in the little mirror and puts some more powder on. Her nose is shiny, and the rings under her eyes look dark. She reapplies lipstick, blots her lips on a letter from the police union, adjusts her hair, and then calls Jenny on Skype.

She can see herself on the screen, and as the call is connected, she undoes one button on her blouse and moves backward slightly so her cheeks are framed better.

Jenny answers almost immediately. She looks angry but attractive, with her messy black hair tumbling over her thin shoulders. She's wearing a washed-out shirt, and the little golden heart is shimmering against her neck.

"Hi, baby," Margot says.

"Did you catch the bad guy yet?"

"I thought I was the bad guy," Margot says.

Jenny smiles and stifles a yawn.

"Did you call the bank about that ridiculous charge?"

"Yes, and apparently there's nothing wrong with it," Jenny replies.

"That can't be right."

"So call them yourself."

"I just meant . . . okay, never mind. It's so irritating when they deduct payments for . . . oh, what the hell."

"What did you want?" Jenny asks, picking at her armpit.

"How are the girls?" Margot asks.

"Fine." Jenny glances off to one side. "But Linda's still a little down. She needs to learn to make new friends. She's too nice."

"Being nice is a good thing, isn't it?" Margot says.

"But she doesn't know what to do when her best friend says she's sick of her. She gets upset and becomes passive."

"She'll learn."

Margot would like to be able to tell Jenny about the investigation, about the inexplicable hatred fueling the murders and her feeling that the preacher is close by, watching them all.

She's worried, because she keeps forgetting all the things that normal people know, and the fact that she's going to have a baby, and that people can be happy and secure.

"You look nice," Margot says, tilting her head.

"No, I don't." Jenny grins, then yawns loudly. "Well, I guess I'm going to get back to watching TV."

"Okay. I'll call you later." She pauses. "Jenny, you know I love you."

Jenny blows her a kiss and ends the call, leaving Margot looking at her own face. *I have my father's nose and those thick, colorless eyebrows. I look like someone's aunt,* she thinks. *Like my dad, only a woman.*

The thought that she has to do something to make it up to Jenny is snaking through Margot's head when Adam comes in and opens the window facing the park.

He's been in a meeting with Nathan Pollock and Elton Eriksson from the Homicide Commission in an attempt to prune the list of potential perpetrators and move the investigation forward.

"I had Pollock as one of my lecturers when I was training," Margot says.

"So he said," Adam replies as he sits and leafs through a bundle of papers.

"Do you have the new profile?" Margot asks.

Adam runs his hands through his thick hair in frustration. "They just keep repeating things we already know."

"That's how it works, setting up things that seem obvious as the parameters," she replies, leaning back.

"The murders are characterized by a high degree of risk-taking, forensic awareness, and excessive brutality," he reads. "The victims are women of childbearing age, and the crime scenes are the victims' homes. The motive may be instrumental, but the violence is probably expressive."

Margot listens to the generalizations and thinks about the fact that Anja's list of names has grown even longer.

There are an awful lot of priests and preachers in Sweden, considering that it's the most secular country in the world. Almost five hundred people with direct connections to faith organizations in the Stockholm area now match the general profile.

This investigation has ground to a halt, she finds herself thinking. If only they had one sighting, just one decent piece of information to go on.

They need to bring things into focus. There isn't enough time to check out more than five hundred men. Given the murderer's momentum, the video of his next victim could appear at any moment.

To limit the search, we need to add some new parameters, she thinks. Previous violent crimes, for instance, or personality disorders.

"There are forty-two men who've been suspects in other cases. Nine have been convicted of violent crimes, none for stalking, none for murder, and none for brutality that bears any resemblance to our serial killer's," Adam says. "Eleven have convictions for sexual offenses, thirty for drugs."

"Just give me someone to shoot," she says wearily.

"I have three names. None of them is a perfect match, but two have been investigated for violent crimes against more than one woman."

"That's something to go on."

"The first one is Sven Hugo Andersson, a vicar in the parish of Danderyd. The other one's Pasi Jokala, who used to be active in the Philadelphia Church but now he has his own congregation, known as the Gärtuna Revivalists."

"And the third one?"

"I'm not sure, but he's the only one of the five hundred who has a documented personality disorder that matches the profile. A twenty-year-old diagnosis for borderline psychosis. But he has no criminal record and doesn't feature in police or social service registers. And he's been married for ten years, which doesn't fit the profile at all."

"Better than nothing," she says.

"Anyway, his name's Thomas Apel, and he's the so-called stake president of the Church of Jesus Christ of Latter-day Saints, out in Jakobsberg."

"We'll start with the violent ones," she says, standing up.

Adam goes to his office to call his wife and tell her he's going to work late, and Margot stops in the kitchen, looks in the cupboard, and pops Petter Näslund's package of jam cookies into her bag before she walks out.

Adam's account of the perpetrator profile has made her think about the stalker and serial killer Dennis Rader, whom she wrote an essay about when she was training. He used to call the police and media to tell them about his murders. He even used to send the police objects he'd taken from his victims.

In his case, the perpetrator profile was completely wrong. They had been looking for a divorced, impotent loner, whereas Rader was married, had children, and was active in both the church and the scouting movement.

81

MARGOT AND ADAM ARE SITTING IN MARGOT'S LINCOLN. TO make room for her stomach, she's had to move the seat so far back that her feet barely reach the pedals.

They just checked on Sven Hugo Andersson. It turns out that he was in Danderyd Hospital for a bypass operation when Sandra Lundgren was murdered. Now only two of the three names are left. Margot puts a cookie in her mouth and chews, tasting the crumbly mixture of sugar and butter, then the tart jam.

"Are those Petter's cookies?" Adam asks.

"He gave them to me." She pops another one into her mouth.

"He wouldn't even offer one to his wife."

"But he was very insistent that you have a couple," she says with a wink, passing him the package.

Adam takes a cookie and eats it with a smile, holding one hand under his mouth so he doesn't drop crumbs in Margot's car.

As they drive, the road gets narrower, grit flies up behind them, and Margot has to slow down. They can make out the occasional cottage down by the lake.

Pasi Jokala was convicted of aggravated assault, rape, and attempted rape. "Do you think he's dangerous?" Adam asks.

The two of them know they shouldn't have come out here without the Task Force. Margot has brought her Glock and four extra magazines.

"He has problems with aggression and a lack of impulse control," she says. "But who the hell doesn't?"

Pasi Jokala is registered as living at the same address as the Gärtuna Revivalist Church.

Margot turns off onto a narrow gravel road that leads through sparse forest, and soon she can see the lake again. Some fifty cars are parked along the side of the road, but she drives all the way to the fence before stopping.

"We don't have to do this now," Adam says.

"I'm just going to take a look." Margot checks her gun, then puts it back in its holster and struggles out of the car.

They're standing in front of a rust-red cottage, with a white cross made of LED lights covering the gable end. The light inside the cottage filters out through narrow gaps in the wood. Behind it, a wild meadow stretches down toward the lake.

The windows are covered on the inside.

A loud voice can be heard through the walls.

A man shouts something, and Margot feels a sudden pang of unease.

She keeps walking, her holster rubbing against her. It's sitting too high, now that her stomach has grown. They walk past a rain barrel, thistles a meter tall, and a rusty lawnmower. Dozens of slugs lurk in the shadowy grass beside the wall.

"Maybe we should wait here until they finish," Adam wonders.

"I'm going in," Margot says curtly.

They open the door and walk into the entryway but now everything is completely silent, as if everyone had been waiting for them to arrive.

On the wall is a poster about meetings beside the lake, and a group trip to Alabama. On a table is a bundle of printouts about fund-raising for the Gärtuna Revivalists' new church, next to a buckled cashbox and twenty copies of the Redemption Hymnal.

Adam is hesitant, but she waves him toward her. It may be a church, but she wants him in position in case there's trouble.

She holds her stomach with one hand as she walks through the next door.

She can hear the murmur of voices.

A church hall takes up the entire building. Pillars hold up the roof beams, and everything is painted brilliant white. There are rows of white chairs on the white floor, and up at the front is a small stage.

A couple of dozen people have stood up from their seats. Their eyes are fixed on the man on the stage.

Margot realizes the man is Pasi Jokala. He's wearing a blood-red shirt with open cuffs hanging down over his hands. His hair sticks up from one side of his head, and his face is sweaty. His chair is on its side behind him. The members of the small choir are silent, looking at him with their mouths open. Pasi raises his head wearily and gazes out across the congregation.

"I was the mud beneath His feet, the dust in His eye, the dirt under His nails," he says. "I sinned, and I sinned on purpose. You know what I have done to myself, and to others, you know what I said to my own parents, to my mother and father."

The congregation sighs and shuffles uncomfortably.

"The sickness of sin was raging in me."

"Pasi," a woman whimpers, looking at him with moist eyes.

They all mutter prayers.

"You know that I mugged a man and beat him with a rock," Pasi goes on with growing intensity. "You know what I did to Emma. And when she forgave me, I left her and Mikko. You know that I drank so much I ended up in the hospital."

The congregation is moving agitatedly. Chairs scrape the floor, some topple over, and one man falls to his knees.

The atmosphere grows tenser, and Pasi's voice is hoarse from chanting. The meeting seems to be reaching a crescendo. Margot retreats toward the door, as she sees two women holding each other's hands and speaking a strange language: incomprehensible, repetitive words, faster and faster.

"But I put my life in the Lord's hands and was baptized in the Holy Spirit," Pasi goes on. "Now I am the drop of blood running down Christ's cheek. I am the drop of blood."

The congregation cheers and applauds.

The little choir starts to sing with full force: "The chains of sin are broken, I am free, I am free, I am delivered of my sin, I am free, saved and free, hallelujah, hallelujah, Jesus died for me! Hallelujah, hallelujah, I am free, I am free."

The congregation joins in, clapping along, and Pasi Jokala stands there with his eyes closed, sweat running down his face.

82

MARGOT AND ADAM WAIT OUTSIDE THE CHURCH AND WATCH the congregation emerge. They're smiling and chatting, switching their phones on and reading messages as they head toward their cars, waving and saying their goodbyes.

After a while Pasi comes out alone.

His red shirt is unbuttoned, and the fabric is dark with sweat under the arms. He's holding a plastic bag as he carefully locks the door.

"Pasi?" Margot says, taking a few steps toward him.

"The pallets are in the garage, but I need to get to the co-op before they close," he says, heading toward the gates.

"We're from National Crime," Adam says.

Pasi continues to walk away.

"Would you please stop!" Margot says more sharply.

He comes to a halt with one hand on the gatepost and turns toward Margot. "I thought you were here because of the ad. I have five pallets of Polish Mr. Muscle that I'm looking to unload. I usually sell to a discount store, but they cut their order."

"Do you live here?"

"There's a smaller cottage nearby."

"And a garage," Margot adds.

He doesn't answer, just prods a rusty pipe that's stuck in the ground.

"Can we take a look?" Adam asks.

"No," Pasi says.

"We'll have to ask you to come with us."

"I haven't seen any ID," he says, almost in a whisper.

Adam holds his badge up in front of Pasi, who barely looks at it. He just nods to himself and pulls the pipe from the ground.

"Drop that now!" Margot says.

Holding the pipe with both hands, Pasi walks slowly toward her.

Adam moves aside and draws his Sig Sauer.

"I have sinned," he says softly. "But I—"

"Stop!" Adam shouts.

Something lets go in Pasi's tense frame. He stops and tosses the pipe into the grass.

"I have actively sought out sin, but I am forgiven," he says wearily.

"By God, maybe," Margot replies. "But I need to know where you've been for the past two weeks."

"I've been in Alabama," he explains.

"In the United States?"

"We were visiting a church in Troy. We were there two months, and I got home the day before yesterday. There was a revivalist meeting on a wooden bridge with a roof." Pasi smiles. "Like the barrel of a cannon filled with prayer and song, that in itself made the whole trip worthwhile."

Margot and Adam hold on to Pasi while they confirm his story with the passport authority. It checks out, and they apologize for troubling him, get back in the car, and drive off through the dark forest.

"So did you see the light?" Adam says after a while.

"Almost."

"I need to go home."

"Okay," she says. "I can talk to Thomas Apel on my own."

"No," Adam says.

"We know he isn't violent."

Of the five hundred names on their list, Thomas Apel is the only one who suffers from borderline personality disorder.

"Let's do that tomorrow," Adam pleads.

"Okay," she lies.

He glances sideways at her. "It's just that Katryna doesn't like being at home on her own," he confesses.

"I get it. You've been away a lot recently."

"It's not that."

She drives slowly along the winding forest road. The baby in her stomach moves and stretches out. "I could talk to Jenny," Margot says. "I'm sure she could go and be with Katryna."

"I don't think so," he says.

"What?" She laughs.

"Well . . ."

"Are you worried something would happen?"

"Stop it," Adam says, squirming in his seat.

Margot picks up a cookie and waits for him to say whatever he's trying to say.

"It's just that I know Katta, and she wouldn't want me to arrange for someone to keep her company. She just wants me to prove that I care about our relationship. I'll go home as soon as we've spoken to Thomas Apel."

"Okay." Margot can't help feeling relieved that Jenny isn't going to have to spend the night with Katryna.

83

IT TURNS OUT SOFA ZONE IS ON KVICKSUNDS ROAD, CLOSE to the train station.

Erik and Joona are driving along next to a barbed-wire fence, toward thirty or so parked garbage trucks. Gray drizzle is falling, sparkling like sand.

The little monkey is swinging from the ignition key.

In the distance, white smoke billows from a chimney beyond a tall transmission tower.

They pass wide empty roads between low industrial buildings. Barbed-wire fences glint in front of parking lots. The windshield wipers sweep the rain aside, leaving a dirty triangle beyond their reach.

"Pull over," Joona says.

Erik drives around an old tire by the side of the road, slows, and stops.

They stare at the big, corrugated-metal building. Rust has trickled down from the screws holding up the large sign: SOFA ZONE.

"This is the Zone, isn't it?" Erik says seriously.

"Yes," Joona says, and drifts off in thought.

As soon as the wipers stop, tiny raindrops quickly form little streams on the windshield.

The Zone's only window is in the office at the front; it's grimy and covered with bars. In the parking spaces next to the fence stand nine cars and two motorcycles.

"What are we going to do?" Erik says after a while.

"If Rocky is here, we try to get him out," Joona says. "And if he doesn't agree to that, you'll have to question him here, but . . . we need more than the fact that the preacher takes drugs, wears makeup, and—"

"I know, I know."

"We need an address, a name," he concludes.

"So how do we get inside?"

Joona opens the door, and cool air brings the smell of wet grass into the car. He can hear a train over the worsening rain.

They leave the car and cross the road. As the rain cools the ground, mist rises from the tarmac.

"How does your hip feel?" Erik asks.

"Fine."

They go through the gates. There's wet cardboard on the ground, with disintegrating labels for three-seat sofas and recliners. Through the filthy window, they can see that the office is dark.

A car pulls up in the parking lot, and a man in a dark gray suit gets out and walks around the far end of the building.

They wait a few moments, then follow him along the windowless wall. As they pass the car, Joona takes a picture of its license plate with his phone.

At the end of the warehouse is a concrete loading bay with metal steps. Beside the large garage loading door is a smaller steel door. The man has disappeared.

Erik and Joona exchange glances, then continue around the corner.

Pieces of polystyrene packaging swirl across the wet ground.

At the back of the warehouse is a dumpster surrounded by thistles. All the way to the fence are mounds of wet sand.

Their feet leave prints in the sand. The man they were following didn't come this way.

The steel door by the loading bay must be the entrance to the building.

They cross the sand, feeling the rain drip down their necks. Close to the far corner is another metal door at the bottom of a flight of steps, with metal rails to help move trashcans up and down.

"Give me the car keys."

Erik hands them to him, and he removes the little monkey and the keys from the metal ring and hands them back. He straightens the metal and makes a hook at the end. He pulls a ballpoint pen from his pocket, snaps off the clip, sticks it into the lock, then inserts the straightened key ring, pushes the clip upward, and turns the lock.

84

THE BULB HANGING FROM THE CEILING IS BURNED OUT. THE floor is stained from leaking trash, and the four dumpsters reek of rancid food. The tattered remnant of a list of rules and regulations hangs on the wall. In the weak light from outside, Joona can see another door at the far end of the room.

"Come on," he says to Erik.

He cautiously opens the door and peers into a small kitchen with a buckled drain board. Rhythmic thuds echo through the walls. The ceiling lamp is on, but there's no one around. On a table is a cutting board with a grease-stained paper bag, surrounded by crumbs and sugar crystals.

There are two closed wooden doors at the opposite end of the room. The first is locked, but the second isn't.

Through the second door is an empty locker room, where they can hear music through the walls.

They pass three shower cubicles, a mirrored makeup table, and a row of lockers. Someone flushes a toilet behind a closed door.

They hurry through the room and find themselves in a narrow hallway lined with ten doors. The small rooms off the hallway have no windows and are furnished with thin beds with shiny plastic mattresses.

Behind a closed door someone is moaning mechanically.

The only light comes from strings of fairy lights draped across the ceiling. Little hearts and flowers illuminate the bare walls in weak flickering colors.

The hallway leads to a large storeroom with foil-covered ventilation pipes running across the ceiling.

In the flashing lights from a stage, they can make out some thirty men and maybe ten women. There are sofas and armchairs everywhere. Along one wall is a row of plastic-wrapped pallets of furniture. It's almost too dark to discern faces.

The throbbing music keeps repeating over and over.

On the stage a naked woman is dancing around a vertical metal pole.

Joona and Erik walk forward carefully in the weak light. The room smells damp.

They keep an eye out for Rocky's bulky frame. He should be visible against the light of the stage if he stands up.

They know this is a gamble. Rocky may already have been here and left. But if he managed to get any money, he would have bought heroin, in which case he probably stayed in the Zone.

A drunk is trying to negotiate a price with a woman. One of the guards appears quickly and says something that leaves the man nodding.

The music changes, blending seamlessly into a different rhythm. The woman on the stage squats with her thighs spread wide on either side of the pole.

A guard is over by the bar, gazing out at the room with a motionless face.

Joona sees a black German shepherd moving among the furniture. It looks accustomed to being there as it eats something from the floor, sniffs, and moves on.

A large man emerges from the hallway. He blows his nose and heads toward the bar. Joona moves aside and tries to keep an eye on him.

"It's not him," Erik says.

They stop by the wall not far from the stage. It's almost completely dark, but the reflected glow from the lights on the ceiling illuminates an assortment of shirts and faces.

A man in black-rimmed glasses sits in front of the stage on a red armchair with a label hanging from its arm. On the back of the man's hand is a tattoo of a cross with a shining star at its center.

On a low table, two bottles clink together in time with the rhythm of the bass. There are very few drugs in sight. Someone is snorting cocaine, a couple more slip pills between their lips, but sex is clearly the main commodity being traded here.

A young woman in a black latex bikini and a studded collar comes over to Erik, smiles, and says something he can't make out. She runs a hand through her short blond hair as she bats her eyelids at him. When he shakes his head, she moves on to the next man.

A movie is showing on a television screen behind the bar: an aggressive man is walking around a room, hitting doors and pulling drawers open. A woman is shoved into the room, turns and tries to open the door again. The man goes over to her, pulls her backward by her hair, and hits her face so hard that she falls to the floor. Just off to one side of Erik and Joona stands a man with a coarse face and fleshy forehead. The shoulders of his gray jacket are wet from the rain.

"Anatoly? I handed my money over when I was searched," he says gruffly.

"I know, welcome," says a voice that sounds adolescent.

Joona moves sideways and sees that it belongs to a tall, very young man with yellowish skin and dark rings under his eyes.

"I was thinking of going to the room. Can I buy two wraps of brown?"

"You can buy whatever you want," the young man replies. "We've got some top quality from southern Helmand, smack from Iran, tramadol, or ..."

Their conversation trails off as they move among the sofas and people.

The dog trots after them and licks the young man's hand. Joona falls in behind them and sees them turn off to the right at the side of the stage.

Erik manages to stumble into a low coffee table. A beer bottle topples and rolls to the floor. He goes a different way, squeezing around a leather sofa.

The guard by the stage watches him.

A young woman with round, pockmarked cheeks is sitting astride a man in a leather vest. He twirls a lock of her dark hair around his index finger as he talks on his phone.

In the darkness, Joona can no longer see the young man who was dealing heroin. There are too many people now. He looks around and sees the black dog slip through a swaying beaded curtain. The beads settle long enough to form the Mona Lisa's face briefly before they part again and a young woman with bare breasts and a pair of tight leather pants walks out.

85

THE SMALL BEADS TINKLE AS ERIK AND JOONA PASS THROUGH the Mona Lisa. The air is suddenly thick with sweet smoke, sweat, and dirty clothes. The room is filled with worn sofas and armchairs. They can still hear the thud of the heavy bass from the stage.

Seminaked people are sitting on the sofas or on the floor. Most of them look as though they're asleep, while others twist around lethargically.

They're all moving slowly, drifting through the realm of the high.

Erik and Joona pass a middle-aged woman sitting on a stained sofa with no cushions. She's wearing jeans that are too big for her and a flesh-colored bra. Her face is thin and focused as she holds her lighter under a crumpled piece of tin foil, then hurriedly inhales through a small plastic straw. A slender curl of smoke twines up toward the corrugated metal roof.

The cement floor is littered with cigarette butts, candy wrappers, plastic bottles, syringes, condoms, empty packs of pills, and a bundle of fabric samples.

Through the smoke, Joona can see the man named Anatoly sitting with the new guest on a sofa that's been sliced open, its stuffing hanging out.

Joona and Erik weave through the furniture.

A skinny man in his seventies is sitting on a stained flowery sofa with two young women.

On the floor behind it, a man lies unconscious in underwear and white socks. He looks almost like a child, but his eyes and cheeks are sunken. The syringe is gone, but the needle with its little plastic end sticks out of a vein in the back of his hand. On an armchair beside him sits a woman with a blank expression. After a while, she bends forward and pulls the needle from his hand, then drops it on the floor.

A guard drags a man who has thrown up. Joona can't help thinking that this place is the complete opposite of the rich kids' saturnalias.

No wishes come true in the Zone. Here there are only prisoners and slaves, and the money flows in only one direction. Everyone is alone in their addiction, slowly being drained of all they have until they die.

He glances behind him and sees Anatoly rise and walk through the room. The black dog follows him.

A fat man in camouflage trousers and a black jacket pushes away a woman in pink underwear and high heels. She goes back and tries to kiss his hands as she begs him for a fix. The man, impatient, tells her to pull herself together, that she hasn't earned enough.

"I can't, they hurt me, they—"

"Shut up, I don't give a fuck. You need to do three more customers," he says.

"But, darling, I don't feel good, I need—"

She tries to stroke his cheek, but he grabs her hand, pulls her little finger, and bends it sharply backward. It happens so quickly that at first the woman doesn't seem to realize what's going on. She stares wide-eyed at her broken finger.

A man with a salt-and-pepper mustache walks over to them, exchanges a few words with the other man, then pulls the sobbing woman through the room toward the curtain. She stumbles and loses a shoe. He hits her, and she falls over, dragging a lamp down with her.

Joona and Erik move out of the way.

The man drags the woman to her feet, and the lamp rolls away and shines straight into the face of a large bearded man.

It's Rocky Kyrklund.

He's sitting completely naked in a red armchair, asleep. His head is leaning forward, and his beard looks as if it has grown into the hair on his chest. He's injected himself in his right leg, and dark blood is trickling down his ankle.

Rocky isn't alone. Beside him, on a sofabed with no mattress, sits a woman with bleached-blond hair, wearing a brown bra. Her pale blue panties are on the floor next to her. A Band-Aid is hanging half off her knee.

She holds a lighter under a sooty spoon and stares with glassy eyes at the small bubbles forming in the liquid. She licks her lips as she waits for the powder to dissolve, leaving the spoon full of pale yellow liquid.

Erik steps over a footstool and walks over to them, smelling the acrid aroma of heroin and hot metal. He comes to a halt.

"Rocky?" Erik says in a low voice.

Rocky slowly raises his head. His eyelids are heavy, his pupils like pinpricks of black ink.

"Judas Iscariot," he mumbles when he sees Erik.

"Yes," Erik says.

Rocky smiles happily and slowly closes his eyes. The woman next to him puts a cotton ball in the solution, holds her syringe on top of it to suck up the liquid, then attaches a needle to the syringe.

Joona notices that the man in camouflage pants is sitting on a chair outside the staff room again, looking at his phone. At the other end of the room, the man with the gray mustache disappears through the beaded curtain with the woman.

"Do you remember telling me about the unclean preacher?" Erik asks, squatting down in front of Rocky.

Rocky opens his tired eyes and shakes his head. "Is that supposed to be me? The preacher?"

"I don't think so. I think you meant someone else," Erik says. "You talked about a man in makeup with scarred veins."

Next to them, the woman uses her panties as a tourniquet around her arm, tightening them as hard as she can by twisting a pen through them a couple of times.

"Do you remember him killing a woman here at the Zone?"

"No." Rocky grins.

"She was known as Tina, but her real name was Natalia," Erik goes on.

"Yes, that—that was him, that was the preacher," Rocky mutters.

The woman on the sofabed looks for a vein in the usual places, a soft spot without too many scars.

"I need to know. Are we talking about a real preacher, a priest?"

Rocky nods and closes his eyes.

"Which church?" Erik asks.

Rocky murmurs something, and Erik leans forward until he can smell his rancid breath.

"The preacher is jealous, just like God," he whispers.

The woman inserts the needle, and a drop of blood mixes with the yellow liquid before she injects it. She unties the tourniquet and lets out a long groan as the kick washes through her. She stretches her legs, tenses her ankles, then relaxes as her body goes completely soft.

"We believe the preacher has murdered at least five women, and we need a name, a parish, or an address," Erik says.

"What are you saying?" Rocky mutters, closing his eyes again.

"You were going to tell me about the preacher," Erik persists. "I need a name, or—"

"Stop badgering him," the woman says, lying back against Rocky's hairy thigh.

"Say hello to Ying," Rocky murmurs, stroking her head clumsily.

While Erik tries to get Rocky to remember, Joona is keeping an eye on their surroundings. The fat man in the camouflage pants gets up from the chair outside the staff room and peers across the room. He puts his phone in his pocket and sets off through the sofas, stopping by a man who's lying with his eyes closed, a lit cigarette between his lips. Then he returns to his place.

"You want me to tell you things," Rocky says. "But all I remember from purgatory is that I was sitting in a little monkey cage . . . and there were long wooden poles with glowing ends—"

"Blah, blah, blah," Ying interrupts.

"I howled, tried to get away, tried to protect myself with my food bowl . . . blah, blah, blah." He smiles.

"Seriously," Erik says more loudly. "I'll leave you alone, if you can just tell me something that will help us find him."

It looks as though Rocky's dozed off. His mouth slips open a few millimeters, and a string of saliva dribbles into his beard.

The man with the gray mustache comes back from the other side of the room. The curtain sways behind him, letting a yellow glow into the room before the Mona Lisa's face re-forms.

"We can't stay here much longer," Joona tells Erik.

Ying tries to put her panties on, but they catch between her toes, and she leans back and rests with her eyes shut.

"My brain is mush," Rocky mumbles. "You need to—"

"Blah, blah, blah," Ying says.

"Give me a name," Erik persists.

"You're probably going to have to hypnotize me if . . ."

"Can you stand up?" Erik asks. "Let me help you."

Joona sees the fat man in the camouflage pants get up from his chair again. He's speaking on his phone as he makes his way toward them.

The woman in the studded collar is in the doorway leading to the stage, holding the curtain open. She seems to be hesitating about whether to come in.

Behind her, Joona catches a glimpse of a tall hooded figure in a baggy yellow oilskin raincoat, the kind fishermen used to wear.

At first he doesn't understand how he knows he's staring at the preacher, but his mind suddenly brings a moment from the past into sharp focus.

"Erik," Joona says quietly. "The preacher is here. He's over there behind the curtain, in a yellow raincoat."

The woman in the studded collar waves to someone and stumbles into the room. The beads of the curtain swing back and sway in front of the yellow-clad figure.

And now Joona remembers. The last thing he heard before he collapsed in the storage locker was Filip Cronstedt describing the thin man who had been filming Maria Carlsson. The man with the camera was wearing a yellow oilskin raincoat, like the fishermen in Lofoten.

Joona starts walking, but the man in the camouflage pants steps around the flowery sofa and stops him.

"I have to ask you and your friend to come with me," he says.

"Erik," Joona says, "you saw him, didn't you? Over there by the beaded curtain. That's the preacher. You have to follow him, try to get a look at his face."

"This club is for members only," the man says.

"We were thinking of buying a sofa," Joona says, as Erik hurries toward the curtain.

86

THE FAT MAN SHOUTS AT HIM TO STOP, BUT ERIK CONTINUES, weaving quickly between the sofas. The man yells at Joona to move out of the way. An armchair gets shoved backward, making a scraping sound on the floor.

"*Pyydän anteeksi*," Joona says in Finnish, stopping him again.

The fat man brushes Joona's hand away, steps back, and pulls out a projectile Taser.

"*Nyt se pian sattutaa*," Joona goes on with a smile.

He takes a step forward out of the line of fire, pushes the Taser aside, and kicks the fat man in the knee, making his leg buckle. The man gasps, and two projectiles with spiral wires slam into the back of a sofa. Joona twists the Taser out of the man's hand and hits him in the collarbone with it, then wraps the wires around his neck and pulls. The man collapses to the floor, rolls over, and tries to get up. Joona forces him down with his foot, winds the wires around his hand, and pulls them tighter until the man loses consciousness and slumps to the floor.

Erik disappears through the beaded curtain next to the stage.

The door of the staff room at the other end of the room opens. A broad-shouldered man in a shiny jacket emerges with a phone to his ear and looks around.

Joona crouches to stay out of sight but knows he has to stop the man from going after Erik.

Rocky still has his eyes closed, and a cigarette between his lips. The prostitute with the studded collar pushes a used tissue between the cushions of a sofa and walks over to Joona in her high heels.

"Want to go to a room? I can show you a good time," she says, moving closer.

"Stay out of the way," he replies abruptly.

She wipes her mouth and starts toward the beaded curtain.

The man in the shiny jacket has seen Joona and heads toward him, pushing a chair over as he approaches. Joona rises and sees that the man is hiding a weapon by his hip, a high-caliber pistol with a short barrel.

The fat man is lying on his back, untangling the wires from his neck, coughing and trying to get up.

The man in the shiny jacket stops in front of Joona, the flowery sofa between them, and screws a silencer on to his Sig Pro. "I'll shoot you in both knees unless you come with me," he says.

Joona holds up one hand in a calming gesture and tries to back away, but the fat man on the floor grabs his legs.

"I didn't know this was a private club," Joona says, trying to pull his legs free.

The armed man has finished fitting the silencer. He raises the gun and squeezes the trigger. Joona throws himself aside, lands on his shoulder, and hits his temple on the floor.

There's no sound as the gun goes off, but the powder hangs in the air, and a naked man behind Joona stands up with blood streaming from a bullet hole in his stomach. A woman screams and hurries away from him.

"I'm gonna kill you," the man with the gun pants, climbing up onto the sofa to see over the back of it.

Joona grabs the toppled lamp and swings the heavy base in a semicircle. It hits the man in the shoulder, and he staggers to one side. The cable clatters on the floor as it snakes along behind. The man leans against the back of the sofa. Before he has time to fire, Joona reaches him, knocks the pistol aside, and punches him squarely in the throat.

Joona grabs the warm barrel of the pistol and feels a heavy blow to his cheek as he bends the weapon upward.

The man recoils, clutching his throat. He can't breathe, and saliva is dribbling from his gaping mouth.

Joona takes a step back, twists the gun around, and shoots the man through his right lung. Instead of a loud bang, the only sound is a sharp click. The empty shell bounces off the cement floor.

The man staggers, trying to cover the entry hole with his hand, coughs, then slumps back onto the sofa.

The fat man gets unsteadily to his feet holding a knife. One of his shoulders is drooping, and the Taser is still dangling from the wires around his neck.

Joona glances at the beaded curtain.

The fat man takes a couple of steps and jabs with the knife. Joona backs into a table as the tip of the blade touches his jacket. He follows the knife as it moves, holds it aside with the pistol, twists his body, and rams his right elbow into the man's cheek with immense force. The man's head snaps sideways, spraying droplets of sweat in the direction of the blow. Joona moves with him, takes a long stride to keep his balance, and feels a stab of pain from his hip.

As the man slumps unconscious to the floor, Joona moves out of the way and scans the room.

Very soon it will be impossible to get out. Crouching, he makes his way toward the curtain with the pistol pointing at the floor.

The new customer who bought heroin from Anatoly is lying lifeless beside his sofa. His lips are gray, and his eyes are open.

Joona steps around a low glass table and sees the woman in the studded collar heading between the sofas toward him.

"Take me away from here with you," she whispers, with desperation in her eyes. "Please, I'm begging you, I have to get away from here."

"Can you run?"

She smiles at him, and then her head suddenly jerks. A cascade of blood squirts from her temple.

Joona spins around as a bullet slams into the back of the chair next to him and stuffing sprays out across the floor. The man with the gray mustache is approaching with a raised pistol.

Smoke is rising from the barrel.

Joona takes aim, lowers the barrel a couple of millimeters, then fires three times. It sounds like the gun isn't loaded, but a cloud of blood explodes behind the man.

The man takes another two steps before collapsing on top of two women, dropping his pistol, and extending his hand toward a footstool.

The woman in the studded collar is still standing. Blood is pumping from her temple and running down her body. She looks at Joona, and her mouth opens as if she's trying to speak.

"I'll get help," he says.

Bewildered, she touches her bloody hair, then falls sideways onto an armchair and curls up as if to sleep.

In the distance, a round-shouldered man is approaching at a crouch, using the sofas as cover. Joona runs the last part of the way. A bullet hits the wall beside him, throwing out a shower of plaster. He ducks through the beaded curtain, tucks the pistol close to his body, and walks as fast as he can toward the narrow hallway.

A fat man is dancing on the stage with his shirt outside his pants.

There's no sign of Erik. Joona starts running as soon as he reaches the hallway.

He can hear his pursuers behind him as he enters the locker room and quickly locks the door. Someone is in the shower, and the floor creaks with their weight. Joona runs past two women standing in front of the makeup table.

In the kitchen a short man is frying frozen meatballs on the stove. He barely has time to grab a knife before Joona shoots him in the thigh.

The man falls to the floor, and Joona hears him scream as he runs across the old cardboard boxes in the waste storage room and emerges out of the back of the building. He runs around the warehouse as fast as he can, through tall weeds, then out through the gates, along a barbed-wire fence and a van.

Erik's car is gone. Joona sets off with a slight limp toward Högdalsplan to alert the police and emergency services.

87

THERE'S BARELY ANY TRAFFIC, AND ERIK MAKES SURE TO keep a safe distance between his car and the car in front. The preacher is driving a blue Peugeot that is so dirty, it's impossible to see the license plate. Erik's only plan is to follow it as long as he can without being seen.

The amber glow of the streetlights fills the car, then vanishes between the lampposts, like slow breathing.

Erik wonders if the preacher was at the Zone to buy drugs or to meet Rocky.

What has happened to Joona? Concern flutters in his chest.

At the club, Erik didn't look back, just did what he had to do.

He passed through the bead curtain and pushed past the crowd.

In the flickering light from the stage he suddenly caught sight of the yellow raincoat. The preacher was heading for the exit and Erik followed him through the metal door and out onto the loading bay.

Joona seemed so sure of what he had said that the only thing on Erik's mind was that he mustn't lose the preacher now that they were so close.

The yellow oilskin glinted in the darkness over by the cars, and Erik followed as quickly as he could without being heard. The preacher walked out through the gates and stopped in front of the blue Peugeot.

Erik has now been following the red taillights for fifteen minutes. He speeds up a little on a long straightaway past a school.

The sparse lights of a large apartment building flicker through the greenery.

A night bus pulls out from a stop, and Erik has to slow down. He loses sight of the preacher, so he presses his foot down and passes the bus on the wrong side of a double yellow line.

The traffic light up ahead turns red. Erik speeds up, swerves, and just makes it past the back of a car crossing his path.

It's already too late, though. The blue Peugeot has turned off to the right. Its lights flicker between the houses.

There's no time to think. He doesn't want to lose the preacher.

He turns into the next road, trying to guess where the Peugeot is likely to be going as he passes lush gardens and dark houses.

He brakes and turns left, glancing at the side of a mailbox, then accelerates hard past a number of houses. He realizes that there's a dead end up ahead, beyond the next intersection, and brakes, sending the tires skidding across the tarmac. He jerks the steering wheel and swerves sharply to the right.

The back wheels lose their grip, and there's a crash as the rear hits a transmission pole.

He accelerates up a hill, reaches the top, and just manages to spot the preacher drive into a tunnel.

He slows and feels his hands shaking on the steering wheel. The side mirror has come loose again and is dangling by its wires.

Someone has sprayed "Another world is possible" on the tunnel's concrete walls.

Everything goes dark, then a moment later he emerges into an area of attractive four-story buildings.

The blue Peugeot passes a garbage truck, and Erik wonders if the preacher lives here.

The idea of the preacher having an ordinary life seems incredible: a man who stabs knives into the faces of his victims long after they're dead, then goes home to his lovely villa with apple trees and lawn sprinklers and sits down to watch television with his family.

Erik follows the blue car as it turns right off Korpmosse Road and into Klensmeds Road. Just after the third side street, the preacher slows down and stops.

Without changing his speed, Erik drives past the blue car and looks in the rearview mirror just as the light inside the car goes out. He passes a small patch of woods, turns into the next road, stops, and hurries back. The yellow oilskin raincoat is just disappearing into the forest to the left of the road.

88

THE CHURCH OF JESUS CHRIST OF LATTER-DAY SAINTS IS located on Järfalla Road, next to a large parking lot. It's a low building with terracotta-colored walls, a paneled roof, and a red tower rising from the center of a circular stone foundation.

Stake president Thomas Apel lives with his wife and two children in a cement-gray villa very close to the temple. The red tower is visible above the trees and tiled roofs.

Adam and Margot are sitting in the living room with glasses of lemonade. Thomas and his wife, Ingrid, are across from them. Thomas is a skinny man, dressed in gray pants, a white shirt, and a pale gray tie. His face is clean-shaven and thin, and he has fair eyebrows and a narrow, crooked mouth.

Thomas has told Margot he was at home with his family when the murders were committed.

"Is there anyone who can vouch for that?" Margot asks, looking at Ingrid.

"Well, of course, the children were at home," Thomas's wife says amiably.

"No one else?" Adam asks.

"We lead a quiet life," Thomas replies, as if that explained everything.

"You have a lovely home," Margot says, glancing around the room.

An African mask is hanging on the wall next to a painting of a woman in a black dress with a red book in her lap.

"Thank you," Ingrid says.

"Each family is a kingdom," Thomas says. "Ingrid is my queen, the girls princesses."

"Naturally." Margot smiles.

She looks at Ingrid's face, free of makeup, at the small pearls in her earlobes, and at the long dress that reaches to her neck and halfway over her hands.

"You probably think we dress in a very old-fashioned, boring way," Ingrid says when she sees Margot looking.

"You look nice," Margot lies, as she tries to find a comfortable position on the deep sofa with the crocheted throw on the back.

Thomas leans forward and pours more lemonade into her glass, and she thanks him soundlessly.

"Our lives aren't boring," Thomas says. "There's nothing boring about not using drugs, or alcohol or tobacco, or coffee or tea."

"Why not coffee?" Adam asks.

"Because the body is a gift from God," he replies simply.

"So you've never had coffee?" Adam asks.

"Of course, it isn't set in stone," Thomas says lightly. "It's just guidance."

"Okay." Adam nods.

"But if we listen to this guidance, the Lord promises that the angel of death will pass our home and not kill us." Thomas smiles.

"How quickly does the angel come if you mess up?" Margot mutters.

"You said you wanted to look at my calendar?" Thomas says, the veins in his temples darkening slightly.

"I'll get it," Ingrid volunteers, rising to her feet.

"I'll just get some water," Margot says, and follows her.

Thomas makes a move to rise, but Adam stops him by asking about the role of the stake president.

Ingrid is standing at a desk looking for the calendar when Margot walks into the immaculately tidy kitchen. "Could I have some water?" Margot asks.

"Yes, of course," Ingrid says.

"Were you here last Sunday?"

"Yes," the woman replies, and a tiny frown appears across the bridge of her nose. "We were at home."

"What did you do?"

"We did . . . the usual. We had dinner and watched television."

"What was on television?" she asks.

"We only watch Mormon television," Ingrid says, checking that the faucet is properly turned off.

"Does your husband ever go out alone in the evening?"

"No."

"Not even to the temple?"

"I'll take a look in the bedroom," the woman says, her cheeks flushing as she leaves the kitchen.

Margot drinks, then sets the glass down on the counter and goes back out to the living room. She can see tension in Adam's face, and a sheen of sweat above his top lip.

"Are you on any medication?" Adam asks.

"No," Thomas replies, wiping his palms on his pale gray trousers.

"No psychoactive drugs, no antidepressants?" Margot asks, sitting down on the sofa again.

"Why do you want to know that?" he asks, looking at her with calm, blank eyes.

"Because you received treatment for mental illness twenty years ago."

"That was a difficult time for me, before I listened to God."

He falls silent and looks warmly at Ingrid, who's just come back in. She's standing in the doorway with a red planner in her hand.

Margot takes the planner, puts on her reading glasses, and leafs through the pages.

"Do you have a video camera?" Adam asks as Margot skims through the planner.

"Yes," he replies with a quizzical look.

"Can I see it?"

Thomas's Adam's apple bobs above the knot of his tie. "What for?" he asks.

"Just routine," Adam replies.

"Well, unfortunately it's being repaired." Thomas smiles, stretching his crooked mouth.

"Where?"

"A friend's fixing it for me," he says softly.

"Can I have the name of the friend, please?"

"Of course," Thomas murmurs.

Adam's phone rings inside his jacket. "Excuse me," he says, standing and looking for his phone in his jacket as he turns his back on Thomas.

Through the window, he sees a neighbor on the other side of the fence looking at them. In the reflection he can also see himself, his thick hair and heavy eyebrows. He finds his phone: Adde, an IT technician with National Crime, who also happens to live in Hökmossen.

"Another video!" Adde practically screams.

"We'll be there as soon as—"

"It's your wife on the video, it's Katryna—"

Adam doesn't hear anything after that. He walks straight into the entryway, reels into the wall with his shoulder, pulling down a framed photograph of two smiling girls.

"Adam?" Margot calls. "What's going on?"

She leaves the planner on the sofa, stands up, and accidentally knocks over a glass of lemonade on the coffee table.

Adam has already reached the front door. Margot can't see his face. She feels sick, clutches her stomach, and follows him.

He runs down the path to the car.

He's started the car before she's even out the door. She stops, panting for breath, and watches him rev the engine, perform a sharp U-turn in the road, skid, and drive into a hockey net that some children have erected near the roadside. She heads toward him and is gesturing for him to stop when her phone rings.

89

KATRYNA YOUSSEF IS SITTING ON THE WHITE SOFA IN FRONT of the television. She's wearing her soft blue Hollister sweatpants and a pink T-shirt.

She knows the polish on her new nails dried a long while ago, but she still spreads her fingers out as she reaches for her glass of wine. Since Adam isn't home, she can do her nails. Otherwise he goes outside and sits in the car to avoid getting a headache from the fumes.

She takes a sip of wine, then looks down at the iPad in her lap. Caroline hasn't updated her status yet. She hasn't said anything for an hour now, and she can't have been in the shower all that time, surely?

Katryna is watching an old movie called *Face/Off* on television but is finding it rather far-fetched.

She has to work tomorrow, so shouldn't really wait up for Adam.

I'm not going to either, she thinks, glancing at the window as a bush in the garden brushes hard against the glass.

She slips her hand inside her loose sweatpants and starts to masturbate, shuts her eyes for a few seconds, then stares out at the yard, still masturbating. But she stops when it occurs to her that their neighbor might be bringing back the rake he borrowed earlier that evening. She can't be bothered to close the curtains, and anyway, she's more bored than horny.

Katryna yawns and scratches her ankle. Even though she ate a tuna salad earlier, she's hungry. She continues looking at the iPad, scrolls back, and reads her own comments, then writes another one.

She looks at the latest pictures of Caroline Winberg, the woman she's practically stalking.

Caroline was discovered on the subway on her way to soccer practice and is now a supermodel. It's rumored that she won't get out of bed for less than twenty-five thousand dollars.

Katryna follows her on social media and always knows where she is and what she's doing. She reaches for the glass of wine again and shivers when she realizes that the outdoor lights aren't working. The bushes look black against the glass. She's not sure if the lights have worked at all that evening. It's not the first time they've gone out. Adam will have to check the fuse box. There's no way she's going down into the basement. Not after the break-in.

She sees her reflection in the dark window, drinks some more wine, and looks at her nails.

Someone broke in last Thursday when she and Adam were both at work, and now the lock on the basement door is broken. They tied a piece of rope around it so it feels locked if you pull it. Nothing of value was stolen—not the home theater system, the stereo, or the Xbox.

It's strange. Maybe they realized Adam is a detective and changed their minds.

Adam thinks it was just some bored teenagers. But it's still a little weird, Katryna thinks. They could have taken their whiskey and wine, or her jewelry or the Prada handbag that Adam gave her two years ago.

She's only discovered one missing object. A little cloth embroidered by her grandmother. Adam doesn't believe her. He figures it will turn up and refused to mention it in the police report.

Lamassu, the protective deity that her grandmother embroidered in pale red thread on white fabric, has always lain on the bookcase next to the silver crucifix.

Katryna knows someone took it.

The close-stitched cloth depicted a man with a braided beard, with the body of a bull and enormous angel's wings arching out from his back. When she was little, she didn't like the embroidery at all. Her mom said Lamassu watched over their home, but she could only see a monster.

Once again she thinks of the rope that Adam wound around the handle of the basement door and then tied to the water pipe. She's made him look through the house several times.

Other than the basement, the part of the house she finds creepiest is the large closet between the living room and the kitchen.

It's like a dressing room, with two unusually thick wooden doors. It used to be locked with a revolving wooden catch, but that's come loose. Now she and Adam just push the doors shut, but they move, rubbing against each other and opening slightly, as if someone's trying to peer out. Every home has its creepy corners, she thinks with a shudder. Rooms and spaces that have stored up childhood fears over the ages.

She drinks the last of the wine and gets up to go to the kitchen.

90

KATRYNA MOVES THE WINE BOX TO THE EDGE OF THE COUN-ter, then fills her glass under the little spigot, splashing some tiny red droplets on her hand.

The wind is rattling in the kitchen air vent. Through the glass door, she can see the empty street.

The two wooden doors of the large closet knock against each other, then close tighter.

She sets her glass down on a flyer from Sephora, licks the drops of wine from the back of her hand, and decides to keep the baby and not go through with the abortion.

The decision shouldn't be about Adam.

If he doesn't change, she can leave him.

Should she text Adam, explaining what she feels, and that this could be a new start for them? She walks slowly, keeping her eyes on the heavy wooden doors. She feels almost compelled to look at them—and stops when the far one opens slightly. She takes a deep breath and hurries past. She forces herself not to run, but the movement of the door sends a shiver down her spine. She thinks about their neighbor. He gave her a funny look when he borrowed the rake, and she wonders if he knew she was home alone.

Her iPad is dark, and she puts her finger on the screen and finds herself pointing straight at Caroline's smiling face when the screen comes back to life.

Katryna knows that if she turns her head to the left, she will see the closet doors reflected in the window at the back of the house.

She needs to stop this, it's turning into an obsession.

What if it was their neighbor who broke in and stole the cloth?

If you knew that the basement door was held shut only by a rope, you could get in without making any noise at all.

Katryna stands up and goes over to the window and is drawing the curtains when she thinks she sees someone running across the grass.

She leans closer.

It's hard to see in the dark.

A deer, it must have been a deer, she thinks, and closes the curtain with her heart pounding.

She sits on the sofa, switches the television off, and starts to text Adam. In the middle of a sentence her phone rings, scaring her so much that she jumps.

She doesn't recognize the number.

"Katryna," she says warily.

"Hello, Katryna," a man says quickly. "I'm one of Adam's colleagues at National Crime, and—"

"He's not—"

"Listen now," the man interrupts. "Are you at home?"

"Yes, I'm—"

"Go to the front door and leave the house. Don't worry about clothes or shoes, just go straight out into the street and keep walking."

"Can I ask why?"

"Are you on your way out?"

"I'm going now."

She stands up and starts through the room, looking toward the closet doors as she goes around the sofa, then turns toward the front door.

A person wearing a yellow raincoat is standing on the doormat with their back to her, closing the front door.

Katryna quickly moves backward, goes around the corner, and stops.

"There's someone in here," she whispers. "I can't get out."

"Lock yourself in a room, and leave your phone on."

"God, there's nowhere to—"

"Don't speak unless you absolutely have to. Go to the bathroom."

She walks on unsteady legs toward the kitchen when she sees that the doors to the closet have slid open slightly. She can't think straight and opens one of them, slips quickly inside, and stands beside the vacuum cleaner. She pulls the door closed behind her.

It's hard to close it properly when her fingers won't fit in the gap. She tries to hold the edge with her nails and pull it toward her.

She holds her breath when she hears footsteps in the room. They move off in the direction of the kitchen, as the doors knock against each other and slip open a couple of millimeters.

She waits in the darkness with her eyes wide and hears a kitchen drawer being opened. There's a metallic clattering sound, and she's breathing in short gasps, and suddenly she thinks of the relic in the church in Södertälje. Adam didn't want to go in with her, but she went and looked at it anyway. It was a fragment of bone belonging to Thomas, one of the apostles. The priest claimed the Holy Spirit was still present in the relic, in the yellow fragment of bone inside the glass tube on the marble table.

She reaches out her hand and tries to close the door but can't get a grip—her nails just slide over the wood. She moves carefully to the side, but the mop and bucket are in the way. The mop handle touches her winter coat, and a few empty hangers rattle softly.

She manages to pull the door closed but then loses her grip. It swings open slightly, and she can see a dark figure standing right outside.

91

THE DOOR IS YANKED OPEN, AND A MAN WITH A PISTOL STEPS backward. His mouth is half open, and his dark brown eyes are staring at her. A smell of sweat reaches her. She registers every detail in that moment: his worn jeans with turned-up cuffs, the grass stain on his right knee, his padded black nylon jacket, and the New York Yankees logo sewn badly onto his cap.

"I'm a police officer," he gasps, and lowers his gun.

"Oh, God," she whispers, and feels tears begin.

He takes her hand and leads her toward the entryway as he reports on his radio, "Katryna is unharmed, but the suspect fled through the kitchen door. . . . Yes, get the roadblocks set up, and send some dog units over here."

She walks beside the police officer, leaning against the wall, brushing against her beauty school diploma.

"Give me a moment," the officer says, and opens the front door to secure their exit.

Katryna bends down to put her sneakers on—as a cascade of blood sprays across the hall mirror. Then she hears the sharp crack of a gunshot, and the echo from the house on the other side of the road.

The plainclothes officer throws his arm out, manages to grab the coats, and pulls them down with him as he falls. He collapses on his back among the shoes. The hangers rattle as blood pulses from the bullet hole in his black jacket.

"Hide," he gasps. "Go and hide again."

Two more shots ring out, and Katryna moves backward. Someone is screaming like an animal outside. She stares at the wounded police officer, at the blood seeping along the cracks in the tile floor. A windowpane shatters as another shot echoes through the neighborhood.

Katryna runs at a crouch through the living room. She slips on the Tabriz rug and hits her shoulder against the wall but manages to keep her balance. In the hallway, she opens one of the closet doors. The mop handle falls out, pulling the red bucket with it, and the strainer comes loose and clatters to the floor. Katryna picks up the mop and tries to get it to stand up among the clothes. A jacket falls down, and the thick hose of the vacuum cleaner pushes the other door open.

She hears two more shots, leaves the closet, and hurries toward the kitchen. She sees the glass door and the darkness outside, opens the basement door, and starts down the steep staircase.

She's so frightened she can barely breathe. This must be a hate crime. The racists are upset about Adam buying a new Jaguar.

She can hear police cars through the stone walls and thinks she can hide in the boiler room until they catch the intruder.

Her anxiety increases as she heads farther down into the darkness.

She clings to the cool handrail, blinks, and opens her eyes wide but can hardly see a thing. She's walking carefully, but the steps still creak under her weight. Finally she reaches the tile floor. She blinks and can make out the washing machine, a paler shape in the darkness, next to the door with the rope around its handle. She turns around and moves in the opposite direction, past Adam's old pinball machine, and into the boiler room. She carefully closes the door behind herself and hears a whining sound.

Katryna stands still with her fingers on the door handle, listening. The pipes are clicking faintly, but otherwise everything is quiet.

She moves farther in, away from the door, thinking she'll just sit here. It won't be long, now that the police have arrived.

She hears the whimpering sound again. Very close to her.

She turns her head but can't see anything.

The whimpering becomes a weak wheezing sound.

It's coming from the safety valve of the hot water tank.

Katryna feels her way forward and finds the paint-stained stepladder standing against the wall. She unfolds it in silence and moves it to the wall, beneath the window up by the ceiling.

Someone has stolen Lamassu, she thinks. The embroidered cloth with her protective deity, her protector—that's why this is happening.

She can't stay in the house. She twists the two window latches and is pushing the little window open against the weeds when she feels a cold draft around her ankles.

Someone's coming up behind her, she's convinced of it. Someone got in through the basement door. They've cut the rope holding it closed and are on their way inside.

It's impossible to open the window. She tries again, but it keeps hitting something. Panting, she reaches out into the weeds and feels the lawnmower parked too close.

She tries to push it away with her hand, even though she can feel the stepladder sliding backward beneath her. She turns the wheel of the lawnmower by hand and manages to roll it a few centimeters. The window opens, and she starts to crawl out.

The door to the boiler room bursts open, and the light is switched on. The old starter switch makes the fluorescent tube flicker. She tries to scramble out as the stepladder is yanked away and clatters to the floor. Her legs thud against the wall, her knees sting, but she clings on to the frame and fights to pull herself up.

The first stab of the knife hits her back so hard, she hears the point scrape the concrete wall in front of her.

92

ADAM YOUSSEF IS LYING ON HIS STOMACH ON THE PAVED
path outside his home, with his hands cuffed behind his back.
His thigh is throbbing, and his black jeans are wet with blood,
but the superficial gunshot wound doesn't really hurt. Blue lights
from various vehicles are pulsing over the yard's dark greenery in
a peculiar rhythm.

A police officer presses his knee into Adam's shoulder blades
and yells at him to be quiet while he explains the situation to the
operational team.

"Katryna's still in there," Adam pants.

The operational lead officer is in direct contact with the head
of the Stockholm Rapid Response Unit, trying to coordinate their
efforts. The first team is forcing the windows and doors, securing
the entryway, and letting the paramedics through.

The officer who has been shot is rolled out onto a stretcher.

Adam tries to pull free but is struck so hard across the kidneys
that he loses his breath. He coughs and feels the police officer press
his knee against the back of his neck, grabbing his jacket, and roaring at him to lie still.

"I'm a police officer, and—"

"Shut up!"

The second officer takes Adam's wallet and backs away slightly.
The gravel crunches beneath his shoes as he looks at Adam's police
badge and ID.

"National Crime," he confirms.

The officer removes his knee from Adam's back and stands up, breathing hard. As the pressure is removed from his neck and lungs, Adam catches his breath and tries to roll over onto his side.

"You shot a plainclothes police officer," the officer says.

"He had my wife, I saw her with him and thought—"

"He was the first officer on the scene, and he was on his way out with her. Everyone had received that information."

"Just get her out!" Adam begs.

"What the hell are you two doing?" a woman shouts.

It's Margot. Adam sees her legs through the blackberry bushes by the road, as she walks through the gate and stops.

"He's a police officer," she says, and takes several shallow breaths. "It's his wife who—"

"He shot a colleague," one of the officers says.

"It was an accident," Adam says. "I thought—"

"Don't say anything more," Margot interrupts. "Where's Katryna?"

"I don't know. I don't know anything. Margot—"

"I'm going in," she says, and her feet move along the path.

"Tell her I love her," he whispers.

"Help him up," Margot tells the two officers. "And get those handcuffs off. Put him in one of the cars for now."

She starts toward the house with both hands around her stomach.

A young man from the rapid response unit comes out through the front door carrying his helmet. He passes Margot, throws up across the front steps, then continues down the garden path with a glazed look. He unfastens his bulletproof vest and lets it fall to the ground, makes it to the street, then leans on the hood of one of the cars.

The two officers take hold of Adam's arms, pull him up onto his feet, and lead him away from the house. He feels blood trickling down his thigh. They lead him to a patrol car and seat him in the back but leave the handcuffs on.

Another ambulance passes the cordon and is waved forward by

the police. Hearing the sharp clatter of a helicopter, Adam looks toward the front door to see if Margot is coming out with Katryna.

When National Crime received the fourth video, the system spun into action instantly, as it should.

One of the technicians was Adam's good friend. He recognized Katryna on the video and issued immediate emergency information to all of National Crime, then called Adam.

The officer closest to the house was a plainclothes detective. He was on the scene seven minutes after the police received the video.

93

IT FEELS LIKE AN ETERNITY BEFORE ADAM SEES MARGOT again. She's walking slowly, holding the handrail, then stops with her hand around her stomach. Her nose is pale, and her forehead is shining with sweat as she comes toward him out in the street.

"Get those fucking handcuffs off," she says with barely suppressed anger to the police officers.

They open the car door and hurry to free Adam. He massages his wrists and looks into Margot's dilated pupils. A wave of nausea rises in his stomach. "What's going on?" he asks, frightened.

She shakes her head, glances toward the house, and then looks back at him.

"Adam, I'm sorry. I can't tell you how sorry I am."

"What for?" he asks stiffly.

"Sit down," she says.

But he gets out of the car and stops in front of her, feeling strangely weightless. "Is it Katryna?" he asks. "Just tell me. Is she hurt?"

"Katryna's dead."

"I saw her in the doorway, I saw her . . ."

"Adam," she pleads.

"Are you sure? Did you speak to the paramedics?"

She hugs him, but he pulls free and takes a step back.

"I'm so terribly sorry," she says again.

"You're sure she's dead? I mean, the ambulance . . . what's the ambulance doing here if she's . . . ?"

"Katryna will stay here until forensics is finished."

"Can you tell me where she is?"

"In the boiler room. She must have hidden there."

The pain in Adam's thigh is suddenly throbbing and all-encompassing. He watches all the police officers leave the house and gather for a debriefing over by the command vehicle.

A flash of insight passes through his mind. His wife was almost safe, but he shot the police officer who was on his way out with her.

"I shot a colleague," he says.

"Don't think about that now. You're sleeping at my place tonight. I'll call the boss." She tries to take his arm, but he turns away.

"I need to be alone. Sorry, I . . ."

The helicopter is hovering a short distance away.

"Did they get the preacher?" he asks.

"Adam, we're going to get him. He's in the area, and we're deploying everything we have. Absolutely everything."

He nods a few times, then turns away. "Just give me a second," he whispers. He takes a few steps and picks at the branch of a bush.

"You have to stay here," Margot says.

Adam looks at her for a few seconds, then wanders slowly into the yard. He covers his face with his hands, pretending to try to absorb what Margot said, but he knows he needs to see Katryna, because he doesn't believe her. It can't be true, it isn't true, Katryna has nothing to do with this.

Adam starts walking around the house. The green hose is lying in the unmown grass. A swarm of gnats is visible in the shimmering blue light. It gets darker when he reaches the back of the house.

He sees himself as a black silhouette in the red dome of the round grill. He goes around the corner. The basement door is open. The rope has been cut. He moves inside. The lights are all on.

He can hear people walking around upstairs. A forensics officer is laying out walking plates.

Adam takes another step inside, and that's when he sees Katryna in the cold neon light of the boiler room. There's blood everywhere, on her sweatpants, her tank top, the floor. Her hair is tucked behind one ear, but most of her face is gone, hacked off. Dark blood glints across her rib cage, and her left hand appears to be squeezing the fingers of her right hand.

Adam staggers backward, hears the sound of his own breathing, stumbles over his own Wellington boots, and emerges into the garden again.

He's gasping for breath but can't get enough air into his lungs, and starts poking at his mouth.

Nothing makes sense. He turns to walk to the police car and is passing the compost heap when he hears a twig snap in the forest. An officer comes around the corner of the house and calls for him, but he heads in among the trees, following the sound of someone moving.

Behind him the floodlights are switched on, bathing his home and garden in light. The tree trunks shine gray, as if they were covered by a layer of ash. As if he were in an underground forest.

Twenty meters in, a man stands looking at him. Their eyes meet between the gently glowing stems, and it takes Adam a few seconds to recognize the man.

The psychiatrist, Erik Maria Bark.

It's like a lightning flash in his head when he realizes everything. Awareness hits him like an ax striking a block of wood.

Adam reaches down and pulls the little pistol from his ankle. There's a rasping sound as the Velcro comes loose. He feeds a bullet into the chamber, raises the pistol, and fires.

The shot hits a branch in front of Erik's face and is deflected, splinters flying up. The psychiatrist flinches.

Adam's hand is shaking as he tries to aim lower. The psychiatrist moves backward, and he fires again. The shot simply disappears, as dark branches sway between the two of them.

He sees the psychiatrist crouch and run, then slide down a slope and vanish behind a thick tree trunk. Adam follows but can no longer see him and runs straight into some fir branches. Police officers who heard his shots come running from the yard, and the edge of the forest is suddenly full of bright light.

"Put your gun down!" someone calls out. "Adam, put your gun down!"

Adam turns around and raises his arms.

"The killer's in the forest!" he gasps. "It's the hypnotist, it's the fucking hypnotist!"

94

ERIK TAKES A DEEP BREATH AND STARES UP AT THE NIGHT sky. He must have passed out after he fell. His back hurts badly. He scraped himself as he slid down the slope.

He stands up and reaches his hand out to the wet rock-face. He can smell moss and ferns, and a glow of bright lights flickers through the trees above.

He crouches and pushes through the undergrowth, moving a branch out of the way.

The distant barking of dogs merges with the noise of an approaching helicopter.

Erik followed the preacher down a narrow path, but the trees became denser, and it got so dark he lost track of him. He stood for a while and listened but heard only the wind through the branches high above. In the end he decided to go back to the car and wait there. Then sirens from a number of emergency vehicles all seemed to converge on the road on the far side of the woodland.

He began to walk in that direction. Maybe the police were closing in on the preacher.

The forest was overgrown and rocky, and it took time to make his way in the dark, but after a while he could see blue-gray lights flashing between the trees, and suddenly he was in front of Adam Youssef from National Crime.

Adam looked me in the eyes and shot at me, Erik thinks.

Loose stones slide under his feet, and he almost falls, so he grabs a branch, cutting his hand on something. His palm grows wet with blood, and he stops, gasping, trying to calm his breathing as he hears the helicopter above the treetops again.

Did they find out he hadn't told the whole truth? Do they think he's involved in the murders?

Erik thinks about how he lied to the police, how he withheld Rocky's alibi and kept quiet about what Björn Kern said under hypnosis.

The helicopter hovers above the trees, searching with spotlights, getting closer and closer. He needs to hide.

This is completely insane, Erik thinks, feeling the whirling air tug at his clothes. I was almost shot.

The helicopter sweeps on, and the searchlight moves through the forest, flickering through the tree trunks.

He's the person they're hunting.

Twenty meters away he sees two heavily armed officers with helmets, vests, and assault rifles. One of them turns in Erik's direction just as the light of the helicopter illuminates him through the tree canopy.

Adrenaline shoots through Erik's blood like an injection of ice.

A shot fires just as everything goes dark again. He sees the flare of the barrel. The bullet slams into the tree trunk immediately above his head.

Erik rushes at a crouch across a clearing without looking behind him, sliding down on his back, running through dense undergrowth until he can see streetlights through the branches.

He approaches the road with caution. A car drives past and some distance away he can see a roadblock, spike strips, patrol cars, and officers in black uniforms.

Erik hides behind some bushes, his back wet with sweat. The uniformed officers are close now. He can hear them talking into their radios, then they walk in the other direction.

His heart is beating so hard it hurts his throat.

He emerges on the street, not looking at the police, and walks straight across the tarmac road. With every meter the distance between him and the police is growing. He passes the Telefonplan subway station and is still heading away from the police operation when his phone rings, and it's Joona. "What's going on?" Erik tries to keep his voice steady. "The police are hunting me with a helicopter. They shot at me. This is crazy. I haven't done anything—I was just following the preacher—"

"Hang on, Erik, just hold on. Where are you now? Are you safe?"

"I don't know, I'm walking along an empty street, past Telefonplan. I don't understand any of this."

"You followed the preacher to Adam's home," Joona says. "His wife is the latest victim. She's dead."

"No . . ." Erik gasps.

"They're all panicking," Joona says darkly. "They seem to think you're guilty because—"

"So talk to them!" Erik interrupts.

"You were seen near the house right after the murder."

"Yes, but if I . . ." Erik hears a car approaching. He ducks into a doorway and turns his back to the street. "Can't I just turn myself in?" he asks after the car passes.

"Not right now," Joona replies.

"You don't trust the police?" Erik asks.

"They just tried to shoot you," Joona says. "There are people in the force who are out for revenge."

Erik runs his hands through his wet hair, struggling to understand all the improbable things that have happened in the past few days.

"What are my options?" he asks. "What do you think I should do?"

"If you can give me some time, I'll try to find out what's happening," Joona says. "I'll find out what they're saying about you internally, and if there's a safe way for you to turn yourself in."

"Okay."

"But you need to lie low," Joona says.

"How do I do that? What do I do?"

"They have your car, so you can't go home. You can't go to any of your friends. Ditch your phone after this conversation, because they can track it even when it's switched off. They're probably tracing it now, so we don't have much time."

"I understand."

Sweat is running down Erik's cheeks as he listens to Joona's advice.

"Find an ATM and take some money out. As much as you can, because this will be your only chance to do that. But before you withdraw the money, you need to figure out how to get to another part of town quickly, because they'll be ready if you make the slightest mistake."

"Okay."

"Buy a used pay-as-you-go phone and call me so I have the number," Joona goes on. "Don't contact anyone else. Sleep in a shelter that doesn't require ID."

"Everyone's going to believe I'm guilty," Erik says.

"Only until I find the preacher," Joona replies.

"If I can hypnotize Rocky, I know I could find out details that—"

"That's no longer possible," Joona interrupts. "He's back in custody."

95

WHEN JOONA GETS BACK TO HIS OLD OFFICE EARLY THE NEXT morning, Margot is sitting behind her desk wearing a T-shirt that says HEAD SUCKS. Her thick braid is almost unraveled, and she has dark rings under her eyes and deep lines around her mouth.

"I've been in an emergency meeting for senior officers," she tells him, helping herself to a bag of candy. "The investigation is now top priority. We're getting a lot more resources. A national alert has been issued, and they're preparing for a press conference tomorrow."

"How's Adam?" Joona asks.

"I don't know. He's been relieved of duty and doesn't want to see a counselor. He has his family around him, but—"

"Terrible," Joona says. He hopes Erik took his advice and destroyed his phone.

The large police and emergency services operation at Sofa Zone had to charter a bus to take everyone they'd apprehended to the custody unit in Huddinge while they waited for a decision from the prosecutor about arrests. The many dead and injured were assumed to be victims of a bloody power struggle for control of the heroin trade.

Rocky Kyrklund was taken into custody for possession of narcotics. He had eleven capsules each containing 250 milligrams of thirty percent heroin hidden in his clothes.

"We saw the murderer at the Zone. Erik followed him to Katryna," Joona says, leaning forward.

"How do you know that?"

"Erik didn't do it," Joona says.

"Joona"—Margot sighs—"you can talk about this with me. I know the two of you are friends, but be careful with the others."

"They need to know he's innocent."

"You don't want it to be Erik, but maybe he's been deceiving you," she says patiently.

"I saw a man in a yellow raincoat at the Zone, and I remembered what Filip Cronstedt said about a yellow oilskin. Erik followed him and ended up at Adam's."

"So how do you explain the fact that he knew all the victims, including Katryna?" Margot says, holding his gaze.

"When did he meet Katryna?"

"She came with us when Adam and I went to his house," she replies. "And Susanna Kern worked at Karolinska as a nurse. She was in a class where Erik was one of the lecturers. We have security camera footage of him talking to her."

Joona gestures with his hand as if to say the information is irrelevant.

"So why would Erik be known as the preacher?" he asks.

"He's smart. He tricked you. He can make Rocky remember anything he wants him to."

"Why?"

"Joona, I don't know everything yet, but Erik has been close to the investigation, and has been hampering our progress. We finally got a witness statement from Björn Kern, and he remembered that he had told Erik that Susanna's body was posed with her hand over her ear under hypnosis."

"So?"

"Erik knew the information about the ear would lead us to Rocky, and then to him, and—"

"That doesn't really make sense, Margot."

"And Erik visited Rocky at Karsudden a few days before we asked him to."

Joona's eyes turn cold as ice as he puts his hand on the folder. "This is all circumstantial," he says. "You know that, don't you?"

"It's enough to bring him into custody, and enough for a search warrant, enough for a national alert," she replies stiffly.

"It sounds to me like he's been conducting his own investigation, and the rest is just coincidence."

"He fits the profile. He's divorced, single, has a history of substance abuse, and—"

"So does half the police force," Joona interrupts.

"The murders are extremely voyeuristic. We know that Erik is obsessed with filming his patients, even under hypnosis."

"That's just so he doesn't have to take notes."

"But he has thousands of hours in his archive, and . . . and a stalker is almost always slow, methodical. The investment in time is part of the ownership process, part of the relationship they create with the victim."

"Margot, I hear what you're saying, but could you at least entertain the possibility that Erik is innocent?" Joona asks.

"That's possible, certainly," she replies honestly.

"In which case you also have to consider the possibility that we're losing sight of the real murderer, the one we're calling the preacher."

She forces herself to look away from him and glances at the time. "The meeting's about to start," she says, getting to her feet.

"I can find the preacher if you want me to," Joona says.

"We already have," she replies.

"I need my gun, and I need all the material, the reports from the crime scenes, the postmortems."

"I shouldn't agree to that," she says, opening the door.

"And can you arrange for me to see Rocky Kyrklund in prison?" Joona asks.

"You don't give up, do you?" she says with a smile.

They walk slowly along the hallway together. Margot stops Joona outside the meeting room.

"Bear in mind that the people waiting in here are Adam's colleagues," she says with her fingers on the door handle. "The tone of the meeting is likely to be pretty hostile, they need to vent their anger. It's their way of showing their support for him, and the force as a whole."

96

JOONA FOLLOWS MARGOT INTO THE LARGE MEETING ROOM. She makes a gesture that simultaneously says hello to everyone and tells them to remain seated.

"Before we start . . . I know emotions are running high at the moment, but I'd still like to encourage everyone to stick to a civilized tone," she says. "The investigation is entering a new phase, and the prosecutor will now take the lead while we focus on making a quick arrest."

She stops and catches her breath.

"Carlos asked me to bring in Joona Linna, because he's the homicide detective with the best results. There's no contest, frankly."

A few of the officers clap while others stare at the table.

"Naturally he won't be officially involved in the investigation, but I hope he'll be able to give the rest of us mere mortals a few tips along the way," she jokes, even though she's clearly not amused.

Joona takes a step forward and looks at his former colleagues seated around the pale wooden table before speaking: "Erik is no murderer."

"What the fuck?" Petter mutters.

"Let's hear him out," Margot says curtly.

"I appreciate that there's a lot of evidence pointing at Erik, and he should certainly be brought in for questioning. But I was asked to tell you what I think—"

"Joona, I had a meeting with the prosecutor," Benny says. "Her opinion is that we have very compelling evidence."

"The puzzle isn't finished just because three pieces fit together."

"For fuck's sake, Erik was there," Benny goes on, "outside the house. We found his car, he knows the victims, he's lied to the police, et cetera, et cetera."

"I understand you shot at him," Joona says.

"He's considered extremely dangerous and probably armed," Benny says.

"But I can tell you it's all a mistake," Joona says. He pulls out a chair, sits, and leans back, making the chair creak.

"We're going to bring Erik in," Margot says. "And he'll be remanded in custody and given a fair trial."

"I don't think that's going to happen," Joona mutters, thinking how the law is doomed never to achieve justice.

"What's he talking about?" Benny asks.

"You're directing your anger at an innocent man—"

"You're right. We're fucking angry," Petter interrupts.

"Calm down," Margot says.

"I'm not going to sit here and listen to—"

"Petter," she warns. The room goes quiet.

Magdalena Ronander fills her glass of water and catches Joona's eye. "Joona, maybe you're thinking about things slightly differently because you're no longer a police officer," she says. "I don't mean any offense, but that might be why we don't understand what you're saying."

"We all want to catch the person who did this, and I'm saying that you're letting the real murderer get away," Joona replies.

"Right, that's enough bullshit," Benny roars, slamming both hands onto the table.

"Is he drunk?" someone whispers.

"Joona doesn't give a shit about the force, and he doesn't give a shit about us," Petter says loudly. "There's so much fucking hype about him, I don't get it. Look at him—he dropped his fucking gun! It was his fault Adam got shot, and now—"

"Maybe it would be best if you left," Margot says, putting a hand on Joona's shoulder.

"—and now he comes here and tries to tell us how to run an investigation," Petter concludes.

"One more thing," Joona says, standing up.

"Just shut up," Petter snaps.

"Let him speak," Magdalena says.

"I've seen this plenty of times," Joona says. "When family, friends, or colleagues are directly affected, it's easy to start thinking about revenge."

"Are you trying to say we aren't going to act professionally?" Benny asks with a cold smile.

"I'm saying there's a chance that Erik will contact me, and I'd like to be able to offer him safe passage," Joona says seriously, "so he'll turn himself in and have his innocence proven in court."

"Of course," Magdalena replies, looking at the others.

"But if you've already fired at him, how am I supposed to convince him to hand himself in?"

"Just tell him we guarantee his safety," Benny says.

"And if that isn't enough?" Joona says.

"Lie better." He grins.

"Joona, have you seen the pictures of Katryna?" Petter says agitatedly. "I can't believe it's even her. What do I say to my wife? This is so fucking sick. I mean, think about Adam. Think about what he's going through right now. I have to say, I personally don't give a fuck what happens to your friend."

"Everyone's upset," Margot says. "Obviously, we want to make it easy for him to turn himself in, and naturally, he'll get a fair trial—"

"Assuming he doesn't hang himself in his cell before then," says a young officer who has been quiet up to now.

"That's enough," Magdalena says.

"Or swallow some broken glass," Benny mutters.

Joona pushes his chair back and nods toward the others. "I'll be in touch when I find the real killer, and trust me, it's not the hypnotist," he says, and leaves the room.

"He's totally fucking pathetic," Petter mutters as his steps fade down the hallway.

"Before we continue, I want to say something," Margot begins. "Like you, I believe Erik is the murderer, but if we all take a step back . . . can we even entertain the possibility that we might be wrong, that Erik is actually innocent?"

"Aren't you supposed to be giving birth soon?" Benny asks sarcastically.

"I'll give birth when I'm finished with this case," she replies drily.

"Let's get to work," Magdalena says.

"Okay. This is how things stand," Margot says. "We've issued a national alert, but we know Erik has enough money to leave the country. We started our searches of Erik's home and his office. We're trying to trace his cellphone. His credit cards have been blocked, but he managed to withdraw a large amount last night. The area around the ATM is being searched. We're watching five addresses, and . . ."

She trails off when there's a knock at the door. Anja Larsson enters the room. Without acknowledging the others, she leans over and has a whispered conversation with Margot.

"Okay," Margot says after a while. "It looks like we've managed to trace Erik's cellphone. He's somewhere close to Växjö, in Småland. It looks like he's heading south."

97

ERIK IS LYING WRAPPED UP IN THE GRAY COVER HE TOOK from a parked motorcycle. He wakes up, freezing. It's light now, and he realizes he's underneath a sugarplum tree in a thicket of ornamental shrubs. He's slept maybe three hours, and his body feels stiff with cold, aching all over, as he sits up and looks around.

The sun is shining off the green leaves, sparkling in the cold.

He climbs over a red fence and crosses to the shady side of the street. He slowly warms up as he walks. He can't believe what's happened since he spoke to Joona.

He found a bus parked in front of a bike shop on Hägerstens Road. A group of weary-looking youngsters in crumpled clothes were gathered on the sidewalk, and parents were helping to unload backpacks and sleeping bags from the bus's open baggage compartments.

Erik went inside the bus, pretending to look for something left behind, and pushed his cellphone between two seats.

He stepped out the rear door, grabbed a cap from a duffel bag, tucked it inside his jacket, and continued toward the subway station. He pulled on the baseball cap and stopped at the ATM in front of the Nordea Bank. He didn't look up but was very aware of the security camera as he withdrew the maximum amount possible from his account.

Now Erik runs his fingers through his hair to flatten it. His clothes are creased but not dirty enough to attract attention. He needs to stay hidden until he can talk to Joona. He can't afford to take any risks, even if the misunderstanding has hopefully been cleared up by now.

Erik starts to cross the street but stops between two parked cars when he sees a convenience store.

His stomach gurgles with unease.

Among the notifications of lottery wins and ads for sports betting, the headlines of the evening tabloids scream: POLICE HUNT SWEDISH SERIAL KILLER.

He recognizes himself in the pixelated photograph. In accordance with press ethics, they've kept his identity hidden. It's only a matter of time, but for the moment his features are concealed by a mass of grainy squares.

The early edition of the other tabloid has no picture, but the headline covers the whole page in capital letters:

NATIONAL ALARM—SWEDISH PSYCHIATRIST SOUGHT FOR FOUR MURDERS.

Under the headline, the paper's contents are listed: VICTIMS, PICTURES, BRUTALITY, POLICE.

He steps back onto the sidewalk and walks past the shop as it dawns on him that the police really do believe he murdered Katryna and the other women.

He turns into a side street, but his legs shake so badly he has to slow down and eventually stop. He stands there, clutching a trembling hand to his mouth. "Oh God," he whispers.

Everyone Erik knows will figure out that he's the man they're talking about when they read the articles.

Benjamin will know it isn't true, Erik thinks, and starts walking again. But Madeleine will be scared.

He pulls out a blister pack containing four Mogadon pills and presses one into his hand, then changes his mind and throws the whole pack into the trash.

On Östgöta Street he finds a small shop selling secondhand cellphones. While he's waiting to be served, he listens to the news on the radio. A neutral voice explains coolly that the hunt for the suspected serial killer is now in its second day.

He almost throws up when he hears the voice say that an arrest warrant has been issued for a psychiatrist at Karolinska Hospital on reasonable suspicion of having murdered four women in the Stockholm area. The police are saying little otherwise, out of consideration for the ongoing investigation, but are hoping to receive further information from the public.

The man behind the counter, his glasses held together by a piece of tape, asks how he can help, and Erik tries to smile as he explains he'd like a pay-as-you-go phone.

On the radio, a senior police officer is discussing the progress of their search and the resources that have been deployed.

Erik changes direction as soon as he leaves the shop. He switches streets a number of times, but is aiming to leave the center of the city via Danvikstull.

He doesn't dare stop and take out the phone until he's passed the Tram Museum. Then he stands facing a yellow-brick building and calls Joona.

"Joona, this is impossible," he says quickly. "Have you seen the papers? I can't keep on hiding."

"You have to give me more time."

"No, I've made up my mind. I want you to arrest me and take me to the police."

"I can't guarantee your safety."

"I don't care," he says.

"I've never seen the police so worked up," Joona says, "and not just Adam's colleagues. It's all across the board. It's one thing for the police to risk their own lives, you know the risks when you join, but violence like this, directed at a police officer's wife—"

"You have to tell them I didn't do this, you—"

"I have, but they've linked you to each of the victims, and you were seen at the crime scene."

"What do I do?" Erik whispers.

"Stay hidden until I find the preacher," Joona replies. "I'm going to talk to Rocky. He's at Huddinge Prison."

"I could hand myself over to one of the evening tabloids," Erik says desperately. "I could tell my own story, my version, and then I'd have journalists with me when I went to the police."

"Erik, even if that were possible, they're already talking about your suicide in custody, about you hanging yourself or swallowing a piece of glass before the trial. It might all be talk, but I don't want you to take the risk right now."

"I'll call Nelly. She knows me, she knows I can't have done this—"

"You can't do that. The police are watching her house. You have to find someone else, someone more distant, unexpected."

98

HUDDINGE PRISON IS ONE OF THE LARGEST IN SWEDEN. Rocky is suspected only of basic narcotics offenses and is therefore not subject to any particular restrictions, but he is considered a flight risk.

The prison is a vast V-shaped, brown-brick building, with an entrance flanked by tall pillars. At the rear are two wings shaped like fans, each of whose top floors contain eight individual exercise areas.

Rocky is the only person who knows who the unclean preacher is. He's met him, spoken to him, and seen him kill.

Joona has to hand over his keys and phone at the security check. They X-ray his shoes and jacket, and he is searched after passing through the metal detector. A black and white cocker spaniel circles him, sniffing for explosives and drugs.

The prison officer waiting for him at the door introduces himself as Arne Melander. As they head toward the elevators, he tells Joona that he's a fisherman, a competitive angler, that he came third in the Swedish fishing championships at the beginning of the summer, and that he's heading to the Fyris River this weekend.

"I went for bottom fishing," Arne explains, pressing the elevator button. "I used pink-and-bronze-colored maggots."

"That's smart," Joona says.

Arne smiles, his cheeks lift and grow rounder. He has a large gray beard and is wearing glasses and a dark blue sweater stretched tight across his big stomach.

His baton and alarm swing from his belt as they leave the elevator and pass through the security doors. As Joona waits, the prison officer pulls his card through the reader and taps in the code.

They say hello to the duty officer, a white-haired man with a lazy eye and thin lips.

"We're running a little late today," the duty officer says. "Kyrklund just went out for some air. But we can check if he wants to come back in."

"Please do," Joona says.

After the murder of a prison officer, Karen Gebreab, the rules have been tightened, and no staff member is allowed to be alone with a prisoner. The inmates are often desperate, in a state of turmoil after their arrests.

Joona watches Arne Melander a little way off talking into a radio. He stares at the bare walls, the doors, the shiny linoleum floor, and the locks.

Huddinge Prison is high security, totally enclosed, with reinforced doors and walls, entrance checks and camera surveillance. But the staff are armed only with batons. Maybe they have tear gas or pepper spray, but Joona doesn't think they have guns.

A few years before he entered the Police Academy, Joona was picked to join the paratroopers' newly formed special ops unit, where he was trained in military Krav Maga, with a particular focus on urban warfare and innovative weaponry.

The old training runs deep. He still finds himself automatically scanning for potential weapons whenever he enters a room.

He's already spotted the stainless steel baseboards and door lintels. The grooves on the heads of the screws have been planed off so they can't be removed with ordinary tools, but the baseboards have started to drop toward the floor with the passage of time. Maybe the food carts have caught on them.

Joona notices that some of the baseboards could be nudged off with his foot. If you wrapped your hands in some cloth, you could pull the whole length of baseboard off, bend it twice, and in twenty seconds create a sort of noose that could be wrapped around an opponent's neck and tightened using the protruding lengths of metal.

Joona remembers the Dutch lieutenant Rinus Advocaat, a sinuous man with a scarred face and dead eyes, who demonstrated that technique and showed how to control your enemy's movements and basically decapitate him by tightening the noose.

"He's on his way," Arne says amiably to Joona.

Rocky is walking behind two prison officers. He's wearing pale green prison overalls and sandals, and has a cigarette tucked behind his ear.

"Thanks for cutting your time outside short," Joona says, walking toward him.

"I don't like cages much anyway," Rocky says, and clears his throat.

"Why not?"

"Good question." He shoots Joona an interested glance.

"You'll be in a monitored interview room, number eleven," Arne tells Joona. "So I'll be sitting on the other side of the glass."

"Maybe it's because cages make me think of the crayfish traps I used when I was little," Rocky says. "I'd catch them at night, around this time of year."

They stop outside the door while Arne unlocks it.

"I used to shine my flashlight at the crayfish, and using just the beam, I could force them into the traps."

Interview room 11 is shabby and contains a table, four chairs, and an internal phone to summon the prison staff.

The legs of the chairs are supposed to be unbreakable, Joona thinks, but if you were to lay one of them on the floor, climb up onto the table, and jump onto the curved back, the laminate would shatter, and you could quickly fashion a shiv out of it.

"So the guard can see me through glass?" Rocky asks, nodding toward the dark window.

"It's just a security precaution."

"But you're not afraid of me?" Rocky smiles.

"No," Joona replies.

The large priest sits down, and his chair creaks beneath him. "Have we met before?" he asks with a frown.

"At the Zone," Joona says evenly.

"At the Zone," Rocky repeats. "Should I know where that is?"

"It's where the police arrested you."

Rocky screws up his eyes and gazes into the distance. "I don't remember any of that. They say I had a load of heroin on me, but how could I afford that?"

"You don't remember the Zone? Sofa Zone in Högdalen?"

Rocky purses his lips and shakes his head.

"An industrial unit with tons of sofas and armchairs, prostitutes, people openly dealing drugs, guns . . ."

"Well, I have a neurological injury from a car crash. I have trouble remembering things," Rocky explains.

"I know."

"But you want me to confess to the drug offenses?"

"I don't care about that," Joona says, sitting opposite him. "You should just say it wasn't your jacket, that you picked up a jacket you found on the floor."

Neither of them speaks for a short while.

Rocky stretches out his long legs. "So you want something else," he says warily.

"You've mentioned a person you call the 'unclean preacher' several times. I need your help to identify him."

"Have I met this preacher?"

"Yes."

"Is he a priest?"

"I don't know."

Rocky scratches his beard and neck. "I have no idea," he says after a while.

"You described how he killed a woman called Natalia Kaliova. He chopped her arm off," Joona goes on.

"A preacher . . ."

"He was the one who murdered Rebecka Hansson."

"What the hell are you trying to do?" Rocky roars and stands up suddenly, toppling his chair. "I murdered Rebecka Hansson.

Do you think I'm stupid or something?" He backs away, stumbles over the overturned chair and almost falls, throws his arm out, and plants his large hand on the reinforced glass.

The prison officer comes in, but Joona holds up a calming hand toward him. He sees several more guards running along the hallway.

"We don't believe you did it," Joona says. "Do you remember Erik Maria Bark?"

"The hypnotist?" Rocky licks his lips and brushes his hair back.

"He found a woman who can give you an alibi."

"And I'm supposed to believe that?"

"Her name is Olivia," Joona says.

"Olivia Toreby," Rocky says slowly.

"You started to remember under hypnosis. Everything suggests you were convicted of a murder that the preacher committed."

Rocky comes closer to him. "But you don't know who this preacher is?"

"No," Joona replies.

"Because everything is locked inside my mashed-up brain," Rocky says hollowly.

"Would you agree to be hypnotized again?"

"Wouldn't you if you were in my position?" he asks, and sits down again.

"Yes," Joona replies honestly.

Rocky opens his mouth to say something but puts his hand to his forehead instead. One of his eyes has started to quiver, the pupil seems to be vibrating, and he leans forward, holding on to the table and breathing hard.

"Christ," he says after a while, and looks up.

His forehead is covered in sweat. He gazes up at Joona and the prison officers who have entered the room with a look of dreamy bemusement.

99

JOONA STOPS DISTRICT PROSECUTOR SARA NIELSEN OUTSIDE
the district court. Because he can't bring Erik into the prison, he
needs to persuade the prosecutor to release Rocky on bail before
his trial.

"I called you about Kyrklund," he says, standing in front of her.
"He can't stay in prison."

"That's for the district court to decide," she replies.

"But I don't understand why," Joona persists.

"Buy a book on Swedish law."

A strand of blond hair blows across Sara's face, and she brushes
it aside with a finger. She raises her eyebrows as Joona starts to
speak.

"According to chapter twenty-four, paragraph twenty," he says, "a
prosecutor can revoke the decision to remand a suspect in custody
if that decision is no longer justified."

"Bravo." She smiles. "But there's a clear risk that Kyrklund will
evade the course of justice, and a tangible danger that he would
commit further offenses."

"But we're only talking about minor narcotics offenses, punish-
able by a year's imprisonment at most, and it's extremely doubtful
that possession could even be proven."

"You said it wasn't his jacket over the phone," she says brightly.

"And that the reason for holding him in custody in no way war-
rants this degree of intrusion into his life."

"Suddenly it feels like I'm holding fresh custody negotiations with a former police officer."

"I can arrange for supervision," Joona says, following her down the steps.

"It doesn't work like that, as you well know."

"I understand that, but he's sick and needs constant medical attention," Joona says.

She stops and lets her eyes roam over his face. "If Kyrklund needs a doctor, the doctor can come to prison."

"But if I were to say that this particular treatment can't be carried out in prison . . ."

"Then I'd say you were lying."

"I can get a medical certificate," Joona persists.

"Go ahead, but I'm pressing charges next Tuesday."

"I'll appeal."

"Nice try," she says, smiling.

100

JOONA IS SITTING ON ONE OF THE REAR PEWS IN ADOLF Fredrik Church. A girls choir is rehearsing for a concert up at the front. The choir leader gives them their note, and the teenagers start to sing "O viridissima virga."

Joona sinks into memories of the long, light nights in Nattavaara after Summa's death, and the way sunlight would flood through the arched windows of the church and mix with autumn leaves and stained glass.

The choir pauses after a few minutes. The girls take out their phones, gather in groups, and walk through the aisles chatting.

The door to the porch opens and closes quickly. The church-warden looks up from her book, then continues reading.

Margot comes in carrying two heavy plastic bags. They hit the pew as she squeezes in next to Joona. Her stomach has swollen so much that it presses against the shelf for hymnbooks.

"I really am sorry," Margot half whispers. "I know you don't want to believe it, but look at this."

With a sigh she lifts one of the bags onto her lap and pulls out a printout showing a fingerprint match. Joona quickly reads through the various parameters of the comparison, then checks the details himself and sees the similarities in the lines and patterns.

There are three perfectly defined fingerprints, and the match with Erik Maria Bark is one hundred percent.

"Where were the prints found?" Joona asks.

"On the little porcelain deer's head that was in Susanna Kern's hand."

Joona gazes out into the nave. The choir is gathering once more, the leader clapping her hands to get their attention.

"You asked for evidence before," Margot continues. "These fingerprints are evidence, aren't they?"

"In a judicial sense," he says in a low voice.

"The searches are still going on," she says. "We've found our serial killer."

"Have you?"

Margot puts the bag containing material from the investigation on Joona's lap.

"I really wanted to believe you, and the idea of the preacher," she says, leaning back and breathing hard.

"You should," Joona replies.

"You met Rocky. I arranged for you to be able to question him," she says with a hint of impatience. "You said you needed to do that before you could find this unclean preacher."

"He doesn't remember anything now."

"Because there isn't anything to remember," she concludes.

The choir starts singing, and the girls' voices fill the church. Margot tries to make herself more comfortable and tucks her braid over her shoulder.

"You traced Erik to Småland," Joona says.

"The rapid response team stormed a charter bus and found his phone tucked between two seats."

"Oops," Joona says drily.

"He hasn't put a foot wrong so far. He's staying out of the way like a professional," she says. "It's almost like he's been given advice."

"I agree," Joona says.

"Has he contacted you?" Margot asks.

"No," Joona replies simply.

He looks down at the other bag, still on the floor between them. "Is that my pistol?"

"Yes." She pushes the bag toward him with her foot.

"Thanks," Joona says, gazing down into it.

"If you continue looking for the preacher, I have to remind you that you're not doing so on my orders," Margot says, starting to squeeze out of the pew. "You haven't received any material from me, and we never met here. Do you understand?"

"I'm going to find the murderer," Joona says.

"Fine, but we can't have any more official contact."

Joona pulls out his pistol, under cover of the pew, ejects the magazine into his lap, pulls the bolt back, checks the mechanism, trigger, and hammer, then puts the safety catch back on and reinserts the magazine.

"Who the hell uses a Colt Combat?" Margot asks. "I'd have a sore back within a week."

Joona just tucks the pistol into his shoulder holster and slips the spare magazine into his jacket pocket.

"When are you going to accept that Erik might be guilty?" she asks roughly.

"You'll see that I'm right," he says, meeting her gaze with icy calmness.

101

NELLY BRANDT IS SITTING AT HER COMPUTER, TYPING. SHE'S
wearing a beige suede skirt and a gold sweater that fits tightly
around her body.

When Joona comes in and says hello, she doesn't answer, just
stands up and goes over to the window and picks a deep pink
flower from the bush outside.

"There you go," she says, giving the flower to Joona. "With my
heartfelt thanks for the magnificent detective work—"

"I know how you feel—"

"Wait," she interrupts. "I need to pick another one."

She reaches out, picks a second flower, and hands it to Joona.

"For the entire Swedish police force," she says. "Fucking impressive. No, I'm going to have to go out and dig up the whole bush."

"Nelly, I know the police have the wrong man," Joona says.

It's as if all the air goes out of her. She sits down at the desk
and rests her head on her hands, tries to say something but can't
get the words out.

"I'm still trying to find the real murderer," he goes on. "But I
need someone who can take over where Erik left off."

"I'd be happy to help," she says, looking up at him.

"Can you hypnotize people?"

"No." She laughs, taken aback. "I thought . . . that's not my area.
I actually find the experience a bit unsettling."

"Do you know anyone who could help me?"

She twists the engagement ring on her freckled finger a couple of times and tilts her head. "Hypnosis is tricky," she says bluntly. "But there are a few people with a good reputation. Not that that's the same thing as being brilliant."

"You mean there's no one as good as Erik?"

She laughs, flashing her white teeth. "Nowhere near as good."

"Is there someone I could talk to?"

"Anna Palmer here is supposed to be pretty good. It depends what you need. She doesn't have Erik's experience when it comes to psychological trauma and states of shock, of course."

Nelly leads Joona along the hallway, but after a little while she slows down and asks him if she's in danger.

"I can't answer that," Joona replies honestly.

"My husband's working late all week."

"You should ask for police protection."

"No, no," she says, waving the idea away, "that seems extreme. But this is all just too much. We noticed the lock at the back of the house was damaged yesterday."

"Do you have someone you can stay with?"

"Yes, of course," she says, blushing slightly.

"Do that, until this is over."

"I'll think about it."

102

ANNA PALMER SEES JOONA IN A SMALL, BOOK-LINED ROOM. There's a desk, and a narrow window overlooking the hospital grounds. She's a tall woman with short lead-gray hair and visible veins beneath her eyes.

"I know someone who was in a car accident ten years ago," Joona begins. "He suffered fairly severe brain damage. I'm no expert, but the way it's been explained to me, he suffers from ongoing epileptic activity in the temporal lobes of both sides of his brain."

"That can certainly happen," she says, jotting down what he says.

"His big problem is his memory," Joona goes on. "Short and long term. Sometimes he remembers every detail of an event, but sometimes he forgets it ever took place. I'm hoping that hypnosis might help him break through the barriers."

Anna lowers her notepad and folds her hands on the desk. Joona notices tiny red eczema scabs on her knuckles.

"I don't want to disappoint you," she says wearily, "but a lot of people have unrealistic expectations about what hypnosis can be used for."

"It's very important for this person to remember," Joona replies.

"Clinical hypnosis is about making suggestions and helping patients sort out their memories. It has nothing to do with revealing truths," she explains apologetically.

"But this type of brain injury doesn't mean that his memory has been erased. It's all there, it's just that the path to it is blocked. Couldn't hypnosis help him find a different path?"

"It would certainly be possible to get to that point, if you were very skillful," she concedes, scratching the red marks on her hands. "But what do you do when you get there? No one would be able to differentiate between his real memories and his imagination because his brain can't tell the difference."

"Are you sure? We think we can tell the difference between memory and imagination. We're convinced that we can."

"Because we store certain information with an awareness that it reflects genuine memories—like a sort of code."

"So shouldn't that code still be in his brain?" Joona persists.

"But extracting that while we extract his memories . . ." she says, shaking her head.

"Is there anyone who could do that?"

"No," she replies, closing her notepad.

"Erik Maria Bark claims he can."

"Erik is very good at . . . he's probably the best person in the world at putting patients into a state of deep hypnosis, but his research isn't evidence-based," she says slowly, and there's a glint of something in her eyes.

"Do you believe what the papers have been saying about him?" Joona asks.

"I have no way of judging that, but he does gravitate toward the perverse, the psychotic—" She stops herself. "Is this conversation about him?" she asks bluntly.

"No."

"But it's not about a friend of yours, is it?"

"It never is. I'm a detective with National Crime, and I need to question a witness suffering from organic memory loss."

The corners of Anna Palmer's mouth twitch. "That would be unethical. Anything said under hypnosis cannot be deemed reliable and has no place in a legal context," she says curtly.

"This is about detective work, not—"

"I can promise you that no serious practitioner of clinical hypnosis would do this," she says, raising her voice and looking him in the eye.

103

WITH HIS CAP PULLED DOWN AND HIS HEAD LOWERED, ERIK makes his way around the heights of Hammarbybacken and heads into the forest.

It's practically impossible to move in Stockholm without getting caught on camera. There are traffic cameras along the roads and surveillance cameras at junctions, tunnels, and bridges. There are security cameras in shops, trains, buses, ferries, and taxis. Twenty-four hours a day gas stations, parking lots, harbors, terminals, railway stations, and platforms are monitored. Banks, department stores, shopping centers, plazas, pedestrian streets, embassies, police stations, prisons, hospitals, and fire stations are all watched.

Erik is extremely tired, and the blisters on the soles of his feet burst as he makes his way through the forest toward Björkhagen.

The sky is growing dark, and Erik's legs shake when he stops in the little park behind the apartment building where Nestor, his former patient, lives.

Erik follows the path to a wooden door with tarnished bronze mailboxes. The color of the building reminds him of putty.

There's a light on in the kitchen in the ground-floor apartment. From here he can see right into Nestor's living room. Erik switches windows and sees Nestor sitting in an armchair. There's no sign of anyone else in the apartment.

Erik feels as though he can't take another step, and his hands are shaking as he rings Nestor's doorbell.

"Can I come in?" he asks as soon as Nestor opens the door.

"This is unexpected," Nestor mutters. "I'll p-put some coffee on." He lets Erik in, closes and locks the door, then disappears inside.

Erik takes his shoes off with a sigh, hangs up his wrinkled jacket, and smells his own sweat. His socks have stuck to his bleeding heels, and his cold fingertips are itching in the heat of the hallway.

He knows that Nestor lives in the same apartment he grew up in. The ceilings are low, and the oak floor is so old, the varnish has worn off. There are dog-shaped ornaments everywhere.

Erik walks through the living room. The single cushion on the sofa is threadbare, and on the low table are a pair of glasses and a crossword puzzle, beside a large statuette of hunting dogs and dead pheasants.

In the kitchen, Nestor is setting out cups and a plate of cookies. There's a frying pan containing sausage and potatoes on the stove.

"You told me I could ask for a favor, anything at all," Erik says, sitting at the table.

"Yes," Nestor says, nodding emphatically.

"Can I stay here for a few days?"

"Here?" A skeptical, boyish smile flits across Nestor's face. "What for?"

"I've had a bit of a fight with my girlfriend," Erik lies, leaning back.

"You have a g-girlfriend?"

"Yes," Erik replies.

Nestor pours coffee into their cups and says he has a spare room with a guest bed already made up.

"Could I have some of the leftover food?"

"Of c-course, I'm sorry," he says, switching the hotplate on.

"You don't have to warm it up for me," Erik says.

"Don't you want . . . ?"

"No, it's fine."

Nestor scrapes the food onto a plate and puts it in front of Erik before sitting across from him.

"Have you thought any more about getting a dog?" Erik asks.

"I n-need to save up some money," Nestor replies, lifting his coffee spoon a few millimeters and surreptitiously looking at his reflection.

"Of course," Erik says as he eats.

"I work over there at the ch-church." Nestor gestures toward the window.

"At the church?" Erik asks, a shiver spreading down his spine.

"Yes . . . well, not really." Nestor smiles, holding a hand in front of his mouth. "I w-work in the pet cemetery."

"The pet cemetery." Erik nods politely, looking at Nestor's slender hands.

Erik finishes the food and drinks his coffee as he listens to Nestor tell him about the oldest cemetery for domestic pets in Sweden, over on Djurgården. It was established in the nineteenth century, when the author August Blanche buried his dog there.

"I'm b-boring you," Nestor says, getting to his feet.

"No, I'm tired, that's all," Erik says.

Nestor goes over to the window and looks out. Black shapes are moving against the paler sky, trees and bushes blowing back and forth. "It'll soon be dark," he whispers to his reflection.

There are two ceramic greyhounds on the windowsill, next to a potted plant. Nestor touches their heads, out of Erik's view.

"Can I use the bathroom?" Erik asks.

Nestor shows him through the living room and points to an extra door behind a curtain.

"This is the old c-caretaker's flat, but I think of that d-door as an emergency exit," he says.

The bathroom has tiles halfway up its walls, with a deep bathtub and a shower curtain with seahorses on it. Erik locks the door and takes his clothes off.

"The red toothbrush is Mother's," Nestor calls through the door.

Erik stands on the moldy mat in the scratched bathtub, showers, and washes the wounds on his body. On top of the bathroom cabinet above the sink is an old lightbulb box with some lipsticks and a mascara tube sticking out of it.

When Erik emerges, Nestor is standing in the hall waiting for him. His wrinkled face looks worried. "I'd really like to t-talk about something. . . . It's something that . . ." he begins.

"What is it?"

"I . . . what do I d-do if the new dog dies?"

"We can talk about that tomorrow."

"I'll show you to the g-guestroom," Nestor whispers, turning his face away.

They go back into the living room, past the kitchen, to a closed door that Erik hasn't noticed before.

Above the bed in the spare room is a large poster of Björn Borg kissing the Wimbledon trophy. On the wall opposite is a shelf full of porcelain dogs.

There's an old corner cupboard painted in a traditional folk art style. The top door is decorated with a hand-painted motif: the ages of man, from cradle to grave. A man and woman are side by side on a bridge where each step represents a decade. On the top step, the pair stand tall as fifty-year-olds, but death lurks beneath the bridge in the form of a skeleton with a scythe in its hand.

"That's lovely," Erik says, looking at Nestor, who is still in the living room.

"I sleep in . . . M-mother's room. I moved in there when . . ." Nestor cranes his neck oddly, as if he wanted to look at someone behind him.

"Goodnight," Erik says.

He starts to close the door, but Nestor puts his hand on it and looks at him anxiously. "The r-rich need it, the poor already have it, but you f-fear it more than death," Nestor whispers.

"I'm a little too tired for riddles, Nestor."

"The rich need it, the p-poor already have it, but you fear it more than death," Nestor repeats, then licks his lips.

"I'll think about the answer," Erik says, and closes the door. "Well, goodnight."

He sits down and stares at the hideous wallpaper. Its repeated pattern looks like ornate coats of arms, garlands, peacock feathers, and hundreds of eyes.

The blinds are already closed, and he switches the light off and detects a faint smell of lavender as he folds back the heavy covers and gets into bed.

He's so exhausted that his thoughts drift away and lose their shape. He's just about to tumble over the boundary into sleep, when he hears a small creaking sound in the room. Someone is trying to open the door quietly.

"What is it, Nestor?" Erik asks.

"A clue," the soft voice says. "I c-can give you a clue."

"I'm very tired, and—"

"Priests think it's b-bigger than God Himself," Nestor interrupts.

"Can you close the door, please?"

The handle clicks as Nestor lets go and pads across the living room parquet.

Erik falls asleep, and in his dreams little Madeleine is standing by his bed, blowing on his face and whispering the answer to Nestor's riddle.

"*Nothing*," she whispers, blowing on him. "*The rich need nothing, the poor have nothing . . . and you fear nothing more than death.*"

104

ERIK IS PULLED FROM SLEEP BY A BREEZE ON HIS FACE. SOME-
one is whispering frantically but stops the moment he opens his
eyes. The darkness is almost impenetrable, and it takes him a few
seconds to realize where he is.

The old horsehair mattress creaks when he rolls over.

Even though he was fast asleep, some part of him was alert, a
force that yanked him from sleep.

Maybe he just heard water running through the building's pipes,
or the wind pressing against the window.

No one has been whispering in his room, everything is still and
dark.

Was this where Nestor was sleeping when he slipped into psychosis? Erik wonders. When the rattling of the pipes turned into
voices, into the old woman brushing dandruff from her long gray
hair who told him you shouldn't look your nearest and dearest in
the eye when you kill them?

Erik knows it all stemmed from the dog Nestor was forced to
put down when he was a child, but he still used to shiver every time
Nestor imitated the woman's creaking voice.

He thinks of the way Nestor used to sit with his hands clasped
in his lap and his head lowered. A little smile would play on his
lips, and he would flush slightly as he dispensed advice on how to
murder a child.

The old closet creaks, and the shadows by the door are hard to interpret. He closes his stinging eyes and goes back to sleep but wakes up again when the door to the guestroom closes.

Erik has to tell Nestor to leave him alone when he's sleeping, that he doesn't have to keep checking on him, but he can't be bothered to get up now.

A car passes on the street outside, and its light finds its way past the roller blind, slides across the patterned wallpaper, and disappears.

Erik stares at the wall. A trace of the light seems to linger on the wall after the car passes. He thinks there must be a weak lamp by the shelf that he hasn't seen.

He blinks, stares at the motionless blue light, and realizes that there's a peephole in the wall between the rooms.

The light is coming from the other bedroom, Erik thinks. Then everything suddenly goes dark.

Nestor is looking into his room right now.

Erik lies absolutely still. It's so quiet he can hear himself swallow.

The blue light becomes visible again, and he can hear intense whispering through the wall.

Erik quickly gets dressed in the darkness and moves closer to the light.

The peephole is between two low bookshelves. It would be invisible if the porcelain animals on the lower shelf were arranged differently.

It's positioned in the very darkest part of the pattern on the wallpaper, so small that he realizes he's going to have to press his face to the wall and put his eye right next to the hole to be able to see anything.

He moves a porcelain puppy in a basket, presses his hands to the wall, and carefully puts his head between the shelves, feeling the wood against his hair and the wallpaper touching the tip of his nose.

When he is right next to the hole, he can see straight into the next room.

There's a cellphone on the bedside table. The screen is lit up, illuminating the alarm clock and the oval pattern on the wallpaper. Erik glimpses a neatly made bed and a framed photograph of a young child in a christening gown, then the light from the phone goes out.

He hears rapid footsteps somewhere in the apartment and tries to pull his head back, but his hair catches on a splinter in the wood. The porcelain figures tinkle ominously.

Erik puts his hand up and tries to free his hair as the door opens behind him. He pulls his head out and hears the figurines on the shelf rattle.

Nestor comes toward him, and he backs away. "I called the p-police, I c-came back to tell you," Nestor whispers. "It's your t-turn to get h-help now. I've spoken to them several times. They're here now."

"Nestor, you don't understand—" Erik says forlornly.

"No, no, you d-don't understand," Nestor interrupts in a friendly voice, and switches on the lamp in the window. "I said it's your t-turn to get medicine, and—"

There's a sudden noise, like a stone hitting the window. The dark roller blind quivers in the light from the lamp, and a cascade of glass falls behind it and tinkles over the radiator.

Nestor lurches. He's been shot, right through his body, with a high-velocity weapon. Blood sprays out of the exit hole in his shoulder.

He looks at the blood in surprise. "They p-promised . . ."

Nestor stumbles, falls onto his hip, and looks up with a confused expression.

"G-get out through the extra door," he hisses. "Go down into the laundry room, straight through, and you'll be in the next building." He puts his knuckles on the floor as if to push himself up.

"Lie down," Erik whispers. "Just lie flat."

"Run across the schoolyard, then follow the church wall t-to the forest and the pet cemetery."

"Lie still," Erik repeats, then runs at a crouch toward the door.

When he reaches the living room, Nestor's apartment door is

being forced open. There's a crash and splinters and pieces of metal from the lock clatter across the floor.

"Hide in the little r-red house," Nestor gasps behind him.

Erik turns around and sees that Nestor has stood up to point. The glass in front of Björn Borg's smiling face explodes, and the echo of the shot resounds between the buildings. Nestor is holding one hand against the side of his neck as a torrent of blood pulses out between his fingers.

Three of the apartment's windows shatter, and distraction grenades explode, flashing with such ferocity that time seems to stand still.

Erik staggers backward.

The silence is like water on a sandy beach. Slow waves roll in, then pull back with a crackle.

He makes his way through the living room, unable to see anything but the freeze-frame image of the bedroom with Nestor's silhouette against the window.

Erik's hearing has been knocked out, but he feels pressure waves against his chest. He walks into the battered sofa and feels his way along its back.

Then the shock lifts, his eyes are working again, and he makes his way around the table and magazine rack, but he's still as giddy as if he were very drunk.

Lights from guns sweep around the entryway and kitchen.

His ears ring, but he still can't hear anything.

He locates the extra door behind the curtain, unlocks it, and creeps out onto the back stairwell.

He makes his way down the stairs on unsteady feet, then walks until he reaches a metal door and finds himself in the basement laundry room. He feels his way along the wall until his fingers make contact with the light switch. He turns the lights on and hurries past washing machines as he tries to remember what Nestor said.

His head feels strangely detached, as if none of this really concerns him.

He still can't see clearly. Silvery spots float in his line of vision, and everything seems slightly out of sync.

At the end of the long hallway is a door, and he runs up a narrow flight of steps and finds himself in a different stairwell.

He walks out into the cool night air. There are no emergency vehicles on this side of the block. Presumably the rapid response team is far away.

He hurries through the little park. In the cold he can feel that one of his ears is wet. He touches his cheek and realizes he's bleeding. Without looking around, he walks straight across Karlskrona Road and past a parking lot and some dirty recycling bins. Broken glass crunches beneath his feet.

The schoolyard is empty. A beer can rolls in the wind, and the basketball hoops on their posts have no nets.

High above a helicopter is approaching. Erik hears the rotors and realizes that his hearing is coming back.

He walks more slowly, gasping for breath, then creeps around the building and in among the trees. It's almost pitch-black here.

Fear is beginning to catch up with him as he follows the wall through tall nettles.

Deep within the forest, he comes to a sudden concentration of tiny graves, decorated by children. He sees headstones with dogs' collars hanging off them, graves with squeezy toys, drawings, photographs, flowers, homemade crosses or painted stones, burned-out candles, and sooty lanterns.

105

IT'S AFTER TWO IN THE MORNING, BUT JOONA IS STANDING in the middle of his room. The floor is covered with photographs from the crime scenes. Because Erik's house has been cordoned off as part of the search, the police have sent him to a hotel.

His jacket and pistol are lying on the untouched bed, and the leftovers from the room service he ordered are on the low coffee table.

As Joona reads the analyses of the crime scenes, he compares them with the pictures, postmortem reports, and test results from the lab.

Rocky's nightmares were genuine memories. Everything he said under hypnosis was true. The unclean preacher has started killing again. After the murder of Rebecka Hansson, the serial killer went into a long cooling-off period until the next escalation began.

For a stalker, following someone is an addiction—it's impossible to stop. He has to get closer, make contact, give gifts, and as time passes develop a real relationship with the victim inside his own head. Outwardly he can exhibit gratitude, but in reality he is resentful and jealous.

The police have a list of almost seven hundred names that fit the basic perpetrator profile: bishops, pastors, priests and members of their families, deacons, churchwardens, caretakers, undertakers, preachers, and faith healers.

Joona believes that the perpetrator is intentionally trying to make it look like Erik is guilty, but he can't find a connection between Erik and any of those men.

What Joona is looking for now is something definite that will allow him to cross most of the names off the list.

Nothing stands out in the material, but perhaps elements of the puzzle could be combined in an unexpected way.

He stops in front of the photograph of Sandra Lundgren's murder weapon. The stained knife was photographed where it was found, on the floor beside her dead body. The flash from the camera shimmers like a dark sun in the brown blood.

He reads that it is a chef's knife, with a twenty-centimeter-long stainless-steel blade. Then he examines Erixon's careful reconstruction of the brutal attack from blood traces and spatter patterns.

The perpetrator has worn the same shoes each time: size eight and a half hiking boots.

Joona tries to identify clues that have been missed, things that don't match the overall picture. He pores over picture after picture and stops at a photograph numbered 311: a blue pottery fragment that resembles a bird's skull, with white bubbles along one edge and a sharp point that's as smooth as ice.

He leafs forward to the item in Erixon's report and reads that it was tucked between the cracks in Sandra's floor. According to the laboratory analysis, the two-millimeter-long fragment consists of glass, iron, sand, and chamotte clay.

Joona moves to the report from Adam Youssef's home. In spite of the gunfire, the murderer chose to go through with his plan, and according to the preliminary report, Katryna was missing the false fingernails from both her hands.

The preacher takes trophies, then marks the places he's taken them from with the victim's hands.

At three-fifteen, Anja calls to say she's just been informed that the police have received a highly credible tip. A man claims that Erik is sleeping in the guestroom in his apartment. Erik was his psychiatrist years ago. "The man has been told to leave the apartment."

"Who's leading the operation?" Joona asks.

"Daniel Frick."

"He's one of Adam's best friends."

"I understand what you're saying," Anja says. "But I don't think there's anything to worry about. The operation is being led by the response unit."

Joona goes to the window and looks down at his rental car. It's a gunmetal-gray Porsche with six cylinders and 560 horsepower that he paid for with the last of his money.

"Where's the apartment?"

"Everyone knows I'm loyal to you, so Margot decided to exclude me from the current investigation. She has a point, because if I knew the address I'd tell you." Even though she doesn't know the exact location, she's figured out it must be somewhere south of Stockholm. She says the response unit has been given permission to arm themselves heavily.

After the call, Joona stands and gazes around the hotel room. Hundreds of pictures, lined up in rows, from wall to wall.

He continues reading Erixon's crime scene analysis, but his mind keeps wandering to Erik.

He reads a lab report about a piece of trampled leaf left on the kitchen floor in Maria Carlsson's home. It turned out to be a fragment of stinging nettle.

He looks at the enlargement on the photograph. The tiny piece of leaf looks like a spiky green tongue.

Dawn comes, and the sky in the east grows pale. Narrow streaks of sunlight filter past chimneys and gables, over roofs and copper ornaments.

The operation must be over by now, Joona thinks, and calls Erik on his new phone.

He tries a second time, but gets no answer.

Even though it's only five-thirty in the morning, he decides to call Margot. He has to know if they caught Erik, but he can't ask straight about the operation because he doesn't want to get Anja in trouble.

"Did you arrest an innocent suspect yet?"

"Joona, I'm asleep."

"Come on, what's going on?"

"What's going on?" she replies tiredly. "You're not actually allowed to ask, but since you did, a former patient of Erik's called and said Erik was in his apartment."

"Can I have a name?"

"Confidential. I can't talk to you, I told you that."

"Just say if it's something I should know about."

"The ex-patient told the police he'd left Erik alone in the apartment. The response unit went in, saw an armed man, and shot live ammunition. It turned out the person in the window was the patient, who had returned."

"And Erik wasn't there?"

He can hear her trying to sit up in bed.

"We don't even know if he'd been there at all, and the patient's on an operating table right now and can't be interviewed or—"

"What if he's the preacher?" Joona interrupts.

"Erik's guilty. But maybe the patient knows where he is. We'll question him as soon as we can."

"You should station armed guards at the hospital."

"Joona, we found blood in Erik's car. It might not mean anything, but it's been sent for analysis."

"Did you look for a yellow raincoat in the patient's apartment?"

"We didn't find anything special," she replies.

"Are there stinging nettles outside the flat?"

"No, I don't think so," she says in a bemused tone.

106

JOONA SITS DOWN FOR THE FIRST TIME IN SEVERAL HOURS and reads more about the killer's steps in Sandra Lundgren's apartment. He looks at the sketches and thinks that there's something unusually agitated and frenetic about the murders. They're planned, but they aren't rational.

Joona compares this with the description in the postmortem of the perpetrator's theatrical aggression. He can't help thinking the controlled preparation is actually a pose, and the aggression is the perpetrator's natural state.

He is about to make a note to investigate Erik's former patients' medical histories when his phone rings.

"Joona, it's me," Erik whispers. "They tried to kill me. I was hiding out at Nestor's, he's an old patient of mine. The police must have thought I was the one they could see in the window. They shot him twice. It was like an execution. I didn't think the police in Sweden could do something like that. It's completely insane."

"Are you somewhere safe now?"

"Yes, I think so. You know, he only came back to tell me what he'd done, to say that the police had promised not to hurt me, and then they shot him through the window."

"Has it occurred to you that he could be the preacher?"

"He isn't," Erik replies instantly.

"What was his problem when he was—"

"Joona, that doesn't matter, I just want a trial, I don't care if they convict me, I can't stay—"

"Erik, I don't think I'm being monitored, but don't tell me where you are," Joona interrupts. "I just want to know how long you can stay hidden where you are."

The phone crackles as Erik moves. "I don't know, twenty-four hours, maybe," he whispers. "There's a spigot here, but nothing to eat."

"Are you likely to be found?"

"There's probably not much risk of that," Erik replies, then the line gets quiet.

"Erik?"

"I don't understand how I could have ended up in this situation," he says, shaking his head. "Everything I do only makes things worse."

"I'm going to find the preacher," Joona says.

"It's too late for that now. I just want to give myself up without being killed!"

Joona can hear Erik's agitated breathing. "Even if we manage to hand you over and keep you alive in prison, these crimes carry a life sentence."

"But I don't think I'd be convicted. I can hypnotize Rocky before the trial."

"They'd never let you do that."

"No, maybe not, but—"

"I went to see Rocky," Joona says. "He's in Huddinge Prison for drug possession. He remembered you, but nothing about the Zone or the preacher."

"It's hopeless," Erik says.

Joona leans against the window and feels the cool glass against his forehead. Down in the street, a taxi stops outside the hotel. The driver's face is gray as he walks around the car to take the luggage out.

Joona glances down at his rental car, watches the taxi drive off, and when he looks up again, he's made up his mind.

"I'll try to find a way to get Rocky out today. And then we'll meet up so you can hypnotize him," he says.

"Is that your plan?" Erik asks.

"You said you could unearth specific details about the preacher if you were able to hypnotize Rocky again."

"Yes, I'm pretty sure I can."

"In that case, I'll be able to find the real killer while you stay in hiding."

"I just want to hand myself in and—"

"You'll be found guilty if it goes to trial."

"That's ridiculous. I just happened to be nearby when—"

"It's not just that," Joona interrupts. "Your fingerprints were on an object found in Susanna Kern's hand."

"What object?" Erik asks in astonishment.

"Part of a porcelain animal."

"I don't get it. That doesn't mean anything to me."

"But the fingerprint match is a hundred percent."

Joona hears Erik walk up and down, as if he's across a wooden floor.

"So everything points to me," he says in a low voice.

"Do you have a picture of Nestor?"

Erik tells him how to log into the medical records of the Psychology Clinic. Then they end the call. Joona puts his pistol and jacket on, then goes down to reception to get a printout of Nestor's picture.

After leaving the hotel, he walks past his rental car and turns into much narrower Frej Street. Outside a doorway is an old Volvo. Joona looks around quickly. The street is deserted. He takes a step back, then kicks in the rear side window.

The alarm of a car farther down the street goes off.

Joona opens the front door from the inside, moves the seat back, pulls his screwdriver out of his pocket, pries off the cover around the ignition, and loosens the panels on the steering column. He leans over and inserts the screwdriver into the upper part of the column and carefully breaks the steering lock.

Quickly he pulls on a pair of gloves, loosens the red cables on the ignition cylinder, and peels back their plastic covering. As soon as he twists the ends together, music starts to play on the radio, and the inside light comes on. He shuts the door, pulls out the brown wires and puts them together, and the engine starts.

The streets aren't busy yet as he drives out to Huddinge. A plastic rosary hangs off the rearview mirror. There are trucks on the road, but the commuters are still drinking coffee in their homes.

In Huddinge, he drives past the imposing prison building and continues south, pulls onto a track leading into the forest, then starts walking back toward Stockholm.

107

JOONA GETS OUT OF THE TAXI ON SURBRUNNS STREET, PAYS, and walks across the street to his gray rental car. The engine starts with a gentle hum. He leans back in the leather seat and pulls away from the curb.

When he reaches Huddinge Prison, he parks right in front of the entrance, next to a metal fence, and calls Erik's number.

"How are you doing?" he asks.

"Okay, but I'm getting hungry."

"I changed my SIM card, so you can tell me where you are now."

"Behind St. Mark's Church, outside the wall. There's a pet cemetery in the woods. I'm hiding in a red wooden shed."

"That's pretty close to Nestor's apartment, isn't it?"

"Yes, I heard the ambulance last night," Erik says.

"I'll bring Rocky out to you in an hour." Joona glances up at the imposing edifice of the prison.

He puts his pistol and phone in the glove compartment, leaves the key in the ignition, gets out of the car, and walks in.

He buys three sandwiches at the kiosk in the lobby, asks for a bag, then approaches the front desk to say why he's there.

After going through the usual security procedures, Joona is shown inside the prison. Arne, the same prison officer as before, is waiting for him.

Joona notes that Arne has a telescopic baton from Bonowi. It's made of spring steel and designed to hit the muscles in the upper arms and thighs.

His name badge sits slightly crooked on his pilled sweater. Handcuffs are dangling from his belt at the base of his broad back.

In the elevator, Arne takes off his glasses and polishes them on his sweater.

"How's the fishing?" Joona asks.

"I'm heading to Älvkarleby with my brother-in-law later this autumn."

One wall of the interview room consists of a pane of glass, making it possible for people in the next room to observe everything going on inside.

Joona sits in a chair and waits with both hands resting on the tabletop until he hears voices approaching along the hallway.

"He's called the naked chef because he was naked when he started," the duty officer is saying as the door opens, and Rocky is led into the room.

"No," Arne says, "that's not right . . ."

"My wife and I saw Jamie Oliver at the book fair in Gothenburg fifteen years ago. He was completely naked. Stood there making spaghetti alle vongole."

"My shoulders hurt," Rocky sighs.

"Just keep quiet," Arne says, pushing him down into a chair.

"Give me a scribble, and he's all yours," the duty officer says as they leave the room.

108

ROCKY LOOKS PALER TODAY, AND HE HAS DARK PATCHES under his eyes—he's probably suffering from withdrawal. Arne Melander sits in the adjoining room watching them, but he can't hear what they say. The soundproof glass wall is intended to protect the confidentiality of conversations between lawyers and their clients, and to allow the police to question suspects without the contents of their conversations leaking.

"They say they can keep me locked up in this fucking place for six months," Rocky says gruffly, rubbing his nose.

"You talked about a preacher," Joona says, in a final attempt to avoid putting his plan into action.

"I have problems with my memory after—"

"I know," Joona interrupts. "But try to remember the preacher. You saw him kill a woman named Tina."

"That's possible," Rocky says, his eyes narrowing.

"He chopped off her arm with a machete. Do you remember that?"

"I don't remember anything," Rocky whispers.

"Do you know someone named Nestor?"

"I don't think so."

"Look at this picture." Joona hands him the printout.

Rocky studies Nestor's thin face carefully, then nods. "He was in Karsudden, I think."

"Did you know him?"

"I don't know, there were different sections."

"Are you prepared to meet Erik Maria Bark and let yourself be hypnotized?"

"Okay," Rocky says with a shrug.

"The problem is that the prosecutor is refusing to let you out," Joona says slowly.

"Erik can always hypnotize me here."

"That isn't possible, because the police think Erik committed the murders."

"Erik?"

"But he's as innocent as you were."

"*Vanitas vanitatum*," Rocky says with a broad smile.

"Erik found Olivia, who—"

"I know, I know. I get down on my knees and thank him every night. But what do you expect me to do about it?"

"We're leaving together, you and me," Joona replies calmly. "I'll take one of the guards hostage, and all you have to do is come with me."

"Hostage?"

"We'll be out in seven minutes, long before the police get here."

Rocky looks at Joona, then at Arne sitting behind the glass.

"I'll do it if I can have my wraps back." Rocky leans back and stretches his legs.

"What kind of heroin was it?" Joona asks.

"White, from Nimroz . . . but Kandahar would do just fine."

"Okay," Joona says, taking a flattened roll of duct tape from his pocket.

With his eyes half closed, Rocky watches the former police officer wrap heavy-duty tape around his hands.

"I'm sure you know what you're doing," Rocky says.

"Bring the bag of sandwiches," Joona says, pressing the button on the intercom to indicate that the meeting is over.

A few seconds later Arne opens the door and lets Joona out into the hallway. The idea is for him to lead Joona out of the prison, then take Rocky back to his cell.

While the prison officer locks Rocky inside the interview room, Joona goes over to the other door with the loose baseboard. He leans over, slips his fingers into the gap, and pulls upward. The screws pull free from the concrete wall.

"You can't do that!" Arne exclaims.

Crumbs of cement rain down on the floor as Joona yanks the baseboard upward. The top screws are stuck, and Joona jerks hard, twisting the metal until there's a bang as the last screws come loose.

"Are you listening?" Arne says, drawing his baton. "I'm talking to you."

Joona ignores him. He holds the baseboard out in front of him, stamps down hard with his foot, bends and turns it, then stamps again.

"What the hell are you doing?" Arne asks with a nervous smile, coming closer.

"I'm sorry," Joona says simply.

He knows what kind of training Arne received, and that he's going to approach with his left hand outstretched, trying to hold him off while he attempts to strike Joona on the thighs and upper arms with sweeping movements of the baton.

Joona moves toward him with long strides, knocks his arm away, and then lands his elbow in the heavy man's chest, making him stagger back. His knees give out, but he puts out a hand to support himself and manages to sit down on the floor.

Joona stumbles from the momentum of his blow but stays on his feet and snatches the prison officer's alarm from Arne before he has time to react. He cuts his lower arm as he puts the bent part of the baseboard around Arne's neck, then pulls the handcuffs from his belt and attaches one cuff to the point where the ends of the baseboard intersect.

"Stand up and let Rocky out," he says.

Arne coughs and turns heavily, crawls to the wall, and leans against it as he gets to his feet.

"Unlock the door."

Arne's hands are free, but Joona is steering him from behind with the protruding ends of the baseboard. His neck is trapped in the nooselike bend, the sharp edges of the metal pressing against it.

"Don't do this," Arne pants.

Sweat is running down his face, and his hands are shaking as he unlocks the door of the interview room. Rocky comes out, picks up the baton, and presses it onto the floor to make it contract again.

"Arne, if you help us, we'll be out in four minutes and then I'll let you go," Joona says.

The prison officer limps ahead of Joona and keeps trying to slip his fingers under the metal noose.

"Use your passcard and type in the code." Joona steers him toward the elevator.

As they travel down through the building, Arne holds one hand against the mirror and keeps looking up at the camera in the hope that someone will see him.

The metal has already cut through one layer of the duct tape around Joona's hands.

When they emerge into the lobby, it takes just a few seconds for the rest of the prison staff to realize what's going on. Like a pressure wave, the atmosphere goes from relaxed to intense. Some sort of silent alarm has evidently been activated. A light flashes beneath a desk, and prison officers who had been sitting around talking moments before hurry to their feet. Chairs scrape the floor, papers fall to the ground.

"Let us through!" Joona calls, steering Arne toward the exit.

Seven guards approach anxiously from the hallway. They're clearly having trouble reading the situation. Joona tells Rocky to watch his back.

Rocky extends the baton and walks backward behind Joona toward the airlock.

The officer who was sitting in the security command center hurries over. His task is to slow things down and delay the escape for as long as possible. "I can't let you out," he says. "But if you give yourselves up, then—"

"Look at your colleague," Joona interrupts.

Arne whimpers as Joona pulls on the ends of the metal. The noose tightens around his neck. He tries to hold the metal back with his hands but stands no chance.

"Stop!" the security officer yells. "For God's sake, stop!"

Arne stumbles sideways into an information display, sending brochures falling to the ground.

"I'll let him go when we get outside," Joona says.

"Okay, everyone move back," the security officer says. "Let them through, let them go."

They pass through the beeping metal detector. The staff get out of the way. One officer is recording everything on his phone.

"Forward," Joona says.

Arne moans as they approach the exit. "Oh God," he whispers.

A dog is barking frantically on the other side of the security airlock, as guards rush outside the glass doors to get into formation.

"Let them through!" the security officer calls, following them out through the airlock. "I'll come with you, make sure you get out." He pulls out his card, taps in the code, and opens the door. "Who the hell are you?" he gasps at Joona.

Outside the prison, the sun is shining and the sky is radiant blue as they walk across the paved entrance area toward Joona's gray Porsche.

Joona walks around the vehicle, pushes Arne to the ground, and apologizes as he attaches the other handcuff to the metal fence behind the car. The security officer stands and watches them as the prison guards mill around inside the glass doors a dozen meters away.

Joona gets in quickly and starts the car.

Before Rocky has time to close the door, Joona drives over the curb, down the grass slope, past the cement blocks, and out onto the road, where he accelerates hard toward the forest where the old Volvo is waiting.

109

NESTOR WAS TAKEN TO KAROLINSKA, WHERE A TEAM OPER-
ated on him and managed to stop the bleeding. Nestor is lucky, his
condition is already stable, and he's been moved from the intensive
care unit.

Margot has stationed two uniformed officers outside his hospital room.

Nestor is conscious again but in a state of severe shock. He's
being given extra oxygen through a tube in his nose, and a pleural
drain has been inserted above his diaphragm. Bubbly blood is running out through the tube.

Nelly has spoken to Nestor's psychiatrist and suggested a low-
level sedative out of consideration for his medical history.

Nestor cries as Margot tries to explain the chain of events from
the police's point of view, up to the storming of his flat.

"But Erik wasn't there—so where was he?" she asks.

"I d-don't know," Nestor sobs.

"Why did you call and say that . . ."

"Nestor, you have to understand that none of what happened
is your fault. It was just an accident," Nelly says, holding his hand.

"Has Erik been in touch with you at all?" Margot asks.

"I d-don't know," he repeats, staring past her.

"Of course you know."

"I d-don't want to talk to you." He turns his face away.

"What line of work are you in?" Margot asks, taking a ham
sandwich out of her large bag.

"I'm retired . . . but I d-do a bit of gardening work."

"Where?"

"For the council . . . d-different places," he says.

"Do you have a lot of trouble with weeds?" Margot asks.

"Not really," he says curiously.

"Stinging nettles?"

"No," he says, picking at a tube.

"Nestor," Nelly says gently, "you know that Erik and I are good friends, and like you, I think it would be best for him to turn himself in to the police."

Tears well up in Nestor's eyes again, and Margot goes over to the window so she doesn't have to watch him cry.

"I'm riddled with b-bullets," he says loudly, and puts his hand on top of the bandage covering the wound in his chest.

"It was a terrible accident," Nelly says.

"God wants to k-kill me," he says, pulling the oxygen tube from his nose.

"Why do you think that?"

"I can't bear it," he whimpers.

"You know, the Jews say that a righteous man can fall seven times and get up again, but the ungodly stumble when calamity strikes. And you're going to get up."

"Am I r-righteous?"

"You tell me," she says.

"That's what you m-meant, isn't it?"

Nelly can see that the oxygenation of his blood is falling and reattaches the tube to his nose.

"Erik saved me, and I just wanted to save him," he whispers.

"Yesterday, you mean?" she asks tentatively.

"He c-came to me, and I gave him food and l-lodging," he says, coughing lightly. "They p-promised not to hurt him."

"How did he look when he came to you?"

"He had an ugly c-cap on, and his hand was bleeding. He was d-dirty and unshaven and had scratches on his face."

"And you just wanted to help him," Nelly says.

"Yes." He nods.

Margot is standing by the window eating her sandwich but can hear Nestor's careful answers. His description of Erik fits someone on the run.

"Do you know where Erik is now?" she asks slowly, turning around.

"No."

Margot meets Nelly's gaze, then leaves the room to set a large-scale police operation in motion.

"I'm getting t-tired," he says.

"It's a little early for the medicine to take effect."

"Are you Erik's g-girlfriend?" Nestor asks, looking at her.

"That's none of your business," Nelly says but can't help smiling. "Did Erik tell you his plans before he left? Do you think he's planning to give himself up?"

"You m-mustn't be angry with Erik."

"I'm not."

"My mother says he's b-bad, but . . . she c-can just shut up, I think."

"Get some rest, now."

"He's the nicest m-man you could get," Nestor goes on.

"I think so too," she says, and pats his hand.

"We meet sometimes . . . but you c-can't see me," Nestor says. "You can't hear me, and you c-can't smell me. I was b-born before you and I'll be waiting for you when you die. I can embrace you, b-but you can't hold on to me."

"Darkness," she replies.

"Good," Nestor nods. "If a man carried my b-burden, he . . . he would . . ."

Nestor closes his eyes and gasps for breath.

"I'm going home now," Nelly says quietly, as she carefully gets up from the edge of the bed.

When she leaves the post-op unit, she notices that the police officers are no longer guarding the door.

110

THE BELL IN ST. MARK'S CHURCH IS RINGING. THE HEAVY clapper hits the metal, and the peal reaches across the wall of the churchyard, in among the trees, all the way to the pet cemetery.

The dirty single-pane window of the shack in which Erik is hiding rattles. The red shed in the pet cemetery consists of thin timber walls and a stained particleboard floor. In recent years, only Nestor has been here, as the solitary but conscientious guardian of the animals' last resting place.

On one wall there is a cold-water faucet above a large zinc trough.

Erik has lined five sacks of compost up on the floor to form a bed.

He's lying on his side listening to the church bell. The smell of earth around him is pervasive, as if he's already lying in his grave.

He watches the morning light shine in through the gray curtain and wander slowly across the sacks of grass seed, grit, and shovels, then down across the floor to an ax with a rusty blade.

His gaze lingers on the ax, on the blunt edge with its deep indentations, and he thinks Nestor must use it to chop off roots when he's digging graves.

He turns on his bed, trying to get more comfortable. He spent the first few hours curled up in the corner behind the sacks. He felt nauseated and was shaking all over.

Eventually silence enveloped him.

After a few hours, he began to feel a little safer, dared to stand up, and went over to the faucet, where he drank some cold water and washed his face. The water splashed up onto a plastic sleeve that had been pinned to the wall. The drips ran down a price list from the Association of Stockholm Pet Cemeteries.

He called Joona and told him what had happened, aware of how incoherent and repetitive he sounded, and he realized he was in shock. He lay back down on the sacks but couldn't sleep—his heart was beating too fast.

His ear has stopped bleeding now but is still humming, as though he were hearing everything through a piece of thin fabric. Gradually the jagged, dazzling halo of light fades, and he closes his eyes.

He thinks about Jackie and Madeleine and hears children's voices in the distance. He creeps over to the window. They're probably playing in the woods behind the school.

Erik has no idea what he'd do if they came over here. His face could be on the front pages of all the papers today. A wave of anxiety washes through him, leaving him feeling utterly chilled.

Spiderwebs rustle when he slides the curtain aside a few more centimeters.

The pet cemetery is a beautiful place, lots of grass and deciduous trees. A small path leads from the church and over a wooden bridge, lined by tall stinging nettles.

On one grave, a number of round stones form a cross, and a child has made a lantern out of a jam jar, with red hearts painted around the outside.

Erik thinks about his conversation with Joona. He knows he can find his way into Rocky's memories if he gets the chance. He's already hypnotized him, but he wasn't looking for the preacher then.

But how long can he stay here? He's hungry, and sooner or later someone is going to find him. He's too close to the school, the church, and Nestor's apartment.

He swallows hard, gently touches the wound on his leg, and tries again to figure out how his fingerprints ended up in Susanna

Kern's home. There has to be a simple explanation. Joona seems to think someone's trying to frame him, but the thought is so ridiculous that he can't take it seriously.

There has to be a rational explanation.

I'm not afraid of a trial, Erik thinks. The truth will come out, if I can defend myself.

He has to turn himself in.

Erik thinks he could seek refuge in the church. The police can't shoot me in a church, he thinks. He decides to creep out and see if the church is open, but then hears someone crossing the little wooden bridge to the pet cemetery.

Erik ducks into the corner. Someone is walking along the path, groaning oddly. There's a tinkling sound, as though whoever it is kicked over the homemade lantern on the grave.

The footsteps stop, and everything goes silent. Maybe he's putting flowers on a dog's grave. Or maybe he's listening for sounds inside the shed.

Erik sits in the corner thinking about the dog that Nestor was forced to drown. In his mind's eye, he sees the flailing legs, the animal's attempts to swim as the sack filled with water.

The man outside spits noisily and keeps walking. Erik hears him come closer, walking through the dead bushes.

He's right outside the shed now, Erik thinks, looking around for a weapon, glancing at the shovels, then at the ax with the short handle and blunt blade.

Something trickles down the wall of the shed, splashing the tall grass. The man outside is urinating, slurring to himself as he does so. "You do your best," his deep voice mutters. "You come home, nice and quiet, but . . . nothing's good enough anymore."

The man lurches over to the window and peers in. The grass scrapes, and his shadow falls across the wall with the shovels. Erik presses himself against the wall next to the window, clearly hearing the man's breathing, first with his mouth open, then through tight nostrils.

"Honest work," he mutters, moving on through the low-lying blueberry bushes.

Erik decides to wait for the drunk to disappear before going to the church and turning himself in.

He tries again to imagine Nestor as the killer but can't honestly believe it.

The sun goes behind a cloud, and the gray curtain becomes dark again.

On a shelf stands a dusty thermos flask, with a plastic bag tucked between it and the wall, a little gray urn, and a painted plaster bulldog.

Erik just has time to see Nestor's shaving mirror quiver on the wall, sending a glint of a reflection across the floor, before the door of the shed swings open.

111

ERIK SCRAMBLES BACKWARD, AND A GREEN FOLDING CHAIR clatters to the floor. The door hits the wall, then bounces back against a very large shoulder. Dust is swirling around the bulky figure, who's panting as he makes his way into the shed. Rocky Kyrklund coughs and bangs his head on the dangling lightbulb. He's dressed in prison-issue clothing, his face is sweaty, and his hair is hanging pale and gray around his big head.

Joona comes in behind him, shuts the door, and stops the swaying bulb with his hand.

"*Viihtyisä*," Joona says.

Erik tries to say something, but he can barely breathe. When the door flew open he got so scared that his cheeks felt like they were burning.

Rocky mutters to himself, picks up the folding chair, and sits down. He's out of breath as he glances around the little room.

"You came," Erik says weakly.

"We made our way through the forest from Nacka Gård," Joona says, taking three cheese sandwiches out of a bag.

They eat in silence. Rocky is sweating from withdrawal and breathing hard between mouthfuls. When he's finished, he goes over and drinks some water from the faucet.

"It's more expensive to bury people," he says, gesturing toward the price list. Drops of water glisten in his beard.

Shadows dance behind the curtain. "I think we're fairly safe here," Joona says, removing the last of the duct tape from his hands. "The operation has already been downgraded. Publicly they're claiming they received inaccurate information, because Nestor wanted to commit suicide."

"But he is still alive, isn't he?"

"Yes." Joona meets Erik's gaze. His blond hair is sticking up, and his eyes have regained the chilly gray of an October sky.

Erik chews the last of the bread. "If this doesn't work, I thought I'd turn myself over inside the church," he says, trying to keep his voice steady.

"Good," Joona replies quietly.

"They can't shoot me inside a church," he adds.

"No, they can't," Joona replies, even though they both know this isn't true.

Rocky is smoking by the price list and muttering to himself.

"I'm ready to start," Erik tells him, crumpling his sandwich wrapper into a ball.

"Okay." Rocky nods and sits in the chair.

Erik looks at him, his dilated pupils, the color of his face, listens to his breathing. "You've marched through the woods, your body is still working hard," he says.

"Maybe it won't work, then?" Rocky asks, stubbing his cigarette out with his foot.

"I'd like to start with some relaxation. The fact that the brain is active is no problem. You're not supposed to be asleep, after all. What we want to do is gather all that activity and focus."

"Okay." Rocky leans back.

"Sit comfortably," Erik goes on. "You can change position as much as you like during the hypnosis, don't worry about that, but every time you move, you'll sink deeper into a state of relaxation."

Joona and Erik know this is the chance they've been waiting for. They don't need much, just a name, a location—some definite detail. If they get that, they should be able to find the preacher.

Erik can't force the process. He has to take his time, leading Rocky into a very deep trance in order to reach his most inaccessible memories.

"Rest your hands on your lap," Erik says quietly. "Clench them tight, then relax. Feel how heavy they are, feel them sink. They're being pulled down toward your thighs. Your wrists are feeling soft."

Erik concentrates on keeping his voice neutral, as he slowly works his way through Rocky's body, watching as his shoulders gradually relax. He talks for a while about his neck, about how heavy his head feels, and about breathing from deep down in his stomach, as he almost imperceptibly approaches the moment of induction.

In a monotone, he describes a wide, sandy beach, with gentle waves rolling in and out of the shore, as the white sand shimmers like porcelain.

"You're walking along the water's edge toward a bluff," Erik says. "The wet sand feels solid under your feet. It's easy to walk on. Warm waves lap against your legs, and grains of sand swirl around your feet." He describes tiny ridged seashells and coral rolling in the bubbling surf of the waves.

Rocky is slumped on the creaking folding chair. His jaw has relaxed, and his eyelids look heavy.

"All you're doing is listening to my voice, and you feel fine, everything is nice and safe . . ."

Joona is standing next to the window looking out at the pet cemetery. His jacket is open, and the butt of his pistol shimmers red against his chest.

"In a little while," Erik says, "I'm going to count backward from two hundred, and with each number, you're going to sink deeper and deeper into a relaxed state. And when I tell you to, you'll open your eyes and remember every detail from the first time you met the man you call the unclean preacher."

Rocky remains still, with his lower lip drooping slightly and his huge hands on his thighs. He looks like he's asleep, dreaming.

Erik counts down in a deep, soporific voice, his eyes monitoring Rocky's breathing, the movement of his bulging stomach.

Parallel to the hypnosis process, Erik sees himself sinking through murky water. It's so dark with mud, he can barely see Rocky in front of him. Air bubbles rise from his beard, and his hair sways in the current.

Erik breaks the sequence of numbers, skipping a few, but keeps counting down at an imperceptibly slowing rate.

He knows he needs to find precise memories.

The water gets darker, the deeper he goes. The current is stronger, pulling at his clothes. The whole time Rocky looks like he's undergoing grotesque changes in the muddy water, as if his face were made from loose sacking.

"Eighteen, seventeen . . . thirteen, twelve . . . soon you're going to open your eyes," Erik says, and watches Rocky's slow breathing. "There's nothing to worry about here, nothing dangerous."

112

ROCKY HAS ENTERED SUCH A DEEP TRANCE THAT HIS HEART rate is lower than during deep sleep. His breathing is like that of a hibernating animal, but at the same time parts of his brain are in a state of extreme focus. "Four, three, two, one. And now you open your eyes and remember exactly where you first met the unclean preacher."

Through the streaming brown water, Erik sees Rocky shake his head, although in reality he is sitting on the chair with his eyes open, trying to lick his lips.

His stomach is moving in time with his slow breathing. His chin rises, and his eyes stare straight ahead, unseeing.

"As soon as you feel ready, you can . . . *tell me what you see.*"

Rocky licks his cracked lips. "The grass is white . . . crunching underfoot," he says slowly. "A black veil flutters from the top of the staff . . . and small snowflakes are drifting to the ground." He mutters something Erik can't make out.

"Listen to my voice and tell me what you remember," Erik reminds him.

Rocky's forehead is wet with sweat. He stretches out one leg, and the chair creaks again under his weight.

"The light is the color of chalk," he murmurs, "falling through the windows in the deep alcoves. . . . Against a gold-leaf ceiling hangs the defeated savior . . . together with the other criminals."

"You're inside a church now?"

Deep down in the fast-flowing, dirty water, Rocky nods. His eyes are open wide, and his hair is floating next to his head.

"Which church is it?" Erik's voice trembles, and he tries to force himself to be calm, to find tranquility within the hypnotic resonance.

"The preacher's church."

"What's it called?" Erik feels his heart beat faster.

Rocky's mouth moves slightly, but the only sound that comes out is a few clicks from his lips. Erik leans forward and hears the slow exhalation, then the voice coming from deep in his throat.

"Sköld-inge," Rocky says groggily.

"Sköldinge Church," Erik repeats.

Rocky nods, leans his head back, and forms a soundless word with his lips.

Erik exchanges a glance with Joona. They have what they need. He should bring Rocky out of his deep trance now but can't help asking: "Is the unclean preacher there?"

Rocky smiles sleepily and raises a weary hand as if to point at the tools on the wall of the little shed.

"Can you see him?" Erik persists.

"In the church," Rocky whispers as his head lolls forward.

Over by the streaked window, Joona is looking stressed. Maybe some visitors have arrived in the pet cemetery.

"Tell me what you can see," Erik says.

Rocky trembles, and a drop of sweat falls from the tip of his nose. "I see the old priest . . . with rouge over the stubble on his drooping cheeks . . . the lipstick, and his stupid expression, morose and silent . . ."

"Go on."

"*Ossa . . . ipsius in pace*," Rocky whispers to himself, his face twitching, and he shifts uneasily on the creaking folding chair. Flakes of green paint fall on to the particleboard floor.

Joona moves backward and silently draws his pistol.

"Do you know what his name is?" Erik asks. "Say his name, loud enough for me to hear."

"The ugly old priest . . . with his scrawny arms, covered in tracks from all the fucking junk he's injected over the years," Rocky says, and his head jerks to one side. "Cloudy from bleeding under the skin and wrecked veins, but now he's wearing his snow-white surplice, no one's seen anything, no one knows what's going on . . . his sister and daughter by his side, his closest colleagues . . ."

"Are there other priests in the church?"

"The pews are full of priests, row after row after row."

Even though Joona is gesturing for him to bring the hypnosis to an end, Erik urges Rocky to go deeper, "Go down to a place where there are only real memories. . . . I'm going to count down from ten . . . and when I get to zero, you'll be in Sköldinge Church, and—"

Rocky stands up, his head jerks, his eyes roll backward, and he collapses over the chair. He hits the floor, his head striking the bags of compost, and his feet twitch spasmodically. His body arches. His shirt slides up, and he's gurgling gutturally with pain as his mouth gradually stretches open and his neck pulls back. His spine creaks.

Erik hurries over and moves tools and equipment out of his reach.

The floor thuds as Rocky rolls onto his side, and a moment later his epileptic attack switches to muscle spasms.

Erik kneels and holds both hands under Rocky's big head to keep him from hurting himself.

His legs are kicking and jerking hard, crashing his heels down on the floor. Joona is holding his gun close to his body and looking at Erik with ice-gray eyes.

"You need to find a new hiding place," he says. "I saw police officers in the woods by the school. They probably got another tip, otherwise they wouldn't be here. They'll be bringing in dogs if they haven't already, and searching with helicopters."

Rocky's attack is fading, but he's still breathing fast, and one of his legs jerks a few more times.

Erik rolls him gently onto his side.

Rocky blinks. He's soaked with sweat as he lets out a tired cough.

"You had an epileptic fit while you were hypnotized," Erik explains.

"God," he sighs.

"Erik, you have to go. Get as far away as you can, and hide," Joona says again.

113

ERIK OPENS THE DOOR CAUTIOUSLY AND LOOKS OUT AT THE pet cemetery, then leaves the shed. Without looking back, he walks along the path between the trees and the little graves. When he reaches the forest, he starts to walk faster. He gets to a wider path and runs.

He can hear dogs barking over toward the school. He leaves the path and heads into denser forest. He forces his way through pine thickets, scratching his cheek and one eyelid and making them sting. He crouches and makes his way through the trees, through spiderwebs, and over glossy fungi and mushrooms.

He's out of breath, and his body is dripping with sweat. The ground slopes down steeply in front of him. The barking is getting closer, and he can hear police shouting instructions to their dogs.

Erik runs through the forest, which has suddenly opened up. He can see reeds and bulrushes between the trees. Just as he detects the acrid smell of a marsh, one foot sinks into wet moss. He can hear a helicopter farther away over the treetops.

Erik hurries forward, but the ground feels like it's rocking. Water rises around his feet, up over his ankles, and he realizes he can't get across the bog. He needs to turn back, but he sinks deeper and almost falls. He leans one hand against a tree trunk. Cool moisture is rising out of the ground, and there's a sucking sound as the wet moss lets go of his foot. He has to crawl back, getting his knees wet and cold. He eventually reaches firm ground and starts running.

Twigs snap under his feet and after a while he can't run any farther, and instead walks as fast as he can.

The dogs have picked up his scent. Soon they'll catch up with him.

A strong impulse to turn himself over to the police overwhelms him. Imagine, this could all be over, he could be warm again.

Then he remembers Nestor getting shot through his chest. The calls are drawing nearer, a hunting team surrounding their prey.

Erik goes cold inside.

He has to move around the bog in a wide arc, then find his way through the forest.

He starts running again.

He's so out of breath that his throat feels raw, and he knows he has no chance of outrunning the dogs if they've been set loose.

A tall rock face covered in sphagnum moss and lichen rises up between the trees. He forces himself upward when the moss slips beneath him, and he slides. He scrapes his hands against the rock to stop himself.

When he's finally at the top, he lies down flat. His heart pounds against the rock beneath him. He wipes the sweat from his eyes and sees the ocher-colored high-rises of Björkhagen above the trees. Below him, on the edge of the marsh, the police officers are circling, their dogs straining at their leashes. The police are talking into their radios and shouting to one another, pointing across the bog. Suddenly one dog signals that it's picked up a scent. It turns back into the forest, following Erik's trail through the trees. Its leash stretches tight, and the dog barks loudly.

Erik shuffles backward, aware that he has to put some distance between himself and the dog patrol. His legs tremble with the exertion as he runs sideways down the slope. He follows a path and emerges onto a running track covered with damp bark chips. A woman in a pink tracksuit is standing still, stretching her muscles, and he hesitates briefly before running past her. Her neck and chest are sweaty. She has a distant look on her face, and he sees that she's listening to music on her headphones. Just as he passes her, she looks up at him. Her face stiffens, and she looks away a little too quickly. He realizes she's recognized him, and sees her move away out of the corner of his eye.

He hurries around the next bend and stops in front of a map of the nature reserve. He looks along the route of the Sörmland Trail, then decides to go down toward the water at Sicklasjön.

114

ERIK RUNS PAST A FALLEN TREE AND THROUGH THE FOREST as he hears the barking of the dogs echo between the tree trunks.

After half a kilometer or so he reaches a stream. The bottom is covered with red stones, and the water shimmers brown with iron.

Erik steps into the ice-cold water and wades along the stream, hoping the dogs will lose his scent for a few minutes.

He wishes he could call Jackie to tell her he's innocent. He can't bear the thought of her believing he's a murderer. The news must be full of exaggerated accusations, details from his life, things from long ago that are now being dragged up as proof of his guilt.

Erik tries to wade faster but slips on a stone, falls, and hits his knee on the bottom. He lets out a gasp. Cold and pain shoot up through his bones, up into his spine and neck.

The banks are steeper here, the water channel narrower and faster ahead of him.

The trees lean over the water, and he has to bend beneath their branches. He continues wading as the stream passes through thicker forest. He can no longer hear the dogs, just the water lapping around his legs.

He scrambles out of the water and hurries through the forest on squelching shoes. Exhaustion and his clinging clothes cause him to keep stumbling.

This is hopeless, he thinks. It's over. I don't have anywhere to go. I have no one I can ask for help.

He has a lot of acquaintances, people he socializes with, colleagues of many years' standing, and a few good friends, but no one he can call right now.

He's pretty sure Simone would be willing to help, but she's probably being watched. And Benjamin would do whatever he could, he knows that, but Erik would rather die than put his son in any danger.

There are only a few people he knows he can call. Joona, Nelly, and maybe Jackie.

If Jackie has gone to see her sister, maybe he could even borrow her apartment—assuming she doesn't believe what the papers have been saying.

Erik looks at his phone—the charge is at four percent. He doesn't want to put Nelly at risk but calls her number anyway.

If her phone's being monitored, that's that, but if he's going to stand any chance at all, he has to take the risk. He's surrounded out here, he has no other option.

His phone crackles, he hears the ringing tone, and then there's a click.

"Nelly," she answers calmly.

"It's me," he says. "Can you talk?"

"Erik? Where are you? What the hell is happening?"

"Nelly, listen, I need help. I didn't do the things they're saying about me. I have no idea what this is all about."

"Erik, I know you're innocent. But you need to turn yourself in to the police. Surrender, and I'll support you, be a witness, anything."

"They'll shoot me the second they catch sight of me. You've no idea what—"

"I understand how you feel," she interrupts. "But won't it just get worse the longer you wait? The police are everywhere."

"Nelly—"

"They've taken your computer, they've packed your whole office into boxes, they're outside our house in Bromma, they're at Karolinska, and—"

"Nelly, I need to stay in hiding for a while. There are no other options. But I understand if you can't help me. I don't want to cause you any trouble."

"This is crazy," she says.

"Please, Nelly, there's no one else I can ask."

He can hear the dogs barking again, closer now.

"It would be a disaster for me to get involved," she says. "It would ruin my career, and it would ruin Martin's, but I—"

"Sorry I asked," Erik says, despair creeping over him.

"—but I have an old place," she continues. "Have I ever told you about Solbacken? It used to belong to Dad's parents. It's pretty out of the way."

"How do I get there?"

"I—I can't believe I'm doing this. I don't know, maybe I can rent a car at Statoil or something."

"You'd do that for me?" he asks.

"Where can I find you?"

"Do you know the public beach at Sickla Strand?" Erik asks.

"No, but I'm sure I can get there."

"There's a school right next to the beach. Wait there until I show up."

Erik crouches and runs through the dense undergrowth at the edge of the water, then pulls off his shoes and heavy pants. He bundles his clothes and hides in the bushes as a helicopter passes low overhead.

His pursuers are getting closer.

Dressed in just his underwear and undershirt, he wades out into Sicklasjön. The chill stabs at his feet and legs.

He sees blue lights flashing over on Älta Road, on the bridge across the inlet leading to Järlasjön. There are at least three police cars. The vehicles' lights reflect off the metal struts of the bridge and across the tops of the trees on both shores.

He sinks quickly into the water. He holds his breath but can clearly feel the current change as the helicopter passes. The water of the lake forms small waves radiating out in rapid circles.

He keeps going, farther out, slipping down among the water lilies, between their long stalks and the slimy bottom of the lake.

There he lets the bundle of clothes and his phone fill with bubbling water and sink.

In the other direction, beyond the dam, he can see that the bridge over the Sickla Channel has been blocked off, too. There are police cars everywhere. The tall fiberglass railings shimmer like huge plates of blue light. A helicopter is hovering above the ski slope.

Erik starts to swim, taking big strokes, feeling the cold against his body and the smell of seawater in his nose.

115

ERIK KEEPS HIS HEAD LOW AND TRIES NOT TO DISTURB THE surface of the lake too much. He's already more than one hundred meters out. The water laps softly as he takes his broad strokes but thunders in his ears when he's underwater.

He raises his head enough to be able to look ahead. Drops of water sparkle on his eyelashes as he sees the two jetties before they disappear behind the swell. The current is pulling him to one side.

High above the nature reserve, the helicopter is hovering, but he can no longer hear dogs.

He swims, thinking about how he lied nine years ago and stole Rocky's whole life from him—and didn't spare him a thought until now.

He slows down and treads water when he sees he's just fifty meters from the two protruding jetties. A few children in bathing suits are running around on the damp wood. There are people sitting with picnic baskets, blankets, and folding chairs in the late-summer warmth.

A motorboat appears to be approaching from the channel.

Erik swims toward the shore, beyond the beach. At the far end, gnarled weeping willows hang over the water. The tips of their bright green branches trail in the undulating water.

The motorboat skims silently toward him, its prow striking the waves as the boat slows down.

Erik takes aim for the trees, fills his lungs with air, then dives below the surface.

He swims underwater with powerful strokes, feeling the coolness of the water against his face and eyes, its taste in his mouth, and the muffled sound as his ears fill.

The dappled daylight shimmers on the bubbles rising from his arms.

Heard beneath the water, the motorboat makes a metallic buzzing sound.

Erik's shoulders are straining from the effort. It's farther to the shore than he thought. The water below him is completely black, but the surface looks like molten tin.

His lungs feel tight. He has to breathe soon. The buzzing of the motorboat gets louder.

He keeps swimming but is closer to the surface. He has no energy left. He needs oxygen.

He kicks out with his legs and feels his diaphragm tighten, cramping in an effort to force his lungs to breathe in some air.

The water gets lighter, full of swirling sand. He can make out the bottom beneath him, rough blocks of stone amid the coarse sand. He takes one last stroke with his arms, then pulls himself forward across the stones with his hands.

Erik breaks the surface, gasps for breath, coughs, and spits out a mouthful of slime. He's bobbing up and down in the swell from the boat. His vision goes dark and he wheezes and wipes the water from his face with trembling hands.

He makes his way up onto the rocks on unsteady legs, then collapses. His whole body shakes as he sits behind the curtain of branches. The police boat is moving along the lake, but its engine is no longer audible.

Even if Nelly manages to leave her house and rent a car, it will be a while before she gets here. It makes sense to wait beneath the trees and dry off a little before he makes his way to the meeting point.

After half an hour or so, he leaves his hiding place, climbs the rocks, crosses the footpath, and steps behind a large hazel bush. The ground beneath the branches is littered with toilet paper. He moves toward the rust-red exterior of Sickla Recreation Center.

Suddenly the sound of a siren echoes loudly between the walls, and he stops abruptly, his heart pounding. People are sitting at an outdoor café a short distance away, eating and drinking, quite unconcerned. The vehicle disappears, and Erik continues walking. He's just thinking he should wait on the other side of the building, hidden by the bushes, when he catches sight of Nelly. She's wearing a green floral-print dress, and her blond hair is tied up with a green scarf.

On the other side of the street is a black Jeep. Nelly shades her face with one hand as she looks toward the water.

Erik walks across the grass and some low bushes, then emerges onto the pavement when Nelly spots him. Her lips part as though she were suddenly frightened. He looks around for traffic, then walks straight across the road in his wet underpants.

Nelly looks him quickly up and down. "Nice outfit," she says, opening the back door. "Get under the blanket."

He huddles on the floor behind the seat and pulls the red rug over himself. The sun-heated car smells like plastic and leather.

He hears Nelly get in the driver's seat and close the door. She starts the engine and pulls away to the left, bumping off the curb, then speeds up. He slides back toward the seat.

"We know Rocky was wrongly convicted of the murder of Rebecka Hansson, but—"

"Not now, Nelly," he interrupts.

"But do we know he's innocent of these new murders? I mean . . . what if he started copying the murder he was convicted of just to put the blame on you?"

"It's not him. I hypnotized him. He saw the preacher and—"

"But couldn't he just have divided himself into different characters? So that he's the unclean preacher when he commits the murders?"

Nelly puts a CD on, and the car fills with Johnny Cash's heavy voice: "Wanted man in California."

Erik can't help smiling at the fact that Nelly is trying to be funny at a time like this.

116

ROCKY IS ASLEEP ON THE PASSENGER SEAT NEXT TO JOONA. His big head lolls to the side when the road bends. The landscape is sparsely populated and desolate, almost abandoned.

Joona is driving fast, thinking about the text message Lumi sent him earlier today. She wrote that she loves Paris but misses their conversations in Nattavaara.

Just beyond Flen, the road and railway come together on two narrow strips of land. A long freight train thunders past next to the car, closer and closer.

The forest gradually thins, and the landscape flattens into huge fields. Combines roll across the fields in clouds of dust.

Sköldinge is on Route 55, not far from Katrineholm. Joona turns off to the right and sees a few red houses through the trees, then the sandy-colored church with its pointed spire, rising from the plain.

Sköldinge Church.

An ordinary Swedish church out in the countryside, dating back to the twelfth century, surrounded by rune stones.

The gravel crunches beneath the tires as he pulls over and stops in front of the parish house.

Maybe they've found the killer now. The preacher from Rocky's nightmarish memories. The old priest with rouged cheeks and arms full of needle tracks.

The church door is closed, and the windows are dark.

Joona pulls his Colt Combat from its holster and notices that the tape is dirty and has started to peel off. He usually wraps athletic tape around the lower part of the butt so his hand doesn't slip.

He pulls out the magazine and makes sure it's full, presses it back in, and feeds a bullet into the chamber even though he can't really believe that the unclean preacher is just waiting for them inside the church.

Nothing is that simple.

The path has been raked, and the churchyard is well tended. Sunlight filters through the leaves of a huge oak.

The preacher is an extremely dangerous man, a serial killer who never rushes, who takes his time, who watches and plans, down to the last detail, until something else takes over and he turns into a wild animal.

His weakness is his arrogance, his narcissistic hunger.

Joona glances at the church, then across the fields. He has two extra magazines of ordinary Parabellum bullets in one pocket, and a magazine of fully jacketed ammunition in the other.

Even if the preacher isn't here, he thinks, even if he's never been here, this is the end of the road.

If he can't find something here that can convince Margot, then it's over. Erik will be found guilty even though he's innocent, just as Rocky was found guilty years ago of murdering Rebecka Hansson. And the serial killer will go free.

Today is the day everything gets decided. Erik can't keep on running—he has nowhere left to go.

And now Joona has broken an inmate out of jail and assaulted a prison officer.

Disa would have said he was just understimulated, that he needed to get back to work. It's too late for that now, but he had no choice.

When Joona opens the car door, Rocky wakes up and looks at him with narrow, sleepy eyes.

"Wait here," Joona says, and leaves the car.

Rocky gets out and spits on the ground, leans against the car roof, and draws a line in the dust on it with his hand.

"Do you recognize where we are?" Joona asks.

"No," Rocky says, looking over at the church.

"I want you to wait in the car," Joona repeats. "I don't think the killer's here, but it could still be dangerous."

"I don't give a shit," Rocky says bluntly.

He follows Joona between the gravestones. The air is fresh, as if it has just been raining. A man in jeans and a T-shirt stands outside the church entrance, smoking and talking on his cellphone. They pass him and go into the church.

The transition from bright sunlight leaves them almost completely blind as they walk into the darkness.

Joona moves quickly to one side, ready to draw his pistol.

He blinks and waits for his eyes to adjust before going in among the pews beneath the organ loft. Huge pillars hold up ornate frescoes leading to the ceiling.

There's a knocking sound, and a shadow flits across the walls. Someone's sitting in one of the front pews.

Joona stops Rocky, draws his gun, and holds it hidden beside his hip.

A bird hits the window. A crow seems to be caught in a piece of twine and keeps hitting the window when it tries to fly away.

The door to the sacristy is ajar. On the wall is a hazy cross in a circle.

Joona slowly approaches the huddled figure from behind and sees a wrinkled hand holding on to the back of the pew in front.

The bird hits the window again. The shrunken figure slowly turns toward the sound.

It's an elderly Chinese woman.

Joona passes her, still concealing his gun, and glances at her out of the corner of his eye. Her face is downcast, impassive.

Beside the medieval font, Mary sits like a child. Her wide wooden dress falls in heavy folds around her feet.

At the center of the altarpiece, Christ hangs on the cross against a sky of gold, just as Rocky described under hypnosis.

This was where he first met the unclean preacher, when the entire church was full of priests.

Now he's back.

Rocky has stopped in the darkened doorway beneath the organ loft. The instrument's pipes stick up above him like a row of quill pens.

He's standing still, irresolute. Like an apostate, he doesn't look up at the altar, just stares down at his big, empty hands.

The Chinese woman gets up and walks out.

Joona knocks on the door of the sacristy, nudges it open slightly, and peers into the gloom. A set of vestments is hanging ready, but the room looks empty.

Joona steps aside and looks into the gap between the hinges and sees the uneven stone wall, like billowing fabric.

He opens the door farther and walks in, holding his pistol chest high. He quickly looks around at the liturgical vestments. High above, pale daylight filters in through a deep alcove.

Joona crosses the floor to the toilet and opens the door, but there's no one there, just a wristwatch on the shelf above the sink.

He raises his pistol and opens the closet door. Chasubles, cassocks, and stoles hang side by side, different colors for different seasons of the religious calendar. Joona quickly pushes the clothes aside and looks toward the back.

There's something on the floor in one corner. A pile of magazines about sports cars.

Joona returns to the nave and walks past Rocky, who is sitting in one of the pews, and goes outside, where he asks the man by the door where the priest is.

"That's me." The man smiles, dropping his cigarette in the empty coffee mug by his feet.

"I mean the other priest," Joona explains.

"It's just me here," he says.

Joona has already looked at his arms—they're free of injection scars.

"When were you ordained?"

"I was ordained as a curate in Katrineholm, and four years ago I was appointed as the priest here," the man replies amiably.

"Who was here before you?"

"That was Rickard Magnusson. And before him, Erland Lodin and Peter Leer Jacobson, Mikael Friis, and . . . I can't remember."

The man has cut his hand—there's a grubby Band-Aid across his palm.

"This probably sounds like a strange question," Joona says. "But when would a church be full of priests? In the pews, like the congregation?"

"When a priest is ordained. But that would be in a cathedral," the priest replies helpfully, picking his mug up off the ground.

"But here?" Joona persists. "Has this church ever been full of priests?"

"It could have been for a priest's funeral, but it's up to the family to decide. It depends who gets invited. There are no special rules for priests."

"Have you buried priests here?"

Joona follows the man as he walks to the church doors and looks out across the headstones, the narrow paths, and the neatly trimmed bushes.

"I know that Peter Leer Jacobson is buried in the churchyard," he says quietly. The young priest's arms are goosebumped from the coolness of the stone.

"When did he die?" Joona asks.

"Long before I got here. Fifteen years ago, maybe, I don't know."

"Is there a record of who was here when he was buried?"

The man shakes his head and thinks for a moment. "No record, but his sister would know. She still lives in the widows' home owned by the parish. He was a widower and took care of her."

Joona goes back inside the dimly lit church. Rocky is smoking underneath the medieval triumphal cross above the choir screen. Jesus's entire emaciated body is dotted with red wounds, like an old heroin addict.

"What does 'Ossa ipsius in pace' mean?" Joona asks.

"Why do you want to know?"

"You said it under hypnosis."

"It means 'his bones are at peace,'" Rocky says roughly.

"You were describing a dead priest. That's why he was wearing makeup."

They walk quickly under the arch toward the door as Joona thinks about Rocky's description of a funeral service with an open coffin. The deceased priest was made up and dressed in a white cassock, but he wasn't the unclean preacher. The funeral was simply the first time Rocky met him.

117

JOONA AND ROCKY APPROACH A FLIGHT OF STONE STEPS leading to Fridhem, the parish house where Peter Leer Jacobson's older sister Ellinor was given permission to stay after his death. Together with a younger woman from Sköldinge village, she runs a café with a small exhibition about the village and what life was like for priests and their families in the past.

Fridhem consists of three red cottages with white window frames and gables, open shutters, and old-fashioned tiles on the roofs. The houses sit on three sides of a neat patch of lawn, with café tables beneath the weeping birch trees.

The two men enter the café and pass through a cramped room lined with framed black and white photographs. Joona glances along the pictures of buildings, teams of workers, and priests' families. Three glass cabinets contain jet mourning jewelry, letters, inventories, and hymnals.

Inside the pleasant café, Joona buys two cups of coffee and a plate of cookies from an elderly woman in a flowery apron. She looks nervously at Rocky, who doesn't smile back when she tells them they get a free refill.

"Excuse me," Joona says. "But you must be Ellinor? Peter Leer Jacobson's sister?"

The woman gives him a quizzical nod. When Joona explains that they've just spoken to the new priest, who said so many nice things about her brother, her clear blue eyes fill with tears.

"Peter was very, very popular," she says tremulously, then tries to catch her breath.

"You must have been very proud of him." Joona smiles.

"Yes, I was."

In a rather touching gesture, she pulls her hands together over her stomach in an effort to calm down.

"There's something I was wondering," Joona goes on. "Did your brother have a particular colleague, someone he worked closely with?"

"Yes, that would have been the rural dean in Katrineholm, and the vicars of Floda and Stora Malm. And he spent a lot of time in Lerbo Church toward the end."

"Did they see each other privately as well?"

"My brother was a fine man," she says. "An honorable man, very well liked."

Ellinor looks around the empty room, then walks around the counter and shows Joona a framed newspaper cutting from the king and queen's visit to Strängnäs.

"Peter was chaplain at the jubilee service in the cathedral," she says proudly. "The bishop thanked him afterward, and—"

"Show her your arms," Joona tells Rocky.

Rocky rolls up his sleeves, without changing his expression.

"My brother was the orator at the diocesan meeting in Härnösand, and he—"

The old woman trails off when she sees Rocky's ravaged arms, uneven and stained from hundreds of injection scars, dark with veins that have disintegrated from the ascorbic acid he's used to dissolve the heroin.

"He's a priest too," Joona says without taking his eyes off her. "Anyone can get trapped."

Ellinor's wrinkled face turns pale and motionless. She sits down on the wooden bench with her hand over her mouth.

"My brother changed after the accident, when his wife passed away," she says quietly. "Grief destroyed him, and he withdrew from everyone . . . thought someone was following him, that everyone was spying on him."

"When was this?"

"Sixteen years ago."

"What did your brother use?"

The woman looks at him with exhausted eyes. "On the boxes it said 'Morphine Epidural.'" She shakes her head, and her old hands flutter restlessly over her apron. "I didn't know anything. He was all alone in the end. Not even his daughter could stand it. She took care of him for as long as she could, but now I understand why she couldn't continue."

"But he was still able to conduct services, do his job?"

She raises her bloodshot eyes toward Joona. "Oh yes, he conducted his services. No one noticed anything, not even me, because we no longer spent any time together. But I used to go to the morning service, and . . . Everyone said his sermons were stronger than ever . . . even though he was growing weaker."

Rocky mutters something and walks away from them. They watch him through the window as he emerges onto the lawn and goes and sits at a table under the weeping birch.

"How did you find out?" Joona asks.

"I was the one who found him," the old woman replies. "I was the one who took care of the body."

"Was it an overdose?"

"I don't know. He'd missed the morning service, so I went into the rectory. There was a terrible stench in there. I found him in the basement . . . he had been dead for three days, naked and filthy, covered in scabs. He was lying in the cage like an animal."

"He was lying in a cage?"

She nods and wipes her nose. "All he had was a mattress and a can of water," she whispers.

"Didn't you think it was strange that he was in a cage?"

The old woman shakes her head. "It had been locked from the inside. I've always thought he tried to lock himself in to escape the drugs."

A younger woman in a similar apron comes out and stands behind the counter when some more customers arrive.

"Could one of your brother's colleagues have helped him write his sermons?" Joona asks.

"I don't know."

"He probably had a computer. Could I take a look at it?"

"He had one in the office, but he wrote his sermons by hand."

"Did you keep them?"

Ellinor slowly stands up from the bench. "I took care of his estate," she says. "I cleaned out the rectory so that there wouldn't be any gossip, but he'd gotten rid of everything. There were no photographs, no letters or sermons. I couldn't find his diaries, and he always kept a diary. He used to keep them locked up in his desk, but it was empty."

"Could they be anywhere else?"

She stands still and her mouth moves silently until the words come. "I only have one diary left. It was hidden in the liquor cabinet. They usually have a secret compartment in the back, where gentlemen could keep their saucy French postcards."

"What did it say in the diary?" Joona says.

She smiles and shakes her head. "I would never read it. You don't do that sort of thing."

"Of course not," he replies.

"But many years ago Peter used to get his diaries out at Christmas and read about Mother and Father, and about ideas for sermons. He wrote very well."

The door to the café opens again, and a draft sweeps through the small room, spreading the smell of fresh coffee.

"Do you have the diary here?" Joona asks.

"It's in the exhibition," she says. "We call it a museum, but it's really just a few things we found here."

She takes him to the exhibition. An enlarged photograph from 1850 shows three thin women in black dresses in front of the home for widows. The buildings look almost black. The picture was taken early one spring, the trees are bare, and there's still snow in the furrows of the field.

Beneath the picture is a short caption about the priest who had Fridhem built so that his wife wouldn't have to marry the next priest if he died before her.

Next to the earrings and necklace of polished jade lies a rusty key and a small color photograph showing the funeral of Peter Leer Jacobson. A man dressed in black is acting as marshal of ceremonies, holding the black veil. The bishop and the priest's daughter and sister are standing by the coffin with their faces lowered.

They walk past pictures of the mine at Kantorp, women and children sorting ore in bright sunshine, the Sköldinge workhouse, and the opening of the railway station. One black and white photograph of the church has been hand-tinted, so the sky is pastel blue, the vegetation looks tropical, and the wooden construction of the new steeple shines like polished bronze.

"Here's the diary," Ellinor says, stopping in front of another glass cabinet containing an array of objects.

118

ON TOP OF A LINEN CLOTH LIES A RUSTY HAIR CLIP, A POCKET watch, a white hymnbook bearing the name ANNA in gold writing, and the priest's diary, with a lilac strap around its stained leather binding.

The old woman looks at Joona with frightened eyes as he opens the case and removes the diary. On the front page, in ornate hand-writing, are the words PETER LEER JACOBSON, PRIEST, VOLUME XXIV.

"I don't think it's right to read other people's diaries," she says with a hint of anxiety.

"No," Joona says, and opens the book.

The first entry is dated almost twenty years ago.

"We don't have the right to—"

"I have to," Joona interrupts. He leafs forward, staring at the diary.

The administration of the parish has become more onerous, the guidelines stricter. I fear that finances will come to govern my church more and more. ~~Why not start selling indulgences again [Sic!].~~

Today is the fifth Sunday after Epiphany, and the liturgical colors are getting darker again. The theme is "Sowing and Reaping." I don't like the warning in Paul's Letter to the Galatians about not mocking God. "For whatsoever a man soweth, that shall he also reap." But sometimes you haven't sown, yet must still reap. I can't say that to my congregation—they want to hear about the riches of heaven.

Joona looks up and sees the old woman leave the room with her hands hanging by her sides.

I met the pasty-faced contract priest in Lerbo for a private conversation. He was probably expecting me to talk about my drinking. He's young, but his faith is so strong, it makes me feel bad. I decided not to visit him again.

My daughter is growing up now. The other day I watched her without her knowing. She was sitting in front of the mirror. She had her hair just like Anna's and was smiling to herself.

Today is the fifth Sunday after Easter. The theme for the sermon is "Growing in Faith." I think about Grandmother and Grandfather who went to Guinea before they moved to the farm in Roslagen. In my congregation there is no place for missionary work, and that makes me wonder.

Joona sits on one of the old chairs beneath the photographs. He leafs through the book, reading about the duties of the liturgical year, Christmas carols, and summer services at some mill or other. He goes back through it again, looking for any further mention of the priest in Lerbo and finds himself in the middle of Easter.

The Gospels turn their attention to the empty grave, but around the dinner table we talked about the Old Testament text describing the last plague to strike Egypt. My daughter said God loves blood and referred to one of Easter's biblical texts: "And the blood shall be to you for a token upon the houses where you are: and when I see the blood I will pass over you."

My wife and I haven't shared a bedroom for a year now. I usually stay up late, and I snore like a mechanical digger (according to her). But we often sneak in to each other at night. Sometimes I go with Anna to her bedroom in the evening just to watch her get ready. I've always liked watching her take off her jewelry at night, pressing the little studs back on to her earrings and putting them in the case next to each other. Anna is quietly attentive to detail. She doesn't reach behind her back when she takes her bra off, but slips the straps over her shoulders, slides the bra down to her waist, and turns it around before unfastening it.

When I sat on her bed last night watching her braid her hair for bed, I thought I could see a face at the dark window. I got up and went over, but I couldn't see anything, so I went out onto the veranda, then into the garden, but everything was quiet, and I looked up at the starry sky instead.

Joona looks out the window and sees that Rocky is still sitting under the tree, with his eyes closed and legs outstretched. He continues reading.

I saw the pasty-faced priest from Lerbo in the supermarket yesterday, but didn't have to say hello.

Fourth Sunday in Lent.
So we have reached the midpoint of Lent. Headache, sat up late drinking wine, reading and writing.
Today we think about "the Bread of Life." The holy days of Easter are almost upon us, and the heavy fist of existence presses us to the ground.

Joona leafs forward, glancing at pages about Trinity Sunday and the transition to the gentler half of the church calendar, then stops abruptly:

It has happened, terrible, impossible. I shall write about it here, and beg God for forgiveness, then I shall never mention it again. My hand is shaking as I write this, two days later:
Like old Lot, I was tricked into breaking the Lord's commandment, but I am writing to understand my role in this, my share of the guilt. It got rather late, and I drank more wine than

I could handle, more than I usually do, and I was drunk when I went to bed and fell asleep.

In hindsight I think I was aware on some level that it wasn't Anna who crept into my bed in the darkness. She smelled like Anna, she was wearing my wife's jewelry and nightshirt, but she was scared, her body was trembling as I lay on top of her.

She didn't whisper at all, she didn't sigh like Anna, she was breathing as if to resist giving in to pain.

I tried to turn on the lamp, I was still so drunk that it fell to the floor. I stood up, staggered, followed the wall with my hand, and turned on the main light.

In my bed sat my daughter. She was wearing makeup and smiling, even though she was scared.

I roared, I shouted, and rushed over and tore Anna's earrings from her ears, I rubbed her face on the bloodstained sheet, I dragged her down the stairs and out into the snow, I slipped and fell, got up again and shoved her away.

She was freezing, and her ears were bleeding, but she was still smiling.

I shall be punished, I must be punished, I should have seen this coming. Isolation and blossoming, her creeping, spying, always fiddling with Anna's jewelry and makeup.

Joona stops reading, looks at the rusty key and the black earrings in the case, and at the text. He leaves the exhibition with the diary, passing the picture of the skinny widows. Out in the café, Ellinor is setting small coffee cups on saucers on the shelf behind the counter. The porcelain tinkles gently as she stacks it. A lethargic fly has flown in through the open doors and is bouncing against the window as it tries to get out.

Ellinor turns when she hears Joona come in. It's clear from her face that she regrets mentioning her brother's diary.

"Can I ask how Peter's wife died?"

"I don't know," she says curtly, and continues stacking cups and saucers.

"You said you were friends, you and Anna."

The old woman's chin trembles. "I think you should leave now," she says.

"I can't," Joona replies.

"I thought you were interested in Peter's sermons, that's why I . . ." She shakes her head, picks up a tray with coffee and two pastries, and starts toward the door.

Joona follows, holding the door for her and waiting as she takes the tray over to the customers in the garden.

"I don't want to talk about it," she says weakly.

"It wasn't an accident?" he asks sharply.

Her face becomes completely helpless and she looks like she's about to cry. "I don't want to," she pleads. "Don't you understand? It's too late." She lowers her face and sobs quietly.

The other woman comes in and puts her hands on Ellinor's shaking shoulders. The nearby customers get up and change tables.

"I'm a police officer," Joona says. "I can find this out, but—"

"Please, leave now," the other woman says, hugging Ellinor.

"It was just an accident," the old priest's sister says.

"I don't want to upset you," Joona goes on. "But I need to know what happened, and I need to know now."

"It was a car accident," Ellinor whimpers. "It was pouring. They drove straight into the church wall. The car buckled and crushed Anna, and she hit her face so badly that . . ." She sits down unsteadily at one of the tables and stares ahead of her.

"Go on," Joona says gently.

The woman looks up at him, wipes the tears from her eyes and nods. "We saw it from the rectory. My brother ran out, down the road . . . and I followed him through the rain, and saw their daughter fighting to get her out, she was using the car jack . . . kept hitting it against the car. And I just screamed and ran off through the willow trees."

The woman's voice cracks, and she opens and closes her mouth a couple of times before she goes on:

"There was broken glass and wreckage from the car everywhere, and there was a smell of gasoline and hot metal. Their daughter had given up. She was just standing there waiting for her father to arrive. I can still remember the look of shock in her eyes, and her peculiar smile."

Ellinor raises her hands and looks down at her palms.

"Dear God," she whispers, "the girl had just gotten home from school, and there she was, standing there in her yellow raincoat looking at her mother. Anna's face was crushed beyond recognition, there was blood everywhere."

Her voice fails her again, and she swallows, then continues slowly.

"Memory is a strange thing," she says. "I know I heard a very high voice as I got closer through the rain. It was like a child talking. . . . And then it started to burn, a blue bubble enclosed Anna, and the next moment I was lying in the wet grass in the ditch, and the flames were spiraling around the whole car. The birch tree caught fire, and I—"

"Who was driving?"

"I don't want to talk about it."

"The daughter," Joona says. "What's her name?"

"Nelly," the old woman replies, looking up at him with exhaustion etched on her face.

119

JOONA TRIES TO CALL ERIK AS HE WALKS BETWEEN THE CAFÉ tables toward Rocky.

His phone is switched off.

He dials Margot Silverman's private number, but there's no answer, so he calls his former boss at National Crime, Carlos Eliasson, instead and leaves a short voicemail.

Rocky is still sitting in the shade under the weeping birch, picking crumbs from his stomach. He's taken his shoes and socks off and is wriggling his toes on the grass.

"We have to go," Joona says when he reaches him.

"Did you find the answers to your questions?"

Joona ignores Rocky and hurries down the steps. Peter didn't keep volume twenty-four of his diary in the bureau with the others because its content was too shameful. And because of that, Nelly missed it when she destroyed the rest of them.

Toward the end of the diary, Peter describes how his daughter was sent to an old-fashioned girls' boarding school.

Joona stops in front of the stolen car. Nelly was fourteen when she started at Klockhammar School outside Örebro. She was at boarding school for six years. It's possible she didn't see her parents at all during that time, but never let go of her fixation on her father.

The feeling of loving and being rejected, of giving everything only to have everything taken from you, led to a serious personality disorder.

She studied her mother, tried to be like her, to take her place.

Rocky has his shoes back on but is holding his socks as he walks to the car and opens the door.

"Is the unclean preacher a woman?" Joona asks.

"I don't think so," Rocky replies, looking him in the eye.

"Do you remember Nelly Brandt?"

"No," he says, getting into the passenger seat.

Joona hot-wires the car again, causing a spark as the engine bursts into life.

"I don't know how much you remember from the hypnosis," Joona says as he drives. "But you talked about the first time you saw the unclean preacher. You met her at a funeral here in Sköldinge, but the person you described was the priest in the coffin, her father, Peter."

Rocky doesn't answer, just stares blankly through the windshield as their speed increases.

The mother went to pick up her grown-up daughter from Klockhammar School and let her drive back.

Her mother was sitting next to her and maybe took her seat belt off when they turned off the main road and drove up to the church.

Nelly probably saw her father in the windows of the rectory as she suddenly put her foot down and drove straight into the wall.

Perhaps her mother wasn't dead, just badly hurt and trapped in the wreckage.

In which case what Ellinor saw through the rain makes sense. Nelly got the car jack from the trunk and beat her mother in the face until she was dead.

Perhaps she lit the car on fire in front of her father's eyes.

But after her mother's death, Nelly isolated him from the world around him, keeping him to herself and becoming everything for him.

Her father lived another four years. Nelly kept him locked up and helpless, keeping him in a cage and making him dependent on morphine.

She would let him out on Sundays to deliver sermons that she had written for him for the morning service.

He was broken, a wreck, an addict.

They may have had fragments of normal life. It isn't unusual for people who are held captive for a long period of time to be allowed short periods of normalcy with their captor. Maybe they ate dinner together, sat on the sofa, and watched television shows.

In the end, he worked out how to lock his cage from the inside and slept on the mattress. It's possible that he died of an overdose or got ill.

A large number of priests attended the funeral, some of them sitting in the pews while others assisted with the ceremony.

One of those priests was Rocky Kyrklund.

Joona takes out his phone, brings up a list of staff at Karolinska, and finds a photograph of Nelly. "Look at this picture," he says.

Rocky takes the phone, holds the screen away from the daylight, and then gasps for breath. "Stop!" he roars. "Stop the car!"

He opens the door as they're speeding along, but it hits a railing and bounces back. Glass from the broken window flies into the car. The door hangs loose, scraping along the tarmac.

Joona pulls over to the shoulder and comes to a halt with two wheels up on the grass. Rocky walks out into the field beside the road, stops, and holds his face in his hands.

120

JOONA PICKS HIS PHONE OFF THE CAR FLOOR AND TRIES TO call Erik again. Rocky stands in the field with his face turned up toward the sky for a long time before returning to the car. He yanks the broken door off, tosses it into the ditch, and gets back in his seat.

"I remember her," he says without looking at Joona. "She had her head shaved, pale as candle wax. She went to Klockhammar School. After the funeral, I had sex with her on the floor of the hall in the rectory. It didn't mean anything. We'd been talking and drinking coffee, and I was in no hurry to get home."

Joona says nothing, aware that even though the photograph triggered Rocky's memory, the flood of information is finite. He could lose touch with his past again at any moment.

"I remember it all," Rocky says dreamily. "She came looking for me in Salem, came to services. She was just there, part of my life, without me really realizing how it had happened."

He drifts off in thought and pokes a cigarette out of the pack with trembling hands. His rough gray hair is frizzy, and his thick eyebrows have tightened across the top of his nose.

"I'm a priest," he says eventually. "But I'm also a man. I do things I might not always be proud of. I'm not boyfriend material, I'm clear about that, I've never been faithful or—"

He falls silent again as if the strength of his memories has taken his breath away.

"Sometimes I slept with her, sometimes she had to wait. I

never promised her anything. I didn't want her fucking sermons. I remember, it was always about me watching out for promiscuous women. . . . 'Her house is the way to hell.'"

The car shakes as a bus drives past, and Joona sees Rocky gaze out across the field and lake at a distant stand of trees.

"When I told her I was finished with her, she disappeared," he goes on. "But I knew she was still creeping around outside the rectory. I opened the door and shouted into the darkness, telling her to leave me the fuck alone."

He stops talking again, and Joona waits in silence.

"The next evening she came to the church with twenty capsules of white heroin, and it all started again. It went fucking fast," he says, looking gloomily at Joona. "I was hooked as good as instantly. We shared needles, and she followed me everywhere, talking about God, preaching. She sank into squalor with me, wanted to be with me, wanted to be part of me." He shakes his head and rubs his face.

"We hung out at the Zone. I didn't care about all her preaching. It was mostly extreme interpretations of the Bible, proof that we should get married . . . a whole worldview in which a jealous God proved her right."

A trace of pain flashes in his eyes as he looks darkly at Joona.

"I was drugged and stupid," he says. "I told her I loved Natalia. It wasn't true, but I still said it."

All the energy goes out of him and his chin sinks to his chest.

"Natalia had such beautiful hands," he says, then falls silent.

His face is suddenly very pale, and he looks out at the fields. His forehead is shiny with sweat, and a drop falls from his nose onto his chest.

"You were talking about Natalia," Joona says after a while.

"What?"

Rocky looks at him uncomprehendingly, leans out the car, and spits on the grass. A car pulling a trailer full of wood pulp drives past.

"Nelly showed you the pictures of the people she was planning to kill," Joona goes on. "But Natalia had to die in front of you."

Rocky shakes his head. "All I know is that God lost me somewhere along the way, and he never came back to look for me," he mutters hoarsely.

Joona doesn't say anything more. He takes his phone out and calls Erik's number again but still can't get through.

He calls Margot but gives up after ten rings.

Now he knows who the preacher is, but he can't prove anything, and he has nothing to give the police. There's a chance that Margot might listen to him, but he may have gone too far when he broke Rocky out of jail.

Joona tries to understand why Nelly has been stalking Erik. It must have been going on for years. It isn't going to end well.

121

GRIT FLIES UP BEHIND THEM AS THEY SET OFF AGAIN. THE car fills with a thunderous, jolting wind.

As Joona pushes the car as hard as it will go, he tries to get a clear picture of the serial killer in his mind. After they had sex at her father's funeral, Nelly transferred her affections to Rocky. She stalked him, made herself part of his life, tried to control him with drugs, and killed the women who threatened their union. She created an impossible life for Rocky by making sure he was the main suspect for the murder of Rebecka Hansson. In the end, she kept him in a cage, was supplying him with heroin, and thought she owned him completely, when he managed to escape. He stole a car in Finsta and crashed on his way to Arlanda. The accident left him with serious brain damage. He lost all appeal for her and ended up being sentenced to secure psychiatric care.

Maybe Nelly first saw Erik when he was called in as an expert witness during Rocky's trial.

Joona shudders at the thought that Nelly probably started stalking Erik that long ago, slowly and systematically getting closer to him.

She studied and got her qualifications, got a job at the same place as him, married Martin, and supported Erik during his separation from Simone.

After his divorce, her assumption of ownership grew stronger, and she started to keep tabs on him, couldn't bear any sign of competition, and became pathologically jealous. She probably wanted him to choose her of his own accord, thought he would have eyes for no one but her, but when that didn't happen, something snapped inside her, and she had to act in order to stop herself from falling apart.

When Erik embarked on an affair with Maria Carlsson, she probably thought everything would be fine if she could just get rid of her rival.

A stalker always develops a relationship with their victim in their imagination, a relationship that they convince themselves is real and reciprocated.

In her head, Nelly may have believed she had a life with Erik, and when she saw him betraying her with Maria Carlsson, attracted by Sandra Lundgren, flirting with Susanna Kern, and maybe even just smiling at Katryna Youssef, a vicious beast woke up.

Joona turns off toward Malmköping, stops in the parking lot outside Lindholm's Floor and Building Services, and switches to a better car.

They're driving along the E20 motorway at 190 kilometers an hour when Margot calls from her private phone. "There's a warrant out for your arrest, did you know that?" she asks.

"I know, but—"

"You're going to end up in prison for this," she cuts him off.

"It was worth it," he replies.

A few seconds of silence follow.

"Now I realize why you're a better detective than me," Margot says in a subdued voice.

"Our forensics team has found strands of Erik's hair in Sandra Lundgren's bathroom. We already have his fingerprints on the deer's head. He's connected to all the victims. He has thousands of hours of video recordings in his basement, and—"

"It's too much," Joona says.

"The analysis of the blood in Erik's car showed that it was Susanna Kern's. And now it's getting too much even for me," she says heavily.

"Good," Joona says.

"It doesn't make sense. All four murders show clear signs of forensic awareness. And Erik is a doctor. Someone like that doesn't end up with blood in his own car. Someone left those traces of blood on the backseat to frame him."

"You've met the real killer," Joona says.

"Is it Nestor?"

"It's Nelly Brandt. She's the preacher."

"You sound sure," Margot says.

"It's Erik she's after. He's the one she's been stalking. The victims are just rivals in her head."

"If you're sure, I'll get an operation organized at once," Margot says. "We'll hit her home and workplace at the same time."

Joona drives on toward Stockholm as he thinks of how Nelly has stalked Erik for years, mapping the life of any woman he showed an interest in, trying to understand what she had that she couldn't offer. She saw them flashing their jewelry, their painted lips, their beautiful nails, and wanted to take that away from them, punish them, and then emphasize their bare ears or ugly hands.

But when that wasn't enough, she tried to take the whole world away from him. Like Artemis with her hounds, she organized a hunt. She's a skillful huntress, Joona thinks. She isolates her prey, wounds it, and harries it toward capture until there's only one way out.

Her intention was for Erik to realize that everything pointed to him and to go on the run before the police caught him. Everyone would shun him, until in the end he turned to the only person who was still prepared to help.

If he hasn't been caught by the police by now, Joona thinks, he must have sought protection from Nelly.

122

JACKIE IS FEELING RESTLESS. SHE GOES OUT INTO THE kitchen and thinks about getting something to eat, even though she isn't really hungry. Maybe she should just drink a cup of tea.

She feels across the counter with her hand, along the tiles, and past the big stone mortar. She finds the pot of tea leaves with the little glass knob.

Her hands stop.

She feels her way back to the mortar. The heavy pestle isn't resting in the bowl like it usually is.

Jackie runs her fingers across the whole countertop but can't find it. She thinks she'll have to ask Maddy about it once things between them calm down.

She stifles a yawn and fills the kettle with water.

During the days following her fight with Erik, Maddy kept saying Erik was sad and would never want to come back to them now. She tried to explain to her mother that everyone forgets. She said she forgets a lot of things and embarked on a long description of how she'd forgotten keys and notes and soccer cleats.

Jackie has tried to explain that she isn't angry anymore, that it isn't anyone's fault when things don't work out between two grown-ups. But then the media witch hunt started.

Jackie hasn't told her daughter why she's keeping her home from school. She postponed all her own lessons with her students and canceled all her work as an organist.

To help the days pass and to stop herself from thinking so much, she's been spending all her waking hours at the piano, practicing scales and doing finger exercises until she feels sick and her elbows hurt so much she has to take painkillers.

Obviously she hasn't told her daughter what they're saying about Erik on the news.

She'd never be able to understand it.

Jackie can't understand it herself.

She doesn't listen to the television anymore. She can't bear to hear the speculation.

Maddy has stopped talking about Erik now, but she's still very subdued. She's been watching shows for younger children, and Jackie has a feeling she's started sucking her thumb again.

Jackie feels a lump of anxiety in her stomach when she thinks about how she lost patience with Maddy when she didn't want to play the piano today. She told her she was acting like a baby, and Maddy started to cry and shouted that she was never going to help with anything ever again.

Now she's hiding in her closet, and she doesn't answer when Jackie tries to talk to her.

I have to show her she doesn't have to be perfect, Jackie thinks. That I love her no matter what, that it's unconditional.

She walks along the cool hallway into the living room, which is flooded with sunlight that feels like streaks of hot water. She knows the piano is going to feel as warm as a large animal.

Out in the street, some sort of engineering work is going on. She can feel the muffled vibration of large machines beneath her bare feet, and she can hear the old windowpanes rattle in their frames.

In the middle of the parquet floor, she feels something sticky beneath her heel. Maddy must have spilled some juice. There's a fusty smell in the room, like nettles and damp soil.

An itchy, electric sense of danger flares up inside her, and a shiver runs up her spine to her neck.

It's hardly surprising that she's shaken up after everything that's happened. The things being said about Erik are terrible, she thinks, as she wonders if she just heard something from the window facing the courtyard.

She listens and walks closer to the glass. Everything is quiet, but someone could easily be waiting there looking at her when the curtains are open.

She moves cautiously toward the window and puts her hand out to touch the glass.

She closes the curtains.

Jackie goes over to the piano, sits down on the stool, lifts the lid of the keyboard, settles more comfortably, lowers her hands, and feels something lying across the keys.

It's a piece of fabric.

She picks it up and feels it. It's a cloth or scarf of some sort.

Maddy must have put it there.

It's a piece of intricate embroidery. She follows the pattern of the stitches with her fingertips.

It seems to be some sort of animal, with four legs, and wings or feathers on its back.

She gets up slowly, and her whole body goes cold, as if she has just fallen straight through broken ice.

There's someone in the room.

She felt it a moment ago, just now.

The parquet floor creaks behind her back under the weight of an adult body.

A feeling of absolute danger makes the world shrink to a compact point in which she is utterly alone with her terror.

"Erik?" she says without turning round.

Something rustles slowly, and the vibration from the floor makes the empty fruit bowl on the table rattle.

"Is that you, Erik?" she asks, trying to keep her voice even. "You can't just show up like this."

She turns around and hears the sound of unfamiliar breathing, shallow and agitated.

She moves slowly toward the door.

He stays where he is, but there's a sort of squeaking sound, as if he were wearing plastic clothes, or rubber.

"We can talk through everything," she says with obvious fear. "I overreacted, I know I did. I wanted to call you."

He doesn't answer, just shifts his weight from one foot to the other. The floor creaks beneath him.

"I'm not angry anymore. I think about you all the time. . . . It's going to be fine," she says weakly.

She moves into the hallway, thinking she has to get out, that she has to lure Erik out of the apartment, away from Maddy.

"Let's go and sit in the kitchen. Maddy hasn't come home yet," she lies.

There's a sudden thudding sound on the floor. He's rushing toward her, and she holds up a hand to stop him.

Something hard strikes her raised arm. It glances off her elbow, and she staggers backward.

The adrenaline rushing through her veins means she doesn't even notice the pain in her arm.

She backs away, holding her injured arm up. She turns and walks into the wall, then hits her knees against the little table, grabs the glass bowl that Maddy usually uses for popcorn, and strikes out hard. She hits him and drops the bowl.

He falls forward into her, and she hits her back against the bookcase.

She can feel his raincoat against her body. She pushes him away with both hands and smells his bitter breath on her face.

Books crash to the floor.

It isn't Erik, she thinks.

That isn't his smell.

She runs, with her hand against the wall, and reaches the front door. She starts to turn the lock with shaking hands.

Heavy footsteps approach from behind.

She opens the door, but something jangles and the door bounces back.

The safety chain, she forgot the safety chain.

She pulls the door shut, fumbles with the chain, but she's shaking too much and can't unfasten it.

The person who wants to kill her is coming closer, making a little purring sound in his throat.

Jackie pushes the twisted chain sideways with her fingers, and suddenly it comes loose. She opens the door and tumbles out into the stairwell. She almost falls but manages to reach her neighbor's door and bangs on it with the palm of her hand.

"Open the door!" Jackie screams.

She feels movement behind her, turns around, and puts her arms up in front of her face to shield it from the blow.

Jackie falls against her neighbor's door. Blood runs down her cheek, and she lets out a deep gasp as the next blow knocks her head sideways.

A bitter taste blossoms in her mouth.

123

FROM WHERE HE'S LYING, ERIK LISTENS TO THE SOUND OF the engine, the monotonous thrum of the tires on the road, and Nelly's inadvertent little sighs as she concentrates on the traffic.

After Sickla Strand, she drove for twenty minutes around central Stockholm, making lots of turns and changing lanes frequently. Then she stopped and got out of the car, saying she needed to pick up a few things if he was going to stay at the house. She was gone for a long time. Erik lay there completely covered by the blanket, occasionally shifting position very carefully, waiting. He fell asleep in the heat of the car but woke up abruptly to the sound of voices right outside.

It sounded like two men discussing something. He tried to hear what they were saying. He thought they sounded like police but wasn't sure.

He lay motionless with the heavy blanket over his back, trying to breathe carefully. His whole right side went numb, but he didn't dare change position until long after the voices left.

After another forty minutes or so, Nelly came back. He heard her open the back of the car and groan as she put some heavy luggage in. The car rocked, and then she got into the driver's seat. She started the engine, and Igor Stravinsky's *Symphony of Psalms* filled the car.

When they emerged onto the highway, he lifted the blanket from his face. Nelly's voice sounded cheerful when she called out to him over the music, saying she must be insane to be doing this, but that she went through a serious punk phase when she was sixteen and maybe this is her way of finally satisfying her desire for revenge on cops and all the other fascists.

They've been driving for over an hour when she slows down.

They turn sharply onto an uneven track. Small stones clatter against the underside of the chassis. She slows down even more, and Erik hears branches scraping against the roof and the windows. The car rocks over lumps and potholes, then comes to a halt. There's a click as the handbrake is pulled on, then silence.

The driver's door opens, and when the cool air carrying a hint of diesel reaches him, he finally sits up on the backseat. Dazed, he looks out across overgrown ruins and sees a white sky, leafy tree-tops, and large fields that have been left fallow.

They're deep in the countryside. Grasshoppers are chirruping in the tall grass. Nelly looks at him with shining eyes. Her floral-green dress is creased around her thighs, and strands of blond hair have escaped from the scarf around her head. One of her cheeks seems oddly red, as if she's been hit. Everything is so quiet, and there's so little wind that Erik can hear the charms on her bracelet jangle as she adjusts the bag on her shoulder.

He pushes the door open and climbs out carefully onto the grass. His undershirt is now dry, and his whole body aches.

Nelly has parked in an overgrown courtyard. A two-story yellow house stands in the middle of the ruins of some sort of factory. A tall brick chimney rises from a sooty oven. The buildings are surrounded by weeds, and through the tall grass, he can make out the remains of a huge grid of railway ties.

"Come on, let's go inside," Nelly says, licking her lips.

"Is this Solbacken?" Erik asks in surprise.

"Nice, isn't it?" she says, and giggles.

Broken glass shimmers in the courtyard, and bricks and soot-blackened sheets of corrugated tin lie in the tall grass. The foundations of some of the buildings have collapsed in on their basements, and the shafts look like empty pools with weeds growing at the bottom, and brick arches leading to underground tunnels.

An old washing machine stands in a clump of young elms, along with a few dirty plastic chairs and a couple of tractor tires.

"Now I want to show you the house. I love it." She tucks her hand under his arm with a contented smile.

The main house is surrounded by dark green stinging nettles. An eave has come loose and rests on the roof of the veranda.

"It's really nice inside," she says, trying to pull him along.

The ground sways, and he feels suddenly sick. He finds himself staring at a pool of brown water with a sheen of oil on its surface.

"How are you feeling?" Nelly asks with an anxious smile.

"It's hard getting a grip on everything—the fact that I'm here now," he replies.

"Let's go inside," she says, walking backward toward the house without taking her eyes off him.

"I hypnotized Rocky this morning," Erik tells her. "He remembered the person who murdered Rebecka Hansson. He said the name of the church where they met."

"We'll have to try to tell the police about that," she says.

"I don't know. Everything's—"

"Come on, let's go in first," she interrupts, and sets off toward the house.

"I haven't had any time to think. I've just been running," he says as he follows her across the yard.

"Of course," she replies distractedly.

A crow hops away and flies up over the roof. Drifts of wet leaves lie beside an old drum of diesel with a grubby Shell logo on the side.

"I need to find a way to turn myself in," Erik says.

He follows her up a green path that has been tramped down through the tall nettles.

"They shot Nestor in front of me. I can't believe it," he goes on. "I know."

"They thought he was me, and they shot him through the window, using snipers. It was like a fucking execution."

"You can tell me everything when we get inside," Nelly says with a little line of impatience between her eyebrows.

Resting against the wall among the nettles is a snow shovel with a broken handle. The paint of the veranda is hanging off in large strips, and one of the windows is broken. There's a piece of plywood covering the hole instead of glass.

"Now you're here, anyway," Nelly says. "You can feel safe. I'm happy for you to stay as long as you want."

"You may need to contact a lawyer once everything's calmed down," Erik suggests.

She nods and licks her lips again, then tucks a lock of hair behind her scarf. "Hurry up," she says.

"What is it?" he asks.

"Nothing," she says quickly. "I just . . . you know . . . all this talk about everyone hunting you. And sometimes the neighbors come by when they see I'm here."

Erik glances along the narrow track at the edge of the field. There are no other houses in sight, just overgrown fields and a strip of forest.

"Come on," she repeats with a tense smile, and takes his arm again. "You need something to drink and some warm clothes."

"Yes," he agrees, and follows her along the path.

"And I'll make something nice to eat."

They go up the steps to the little porch. Grimy bags of trash lean against the outside wall, next to a plastic tub filled with bottles and rainwater. Nelly turns the key in the lock, opens the front door, and walks into the entryway ahead of him. There's a click but nothing more when she tries to turn the light on.

"Oops, need to check the fuse box," she says.

A set of blue overalls covered in oil stains is suspended from a hanger next to a silver down jacket. In the shoe rack are a pair of worn wooden clogs and some work boots with black stains on them. Above a small sofa hangs an embroidered sampler with a biblical quotation: FOR LOVE IS STRONG AS DEATH, SONG OF SOLOMON 8:6.

A sweet smell, like raw chicken and overripe fruit, hangs in the air.

"It's an old house," she says softly.

"Yes," he says. He suddenly feels like he needs to get out of here.

Nelly looks at him with a smile, so close he can see that her face powder has settled in rings around her eyes.

"Do you want to take a shower before we eat?" she asks without taking her eyes off him.

"Do I look like I need one?" he jokes.

"You're the best judge of how unclean you are," she replies seriously, and her bright eyes shine like glass.

"Nelly, I'm incredibly grateful for everything you—"

"Anyway, here's the kitchen," she interrupts.

As she pushes at the heavy door beside the sofa, Erik hears a creaking metallic sound.

The noise rises a couple of notes, then stops abruptly.

He follows her hesitantly into the gloomy kitchen. A stench of rotten food hits him. Weak light filters through the closed venetian blinds. It's hard to see anything. Nelly has gone in and is turning the faucet on.

Erik stands inside the door, and a shiver runs down his spine. The whole kitchen is full of rusty tools and engine parts, blocks of firewood, crumpled plastic bags, shoes, and pans of old food.

"Nelly, what happened here?"

"What do you mean?" she says lightly as she fills a glass with water for him.

"The whole kitchen," he says.

She follows his gaze to the counter and closed blinds. Three dark paraffin lamps are sticking up from an open kitchen drawer.

"We must have had a break-in," she says, holding out the glass.

He walks in and has barely reached her when the kitchen door shuts behind him with a loud slam. Erik spins around, his heart pounding. The powerful spring of an oversize self-closing mechanism is singing metallically.

124

NELLY SWITCHES ON A FLASHLIGHT AND SETS IT DOWN HAP-
hazardly on the counter. The light shines on the layers of cobwebs
on the venetian blinds.

Erik tries to take in what he's seeing. A large fly buzzes around
the kitchen and lands on the door to the basement. From one door-
post hangs an iron bar that seems to function as a barrier across
the door.

"'A woman that feareth the Lord, she shall be praised,'" Nelly
whispers.

"Nelly, I don't understand what all this is about."

Two knives are lying on the floor next to a rolled-up rag rug, the
transmission of a car, and a dirty hymnal.

"You're home," she says with a smile.

"Thanks, but I—"

"There's the door," she points.

"There's the door?" he repeats, uncomprehendingly.

"It's better if you go down on your own," she says, holding out
the glass of water.

"Down where?" Erik asks.

"Now don't argue." She giggles.

"You think I need to hide in the cellar?"

She nods eagerly.

"Isn't that a bit over the top? I don't think—"

"Be quiet!" she yells, and throws the glass of water at him.

The glass hits the wall behind him, falls to the floor, and shatters. He feels the water splash his legs and feet.

"What are you doing?"

"Sorry, I'm just a little stressed out." She rubs her forehead.

He nods and walks over to the door to the entryway and pulls the handle, but the powerful spring-loaded mechanism has locked the door. There's no key in the hole. Adrenaline floods his body as he hears her approach from behind. He yanks at the door, but it doesn't move a millimeter.

"I just want you to do what I say," Nelly explains.

"Well, I'm not going down into some fucking—"

Erik can't understand what's happening, but something hits him hard across the back, and all the air goes out of him as his forehead hits the door. He stumbles sideways. It feels like he's got a cramp in his left shoulder, then realizes that warm liquid is running down his back.

He looks down and sees splashes of blood in the filth on the linoleum floor, turns to face Nelly, and realizes that she hit him with a lump of wood, which is now lying on the floor by her feet.

"Sorry, Erik," she says breathlessly. "I didn't mean—"

"Nelly?" he gasps. "You hurt me."

"Yes, I know. But I'm helping you. Nothing to worry about," she says.

"I didn't do what they're saying about me," he tries to explain.

"Didn't you?"

He moves sideways, then turns back toward her again and sees she's picked up a heavy crowbar from the counter.

"Don't you understand? I'm innocent!"

He backs away and bumps into the table, on top of which is a bowl full of dirty, soapy water. The water slops over the side and splashes onto the floor.

Nelly moves quickly toward him and strikes. He blocks the blow with his lower arm. It hurts so much he almost passes out, and he stumbles backward into the pale blue door of the pantry.

She swings again but misses his head. Splinters fly from the edge of the door. He lurches to the side and manages to knock over a tray of empty jam jars. They roll across the counter and fall to the floor, scattering shards of broken glass.

"Nelly, stop it!" he gasps.

His arm is probably broken. He has to support it with his other hand.

Nelly has a look of intense concentration as she pursues him. He throws his head back, and she turns her body and strikes again. The crowbar misses his face and brushes past the tip of his nose. The back of his head hits an open cupboard door. He tries to get away but puts his foot down on a piece of broken glass just as she lashes out again.

He blocks the powerful blow with his broken arm and shrieks with pain. His vision goes black for a moment, and his legs give out. He falls to his knees. He stares at the filthy floor and the blood running down his injured arm.

"Stop—just stop," he pleads, and tries to get up, but the next blow hits him on the temple.

His head is knocked sideways. Everything goes quiet inside him, as though he has simply come to a stop.

He fumbles for support with his hand.

His field of vision contracts to a narrow tunnel. The kitchen shrinks as Nelly leans forward and smiles at him.

He tries to stand up. He realizes he must have stepped on more glass, because he feels the pain like a distant itch, far away, under his foot, down in the ground somewhere.

He falls backward, rolls onto his side, and lies there panting with his cheek against the floor.

"Oh, God . . ."

"'And the just, upright man is laughed to scorn,'" she mutters. "'But ask now the beasts.'"

Through his limited field of vision, he sees Nelly open the door to the basement and stick a wedge under it with her foot.

He smells her perfume as she bends over, grabs him under his arms, and drags him across the floor. He's completely powerless. His feet just hang limp, leaving a trail of blood across the floor.

"Don't do this," Erik pleads, panting.

As she pulls him toward the staircase, he tries to cling to a cupboard but can't hold on. Blood is trickling over his cheek and down his throat and neck. He tries to grab the doorframe but is too weak to resist.

Nelly walks backward down the stairs, dragging him into the darkness. His feet fall heavily with each step.

He can barely see anything, just feels the pain shooting from his arm with each step. Far above he can make out the glow of the flashlight. Then he loses consciousness.

125

WHEN ERIK OPENS HIS EYES IN THE DARKNESS, HE NOTICES the stench of old excrement and decay. His right arm feels excruciatingly painful, and his head is throbbing.

He can't see anything, and a wave of panic scatters his thoughts. He can't understand what's happened, and his entire body feels tense, wary, ready for flight.

He feels like calling for help but forces himself to lie still and listen. The room is completely silent.

Occasionally he hears a vague rumbling sound, like wind in a chimney.

He carefully touches his wounded arm and discovers it's been wrapped in paper.

Erik's heart beats faster.

This is madness, he thinks. Nelly hit me. My arm is probably broken.

When he tries to roll over, he can feel dried blood sticking his hair and cheek to the mattress.

He raises his head and gasps with dizziness. His temple pounds as he forces himself up onto his knees.

The effort makes him breathe hard through his nose, and he listens again but can't hear any movement, no sound of breathing apart from his own.

He stares out into the darkness and blinks, but his eyes don't get used to it.

Unless I've gone blind, this room is entirely devoid of light, he thinks.

Now he remembers being dragged down a steep flight of steps into a basement before he passed out.

He holds his injured arm tightly to his body as he gets to his feet, but before he manages to straighten up, his head hits something.

There's a faint rattle of metal.

Crouching, he creeps forward with his hand outstretched, but walks only two steps before he reaches some bars.

Something wet pops beneath one of his feet.

He tries to feel his way forward, following the mesh, and reaches a corner.

It's a cage. He keeps moving around, trampling on something that feels like a blanket. He feels the mesh with his good hand, running his fingers along the thick bars, investigating the corners. They've been fused together. With his fingers, he can feel the lumpy joints where the bars have been welded to the mesh on the floor and roof of the cage.

Nelly, he thinks. Somehow she's the unclean preacher. A serial killer, a stalker.

He stands on the mattress and finds the latch with his fingers. There's a dull rattle as he pushes it, and the cage sways around him.

He sticks his fingers out and feels the large padlock, twists it and tries to pull it, but it soon becomes obvious that the lock can't be forced, not even if he had a crowbar.

Erik kneels again and tries to breathe calmly. He leans on his left hand and closes his eyes until a sound startles him. The door up in the kitchen is opening.

Steps creak on the staircase, and a patch of light grows steadily larger.

Someone is coming down, holding a flashlight.

He leans forward and sees the green dress around Nelly's legs.

The beam from the flashlight veers across the steps and wall, where a large patch of plaster has fallen off. The handrail is loose, and some more mortar falls off when she leans on it.

Erik feels like he's going to be sick.

She killed Maria Carlsson, Sandra Lundgren, Susanna Kern, and Katryna Youssef—completely innocent women whom he happened to come into contact with.

Nelly's reached the bottom now. The light sweeps past him, and he sees that the cage is made of welded reinforcement mesh in a close grid pattern. The heavy lock is made of brushed steel, sealing a latch made of a double layer of mesh with welded hooks.

Shadows slide across the walls of the basement as she stops and looks at him.

Her face is flushed with excitement, and she's panting for breath. Erik sees that his left hand is brown with rust from the mesh. His undershirt is torn, hanging in shreds around his waist.

"Don't be scared," Nelly says, pulling an office chair toward the cage. "I know, right now you're trying to figure out how this all fits together, but there's no rush."

Without taking her eyes off him, she sets the flashlight down on an old kitchen table. Erik sees it light up the wall by the stairs and is able to make out the rest of the room in its indirect light.

Beside him is an old mattress. The striped fabric is stained with dark patches in the middle, as if someone lay there for a long time.

In the other corner is a faded plastic bucket full of murky water, next to a china plate with a washed-out floral pattern and a network of fine cracks.

This must be the cage Rocky spoke about.

He was here for seven months before he managed to escape.

He got out of the cage and stole a car in Finsta, only to crash and end up getting sentenced for Rebecka's murder.

In the shadows outside the cage, Erik can see dead rats and a pile of wooden sticks with sooty ends.

Nelly's black bag is under the table.

Erik brushes his hair from his eyes, thinking he has to talk to her, to make himself something more than just another victim.

"Nelly," he says weakly, "what am I doing here?"

"I'm protecting you," she says.

He coughs and thinks he needs to speak in his usual voice, has to sound like her colleague at Karolinska. He can't sound afraid, dehumanized.

"Why do you think I need protecting?"

"Lots of reasons," she whispers with a smile.

Some of her blond hair has slipped out from her headscarf, and her thin dress has dark sweat stains under the arms and across her chest.

She says she's protecting me, he thinks. She hasn't brought me here to kill me.

Rocky sat in this cage and wasn't tortured or mutilated, though he was possibly chastised and beaten.

Old spiderwebs hang from the mesh down by the floor. He looks at the dark opening at the other end of the cage. A faint breeze across the floor seems to be coming from a tunnel.

He needs to think.

She was the person who set the police on him. She knew he would run but wouldn't have anywhere to go, and that sooner or later he'd turn to her of his own volition.

He was the one who called her and begged to come out here.

That was what she wanted. There was nothing coincidental about it—it all fits too well. She's been stalking him.

She's been close to him for so long that she could predict every movement he would make, and she's been able to manipulate all the evidence to make him look guilty.

He may well be stuck here until he dies.

Because no one knows where he is.

Joona is looking in the wrong place. Sköldinge Church is just a confused muddle of memories in Rocky's brain.

His family and friends and the rest of the world will remember him as a serial killer who vanished without a trace.

126

NELLY LEANS FORWARD AND LOOKS AT HIM WITH AN EXPRES-
sion he can't read. Her pale eyes are like shining porcelain globes.

"Nelly, you and I are both rational individuals," Erik says,
aware of the quiver of fear in his voice. "We respect each other,
and I understand that you didn't mean to hurt me as badly as you
did."

"It's just such a pain when you don't do what I say," she sighs.

"I know it feels like a pain, but it's like that for everyone. It's
part of life."

"Sure," she says blankly.

She whispers something to herself and moves an object on the
kitchen table. Sand falls onto a dusty sheet of glass, a small picture
that's leaning against the wall. It's a framed contract of cooperation
between Emmaboda Glassworks, Saint-Gobain, and Solbacken
Glassworks.

"My arm hurts badly, and my . . ."

"Are you saying you need to go to the hospital now?" she asks
derisively.

"Yes, I need to get my arm X-rayed, and—"

"You'll be fine," she interrupts.

"Not with an epidural hematoma," he says, touching the wound
to his temple. "I could have arterial bleeding here, between the dura
mater and the inside of my skull."

She looks at him in astonishment, then laughs. "That's goddamn
pathetic."

"I mean . . . I'm just saying that if I'm going to be happy here, you're going to have to take care of me, make sure I'm okay."

"I am. You have everything you need."

Erik thinks that someone who's capable of what Nelly has done has an insatiable emotional hunger. She desperately needs to control her target and can switch from devoted love to impassioned hatred in an instant.

"Nelly," he asks tentatively, "how long are you thinking of keeping me locked up?"

She smiles at the floor, embarrassed, then gives him an indulgent look. "Initially you'll plead and maybe threaten me," she says. "You'll promise all sorts of things. And soon you'll try to manipulate me in different ways by saying you're not planning to escape, that you only want to help me sweep the stairs."

She adjusts her dress and looks at him in silence. After a while she crosses her legs and moves a little so the light from the flashlight brushes her cheek.

"Nelly, I'm grateful to you for letting me stay here, but I don't like the basement. I don't know why, that's just the way it is," Erik says, but gets no response.

He looks at her and tries to remember how they first met.

She must have been somewhere in the vicinity when he was conducting his examination of Rocky, then applied for a job in his department.

How had she got it?

The head of HR had committed suicide. That was just after she started. She must have forced him in some way to give her the job, then just finished him off.

Nelly was always funny and easygoing, talkative, in a charming, self-deprecating way.

He went through a tough time when he got divorced from Simone. Particularly at night, with all those long, sleepless hours. Nelly persuaded him to go back to using pills. She gave him Valium, Rohypnol, Sobril, and Citodon—all the old pills he'd managed to kick years before.

They drank and took pills together, made light of it. Now he can't understand what he was thinking. They'd kissed, then ended up in bed together. She insisted on putting on a nightie that Simone had left behind, and he tried not to show how uncomfortable it made him.

Now he remembers something that happened very recently. It had been an unusually difficult day. One of his patients had been arrested and put in a straitjacket, and he had spent hours with the relatives listening to their recriminations. Afterward he was tired, and it was so late, he decided to stay at the clinic and sleep on his bunk.

Nelly was there too, working overtime. She gave him a pill and then poured them drinks.

He must have taken too many drugs or drunk too much, because he'd slid rapidly into deep sleep.

He knows he slept for a long time, and very deeply, and that Nelly helped him get undressed before she went home.

But he dreamed that someone was kissing him and licking his closed lips.

In his dream, Nelly returned. Her tongue was pierced, and she took his penis in her mouth. Then he dreamed that a deer came into his office, the same way Nelly had, and walked past his bunk to stand behind the floor lamp, raising its head and looking at him with bashful eyes.

Erik couldn't sleep in the dream. Light filtered through his eyelashes, and he could see Nelly. She was on her knees, pressing a cold, hard object into his hand. It was a small, brown porcelain deer's head.

Now she's sitting there silently watching him.

After a while, she takes some neatly folded clothes out of a trash bag and puts them on her lap.

"Are those clothes for me?"

"Yes, sorry," she says, rolling them up and passing them to him through the mesh.

"Thanks."

He unfolds a pair of dirty jeans with muddy stains on the knees, and a washed-out T-shirt with the words SAAB 39 GRIPEN across the chest. The clothes are damp and smell like sweat, but Erik pulls off his tattered undershirt and gets changed very gingerly.

"You have a cute little tummy," she says, and giggles.

"Yes, don't I?" he says quietly.

With a coquettish gesture, she raises her chin and loosens the scarf covering her hair. Her blond hair is stiff with blood. He forces himself to look her in the eye, not away, even though his heartbeat is speeding up with fear.

"Nelly, we're together," he says, swallowing hard. "We've always been together, but I've been waiting, because I thought you were with Martin."

"With Martin? But . . . you can't have thought that meant anything," she says, blushing.

"The two of you seemed happy."

Her mouth turns serious and her lips tremble. "It's just you and me," she says. "It's always been us."

He's having trouble breathing but tries to sound natural when he speaks. "I didn't know if you regretted what happened that time—"

"Never," she whispers.

"Me neither. I know I've done some silly things, but only because I felt abandoned."

"But—"

"Because I've always felt we had a unique connection, Nelly."

She wipes tears from her eyes and looks away. She rubs her nose with a trembling finger. "I didn't mean to hurt you," she says.

"I wouldn't say no to a couple of Morfin Medas," he says in a lighter tone.

"Okay." She nods, wipes her face, then gets up and leaves.

127

AS SOON AS NELLY REACHES THE KITCHEN, CLOSES THE DOOR behind her, and puts the heavy bar across it, Erik yanks at the mesh. He pulls as hard as he can and manages to bend it a couple of millimeters but realizes it will never give.

He kicks at it with his bare soles, feels the metal burn into the arches of his feet, and hears nothing but a solid thud from the cage. He shifts around desperately and tugs at the corner, seeking a weak point in the construction, pushes up at the roof, but there are no gaps anywhere, no loose welding joints. Then he lies down on his stomach and stretches his left hand out until he can reach one of the wooden sticks with his fingertips. He rolls it closer until he's able to grip it and pull it into the cage. He moves to the other side of the cage, holds the stick out, and can just reach the strap of Nelly's Gucci purse. Carefully he raises the stick, sliding the bag closer to him. He writhes with pain whenever he has to put any pressure on his injured arm. It feels like an eternity before he drags the bag over to the mesh. With shaking hands, he hunts around for the keys to the padlock among Nelly's gold-plated lipstick holders, travel hairspray, and powder. In a side pocket, he finds her cellphone. Because he can use only one arm, he puts the phone on the floor, leans over it, and dials the SOS Alarm number.

"SOS 112. What's the nature of the emergency?" a calm voice says.

"Please listen . . . you need to try to trace this phone," Erik says as loudly as he dares. "I've been locked up in a basement by a serial killer. You have to come and—"

"The reception's very bad," the voice interrupts. "Can you move somewhere—"

"The murderer's name is Nelly Brandt, and I'm in the basement of a yellow house on the way to Rimbo."

"I can't hear anything now. Did you say you were in danger?"

"This is serious. You have to come," Erik explains, glancing toward the staircase. "I'm in a yellow house on the way to Rimbo. There are fields, and I saw ruined buildings on the site, an old factory with a tall chimney, and—"

The door to the kitchen rattles, and Erik ends the call with trembling fingers. He drops the phone to the floor but manages to pick it up and slip it back inside the bag. He hears Nelly coming down the steep steps and pushes the handbag back toward the table with the stick. It almost topples over and he has to nudge its lower side with the end of the stick. He stretches out as far as he can to slide the bag back into place.

She's almost down now.

Erik pulls the stick back and hides it under the mattress. He notices a faint trail through the dirt on the floor.

Nelly reaches the cellar. She's holding a broad-bladed kitchen knife. Her face is sweaty, and she brushes her blood-streaked hair back and looks at her bag on the table.

"You were gone a long time," he says, leaning back against the mesh.

"The kitchen's a bit of a mess," she explains.

"But you have some morphine?"

"To the hungry soul, every bitter thing is sweet," she mutters, and puts the white pill on the end of the knife blade.

She smiles blankly and extends it toward the mesh. "Open wide," she says distantly.

With his heart pounding, Erik leans his face toward the rusty mesh, opens his mouth, and sees the point of the knife come closer.

It's trembling. Nelly's breathing quickens as she puts the tip of the knife into his open mouth.

He feels the underside of the cold blade against his tongue before carefully closing his lips around the knife.

She pulls it out again, and the blade hits the side of the mesh with a clang.

Erik pretends to swallow the pill, but tucks it between his cheek and his back teeth. A bitter taste spreads through his mouth as his saliva dissolves the outer layer. He can't swallow the pill. It doesn't matter how much pain he's in, he can't risk becoming addled.

"You have new earrings," he says, sitting back on the mattress.

She smiles briefly, looking at the knife in her hand. "But I haven't been good enough," she says.

"Nelly, if only I'd known that you were waiting for me . . ."

"I stood in the garden and saw you looking at Katryna," she whispers. "Men like beautiful fingernails, I know that, but my hands have always been strange. There's nothing I can—"

"You have lovely hands. I think they're lovely. They're—"

"Lovelier than she is now, anyway," Nelly interrupts. "That just leaves your little teacher. I've seen you together. I've seen her slippery mouth and—"

"There's no one but you," he says, trying to keep his voice steady.

"But I don't have any children. I don't have a little girl," she whispers.

"What are you talking about?" Erik feels his body go utterly cold.

"Probably best not to take fire into your bosom, unless you want—"

"Nelly, I don't care about them," he says. "I only have eyes for you."

She lunges suddenly with the knife. He jerks his head back, and the knife hits the mesh where his face was a moment ago.

She's panting and looking at him with disappointment, and he knows he's gone too far, that she knows he wasn't telling the truth.

"What you're saying," she gasps. "I don't know, it's a bit like seeking death by chasing the wind."

"What do you mean? I'm not seeking death, Nelly."

"It isn't your fault," she mutters, and scratches her neck with the knife blade. "I don't blame you."

She takes a few steps back, and the shadows close around her pale face, painting big black holes where her eyes should be, and drawing dark shapes across her neck.

"But you'll see what mortality looks like, Erik," she says, and turns toward the stairs.

"Don't do anything stupid," he calls to her.

She stops and turns around. Sweat has run down her cheeks, and her makeup has almost come off.

"I really can't accept that you're going to continue thinking about her," Nelly says steadily. "If you're going to think about her, it should be a face without eyes and lips."

"No, Nelly!" Erik shouts, watching her disappear up the narrow staircase. He sinks down onto the floor, spits out the half-dissolved pill in his hand, and puts the loose remains in one pocket of his jeans.

128

MARGOT KNOWS IT'S PRETTY UNLIKELY THAT NELLY BRANDT is at her home. Even so, she feels extremely anxious as she sits in her car watching the National Task Force spread out around the white modernist house.

If she disregards the black-clad and heavily armed police officers, the entire area is dreamily peaceful.

Margot is following the operation on the radio, and the tension is almost unbearable. She can't help imagining the silence being shattered by screams and the sound of weapon fire.

Her radio crackles as the head of the operation, Roger Storm, reports directly to her. "She's not here," he says.

"Did they look everywhere?" she asks. "Basement, attic, yard?"

"She's not here."

"And her husband?"

"Watching diving on television."

"What does he say?"

"I got straight to the point, but he says he's sure Nelly isn't involved. They've read all about Erik, and he says Nelly is just as shocked as he is."

"I don't give a shit what he thinks. I just need him to tell us where the fuck she is," Margot says, looking over toward the house.

"He has no idea," Roger replies.

"Is the response team finished?"

"They're on their way out."

"Then I'm coming in." Margot opens the car door.

The moment she gets out of the car, she feels a dull ache at the small of her back. She realizes immediately what it means but keeps going, slowly making her way to the open front door.

"I'll give birth when I'm finished with this case," she says to the officer at the door.

The entry is large, but cozy and welcoming. The response unit are on their way out, helmets in hand, their automatic rifles swinging from their straps.

In the gloom of the living room, a rather plump man is sitting in an armchair. He's loosened his tie and undone the top button of his shirt, and there's a microwaved meal on a tray on the coffee table. He looks shocked. He keeps rubbing his thighs and looking in bewilderment at the officer talking to him.

"It's a big house," he's explaining. "It's enough for us. And in the winter we usually go to the Caribbean and—"

"Your extended family—don't they have houses?" Margot interrupts.

"I'm the only one who lives in Sweden," he replies.

"But if your wife were to borrow a house, where would that be?"

"I'm sorry, I have no idea, I—"

Margot leaves him and heads upstairs, looks around, then goes into a bedroom and takes out her phone.

"Nelly Brandt isn't at home, and clearly she isn't at Karolinska," she says as soon as Joona answers.

"Does she have any connection with other properties?" Joona asks.

"We've checked all the registries," Margot replies, gasping as the next contraction hits. "They don't own any other houses, no land."

"Where did she live before?"

Margot takes out the printout of information she requested after she last spoke to Joona. "According to the population registry, she was registered at Sköldinge rectory until ten years ago. Then there's a gap of four years before she shows up here."

"She lived with Rocky Kyrklund in his rectory," Joona says.

"We have people there, but these days it's sheltered housing for—"

"I know, I know."

"Obviously she could have rented an apartment."

"In the diary, there are references to a farm in Roslagen," Joona says.

"There's no farm, nothing she has any connection to. Her family has never owned any land, and she's the last of her line."

"But Rocky escaped from her and stole a car in Finsta. We don't know how far he walked on foot first—"

"There must be a thousand farms around Norrtälje," Margot interrupts.

"Check all her paperwork. If she's renting a farm from someone else, she may have paid electricity bills, things like that."

"We should be getting a decision about an official search warrant in a couple of hours."

"Start looking, and keep going until someone stops you," he says.

"Okay, where do I begin?"

"If you think the husband's telling the truth, you'll need to look through her personal effects."

"I'm upstairs. They have separate bedrooms." She walks into an airy room with dove-blue wallpaper.

"We can keep talking while you search. Tell me exactly what you're looking at."

"The bed is made, and she has a few psychology books on the bedside table."

"Check the drawers."

Margot opens the two drawers and tells him there are no documents. "They're practically empty. A pack of Mogadon, cough drops, and hand cream."

"Ordinary hand cream?"

"Clarins."

She puts her hand in the drawer and finds a little plastic container. "A bottle of dietary supplements."

"What sort?"

"Iron . . . iron hydroxide."

"Why do people take that? Do you?" Joona asks.

"I eat enough meat for five people instead." Margot closes the drawers.

"Is there a closet?"

"I'm on my way into her walk-in closet," she says, walking between the rows of clothes.

"What's in there?"

"Dresses, skirts, suits, blouses . . . don't think I'm envious, but it's all designer: Burberry, Ralph Lauren, Prada." She falls silent as she stares at one wall.

"What's happening?" Joona asks.

"Her shoes . . . I might have to cry after all."

"All right, let's stay focused."

"Where do I look now?"

"Poke around in the back," Joona replies. "Look behind shelves, under boxes. You need to find something."

They end the call, and Margot looks everywhere, leaning against the wall and crawling to the back, but she finds absolutely nothing. Just as she walks back into the bedroom, she sees Roger Storm reach the top of the stairs. His face is sweaty, and he approaches her with wide eyes.

Margot sighs and presses her clenched hand against the small of her back to suppress the next contraction. "What is it?" she asks in a subdued voice.

"We received another video," he says.

129

THE STREETLAMPS ARE COMING ON, AND JOONA AND ROCKY are approaching Södertälje, when Margot calls back.

"We received a new video," she says in anguish. "Presumably it's someone Erik knows, or has at least—"

"Describe it."

"Nelly is already inside the victim's home when she begins filming. The woman seems injured. She's sitting curled up in a corner . . . and at the end, at the end of the video, there's a small foot. It's dark, but it looks like there's a child lying on the floor."

"Go on."

"It's a perfectly fucking ordinary room, old walls and uneven wallpaper. There might be a big chimney outside the window."

"Go on."

"I'm watching the video on an iPad right now. The woman has short black hair, she's thin, and . . . I don't know. She's bleeding. She's almost unconscious, and she's moving her hands as if she can't see anything, or—"

"Listen," Joona interrupts, "her name is Jackie Federer and she lives at Lill-Jans Plan."

"I'll send the Rapid Response Unit," she says, ending the call.

Joona doesn't have time to explain that she may no longer be in her apartment, because Nelly will want to kill Jackie in front of Erik's eyes, just as she killed her mother in front of her father, and Natalia in front of Rocky. "You talked about a cage, about being locked in a cage," Joona says to Rocky.

"When was that?"

"Nelly had you locked up somewhere."

"I don't think so," he replies, staring out at the road.

"Do you know where that might have been?"

"No."

"You escaped and stole a car near Norrtälje."

"I thought you were the one who goes around stealing cars," he mutters.

"Think. It was a farm, and there may have been a chimney."

Rocky watches the landscape flash by and as they pass the junction for Salem, he lets out a deep sigh. He rubs his face and beard with his big hands, then looks back at the road. "Nelly Brandt murdered Rebecka Hansson," he says slowly.

"Yes."

"God came back for me after all." He crumples an empty cigarette pack.

"It looks like it," Joona replies gently.

"Maybe I'll be punished for escaping and for having heroin in my pockets . . . but after that I can go back to being a priest."

"You've already been wrongly convicted. You won't be sentenced again," Joona says.

"Can you stop here?" Rocky says. "I need to take a look at my church."

Joona pulls over to the shoulder and lets him out. The big priest knocks on the roof and sets off toward Salem.

130

WHEN HE WAS ASSIGNING WORK EARLIER THAT DAY, RAMON Sjölin, commanding officer of the Norrtälje Police, decided that Olle and George Broman could take one of the patrol cars.

They're father and son and don't often partner with each other. Their colleagues joked that at last Olle, the father, would get a lesson in police work.

Olle loves his colleagues' teasing and is immensely proud of his son, who is a head taller than him.

As usual the day passed peacefully, and toward evening they drove out to Vallby industrial estate. There had been several reports of break-ins there in the past six months, but tonight everything was calm.

Olle's back is hurting, and he tilts the seat a bit farther and is about to say they'll give it half an hour, then head to the station, when a call from the regional communications center comes in.

Emergency Services received a phone call thirty minutes ago. The operator could barely hear anything, but analysis of the recording of the short conversation suggests that the man needs help. He described a location with a ruined factory on the property somewhere in the vicinity of Rimbo.

They had been able to identify the place as the house built after the big fire at Solbacken Glassworks.

"We're on our way back to the station," Olle mutters.

"You don't have time to take this first?" the operator asks.

"Okay, we'll take it," he replies.

Large drops of rain are falling on the car roof. Olle shivers and closes his window.

"Suspected domestic down in Gemlinge," he tells his son.

George turns the car around and heads south, past large farms that open up the landscape amid black forests.

"Mom thinks you don't eat enough vegetables, so she was going to make carrot lasagna," Olle says. "But I forgot to buy carrots, so we're having hamburgers instead."

"Sounds good." George grins. They stop talking when they turn onto the narrow track. The deep potholes make the suspension creak, and branches scrape the roof and sides of the car.

"For God's sake, this place is derelict," George says.

The car's headlights open a tunnel through the darkness and make the swirling moths and the tall grass beside the track shine like brass.

"What's the difference between a cheese and a hole?" Olle asks absurdly.

"I don't know, Dad," George says without taking his eyes off the track.

"There are holes in the cheese, but no cheese in the holes."

"Great," his son sighs, and drums his hands on the wheel.

They turn into a large yard and see a huge chimney etched against the night sky. The tires crunch slowly over gravel. Olle leans toward the windshield, breathing through his nose.

"Dark," George mutters, turning the wheel. The headlights sweep across bushes and rusting machine parts until they are suddenly reflected back at them.

"A license plate," Olle says. They drive closer and see a car with its trunk open.

The two men look toward the yellow house. It's surrounded by tall stinging nettles, and the windows are black.

"Do you want to wait and see if they carry out a television?" Olle asks quietly.

George lines the car up so that the headlights are pointing straight at the porch, then puts the handbrake on.

"But the call was about a suspected domestic," he says, opening his door. "I'll go and take a look."

"Not alone," his dad says.

They are both wearing light protective vests under their jackets, and they're carrying their service pistols, extra magazines, batons, handcuffs, flashlights, and radios. George pulls out his flashlight and suddenly thinks he sees something move behind the broken glass.

"What is it?" Olle asks.

"Nothing," George replies with a dry mouth.

The leaves rustle in the darkness, and then they hear a strange noise, like someone crying out in anguish from within the forest.

"Goddamn deer, scaring people like that!" Olle says.

George shines his flashlight at a deep shaft between some collapsed brick walls. There are fragments of glass scattered among the weeds.

"What is this place?" George whispers.

"Just stick to the path."

The flat disk of the flashlight moves over the house's dirty windows. The glass is so filthy, it reflects no more than a gray shimmer.

They wade through the tall nettles. "Maybe you can ask them for some gardening tips," George jokes.

One pane has been nailed over with plywood, and a rusty scythe leans against the wall. "The argument was probably about whose turn it was to clean," Olle says under his breath.

131

THROUGH THE MESH OF HIS CAGE, ERIK WATCHES NELLY force Jackie down the stairs. Jackie's frightened and confused, trying to grasp the situation without succumbing to panic. Nelly must have had her locked up somewhere in the house.

Erik doesn't know what Nelly is thinking, but he can see her exultant fury as she glares at Jackie with her chin jutting out.

He doesn't dare to plead with her—anything he says will only make her jealous. Thoughts race through his head as he tries to find something that could break through her wounded rage.

Jackie makes a clicking sound with her tongue and takes a step forward. She walks straight into the flashlight beam and stops for a moment as she feels the slight warmth.

Now Erik can see how badly injured she is. Dark blood shines on her temple, and there are bruises on her face and a cut in her bottom lip. Her shadow fills the wall. Off to one side, just in front of her, Nelly wipes sweat from her right hand onto her dress and picks up the knife from the table.

Jackie hears the movement and backs up until she reaches the brick wall. Erik sees her run her hand across it, feeling for any deviations with her fingers, something to help her orient herself.

"What did I do?" Jackie asks fearfully.

Erik looks down, waits a few seconds, and then looks at Nelly instead. But she has already noticed him looking at Jackie. Her mouth is so tense that the sinews in her neck are visible. She wipes tears from her cheeks, and the knife twitches in her right hand as she approaches Jackie.

Erik sees that Jackie can sense Nelly's presence. She doesn't want to show how afraid she is, but the movement of her chest betrays the shallowness of her breathing. He can tell that she instinctively wants to duck but is forcing herself to stand up straight.

Nelly moves slowly sideways, and grit crunches beneath her shoes.

Jackie tilts her head slightly toward the sound. Blood has congealed across the side of her head.

Nelly holds the knife out toward Jackie and looks at her through narrowed eyes. The point of the blade moves in front of Jackie's face, and a weak reflection trembles on the ceiling. Jackie raises a hand, and the knife glides out of the way, but returns at once and slowly lifts the collar of her blouse.

"Nelly, she's blind." Erik struggles to remain calm. "I don't see the point—"

Nelly jabs the point of the knife between her breasts. Jackie whimpers and touches the superficial injury with one hand. Her fingertips get covered with blood, and fear and confusion fill her pale face.

"Look at her now," Nelly says. "Look at her. Look!"

Jackie feels along the wall with her fingertips, walks straight into the table, and stumbles over a brick, taking a long stride to keep herself from falling.

"Very elegant," Nelly giggles, brushing the bloody hair from her face.

Jackie backs away, and Erik hears her shallow breathing, like a wounded animal.

Nelly circles around Jackie, who moves to face the sound, holding her hands up to protect herself and try to get her bearings in the room.

She walks into the table again, and Nelly creeps behind her and jabs the knife into her back.

Erik forces himself not to scream.

Jackie groans with pain, stumbles, and one knee hits the floor. She gets up quickly as blood runs down her clothes and one leg, and takes a few fumbling steps with her hands in front of her.

"Erik, why are you doing this?" Jackie asks tremulously.

"Why are you doing this?" Nelly mocks.

"Erik?" Jackie gasps, turning around.

"It's over between us," Erik says harshly. "Don't imagine that—"

"Don't talk to her!" Nelly shrieks at him. "I don't give a shit about anything now. I'm not going to let the two of you—"

"Nelly, I only want to be with you, no one else," Erik interrupts. "I only want to look at you, at your face, and—"

"Do you hear that?" Nelly screams at Jackie. "What's wrong with you? He doesn't want some fucking blind bitch. Got that? He doesn't want you."

Jackie says nothing, just sinks to her knees, shielding her face and head with her arms and hands.

"Nelly, that's enough." Erik is no longer able to keep his voice steady. "She understands. She's no threat to us, she—"

"Get up. He says that's enough. He wants to look at you. Show your face, your pretty little face."

"Nelly, please—"

"Get up!"

Jackie slowly gets to her feet, and Nelly lunges with full force, but the blade misses her neck. The knife slides over her shoulder, right next to her throat. Jackie screams and falls backward. Nelly jabs again but hits nothing but thin air. She catches the blade on a shelf on the wall and some cans of food topple over and fall to the floor.

"Nelly, stop it, you have to stop!" Erik cries, tearing at the mesh.

Jackie shoves her with both hands, and Nelly staggers backward, falls across the wooden sticks, and drops the knife.

"'Bray a fool in a mortar among wheat with a pestle,'" Nelly whimpers in a high voice as she sweeps her hands across the floor. She grabs a can, gets to her feet, and hits Jackie with it hard, in her stomach, chest, and collarbone.

Jackie screams and manages to knock the can from Nelly's hand. She rolls over onto her side and tries to get to her feet.

Gasping, Nelly looks around at the dark shadows and finds her knife on the floor by the wall. "Now I'm going to take her face," she screeches.

Jackie is on her knees with her face unprotected; blood pours down her back. She's found a small screwdriver and gets unsteadily to her feet, panting for air.

Nelly wipes sweat from her eyes. Her green dress is smeared with dark stains.

Jackie turns away from her and finds the stairs.

Nelly smiles at Erik, then goes after Jackie. She raises the knife and stabs, but the blade misses and lands wrong, cutting a wound between Jackie's neck and shoulder.

Jackie falls forward onto both knees, hits her forehead on the first step, and collapses.

Nelly staggers back and blows the hair from her eyes—and a bell suddenly rings.

With the knife trembling in her hand, Nelly glares up at the stairs in indecision. The bell rings again. She says something to herself, goes quickly past Jackie up the stairs, then closes and locks the door behind her.

132

THE TWO POLICE OFFICERS WAITING ON THE PORCH CAN'T hear anything from inside, just the wind in the trees and the chirruping of insects in the weeds.

"What's the difference between a ham sandwich with pickles . . . and an old man with a cigarette in his ass?" Olle asks, ringing the bell again.

"I don't know," George says.

"Okay, I'll ask someone else to buy the sandwiches tomorrow."

"Dad . . . really . . ."

Olle laughs and shines his flashlight at the peeling door.

George knocks hard on the window next to them, then steps aside.

"Let's go in." Olle gestures at his son to back away down the steps as he grabs the door handle.

He's about to open it when a warm glow appears. The gray hall window suddenly looks welcoming. The door is opened by an elegant woman wearing a headscarf and holding a paraffin lamp. She's in the process of buttoning a yellow raincoat over her chest and looks at the two police officers with bemused surprise.

"God, I thought it was the electrician—we had a power outage," she says. "What happened?"

"We received an emergency call from this location," Olle replies.

"What for?"

"Is everything okay?" George asks.

"Yes, I think so," she says anxiously. "What sort of emergency?"

The steps creak as George takes a step closer. The woman smells strongly of sweat, and there's a splash of something on her neck.

Without knowing why, he turns and shines the flashlight into the darkness along the front of the house. "It was a man who called. Is there anyone else in the house?"

"Only Erik. Did he call you? My husband has Alzheimer's."

"We'd like to talk to him," Olle says.

"Can't you do that tomorrow? He's just had his Donepezil." She raises her hand to brush the hair from her forehead. Her fingernails are black, as if she's been digging in the earth.

"It won't take long," Olle says, taking a step inside.

"I'd rather you didn't," she says.

The two police officers look down the hallway. The wallpaper is brown, and a homemade rag rug covers the worn linoleum floor. On the wall is a framed biblical quotation, and a few outdoor clothes hung up neatly on hangers.

Olle goes inside, shivers, and glances back at the car. Insects have been drawn to the strong headlights and are swirling like captives in their beam. "I'm afraid we're going to have to speak to your husband," he says.

"Do we have to?" his son murmurs.

"We received an emergency call," Olle tells the woman. "I'm sorry, but this is how it works. We have to come in."

"It won't take long," George says.

They wipe their shoes carefully on the doormat. A curl of fly-paper hangs in the same corner of the hall as the ceiling light. Hundreds of flies cover the sticky paper, like black fur.

"Can you hold this?" the woman says, passing the paraffin lamp to Olle. Its light flickers across the walls.

As George waits behind his dad, the woman pushes the kitchen door open with both hands. A creak of metal echoes through the hall. George hears her talking about her husband's illness as she walks into the dark kitchen. A stench comes through the open door and hits them. Olle coughs and follows the woman, holding the lamp.

The yellow light plays over chaos. There's broken glass, saucepans, and old tools everywhere. The filthy floor is smeared with fresh blood, and the drips are splattered high up the cupboard doors.

Olle turns back to his son, who's right behind him—when the door suddenly slams with immense force. It hits George square in the face, and he's thrown backward, knocking his head on the hallway floor.

Olle, still in the kitchen, simply stares at the door and the huge spring. His son's foot is sticking between the door and the jamb.

When he turns back around, the woman is holding a long-handled ax over her shoulder, and before he has time to move, she strikes. The blade enters the side of his neck from above. The blow sends him careening sideways, and he sees his own blood spatter the woman's raincoat. As she pulls the ax free, he gets jerked off balance and takes a step forward to steady himself.

She calmly takes the paraffin lamp from his hand and sets it on the counter before lifting the heavy ax over her shoulder again.

Olle wants to shout to his son, but he has no voice. He's on the point of losing consciousness. Black clouds are billowing up in his field of vision. He puts one hand to his neck and feels blood running down inside his shirt. He tries to draw his pistol, but there's no strength left in his fingers.

The woman strikes again, and everything goes black.

Out in the hallway, George opens his eyes and looks around. He's lying on his back, and his forehead is bleeding. "What the hell just happened?" he gasps, feeling his nose and bleeding forehead with trembling hands. "Dad?"

He notices that his foot is stuck in the door. His ankle feels broken, but strangely enough, it doesn't hurt. He pulls and realizes he doesn't have any feeling in his toes.

Confused, he looks up at the ceiling and sees the spiral of flypaper swaying above him. He hears thuds from inside the kitchen and pushes himself up onto his elbows but can't see anything through the crack in the door.

Fumbling, he manages to pull his flashlight from his belt and points it into the kitchen. His dad is lying on the floor with his mouth open, staring at him.

Suddenly his head rolls over a few times, as the woman shoves it with her foot. It rolls and spins on the bloody linoleum floor.

George, seized by utter panic, lets out a loud scream. He drops the flashlight and tries to move backward. He kicks at the door with his free foot, but it's like he's caught in a mantrap. He fumbles for his pistol but can't pull it out. He needs to take his glove off. He puts his hand to his mouth to use his teeth. Then the door suddenly opens, and he's free.

Panting, he shuffles backward and hits his back against a small desk. A bowl of coins falls to the floor, scattering money around him.

He manages to get his glove off and pulls his pistol from its holster as the woman in the yellow raincoat comes out into the hall. She raises the ax above her head, striking the lamp and bringing the coil of flypaper down. The heavy blade hits his chest with terrible force, cutting straight through the thin protective vest and his rib cage, down into his heart.

133

ERIK STRETCHES OUT THROUGH THE MESH OF THE CAGE TO reach Jackie, but she's too far away. His fingertips flail at the air behind her back. He keeps talking to her without knowing if she can hear him, saying she needs to get up and make her way out through the tunnel.

Nelly has already been gone for several minutes.

At first he didn't know if Jackie was alive. She lay slumped on the floor without moving. But lying on the floor against the cage mesh, he could hear her breathing.

"Jackie?" he says again.

She'd be dead if the doorbell hadn't rung. In spite of the silence, he knows it's the police—it must be the police responding to his phone call.

As long as they realize how serious it is, he thinks. As long as they sent enough officers.

He picks up the stick, reaches out with it, and gently pokes Jackie with the blunt end. "Jackie?"

She slowly moves one leg, turns her face, and coughs weakly.

He explains what happened, what Nelly has done, how he got blamed, but that Joona knows the truth.

She lifts one hand tiredly to the superficial wound on her neck.

Erik has no idea how much she understands, but he repeats that she needs to get away, she needs to hurry. "You need to fight now," he says. "You won't survive otherwise."

She doesn't have long. He's been listening for pistol shots, for voices, but can't hear anything.

"Jackie, try to get up now," he pleads.

Finally she sits up. Blood is running from her eyebrow and down over her cheek, and she's gasping for breath.

"Can you hear me?" he says. "Do you understand what I'm saying? You need to run, Jackie. Can you stand?"

He says nothing about having called the police. He doesn't want to give her false hope. She needs to get away, because he fears the police will fall for Nelly's lies.

Jackie gets to her feet, groans, and spits blood onto the floor. She lurches forward but stays upright.

"You need to get away before she comes back," he repeats.

Jackie stumbles toward his voice, breathing heavily, with her arms outstretched.

"Go in the other direction," he says. "You have to get out of the ruins and away across the fields."

She makes her way carefully past the cans on the floor and reaches the cage with her hands.

"I'm locked in a cage," he says.

"Everyone's saying you killed four women," she whispers.

"It was Nelly. You don't have to believe me. You just have to get out of here."

"I knew you didn't do it," she says.

He strokes the fingers clinging to the cage. She leans forward and rests her forehead on the rusty metal.

"You have to keep going a little longer," he says, stroking her cheek. "Turn around so I can take a look. You've been wounded, Jackie. You're seriously hurt. You need to get to a hospital. Hurry up and—"

"Maddy's still at home," she whimpers. "Thank God, she was hiding in her closet when—"

"She'll be fine," Erik says. "She'll be fine."

"I don't understand any of this," Jackie whispers, her face crumpled with anxiety.

"How does it feel when you breathe?" Erik asks. "Try to cough for me. Okay. You'll be okay. Your pleural cavity is probably damaged, but you were lucky, Jackie. Listen, there's a little flashlight on the table. You can feel its warmth. You'll know where it is."

She wipes her mouth, nods, and tries to pull herself together.

"Can you get it? There's nothing between you and—"

He breaks off when he hears a loud thud from upstairs. It's the kitchen door slamming shut, thanks to the powerful spring.

"What was that?" she whispers, her lips quivering.

"Hurry up. You can walk straight toward the flashlight. There's nothing on the floor between you and the table."

She turns and walks toward the tiny source of heat, feels across the tabletop, picks up the flashlight, and returns to Erik with it.

"Do you know where the opening to the tunnel is?" he asks.

"More or less," she whispers.

"It's narrow. It's a small brick opening, no door," he explains as he hears someone scream up above. "You need to run away, get as far away as you possibly can. Take this stick—you can use it to feel your way."

She looks as if she's about to break down. Her face is drained of color, her lips already white from the shock to her circulation. "Erik, it won't work—"

"Nelly will kill you when she comes back. Listen, there's a passageway. . . . I don't know what it looks like farther along, it could be blocked, but you have to try to get out."

"I can't," she whimpers, twisting her head back and forth in an anxious, repetitive pattern.

"Please, just listen to me. When you get to the cellar with no ceiling, you'll have to climb up to reach ground level."

"What are you going to do?" she whispers.

"I can't get out. Nelly has the key around her neck."

"But how am I going to find my way?"

"In the darkness, the blind man is king," he says simply.

Her face trembling, she turns and starts to walk, feeling the ground in front of her with the stick.

He holds the flashlight up so he can see where she is and try to guide her. The angled light makes the shadows stretch and shrink.

"There's a pile of roof tiles on the floor ahead of you," he says. "Move a little to your right, and you'll be heading straight for the opening."

Then they hear the bar being lifted from the basement door. It jolts and scrapes against the wall.

"Hold your hand out now," Erik whispers. "You'll be able to feel the wall on your left. Just follow that."

Jackie walks into something that clatters. A can of paint rolls away.

He sees her shrink with fear. "Don't stop," he urges. "You have to get home to Maddy."

The door above them opens, closes, and clicks, but there's no sound of footsteps on the stairs.

Jackie has reached the opening now, and she continues into the passage, holding one hand against the wall and sweeping the ground ahead of her with the stick.

Erik points the flashlight at the floor and sees Nelly come down the stairs and step out into the middle of the basement. Her yellow raincoat is smeared with blood, and she's clutching a smaller kitchen knife.

She's staring straight at him.

He doesn't know how much she's seen, but he switches the flashlight off. Everything goes completely dark, as if someone has swept the whole world away from them.

"Nelly, they'll send more police officers." He is holding his injured arm with his hand. "Do you understand? It's over now."

"It's never over," she replies, and stands still, a meter or so away from him, breathing.

There's a clattering sound from the tunnel. Nelly giggles and crosses the floor. Erik hears her hit the stack of tiles, go around them, and walk through the darkness toward the tunnel.

134

JACKIE IS HEADING ALONG THE NARROW PASSAGE AS QUICKLY as she can. With her right hand, she feels along the wall, as she moves the stick side to side in front of her.

She needs to try to find a way out, then find help.

Fear washes over her. It feels almost like being burned. She kicks a bottle lying on the ground that she missed with her stick. It tinkles as it rolls away across the rough floor.

Her fingertips slip across the bricks and crumbling mortar. She's passing a seventh vertical indentation in the wall, she notices. She keeps count automatically because it will make things easier if she has to find her way back.

She is having difficulty breathing. The pain in her back flares up like a beacon with every step she takes. Warm blood is still trickling from the wound, between her buttocks and down her legs. She coughs and feels a cramping pain in her injured lung, just below her shoulder blade.

Her stick isn't quite quick enough.

Her shin hits some sort of apparatus with sharp tin corners and dangling cables. She clambers over the machine, her legs trembling with effort and fear. She has no way of knowing how long the passageway is, but she has a feeling she's inside a system of underground tunnels.

She's walking too fast and knows there's a risk that she'll trip over something.

She passes a room on her left, sensing it as a gap in the acoustics.

She decides to stop counting the indentations and concentrate on finding a way out.

"Nelly's coming!" Erik calls from the basement room behind her. "She's on her way now!"

His voice sounds frightened, weakened by the long tunnel, but she hears him. Jackie tries to go faster. She makes her way around an armchair and moves along the wall, her fingers brushing a number of shelves. Something rattles behind her, and she almost cries out in fear.

It's getting harder and harder to breathe. Jackie holds her hand over her mouth and tries to cough quietly as she presses ahead. In midstride, her face hits something—an open cupboard door. It slams shut, and glass objects rattle on the shelves.

She remembers the feeling of a sharp knife blade being yanked out with a sigh, and the constricting pain in her back.

She knows she's breathing too hard, but it still doesn't feel like she's getting enough oxygen.

She moves the stick quickly and lets her other hand brush over bricks and joints, past a thick cable, along bare brick again, and then some old window frames that are stacked against the wall.

She's trying to read the space.

Whenever she hears an opening, she stops for a few seconds and checks if it's another passage or just an enclosed room.

She keeps moving forward along the main passageway. The weak draft across the floor seems to be coming from that direction.

A protruding bolt tears the skin of her knuckles, and now she can hear her pursuer behind her.

Nelly shouts something to her, but Jackie can't make out the words.

Panic bubbles up inside her. The hand holding the stick is covered in sweat.

She trips over a brick, loses her balance, and starts to fall. She throws her arm out, putting her hand through some thick spiderwebs, and hits the wall hard. Her back shrieks with pain, cutting through her like a javelin, and she can taste blood in her mouth.

A crash from the tunnel behind her makes her ears ring. It

sounded like the cupboard full of glass objects falling over. Glass shatters on the floor.

Jackie wipes her sweaty hand on her legs, takes a firm grip of the stick, and moves forward as fast as she can. The fingertips of her right hand have gone numb from the rough brick wall.

She can hear footsteps behind her—much faster than her own.

In panic, Jackie turns into a side passage.

Her heart is pounding.

This isn't going to work, she thinks. Nelly knows her way around these tunnels. This is her territory.

She forces herself to go on. This passage is narrower than the last one. She stumbles over some old fabric and feels something catch around her foot and drag along behind her.

"Jackie?" Nelly shouts. "Jackie!"

She tries not to cough and feels herself pass a hole in the wall fairly close to the ceiling. She hears air streaming through it as something grabs at her clothes. It's holding on to her blouse, pulling her backward. She flails her arms in panic and hears the fabric tear. She's stuck and is trying to pull free when she hears Nelly once more.

She must have followed her into the side passage.

Jackie pulls at her blouse and turns around. She puts her hand under her left arm and feels a thick pipe. She walked into a pipe that's somehow hanging from the roof. It's caught in her clothes, and she has to back up to free herself.

Nelly is close now. Mortar crunches under her boots, and her clothes rustle.

Breathing through her nose, Jackie continues along the passageway.

Nelly lets out a bark—she too has walked into the dangling pipe. A metallic clang echoes off the walls.

Jackie hurries forward and emerges into a large room with a slower echo.

There's a smell of stagnant water in the air, like an old aquarium. Jackie keeps moving—and almost immediately bumps into something and drops her stick.

She bends over and feels a large trough filled with dusty soil, twigs, and pieces of bark. The pain in her back almost makes her topple forward, but she keeps searching beside the trough, feeling tentatively across old bottles, spiderwebs, and twigs.

Nelly calls out to her. She's getting closer.

Jackie gives up looking for the stick. She'll have to go on without it. With her arms outstretched, she feels her way past a series of alcoves with brick walls dividing them.

She stops in front of a large object that's blocking the whole room, a long steel sink. She feels along it to one end and has just made her way around it when she hears Nelly's footsteps behind her.

Jackie clicks her tongue loudly, the way she has learned to. The room reflects the sound as vague echoes that her brain turns into a three-dimensional map. She clicks again but is too scared for it to work well. She doesn't have time to listen properly, can't get any real sense of the room.

Panting for breath, she moves on. Her whole body is shaking, and she doesn't know how to stop it. She turns her head and clicks again—and suddenly becomes aware of an opening to her left.

She reaches for the wall, follows it until she finds the opening, and once again feels cool air from outside.

It's a narrow passageway, its floor covered with loose grit and what smells like the charred remains of wood and plastic. One foot goes straight through a windowpane, shattering it with a loud crash. She knows she's cut her foot but stumbles on across the floor. As she reaches out to the wall, her fingers dislodge bits of dry mortar, and then she hears Nelly stand on the glass.

She's right behind her.

135

JACKIE BREAKS INTO A RUN, WITH ONE HAND AGAINST THE wall and the other stretched out in front of her. She runs into a wooden trestle and falls over it, landing on her left shoulder and groaning with pain. She tries to crawl, but something hits the floor right beside her. It sounds like a plastic pipe or a broom handle.

She crawls forward and hits her head on the wall. She manages to get to her feet again, stumbles across some fallen bricks, and leans against the wall.

She isn't entirely sure which way she's facing. She turns and listens but can no longer hear Nelly. Her own breathing is so labored, she has to hold one hand over her mouth in an effort to stay quiet.

Something rustles in front of her, down on the floor, moving slowly.

It's only a rat.

Jackie stands completely still, breathing through her nose. She has no idea how to find her way out. Terror is preventing her from thinking clearly. She's too stressed to be able to interpret her surroundings.

A short distance away, something creaks. It sounds like a heavy door or even an old hand wringer. She desperately wants to hide, to curl up on the floor with her arms over her head, but she forces herself to keep going.

Her feet crunch on stones, charred pieces of wood, and piles of sand and grit. The walls have collapsed in places, blocking the hallway, and she has to clamber over the heaps.

She hears air rushing through a small gap higher up and keeps crawling, leaning on her hands. A broken plank scrapes her thigh, and her feet slide across bricks and mortar.

There's a rustling sound behind her, and she climbs faster until she hits her head on the ceiling. She can feel a breeze on her face but can't locate the opening. She fumbles desperately with her hands, trying to push through stones tangled in metal wire, sweeping aside loose mortar, until she finds the narrow gap. She puts her fingers through a piece of chicken wire and pulls. She manages to loosen a large stone, makes the hole a bit larger, and cuts her palm. She shuffles forward and tries to crawl through. Groaning, she manages to push one arm and her head into the hole. Stones tumble away on the other side of the hole, and she forces her way in, kicking with her legs and panicking that she's going to get stuck.

She fumbles in front of her with her hand, trying to get a grip on anything that might help her pull herself through the hole. She can't hear Nelly and has no idea if she's scrambling up the heap of rubble with her knife raised.

Jackie feels a piece of rope with her hand and pulls as she pushes as hard as she can with her legs. Chicken wire and stones scratch her back, but she makes it out. She shuffles down the other side but catches her foot on the edge of the hole. She angles it differently and finally it comes loose.

Jackie slides down the heap of rubble and reaches a floor. Without having any idea where she is, she walks forward with her hands outstretched until she finds a wall and begins to follow that instead.

The bricks are colder here, and she realizes she must be getting closer to an exit. She turns a corner and finds herself in a larger room. The ceiling is much higher here. Noises rise and spread out like a gentle sea.

She stops and rests for a moment, trying to catch her breath. She leans forward and puts her hands on her knees. Her whole body is shaking with exhaustion and shock.

She has to go on, she thinks.

With bleeding fingers, she feels along the wall. Then she hears a metal door open with a creak off to the right.

She crouches and hopes she's hidden behind something. She tries to breathe silently, but her heart is pounding hard.

Nelly must have gone a different way, she thinks. Nelly knows the layout of the rooms, where the tunnels lead.

The knife wound hurts much more now. It feels oddly stiff, and she's having trouble breathing. She can't help but let out a quiet cough, and as she does, she feels warm blood trickle down her back.

Still crouching, she moves slowly forward, and hits something that scrapes metallically. She lowers her hands and feels that it's a shovel.

"Jackie," Nelly calls.

She stands up cautiously and feels her way along the wall. She clicks her tongue and realizes that there's an opening ahead on her left.

"Jackie?"

The echo of Nelly's voice hits the wall on the other side. Jackie stops to listen. All of a sudden she's sure: Nelly shouted in the wrong direction.

She can't see me, Jackie thinks. It's so dark in here that she can't see me.

Nelly's blind.

Moving slowly, Jackie bends over, picks up a small stone, and throws it. It bounces off a wall onto the floor and hits something. She hears Nelly move toward the sound.

Jackie returns to the shovel and carefully picks it up. The blade scrapes the ground.

Nelly stops, panting. "I can hear you!" she says, laughing.

Jackie moves closer to Nelly. She steps carefully, listening to the gentle crunch of the gravel.

Nelly moves backward and walks into a bucket, which falls over with a clatter.

She can't see me, but I can see her, Jackie thinks as she gets closer, hearing Nelly's strained breathing and smelling her sweat through her perfume.

Jackie can clearly sense Nelly's presence. She hears the knife move through the air and detects the movement of Nelly's feet backing away another couple of steps.

Jackie squeezes the handle of the shovel, cautiously adjusts her grip, clicks with her tongue, and knows at once where the wall is and where Nelly is standing.

Nelly pants and stabs in different directions, but the knife hits nothing but air. She stops and listens, anxiety audible in her breathing.

Jackie approaches silently, feeling the heat radiating from Nelly's body. She follows the movements of the knife, then takes a step forward and strikes hard with the shovel.

The heavy blade hits Nelly on the cheek with a clang. Her head jerks sideways, and she collapses onto her hip, roaring with pain.

Jackie walks around her, listening to every movement, every breath.

Nelly whimpers and tries to get up.

Jackie strikes again, but the shovel passes close to Nelly's head, the metal merely pushing through her hair.

Nelly gets to her feet and jabs with the knife. It cuts into Jackie's lower arm. Jackie backs away instinctively and walks into the bucket that Nelly hit earlier, then steps quickly to the side with her heart thudding. Her arm stings with pain from the cut, and blood is dripping down into her hand. Adrenaline courses through her, making the hairs on her arms stand up. She shakes the blood from her hand, wipes it on her skirt, and takes a fresh grip on the shovel.

She approaches as silently as she can. She can hear Nelly crouching and jabbing with the knife, and she can feel the dampness of her breath. Without a sound, Jackie circles her, then changes direction and strikes with all the strength she can muster. The blow is ferocious. The shovel hits the back of Nelly's head. Jackie hears her sigh and fall forward without putting her hands out to break her fall.

She hits again and strikes Nelly across the head with a wet sound, and after that she doesn't hear anything.

Jackie backs away, panting. Her hands are shaking, and she listens but can't hear the sound of breathing. She approaches Nelly warily, poking her with the shovel, but her body is limp.

Jackie waits, hearing her own pulse thump in her ears. She jabs hard again with the point of the shovel, but there's no reaction.

Jackie is breathing fitfully. Anguish washes over her. Her stomach churns. She puts the shovel down and moves closer to Nelly, her legs shaking. Steaming warmth from the body rises up toward her. Carefully she leans over until she can feel Nelly's back with her fingers. She's wearing a raincoat. The rough fabric squeaks beneath her fingers.

Erik said she had the keys around her neck.

She reaches tentatively up Nelly's back to her neck, where she can feel Nelly's hair wet with warm blood.

Her fingers fumble clumsily inside Nelly's collar, tracking along her sticky neck until she finds a chain. She tugs at it, but it won't come loose.

She needs to roll Nelly onto her back. She's heavy, and Jackie has to use both hands and push with one leg.

The body rolls over, and Jackie ends up sitting astride it. With her fingers shaking, she undoes the first button at the neck of the raincoat. She hears a squelching sound, as if Nelly were moistening her mouth, and stops.

She undoes another button and thinks she can hear little clicks, as though Nelly were blinking her dry eyelids.

Fear pulses through her head. She tears Nelly's dress open at the neck, grabs the key on the chain, and pulls it over her bloody head.

136

JOONA HAS BEEN FOLLOWING THE SIGNS TO RIMBO BUT leaves Route 280 at Väsby. He is heading toward Finsta when Margot calls to tell him that Jackie and her daughter aren't in the apartment at Lill-Jans Plan. Evidence suggests they've been abducted. There are traces of blood on the floor, all the way out into the stairwell. The door to the closet has been smashed, and on the wall inside it Jackie's daughter wrote "The lady talks funny."

Joona repeats several times that they have to find the house near Finsta, that that's where Nelly took Jackie and Madeleine. Erik is probably already there, caged, or will be very shortly.

"Find the house—that's the only thing that matters right now," Joona says before they end the call.

He's passed plenty of farms in the darkness along the way, agricultural premises and sawmills with chimneys of varying sizes.

He's driving fast along the black road, not letting himself think about the fact that it might be too late, that time has already run out.

He has to fit the pieces of the puzzle together.

There are always questions left to ask, answers he can still find.

Nelly keeps repeating herself, returning to old patterns, he thinks.

There has to be a farm in Roslagen that Nelly somehow has access to. The farm didn't belong to her family, but her grandfather might have managed it, Joona reasons. He was also a priest, and the Swedish Church owns a great deal of land and forest, as well as a large number of properties.

As he drives, Joona tries to think through the case again and consider everything he read and saw before he knew Nelly was the person Rocky called the unclean preacher. He needs to find something to connect a farm in Roslagen with the video of Jackie.

Joona thinks about the yellow raincoat, the narcotics, the collection of trophies, and the way she clearly marked the places she took them from on the bodies. He thinks about her completely ignorant husband out in Bromma, her expensive clothes, her hand cream, and the jar of nutritional supplements. Then he picks up his phone and calls Nils.

"You've climbed out onto a very precarious branch," The Needle says. "That escape from prison wasn't exactly—"

"It was necessary," Joona interrupts.

"And now you want to ask me something," The Needle says, clearing his throat.

"Nelly takes iron pills," Joona says.

"Maybe she suffers from anemia," Nils replies.

"How do you get anemia?"

"A thousand different ways. Everything from cancer and kidney disease to pregnancy and menstruation."

"But Nelly takes iron hydroxide."

"Do you mean iron oxide-hydroxide?"

"She has speckled hands," Joona says.

"Freckles?"

"Blacker, with definite pigment change, and—"

"Arsenic poisoning," The Needle interrupts. "Iron oxide-hydroxide is used as an antidote to arsenic. And if she's got dry, speckled hands, then . . ."

Joona stops listening when he remembers one of the photographs he left on the floor of his hotel room. It showed a two-millimeter-long fragment that looks like a bluebird's skull.

The fragment had been found on Sandra Lundgren's floor. It looked ceramic but actually consisted of glass, iron, sand, and chamotte clay.

He drives past a big red barn and realizes the little bird's skull was a tiny shard of slag, a by-product of glass production.

"Glass," he whispers.

The ground around old glassworks is often contaminated with arsenic. In the old days, they used great quantities of it as a refining agent, to prevent bubbles and to homogenize the glass.

"A glassworks," Joona says out loud. "They're at a glassworks."

"That could fit," The Needle says, as if he has been following Joona's internal thought process.

"Are you sitting at your computer?"

"Yes."

"Search for an old glassworks in the vicinity of Finsta."

"No . . . all I'm getting is one that burned down in 1976, Solbacken Glassworks in Rimbo, used to make sheet glass and mirrors. The land is owned by the Swedish Church, and—"

"Send the address and coordinates to my phone," Joona interrupts, "and call Margot Silverman."

137

TRYING NOT TO GASP WITH PAIN, ERIK LISTENS FOR NOISES from the tunnels. He picks up the flashlight and tries to breathe calmer. He thinks that he can hear shuffling steps from the passageway. There's someone there—he heard right—footsteps are approaching. He switches the light off and reminds himself that he has to play along, no matter what happens. He has no choice. It would be far too easy for Nelly to kill him while he's in the cage.

He waits in silence, listening to the crunching footsteps and then the sound of breathing outside the cage.

"Erik?" Jackie whispers.

"You have to get out of here," Erik whispers quickly.

He switches the flashlight on and sees Jackie standing a meter away from him. Her face is dirty and bloody. She's gasping for breath and seems to be in a very bad way.

"Nelly's dead," Jackie says. "I killed her."

"Are you hurt?"

She doesn't answer but takes a couple of steps toward him, reaches the mesh, and sticks her hand in. He strokes her fingers and shines the light on her to look at her injuries.

"Can you manage to get out and call for help?" he asks, stroking the hair away from her blood-streaked face.

"I have the key," she says, and coughs weakly. She leans against the cage, pulls the chain over her head, and gives it to him.

"I killed her." Gasping, she sinks to the floor. "I killed another human being."

"You had to. It was self-defense," Erik says.

"I don't know," she whispers, and her face dissolves into tears.

Erik puts the key into the padlock, turns, and hears the click as the shackle slides out of the casing.

He climbs out with the flashlight and hugs Jackie on the floor. Her breathing is erratic and shallow.

"Let me look at the wound on your back," he whispers.

"Don't worry about that," she says. "I need to get home to Maddy. Just give me a few seconds."

Erik shines the flashlight at the peeling walls, the table, and the shelf.

"I think the door to the kitchen is locked, but I'll go up and check," he says.

"Okay," Jackie nods, and makes another attempt to stand.

"Stay where you are." Erik heads up the steep steps.

On the brown, antislip linoleum, there are bloody bootprints. He gets up to the heavy metal door, jerks the handle down, and pulls and pushes the door, but it's locked.

He yanks the handle and looks around with the flashlight to see if the key's on a hook anywhere, but he can't find one. He goes back down to Jackie, who is leaning on the cage.

"The door's locked," Erik confirms. "We'll have to get out through the tunnels."

"Okay," she replies quietly.

"I think she killed the police officers who came," he says. "The police will come and find us, but we have no idea how long that's going to take, and you need to get to a hospital immediately."

"We can walk." She pants.

"You can do it," Erik says, putting her hand on his shoulder. "I have a flashlight. I can see where we're going."

He leads her into the passageway, around an armchair and a small padded footstool. Some old window frames are leaning against the wall, and dusty lightbulbs sit in yellowed sockets.

They cross another passageway with steep steps leading downward, then pass a toppled cupboard, treading carefully across the broken glass.

With the beam of the flashlight and with Erik's help, getting through is straightforward. They emerge into a large room with long metal sinks, rows of faucets, and cubicles with crumbling plaster.

On the ceiling there are empty strip lights with no coverings. The cables are just hanging down. A large trough full of soil stands in the middle of the floor. Rust has eaten through its green metal, and the stick that Jackie used to guide her is lying on the floor next to it.

They move through the room into a hallway lined with dented lockers. There's a water pipe attached to the ceiling, but one end has come loose and is hanging down like a spear, curving under its own weight.

Erik shines the flashlight along the narrow passageway. The walls have collapsed, and parts of the ceiling have fallen in. The passage is full of bricks and boards, all the way up to the ceiling.

Erik opens a door, and they continue along a different tunnel, turn right, go through a rounded arch, and are suddenly out in the fresh air.

They're standing in a large room, and a sharp wind is blowing. The roof is gone, and the tall chimney is visible against the dark sky. The beam of the flashlight shimmers off a huge metal extractor hood. The tile floor is dirty and cracked.

Tall weeds are growing through an aluminum ladder lying on the ground in front of a huge oven. Erik barely has any strength left in his injured arm, but he manages to lift the ladder and pull it free of the weeds. He shoves some fallen bricks and gravel aside with his foot and props the ladder up against the wall.

He helps Jackie climb and follows right behind her. She slips, and he drops the flashlight when he catches her. It clatters down between the rungs, hits the ground, and goes out abruptly.

The pain in his arm is throbbing as if it's trapped in a piece of machinery, by the time they emerge into the tall grass growing around the ruins. Jackie is leaning hard against Erik as they make their way through thistles and low bushes. They see an empty police car, its headlights shining straight at the yellow house.

138

JOONA IS DRIVING AS FAST AS HE CAN. MARGOT HAS ORGA-
nized a police operation, but he can't risk them getting there too
late. The Norrtälje Police haven't been able to get any response
from their patrol car in the area.

The headlights sweep across the field as he swerves onto the
narrow gravel track through the forest. The tires skid across the
loose surface, unable to get a grip, but he steers into the skid and
manages to overcome it. He puts his foot down again, and the car
lurches along the uneven track.

Two deer run across ahead of him. He brakes, and they leap
through the light and disappear among the trees.

Now he can see the tall chimney of the glassworks between the
trees, like a black obelisk against the lead-gray sky.

Far ahead, at the very limits of the beam of the headlights, he
sees two figures. They're standing in the track, in a motionless
embrace.

It's Erik and Jackie, he's almost certain.

A stone strikes the undercarriage, and the light disappears from
the road for a few seconds.

Branches lash the windshield, and it's hard to see their faces,
unsteady in the wavering light.

A deep pothole in the track forces Joona to slow down and
swerve. There's a bang, and the beam of the headlights lurches high
above the two figures.

And then he sees the light reflect off something yellow at the side of the track.

Nelly.

She's not far behind Erik and Jackie and is moving forward with her face lowered, across a shimmering layer of crushed green glass.

Joona honks his horn, changes gear, and presses his foot on the pedal. Grit flies up onto the underside of the car. The car lurches, and the glove compartment opens, scattering its contents across the seat. He veers off the side of the track, and tall weeds lash the windshield.

Joona honks again as Nelly strides purposefully through the nettles and undergrowth.

Erik squints toward the car, looking relieved as he waves.

Joona honks his horn again and again. He loses sight of them for a moment, rounds a slight bend, and sees that Nelly is holding a knife.

She steps across the ditch, and now she's right behind them, crouching in their shadow.

Still honking, Joona speeds up along the track. The engine roars. In the shaky light of the headlights, he sees Nelly stick the knife into Jackie.

A heavy branch smashes one of the headlights, and the ruins to the right of the car disappear in sudden darkness.

In the weakened light, Joona sees Jackie collapse onto the rough track. Erik is still holding her hand.

Some branches are swaying by the side of the road, but Nelly has vanished.

Joona brakes hard. The tires kick up dust as they slide across the loose grit. He swerves, and the windshield smashes, sending glass swirling into the car and hitting his face. Branches and grass lash the body of the car as it slides to a halt with two wheels in the ditch.

Joona clambers out onto the hood of the unsteady car, jumps down, and runs over to Erik, who's kneeling next to Jackie.

"I didn't see anything," Erik says, tugging Jackie's blouse open and touching the knife to see how deep it goes. "It could have hit one of her kidneys. We need an ambulance as soon as—"

"Where's Maddy?" Joona interrupts.

"At home in the apartment. We have to call—"

"She's not in the apartment," Joona says. "Nelly took her when she took Jackie."

"Jesus," Erik whispers, looking up at him.

"Could she be inside the house?"

"There's a cage in the basement, and a series of tunnels that . . ."

Jackie is gasping for breath, and Erik can feel her pulse getting weaker. He glances toward the house, brushes his hair from his face, and sees a yellow glint in a window on the second floor.

"There's a light in the window," Erik points. "They must be—"

He breaks off when Jackie's pulse disappears completely. He puts his ear to her chest. Her heart has stopped.

"Get an air ambulance!" Erik yells. "Her heart's stopped! It's urgent!"

He leaves her on her side so they don't have to pull the knife out and begins CPR, no longer aware of the pain in his arm as he counts thirty quick compressions, then blows into her lungs twice before resuming the compressions. He hears Joona give the address and coordinates to the emergency services operator.

"Stay with Jackie. Save her. I'll get her daughter." Joona sets off running toward the house.

139

JOONA RUNS ACROSS THE YARD, DRAWING HIS PISTOL. THE headlights of the police car are still shining straight at the yellow house. The smell of fire suddenly fills the still night air. He pushes through the tall nettles and sees white smoke billowing like steam from the weeds around the building's foundation.

He jumps up onto the porch, raises his gun, and opens the front door. He sees the dead police officer on the floor, his torso dark with blood.

Joona aims his pistol at the next door as he steps over the body, leans down, picks up the cracked flashlight, and shines it into the kitchen.

In the dwindling light, he can see a scene of horrific brutality. The floor is covered with blood, and the second policeman's head is lying a meter from his body. He never even managed to pull his pistol from its holster. Blood has splashed the glass of an unlit paraffin lamp standing on a chair. A roaring sound is coming from deep in the basement, and a thin veil of gray smoke slips across the ceiling and envelops an old smoke alarm.

Joona hurries through the kitchen, across a living room, and into a narrow hallway with an open staircase leading to the next floor. Smoke is rolling beneath the ceiling like a murky river.

Parts of the burning floor in the next room collapse into the basement, and sparks and smoke swirl upward. He can feel heat on his face as he rushes up the stairs. The wallpaper is alight. The fire is making its way to the second floor.

Joona realizes Nelly is burning the evidence. If Jackie doesn't survive and the house is gone, all that will be left is the evidence against Erik.

The light glow of the flashlight turns yellow as it weakens.

He reaches the upper floor, aims the pistol in front of him, and makes his way into a girl's room. The pink rose-patterned wallpaper is covered with photographs of Erik. A lot were taken surreptitiously, but some are portraits, and others seem to have come from professional journals and photo albums.

On a shelf in the darkness stands a collection of things she's probably stolen from Erik. Wineglasses, books, deodorant, and a wooden elephant from Malaysia. A brown corduroy jacket is draped over a blue shirt on a wooden hanger.

There's a hissing sound from deep below the floor under his feet. The fire is sucking up more oxygen, and the air is getting harder to breathe.

The flashlight goes out. He shakes it and gets back a weak, unsteady beam.

Nelly has arranged her trophies from the victims in front of a mirror on a vanity table. They don't amount to much, just some bottles of nail polish, a tube of lipstick from H&M, and a red bra. On a pink plate lies the metal tongue stud in the shape of Saturn, a hairclip, Susanna Kern's earrings, some fake fingernails, and a pearl necklace blackened with blood.

The flashlight goes out, and Joona sets it carefully on the floor.

He approaches the door to a bedroom with a sloping roof, moves slightly to one side, and catches sight of Madeleine in the murky light.

She's lying on the floor next to a bed, in the middle of the room. Her mouth is covered with tape, and there's a pool of blood under her head.

The little girl is the trophy Nelly took from Jackie.

She's breathing but seems to be unconscious.

He can't see any sign of Nelly, but the door beside the bed has sticky blood around its handle.

The room is rapidly filling with pale smoke. Time is running out.

Joona glances at the girl, then aims his gun to the right and hurries forward.

The heavy ax comes toward him from the left. Joona has misread the room and sees the movement too late. He just manages to pull his head away, and the blade swings past his face and embeds itself deep in the wall.

The air fills with dust and plaster.

Nelly tries to yank the ax free, but Joona hits her across the face with the butt of his pistol.

Her head flies backward, and saliva sprays from her mouth. She lands crookedly on her back, and the floor seems to rock beneath her as black smoke billows from the gaps between the floorboards.

Joona stumbles backward from the force of his own blow and knocks over a chair holding some plastic hangers.

Nelly sits up, and suddenly she is beside Madeleine. Joona can't understand how it happened so quickly. It took her less than a second.

The bed has moved.

Then he realizes he's been looking at a large mirror. The reflection made him think Maddy was in the middle of the room, at a safe distance.

The fire crackles and hisses as it eats up the oxygen.

Holding his pistol by his side, Joona tries to get a grip on the room. Large fragments of mirrored glass are leaning against the walls and furniture, distorting the perspective and making the room look very different.

Nelly's nose is bleeding. She's pulled the girl toward her and is clutching her tight. Smoke swirls around them, and Joona can't see if she's armed.

"Let the girl go." Joona cautiously moves closer.

The pictures of Erik on the floor are curling up in the heat.

"Let her go," Joona repeats.

"Yes," she replies softly, but keeps holding Madeleine.

Madeleine opens her tired eyes, and Nelly kisses her on the head.

"Nelly, we have to get out," Joona says. "All of us. Do you understand?"

She nods weakly and looks into his eyes. Above the closed door to his left, oily black smoke is filtering into the room.

"Can you help me?" Nelly asks, without taking her eyes off him.

"Yes, I can," he replies, trying to see what she's hiding by her hip.

She smiles at him oddly, almost devotedly.

Sparks and soot are drifting upward on the hot air currents, and the cooler air is being sucked down toward the floor, closer to the fire. The curtains flare up as the flames coil around the fabric.

"What does the fire say?" she mutters, getting to her feet. She pulls Madeleine up from the floor harshly, by her hair.

The girl is frightened. There are tears running down her cheeks.

"Nelly," Joona says again, "we have to get out. I'll help you, but I—"

With a crash, a large panel of the wall to the next room collapses to the floor between them. Tiny sparks flicker in the gray fog above their heads.

"—but I won't let you hurt the girl," he says.

In one of the mirrors, Joona sees that Nelly has pulled out a knife. She's holding Madeleine by the hair with her other hand, pulling it so hard, the girl has to stand on tiptoes.

The floor is vibrating beneath their feet. Heat is flooding in from the side. Black smoke fills the room, and the flames climb toward the ceiling.

"Drop the knife. You don't have to do this!" Joona cries, aiming his pistol toward the shape behind the smoke.

He tries to move sideways but can only just make out the yellow oilskin through the smoke and fire.

"It's never enough," a very high child's voice says.

For a fraction of a second, he thinks it's Madeleine speaking, but when he realizes her mouth is still taped shut, he squeezes the trigger.

He fires through the smoke three times.

The bullets hit Nelly in the middle of her chest, and in the mirror off to one side behind her, Joona sees blood spurt out between her shoulder blades. The large mirror collapses beneath her and shatters.

Madeleine is standing perfectly still, her hand on her neck wound. Blood is running between her fingers, but she's alive.

Nelly's high-pitched voice has been a warning of death every time.

Joona rushes over to the girl and kicks the knife from Nelly's hand. He picks Madeleine up and backs away through the smoke.

Nelly is lying among the fragments of broken mirror, her mouth open. She's lost one of her boots and her foot is twitching in her filthy nylon stocking.

A plastic gas can topples over and paraffin splashes out across the floorboards. There's a hiss and then the fire leaps up through the floor.

Joona stumbles backward with the girl as the floor of the bedroom gives way under Nelly's weight. She's sucked down and vanishes into a shaft of raging flame.

Joona's pant leg catches fire as he shuffles backward with the girl in his arms. The flames are reaching up with a howl all the way from the cellar, striking the ceiling above the collapsed floor. Burning pieces of the lamp fall in a cloud of swirling sparks. The windowsill is ablaze and the glass shatters with a bang.

Joona pulls Madeleine with him farther from the bedroom.

"I'm sorry if this hurts," he says, and pulls the tape from her mouth.

A tall cupboard collapses through the floor of the bedroom and disappears into the shrieking inferno.

He wraps his leather jacket around Madeleine. "The smoke's dangerous, so I want you to breathe through the lining. Can you do that?" She nods, and he picks her up and starts to carry her down the stairs. From somewhere deep in the basement there's a shriek of twisting metal.

The fire is climbing the wall.

There's a crash in the room beneath them as the heat blows out the windows in the living room. Glass rains down onto the floor and air streams in, making the flames leap up toward the ceiling with a roar. The girl coughs and Joona shouts to her to keep breathing through the lining of his jacket.

In the living room the walls are burning from floor to ceiling. The heat forces him toward the television room. The girl screams as burning dust rains down on them.

Joona knows he doesn't have many seconds left, so he holds his breath and, with the girl in his arms, he takes a few faltering steps forward, then stumbles through the thick smoke.

His eyes are tearing and he can barely see. The sofa catches alight and sparks swirl up into his face on the hot wind.

The kitchen is ablaze, and sections of the ceiling are crashing down. An explosion sends splinters of glass and fire across the room.

Joona's lungs are straining. He'll have to breathe soon.

The end of one of the roof beams comes loose and falls like a heavy pendulum, crushing the kitchen table and embedding itself deep in the floor.

The powerful spring mechanism has contorted out of shape, bending the door back on one hinge. Joona steps over the dead police officer's body. Surrounded by fire, he fights his way forward and kicks the burning front door open.

Police and paramedics rush toward them with blankets.

Margot Silverman is forced to take a step back from the heat and lets out a gasp as a powerful contraction hits her. She feels her water break and run down between her thighs.

THE DOWNDRAFT FROM THE CLATTERING HELICOPTER blades sends dust flying in a wide circle.

Erik is holding Maddy's hand as the helicopter takes off. She's lying strapped to a stretcher next to Jackie and smiles up at him before closing her eyes. They rise unsteadily into the air.

Down below, he sees Joona lying on the ground, coughing. He's surrounded by police and paramedics. Margot is trying to resist as she is being led to a waiting ambulance.

Joona slowly gets up, takes his pistol from its holster, and throws it onto the ground. Then he holds out both hands so he can be cuffed.

The helicopter turns, tilts forward, and picks up speed.

EPILOGUE

ERIK SITS IN HIS ARMCHAIR, LOOKING OUT THROUGH THE tall windows at the white October sky. Detective Margot Silverman is walking up and down across the polished oak floor, holding her baby daughter at her breast.

Erik and Rocky Kyrklund have both been cleared of the murders. Margot is outlining the key points of the long reconstruction of events she has been working on for the last month.

Nelly probably began stalking Erik at the time of Rocky Kyrklund's trial. She transferred her fixation from Rocky to him, just as she had transferred her fixation to Rocky at her father's funeral.

It turned out that Nelly once registered for medical school in the United States, but there's no sign she ever received a degree. She has no employment history or specialist training in the field. She probably taught herself everything. Her house in Bromma contained hundreds of books about neurology, psychological trauma, and disaster psychiatry.

There was nothing to suggest that her husband had any idea about her double life. She spied on Erik in secret, slowly getting closer to him and collecting pictures of him that she kept in the house at the burned-out glassworks. After Erik's divorce, she began to imagine that she and he were a couple.

Erik closes his eyes and hears gentle piano music through the walls as Margot talks.

In Nelly's case, her obsessive fixations were linked to a narcissistic personality disorder that made her try to mirror Erik, to become everything for him. And the more she felt she owned him, the more she needed to watch and control him.

She wanted him to see her, to love and desire her. Her need was insatiable, until in the end she was like a fire, burning and burning until everything around her was consumed.

Nelly was deeply marked by her religious upbringing, by the constant presence of the church and her father's sermons. She had studied the Old Testament closely, and its jealous God convinced her that everything she felt was right.

She spied on the women she thought Erik was attracted to and became fixated on their individual attributes. Driven by pathological jealousy, she filmed them to unmask their supposedly coquettish behavior before stripping them of their beauty.

The evidence suggests that each murder accelerated the process. When there was no way back, she turned her hostility against Erik himself.

Tormented by jealousy, she murdered her rivals and at the same time set a trap for Erik, one that would ultimately lead him to her.

Nelly had killed her mother in front of her father. She had killed the woman Rocky claimed he loved in front of him, and she had been planning to kill Jackie in front of Erik.

She would have taken Madeleine as a trophy, leaving Jackie without a face, with her hand over her womb to illustrate her particular crime.

Margot falls silent, carefully moves her baby up toward her shoulder, and strokes her back until she burps.

WHEN MARGOT HAS LEFT THE HOUSE, ERIK WALKS TOWARD the gently rippling piano music and opens the double doors. The grand piano is in the middle of the living room and appears to be playing itself. Only when he walks around the oversize instrument can he see the look of concentration on Madeleine's face as her fingers dart across the keys.

He sits quietly next to Jackie on the sofa, and after a while she leans her head on his shoulder.

The paramedics managed to stabilize her heart with a defibrillator before she was put in the helicopter. She underwent a seven-hour operation at University Hospital in Uppsala.

Erik feels like he's woken up from a long nightmare, and as Jackie laces her fingers between his, all he feels is deep gratitude that they're alive and that Cupid had another arrow in his quiver for him.

Madeleine lets the final notes fade before stopping the strings, then waits for silence to spread through the room before looking up and smiling at them.

Erik stands and applauds and doesn't stop until Madeleine starts to adjust the stool. He walks over and sits down, changes the sheet music, closes his eyes for a few seconds, then begins to play his étude.

ON FRIDAY, OCTOBER 24, THE HEARING IN STOCKHOLM DISTRICT Court comes to an end. The four-judge panel decides the state has proven beyond a reasonable doubt that Joona Linna is guilty of a number of serious crimes in connection with the jailbreak at Huddinge Prison.

The verdict should have been expected in spite of the extenuating circumstances, but when the sentence is pronounced, Erik gets to his feet. Jackie and Madeleine stand up beside him, followed by The Needle, Margot Silverman, and Saga Bauer.

Joona remains seated next to his defense lawyer, his head lowered, as the judge reads out the unanimous verdict.

"The court finds Joona Linna guilty of violence against a public official, aggravated criminal damage, assisting a felon in an escape from custody, impersonating a police officer, and aggravated theft. The defendant is sentenced to four years in prison."